THE
Christmas
COLLECTION

Three new full-length stories from
three favourite Mills & Boon® authors

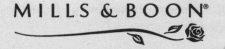

MILLS & BOON®

Lynne Graham—Presents™ author—was born in Northern Ireland and has been a keen Mills & Boon® reader since her teens. She is very happily married with an understanding husband who has learned to cook since she started to write. Her five children keep her on her toes. She has a very large Old English Sheepdog, which knocks everything over, and two cats. When time allows, Lynne is a keen gardener.

Day Leclaire—Enchanted™ author—and her family live in the midst of a maritime forest on a small island off the coast of North Carolina. Despite the yearly storms that batter them and the frequent power outages, they find the beautiful climate, superb fishing and unbeatable seascape more than adequate compensation. One of their first acquisitions upon moving to Hatteras Island was a cat named Fuzzy. He has recently discovered that laps are wonderful places to curl up and nap—and that Day's son really was kidding when he named the hamster Cat Food.

Josie Metcalfe—Medical Romance™ author—lives in Cornwall now with her long-suffering husband, four children and two horses, but as an Army brat frequently on the move, books became the only friends who came with her wherever she went. Now that she writes them herself she is making new friends and hates saying goodbye at the end of a book—but there are always more characters in her head clamouring for attention until she can't wait to tell their stories.

The 1999
Christmas
COLLECTION

LYNNE GRAHAM
DAY LECLAIRE
JOSIE METCALFE

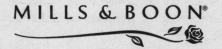

MILLS & BOON®

THE CHRISTMAS COLLECTION
© by Harlequin Enterprises II B.V., 1999

*First published in Great Britain 1999 by
Harlequin Mills & Boon Limited,
Eton House, 18-24 Paradise Road,
Richmond, Surrey, TW9 1SR*

THE SICILIAN'S MISTRESS © Lynne Graham 1999
HER SECRET SANTA © Day Totton Smith 1997
A FAMILY CHRISTMAS! © Josie Metcalfe 1999

ISBN 0 263 82350 4

101-9909

*Printed and bound in Spain
by Litografia Rosés S.A., Barcelona*

THE SICILIAN'S MISTRESS

BY
LYNNE GRAHAM

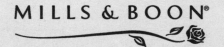

MILLS & BOON®

CHAPTER ONE

STUDIOUSLY ignoring Faith's troubled expression, Edward smiled. 'I never dreamt that Mother would make us such a generous offer—'

Faith sucked in a deep, steadying breath. 'I know, *but*—'

'It makes perfect sense. Why go to the expense of buying another property when there's ample space for us all at Firfield?'

At that precise moment Edward's flight was called. Immediately he rose to his feet and lifted his briefcase. 'We'll talk it over when I get back.'

Faith stood up. A slim, beautiful blonde of diminutive height, she had sapphire-blue eyes, flawless skin and wore her hair in a restrained French plait. 'I'll see you to the gate.'

Her fiancé shook his well-groomed fair head. 'Not much point. I don't know why you bothered coming to see me off anyway,' he remarked rather drily. 'I'm only going to be away for three days.'

Edward strode off and was soon lost from view in the crowds. Faith left the café at a slower pace, genuinely appalled at the announcement Edward had just made. They were getting married in four months and they had been house-hunting for the past three. Now Faith sensed that as far as Edward was concerned the hunt was over: his mother had offered to share her spacious home with them.

It was a really ghastly idea, Faith acknowledged in guilty dismay. Edward's mother didn't like her, but she carefully concealed her hostility. Mrs Benson was no more fond of Faith's two-year-old son, Connor. But then the fact that Faith was an unmarried mother had first fuelled the older

5

woman's dislike, Faith conceded ruefully as she walked back through the airport.

Her troubled eyes skimmed through the hurrying crowds. Suddenly she stiffened, her gaze narrowing, her head twisting back of its own volition to retrace that visual sweep. She found herself focusing on a strikingly noticeable man standing on the far side of the concourse in conversation with another. As her heartbeat thumped deafeningly in her ears, she faltered into complete stillness.

The compulsion to stare was as overwhelming as it was inexplicable. The man was very tall and very dark. His hard, bronzed features were grave, but not so grave that one glance was not sufficient to make her aware that he was stunningly handsome. Her tummy somersaulted. A fevered pound of tension began to build up pressure behind her temples.

A smooth dark overcoat hung negligently from his wide shoulders. He looked rich, super-sophisticated, that cool aura of razor-edged elegance cloaking immense power. Perspiration dampened her skin. Sudden fear and confusion tore at her as she questioned what she was doing. A wave of dizziness ran over her.

Simultaneously, the stranger turned his arrogant dark head and looked directly at her, only to freeze. The fierce intensity with which those brilliant dark eyes zeroed in on her stilled figure disconcerted her even more. But at that point the nausea churning in her stomach forced a muffled moan from her parted lips. Dragging her attention from him, Faith rushed off in search of the nearest cloakroom.

She wasn't actually sick, as she had feared. But as she crept back out of the cubicle she had locked herself in and approached the line of sinks she was still trembling. Most of all, she was bewildered and shaken by her own peculiar behaviour. What on earth had possessed her to behave like that? What on earth had prompted her to stop dead and gape like some infatuated schoolgirl at a complete stranger?

Infatuated? She questioned the selection of that particular

word and frowned with unease, the way she always did when a thought that didn't seem quite *her* came into her mind. But she wasn't feeling well. Maybe she was feverish, coming down with one of those viruses that could strike with such rapidity.

There had to be some good reason why a total stranger should inspire her with fear...unless he reminded her of somebody she had once known. She tensed. That was highly unlikely, she decided just as quickly, and began to scold herself for her overreaction to a fleeting incident.

But she knew what was the matter with her. She understood all too well the source of her basic insecurity. But *that* was something she had learnt to put behind her and never ever dwell on these days. With conscious care, Faith suppressed the scary stirrings at the back of her mind and blanked them out again.

But what if she *had* once known that man? The worrying apprehension leapt out of Faith's subconscious before she could block it again. Aghast, she stared blindly into space, suddenly plunged into a world of her own, a blank, nebulous world of terrifying uncertainty which she had believed left far behind her. *The lost years...what about them?*

A crowd of noisy teenagers jostled her at the sinks, springing her back into awareness again. She blinked rapidly, once, twice, snatched in a shuddering breath to steady herself. Discomfited by her uncomfortably emotional frame of mind, she averted her head and shook it slightly. You saw some really interesting people at airports, she told herself squarely. Her attention had been momentarily distracted and she wasn't feeling too good. That was all it had been.

But when Faith vacated the cloakroom and turned back into the main concourse, she found her path unexpectedly blocked.

'Milly...?' A dark, accented voice breathed with noticeable stress.

Faith glanced up, and it was a very long way up, and met flashing dark eyes so cold and deep her heart leapt straight into her throat. It was the same guy she had been staring at ten minutes earlier! Her feet froze to the floor in shock.

'*Madre di Dio…*' The stranger stared fixedly down at her, his deep, accented drawl like an icy hand dancing down her taut spine. 'It *is* you!'

Faith gazed up at him in frank surprise and sudden powerful embarrassment. She took a backward step. 'Sorry, I think you've got the wrong person.'

'Maybe you wish I had.' The intimidating stranger gazed down at her from his incredibly imposing height, slumbrous dark eyes roving so intently over her face that colour flooded her drawn cheeks. '*Dio*…you still blush. How do you do that?' he drawled very…very softly.

'Look, I don't know you, and I'm in a hurry,' Faith responded in an evasive, mortified mutter, because she couldn't help wondering if her own foolish behaviour earlier had encouraged him to believe that she was willing to be picked up.

Eyes the colour of rich, dark golden honey steadily widened and her heartbeat started to thump at what felt like the base of her throat, making it difficult for her to breathe. 'You don't know me?' he repeated very drily. 'Milly, this is Gianni D'Angelo you're dealing with, and running scared with a really stupid story won't dig you out of the big deep hole you're in!'

'You don't know me. You've made a mistake,' Faith told him sharply.

'No mistake, Milly. I could pick you out of a thousand women in the dark,' Gianni D'Angelo murmured even more drily, his wide, sensual mouth curling with growing derision. 'So, if the nose job was supposed to make you unrecognisable, it's failed. And what sad soap opera did you pick this crazy pretence out of? You're in enough trouble without this childish nonsense!'

Her dark blue eyes huge in receipt of such an incomprehensible address, Faith spluttered, 'A nose job? For goodness' sake—'

'You have a lot of explaining to do, and I intend to conduct this long-overdue conversation somewhere considerably more private than the middle of an airport,' he asserted grittily. 'So let's get out of here before some paparazzo recognises me!'

As Faith attempted to sidestep him he spontaneously matched her move and blocked her path again. She studied him in disbelief. 'P-please get out of my way…' she stammered, fear and confusion now rising like a surging dark tide inside her.

'No.'

'You're mad…if you don't get out of my way, I'll scream!'

He reeled back a full step, a deep frown-line of impressive incredulity hardening his lean, strong features. 'What the hell is going on here?' he demanded with savage abruptness.

Faith broke through the gap he had left by the wall and surged past him at frantic speed.

A hand as strong and sure as an iron vice captured her wrist before she got more than two feet away. '*Accidenti…*where do you think you're going?' he questioned in angry disbelief, curving his infinitely larger hand right round her clenched fingers.

'I'll report you to the police for harassing me!' Faith gasped. 'Let go of me!'

'Don't be ridiculous…' He gazed unfathomably down into her frightened and yet strangely blank eyes and suddenly demanded with raw, driven urgency, *'What's the matter with you?'*

Faith spun a frantic glance around herself. Only her instinctive horror at the idea of creating a seriously embarrassing public scene restrained her from a noisy outburst. *'Please* let go of me!' she urged fiercely.

The ring on her engagement finger scored his palm as she tried to pull free. Without warning he flipped her hand around in the firm hold of his and studied the small diamond solitaire she wore. A muscle jerked tight at the corner of his bloodlessly compressed lips, shimmering flaring eyes flying up again to her taut face.

'*Now* I understand why you're acting like a madwoman!' he grated, with barely suppressed savagery.

And Faith's self-discipline just snapped, right then and there. She flung back her head and tried to call out for assistance, but her vocal cords were knotted so tight with stress only a suffocated little squawk emerged. But surprisingly that was sufficient. Gianni D'Angelo, as he had called himself, dropped her hand as if she had burnt him and surveyed her in almost comical astonishment.

Shaking like a leaf, Faith backed away. 'I'm not this Milly you're looking for...never seen you before in my life, never want to see you again...'

And she rushed away her tummy tied up in sick knots again, her head pounding, a kind of nameless terror controlling her. She raced across the endless car park as if she had wings, and then fell, exhausted, to a slower pace, breathless and winded, heartbeat thundering. Crazy, crazy man, frightening her like that all because she resembled some poor woman who had clearly got out while the going was good. Gianni D'Angelo. She didn't recognise that name. And why should she?

But wasn't it strange that he should have attracted *her* attention first? And only then had he approached her. Almost as if he genuinely had recognised her...

As her apprehensions rose to suffocating proportions release from fear came in the guise of an obvious fact. Of course he *couldn't* have recognised her! She couldn't believe that she had ever been the kind of person to run around using a false name! And she was Faith Jennings, the only child of Robin and Davina Jennings. True, she might have been a difficult teenager, but then that wasn't that uncommon, and her parents had long since forgiven her for the awful anxiety she had once caused them.

Half an hour later, sitting in her little hatchback car in heavy morning rush-hour traffic, Faith took herself to task

for the overwrought state she was in. Here she was, sup-
posedly a mature adult of twenty-six, reacting like a frightened teenager desperate to rush home to her parents for support. And yet what had happened? Virtually nothing. A case
of mistaken identity with a stubborn foreigner unwilling to
accept his error! That was all it had been. A nose job, for
heaven's sake!

And yet as she gazed through the windscreen she no
longer saw the traffic lights; she saw Gianni D'Angelo, his
lean, bronzed features imposed on a mind that for some reason could focus on nothing else. As furiously honking car
horns erupted behind her Faith flinched back to the present
and belatedly drove on, strain and bemusement stamping her
troubled face.

Gianni D'Angelo stared fixedly out of the giant corner window of his London office. An impressive view of the City's
lights stretched before him but he couldn't see it.

His sane mind was telling him that even twelve hours on
he was still in the grip of shock, and that self-control was
everything, but he wanted to violently punch walls with the
frustrated anger of disbelief. He had searched for Milly for
so long. He had almost given up hope. He certainly hadn't
expected her to do something as dumb and childish as try
and pretend she didn't know him, and then compound her
past offences by attempting to run away again. And why
hadn't it occurred to her that he would have her followed
before she got ten feet away from him?

Milly, whom he'd always called Angel. And instantly
Gianni was beset by a thousand memories that twisted his
guts even after three years of rigorous rooting out of such
images. He saw Milly jumping out of a birthday cake
dressed as an angel, tripping over her celestial robes and
dropping her harp. Milly, impossibly beautiful but horren-
dously clumsy when she was nervous. Milly, who had given
him his first and only taste of what he had dimly imagined
must be a home life…

And you loved it, you stupid bastard! Gianni's lean hands suddenly clenched into powerful fists. Punishing himself for recalling only pleasant things, Gianni made himself relive the moment he had found his precious pregnant Angel in bed with his kid brother, Stefano. That had put a whole new slant on the joys of home and family life. Until that moment of savage truth he hadn't appreciated just how much he had trusted her. And instead of proposing marriage, as he had planned, he had ended up taking off with another woman. What else could he have done in the circumstances?

He had wanted to kill them both. For the first time he had understood the concept of a crime of passion. The only two people he had ever allowed close had deceived and betrayed him. A boy of nineteen and a girl/woman only a couple of years older. The generation gap had been there, even though he had been too blind to acknowledge it, he reflected with smouldering bitterness. And naturally Stefano had adored her. Everybody had adored Milly.

Milly, who had called him on the slightest pretext every day and never once failed to tell him how much she loved him. So she had spent a lot of time alone. But business had always come first, and he had never promised more than he had delivered. He had been straight. He had even been faithful. And how many single men in his position were wholly faithful to a mistress?

As a knock sounded on the door Gianni wheeled round and fixed his attention with charged expectancy on his London security chief, Dawson Carter. His child, he thought with ferocious satisfaction. Milly *had* to have had his child. And, whatever happened, he would use that child as leverage. Whether she liked it or not, Milly was coming back to him…

'Well?' he prodded with unconcealed impatience.

Dawson surveyed his incredibly rich and ruthless employer and started to sweat blood. Gianni D'Angelo ran one of the most powerful electronic empires in the world. He was thirty-two. He had come up from nothing. He was tough, streetwise, and brilliant in business. He didn't like or expect disappointments. He had even less tolerance for mysteries.

'If this woman *is* Milly Henner—' Dawson began with wary quietness.

Gianni stilled. 'What do you mean *if*?' he countered with raw incredulity.

Dawson grimaced. 'Gianni…if it is her, she's living under another name, and she's been doing it successfully for a very long time.'

'That's insane, and utterly impossible!' Gianni asserted in instant dismissal.

'Three years ago, Faith Jennings was found by the side of a country road in Cornwall. She had been seriously injured and she had no identification. She was the victim of a hit and run. The police think she was robbed after the accident—'

'*Dio!*' Gianni exclaimed in shaken interruption.

'But she *was* pregnant at the time of the accident,' Dawson confirmed. 'And she does have a child.'

Gianni drew in a stark breath, incisive dark eyes flaming to bright gold in anticipation. 'So the child must be two and a half…right? A girl or a boy?' he prompted with fierce impatience.

'A little boy. She calls him Connor. He'll be three in May. He was born before his mother came out of the coma she was in.'

Gianni screened his unusually revealing eyes as he mulled over those bald facts. 'So…' he murmured then, without any expression at all. 'Explain to me how Milly Henner could possibly be living under another woman's name.'

'It was a long time before she was able to speak for herself, but she was apparently wearing a rather unusual bracelet. Her face had been pretty badly knocked about and she needed surgery.' For the first time in his life Dawson saw his employer wince, and was sincerely shaken by the evidence of this previously unsuspected vein of sensitivity. 'So as a first move the police gave a picture of the bracelet to the press. She was swiftly identified as a teenager who had run away from home when she was sixteen. Her parents came forward and identified her—'

'But Milly doesn't *have* parents alive!' Gianni cut in abrasively.

'This woman never recovered her memory after the hit and run, Gianni. She's a total amnesiac—'

'A total amnesiac?' Gianni broke in, with raised brows of dubious enquiry.

'It's rare, but it does happen,' Dawson assured him ruefully. 'I spoke to a nurse at the hospital where she was treated. They still remember her. When she finally recovered consciousness her mind was a blank, and when her parents took her home she still knew nothing but what they had told her about her past. I gather they also discouraged her from seeking further treatment. The medics were infuriated by their interference but powerless to act.'

'Normal people do not take complete strangers home and keep them as their daughters for three years,' Gianni informed him with excessive dryness.

'I should add that the parents hadn't seen or heard from their missing daughter in seven years, but were still unshakeable in their conviction that the young woman with the bracelet was their child—'

'Seven years?' Gianni broke in.

'The police did try to run a check on dental records, but the surgery which the daughter attended before she disappeared had burnt down, and the most her retired dentist could recall was that she had had excellent teeth, just like the lady in the hospital bed. This is a very well-known story in the town where Faith Jennings lives—her miraculous return home in spite of all the odds.'

'There was no return, miraculous or otherwise…that *was* Milly at the airport! Seven years…' Gianni mused with incredulous bite. 'And Milly was in a coma, at the mercy of people no better than kidnappers!'

Dawson cleared his throat. 'The parents are respectable, comfortably off—the father owns a small engineering plant. If there's been a mistake, it can only have been a genuine one, and most probably due to wishful thinking.'

Gianni was unimpressed. 'While Milly was still ill, that's possible, but when she began to recover they must've have started to suspect the truth, so why didn't they *do* anything?' he demanded in a seething undertone. 'What about the fiancé?'

'Edward Benson. A thirty-eight-year-old company accountant.'

Gianni lounged back against the edge of his desk like a panther about to spring. 'An accountant,' he derided between clenched teeth.

'He's her father's second-in-command,' Dawson filled in. 'Local gossip suggests that the engagement is part of a business package.'

'Check me into a hotel down there.' Gianni straightened, all emotion wiped from his lean, strong face, eyes ice-cool shards of threat. 'I think it's time I got to meet my son. And isn't that going to put the cat among the pigeons?'

Dawson tried not to picture the onslaught of Gianni, his powerful personality, his fleet of limos and his working entourage without whom he went nowhere on a small, peaceful English town…and the woman who against all reason and self-preservation had contrived to forget her intimate involvement with one of the world's richest and most influential tycoons. A lot of people had a lot of shock coming their way…

'So you just tell Edward you *refuse* to live with his mother!' Louise Barclay met Faith's aghast look and simply laughed. A redhead with green eyes and loads of freckles, Louise looked as if she was in her twenties but she was actually well into her thirties, and the divorced mother of two rumbustious teenage boys.

'Sometimes you're such a wimp, Faith,' Louise teased.

'I'm not—'

'You are when it comes to your own needs. All your energy goes into keeping other people happy, living the life *they* think you should live! Your parents act like they own you body and soul, and Edward's not much better!' Louise informed her in exasperation.

Faith stiffened. Louise was her best friend and her business partner, but she had little understanding of the burden of guilt that Faith carried where her parents were concerned. 'It's not like that—'

'Oh, yes, it is.' Louise watched Faith carefully package a beautiful bouquet for delivery and leant back against the shop counter. 'I'm always watching you struggle to be all things to all people. Once you wanted to be a gardener. Your parents didn't fancy that, so here you are in a prissy flower shop.'

Faith laughed. 'Alongside you.'

'But this *was* my dream. And if you don't watch out, you're going to end up living with old Ma Benson. She will cunningly contrive, without Edward ever noticing, to make your home life the equivalent of a daily dance on a bed of sharpened nails!' the lively redhead forecast with conviction. 'You think I haven't noticed how stressed-out and quiet you've been since Edward dropped this on you the day before yesterday?'

Faith turned her head away. For once, Louise was barking up the wrong tree. Faith hadn't told anybody about that incident at the airport, but she still couldn't get it out of her mind. Her mother didn't like to be reminded that her daughter was an amnesiac, and got upset whenever Faith referred to that particular part of the past. Her attitude was understandable: after running away, Faith hadn't once got in touch to ease her parents' distress.

How could she ever have been so selfish and uncaring that she had failed to make even a single phone call to reassure them that she was at least still alive? Conscience had given Faith a strong need to do whatever she could to please her parents in an effort to make up for her past mistakes.

She was also painfully aware that both her parents viewed those missing years as a Pandora's box best left sealed. As far as they were concerned, seven years on she had turned up again, pregnant, unmarried and seemingly destitute. Nobody she might have known during that period had listed her as missing. Those bald realities suggested that prior to the accident she had been homeless, unemployed, not in a stable relationship and bereft of any true friends. Frankly, she'd been desperately lucky to have forgiving parents willing to take her home and help her back to normality again, she acknowledged humbly.

Only what was normality? Faith wondered, with the lonely regret of someone who had learnt not to discuss her secret fears and insecurities with anyone. It could never be *normal* to possess not one single memory of what she'd been told she'd lost—the first twenty-three years of her life. But if she wanted people to feel comfortable with her, if she wanted people to forget that strange past and treat her like everybody else, she always had to pretend that that vast gaping hole inside her memory banks was no longer any big deal...

'A fresh start.' In the early days of her convalescence that had been a much-used parental phrase, the implication being that an inability to recall those years might well prove an unexpected blessing. So Faith had concentrated instead on trying to retrieve childhood memories. She had dutifully studied the photo albums of the much-loved and indulged daughter who had grown into a plump teenager with a sullen face, defiant blue eyes and make-up like war paint. Self-conscious about her weight, the teenage Faith hadn't liked photos, so there had only been a handful after the age of twelve.

Faith had walked through the schools she had once attended, met the teachers, wandered round the town where she had grown up and paid several awkward visits to former schoolfriends, always willing her blank brain to remember, recognise, sense even token familiarity…

Repetition *had* created a kind of familiarity, and she had exercised her imagination until sometimes she suspected that she did *almost* remember and that real memory was hovering cruelly just out of reach on the very edge of her mind. She had rebuilt a quiet, conventional life round her family, but Connor was the true centre of her world. She loved her parents for their unquestioning support, loved Edward for his calm acceptance of her, but she adored her son with a fierce maternal joy and protectiveness that occasionally shook even her.

'There's something more up with you than Edward's sudden penny-pinching desire to regress and stay home with Mother,' Louise remarked with sudden insight.

The silence thickened. Faith reached a sudden decision and took a deep breath.

'A man spoke to me at the airport. He was very persistent. He insisted that he knew me by another name…Milly, he called me.' Trying to downplay the incident even now, Faith loosed an uneven laugh, but the pent-up words of strain continued to tumble from her. 'Maybe I have a *doppelgänger* somewhere. It was daft, but it was a little scary…'

'Why scary?'

Faith linked her hands tightly together in an effort to conceal their unsteadiness. 'You see, I noticed this man first…to be honest, I really couldn't take my eyes off him…' Her voice trailed away as embarrassment gripped her.

'So he was trying to make a move on you—but do tell me more,' Louise invited with amusement. 'Just why couldn't you take your eyes off this guy?'

'I don't know. He was very, very good-looking,' Faith conceded, colour flaming into her cheeks. 'And at first I thought that my staring at him had encouraged him to approach me. But when I thought about it afterwards… I don't think it was like that.'

'Why not? You might wear fuddy-duddy clothes and

scrape your hair back like a novice nun, but your kind of beauty would shine through a potato sack,' her friend advised her drily.

'This man was angry with me...I mean...with this woman, Milly,' Faith adjusted hurriedly. 'He accused her of having run away. And he was really astonished when I said I didn't know him and when I threatened him with the police.'

'That's persistent.' Louise looked more serious now.

'He said his name was Gianni D'Angelo...it means nothing to—'

Louise had straightened, an incredulous light in her eyes. 'Say that name again.'

'Gianni D'Angelo.'

'Did this guy ooze money?'

'He was very well dressed.'

'Gianni D'Angelo owns Macro Industries. He's a hugely important electronics mogul. My ex-hubby once worked on a major advertising campaign for one of his companies,' Louise informed her with dancing eyes. 'And if I thought a gorgeous single guy worth billions was wandering round Heathrow trying to pick up stray women, I'd take my sleeping bag and move in until he tripped over me!'

'It can't have been the same man,' Faith decided. 'I must've misheard the name.'

'Or perhaps you once enjoyed a champagne and caviar lifestyle, rubbing shoulders with the rich and the famous!' Louise teased with an appreciative giggle. 'I think you met a complete nutter stringing you a weird line, Faith.'

'Probably,' she agreed, with a noticeable diminution of tension.

With a sense of relief, Faith decided to put the entire silly episode out of her mind. And, just as she had arranged a couple of days earlier, she called in at the estate agent to collect the keys of the house which was her dream house for a second viewing.

True, Edward had not seen the sadly neglected Victorian

villa in quite the same light. But Faith knew she had to tell
her fiancé why there was no question of her agreeing to
move in with his widowed mother after their marriage.
Perhaps then he would be more amenable to a property
which needed a fair amount of work, she reasoned hopefully.

Set on the edge of town, in what had once been open
countryside, the house rejoiced in a large garden screened
from the road by tall hedges. Faith unlocked the front door
and walked into the hall. The stale air made her wrinkle her
nose, and she left the door wide on the weak morning sunlight. She wandered contentedly through the shabby rooms
and finally into the old wooden conservatory which still possessed considerable charm. Edward had said it would have
to be demolished.

A faint sound tugged Faith only partially from her cosy
reverie. She half turned, without the slightest expectation of
seeing anybody. So the shock of seeing Gianni D'Angelo
ten feet away in the doorway was colossal. A strangled gasp
escaped her convulsing throat, all colour draining from her
face to highlight sapphire-blue eyes huge with fear.

'All I want to do is talk to you. I didn't want to walk into
the shop. I didn't want to go to your home. At least here
we're alone, on neutral territory.' He spread fluid brown
hands in a soothing motion that utterly failed in its intent.
'I won't come any closer. I don't want to frighten you. I just
want you to listen.'

But, in a state of petrified paralysis, Faith wasn't capable
of listening. She started to shake, back away, her entire attention magnetically pinned to him, absorbing every aspect
of his appearance in terrifyingly minute detail. His smoothly
cropped but luxuriant black hair. His fabulous cheekbones.
His classic nose. His perfectly modelled mouth. And the
devastating strength of purpose dauntingly etched into every
feature.

His charcoal-grey suit just screamed designer style and
expense, moulding broad shoulders as straight as axe-

handles, accentuating the lithe flow of his lean, tightly muscled all-male body. 'P-please…' she stammered sickly.

'*Per meraviglia!*' Gianni D'Angelo countered rawly.
'Since when were you a bag of nerves on the constant brink
of hysteria? All right, I'll just give you the proof that we
have had what you might call a prior acquaintance.'

'I don't want to have had a prior acquaintance with you!'
Faith exclaimed with stricken honesty. 'I want you to go
away and leave me alone!'

He withdrew something from the inside pocket of his
beautifully tailored jacket and extended it to her.

Faith stared, but wouldn't move forward to reach for the
item, which appeared to be a photograph.

'This is you just over three years ago,' he breathed in a
gritty undertone. 'And if you had your memory right now,
we'd be having a major fight.'

'A m-major fight…' Faith parroted weakly.

'I crept up on you with the camera. You were furious.
You made me promise to destroy the photo. I said I would.
I lied. I'm afraid it's the only photo of you I have left.'
Stooping with athletic ease, he tossed the glossy snap down
on the pitted tiled floor like a statement.

It skimmed to a halt about two feet from her. Faith stared
down at the snap where it lay. Her eyes opened impossibly
wide. She saw a slim, bare-breasted blonde semi-submerged
in bubbles in a giant bath. She saw a slim, bare-breasted
blonde with her face, her eyes, her mouth…her breasts. She
didn't want that brazen hussy to be her! Shock rolled over
her like a tidal wave.

'Keeping it was kind of a guy thing,' Gianni admitted,
almost roughly.

A strangled moan of denial slowly hissed from Faith's
rigidly compressed lips. Her head swam, the photo spinning
out of focus, her legs turning hollow. And then the great
well of darkness behind her eyelids sucked her down frighteningly fast into a faint.

Gianni caught her before she hit the floor in a crumpled
heap and swore vehemently.

CHAPTER TWO

FAITH drifted back to awareness in a complete daze. Her lashes fluttered and then lifted. A dark male face swam into stark focus, but it was those eyes, those stunning lion-gold eyes fringed by black spiky lashes, that entrapped her attention and held her still. Her breath feathered in her throat.

The oddest little tugging sensation pulled deep down inside her, heralding a slow burst of heat that spread from the pit of her stomach up, and then down to more intimate places. Faith quivered in extreme disconcertion, extraordinarily conscious of the strange sensitivity of her full breasts, the sudden straining tightness of her nipples. She couldn't breathe, she couldn't speak, she couldn't think. Her body had taken on a frightening life of its own, yet she couldn't muster the power to either question or control it.

'Gianni…Gianni,' a breathless voice she barely recognised as her own pleaded achingly inside her mind. Seemingly of its own volition, her hand lifted and began to rise towards that strong, aggressive jawline…

Gianni's eyes shimmered chillingly. He broke the spell by tilting his proud dark head back out of her reach. Then he flashed her a look of raw derision. 'When I want sex, I'll tell you, Milly. In the meantime, keep your hands to yourself.'

That assurance was so shattering it sprang Faith back to full awareness. As he slid back upright from his crouching position by the sagging basketwork chair on which she sat, all that had happened in the minutes before she had fainted flooded back to fill her with frantic, frightening confusion.

She had been viewing the house. He had arrived. He had shown her the photo, that awful photo of herself flaunting her bare breasts like a tart. He *did* know her. He *had* known her. Dear heaven, she conceded in drowning mortification, he had to have known her in the biblical sense. This man had actually slept with her.

Disorientation engulfed her. She heard afresh that pleading voice whispering his name inside her head, and wondered in stunned disbelief if after three long empty years she had *finally* remembered something from the past. Something she didn't want to remember, something that made her squirm with discomfiture. Perhaps it had been her imagination playing a trick on her. Why now and never before? She lifted her head and then suddenly dropped it down again, shutting her eyes tight, unable to meet Gianni D'Angelo's cool, measured gaze. A dulled throb of tension now pulsed behind her temples.

She recalled his derision, the blunt immediacy of what had been a rejection couched in the most humiliating terms. And then she relived what had prompted that crushing response from him. Oh, dear God, she thought with stunned shame, in those first moments of recovering consciousness she had focused on him and experienced the most unbelievably powerful surge of physical hunger. She was shattered by that realisation. It rewrote everything she had believed she knew about that side of her nature.

The sound of brisk footsteps sent her eyes flying open again. She gaped at the sight of the uniformed older man who appeared in the doorway to extend, of all things, a brandy goblet. Gianni took it from him with a nod and a dismissive move of one authoritative hand. He strode back to Faith and slotted the glass into her nerveless fingers. 'Drink it. You're as white as a sheet,' he instructed grimly.

'Wh-where did that man and this drink come from?' she stammered in unwilling wonderment.

Gianni frowned, as if that had been a very stupid question. 'When you passed out, I called my driver on the car phone and told him to bring it in.'

Faith slowly nodded, studying him with slightly glazed

eyes. Did he have a bar in his car? It had to be a big car.
He wasn't giving her a bottle to swig out of. Her sense of
dislocation from reality increased. The gulf between them
felt immeasurable. According to Louise, Gianni D'Angelo
was a very wealthy and powerful tycoon, and certainly he
looked the part. What sort of relationship could she possibly
have had with such a man? Suddenly she really didn't want
to know.

'Drink the brandy,' Gianni pressed with controlled impatience.

'I hardly ever touch alcohol…'

'Well, you weren't on any wagon when I knew you,'
Gianni informed her without hesitation.

Shaken by that come-back, and the daunting knowledge
that was his alone, Faith tipped the glass to her lips. The
spirit raced down her dry throat like liquid fire and burned
away the chill spreading inside her. She swallowed hard and
then breathed in deep. 'It seems you once knew me…I want
that photograph back!' she added the instant she recalled its
existence, anxious eyes lowering to see if it still lay on the
floor. It didn't.

'Forget it; it's mine. But isn't that just like a woman?'
Gianni growled with incredulous scorn. 'I only showed you
that photo to make you accept that we once had a certain
bond, and now you can only concentrate on a complete ir-
relevance!'

It didn't feel irrelevant to Faith. Right at that moment she
saw that revealing photo as shocking evidence of a past she
wanted to leave buried, and she certainly didn't want it left
in his possession. 'Look, Mr D'Angelo—'

'*Mister* D'Angelo?' he queried, with a slashing smile that
chilled her to the marrow. 'Make it Gianni.'

That ice-cold smile was like a threat. It shook her. He was
poised several feet away, still as a predator about to spring.
She recognised his hostility and recoiled from it in sudden
fear. 'You hate me…'

He froze.

The silence thundered.

Suddenly he swung away from her. 'You don't remember me...you don't remember *anything*, do you?'

'No...I don't,' she conceded tautly.

'I thought you would've been full of questions. This isn't any easier for me,' he ground out in a charged undertone, spinning back to her with graceful but restive rapidity. Stormy dark eyes assailed her and she paled even more. 'At the airport, I admit I wanted to strangle you. I didn't know you'd lost your memory. I don't like you looking at me like I'm about to attack you either!'

Intimidated by the powerful personality that he was revealing, Faith did nothing to soothe him when she instinctively cowered back into the chair.

'Milly...'

'That's not my name!' she protested.

He let that go past.

'Look...' He spread the fingers of one lean and eloquent hand. 'You're scared because I'm rocking your cosy little world. It's not me you're afraid of. You're scared of the unknown that I represent.'

Faith gave a slight wary nod that might or might not have signified agreement, but her expressive eyes revealed her surprise that he could make that distinction. She wasn't used to the sensation of someone else trying to get inside her head and work out how she felt.

'I don't want to frighten you, but anything I tell you is likely to cause you distress, so I'll keep it basic.'

'How did you find out where I was living? How did you know I was an amnesiac?' Faith suddenly demanded accusingly.

'Naturally I had you followed from the airport. Then I had some enquiries made,' Gianni supplied with a fluid shrug.

Rising in one sudden motion from the chair, Faith gave him a stricken look of bemusement. 'But why would you do something like that? Why would you go to so much trou-

ble? Why are you here now? Just because we had some
relationship years ago?'

'I'm working up to that. I did have this rather naïve hope
that you might start remembering things when you saw me
again,' Gianni confided with a sardonic laugh, his smooth,
dark features broodingly taut. 'But it looks like I'm going
to have to do this the hard way. I suggest you sit down
again.'

'No.' Faith braced her slim shoulders, a sudden powerful
need to regain control of the situation driving her. 'I don't
need to put myself through this if I don't want to. I don't
need to listen to you—'

Gianni murmured, 'I'm afraid you do...'

'No, I don't. I just want you to go away and leave me
alone,' Faith admitted truthfully, suppressing the little inner
voice that warned her that that was craven and short-sighted.
For here it finally was, the opportunity she had once yearned
for: the chance to knock a window, however small, into that
terrible wall that closed her out from her own memory. Yet
because she didn't know, indeed strongly feared what she
might glimpse through that window, she was rejecting the
chance.

Gianni D'Angelo surveyed her with disturbing intensity,
brilliant eyes semi-screened by his lush lashes to a glimmer
of gold. 'That's not possible. You asked me why I was here.
So I'll tell you. It's quite simple. When you disappeared out
of my life, you were pregnant with my child...'

A roaring sounded in Faith's ears. Her lips parted. She
stared back at him in horror as that cosy little world he had
referred to with such perceptible scorn lurched and tilted
dangerously on its axis.

'Connor is *my* son,' Gianni spelt out levelly.

The very floor under Faith's feet seemed to shift. Her eyes
were blank with shock.

As she swayed, Gianni strode forward. Curving a powerful arm to her spine to steady her, he took her out of the
conservatory and back through the hall. 'No, don't pass out

on me again. Let's get out of this dump. We both need some fresh air.'

The winter sunlight that engulfed her at the front of the house seemed impossibly bright. She blinked and shifted her aching head. 'No, not Connor...it's not possible...not *you*!'

Ignoring those objections, Gianni guided her over to a worn bench and settled her down on it with surprisingly gentle hands. He hunkered down in front of her and reached for her trembling fingers, enclosing them firmly in his. 'There *is* no easy way to tell you these things. I'm working really hard to keep the shocks to the minimum.'

That one shock had temporarily left her bereft of the ability to even respond. And yet he could call that one bombshell keeping the shocks to the ''minimum''? Dear God, what worse could he tell her than he had already told her? Her face was pale as parchment. 'My head hurts,' she mumbled, like a child seeking sympathy in an effort to ward off punishment for some offence.

Gianni's hands tightened fiercely on hers. 'I'm sorry, but I had to tell you. Why do you think I'm here? Why do you think I've spent three endless years trying to trace you both?' he demanded emotively.

Faith focused on him numbly. The father of her child. Why hadn't that possibility occurred to her sooner? But she knew why, didn't she? Connor might as well have sprung into being without benefit of any male input whatsoever.

Once she had been frantic to know who had fathered her child, but when she had admitted that need to her parents they had gone all quiet and looked at each other uncomfortably. And when she had questioned their attitude to what seemed to her an absolutely crucial question that had to be answered, she had recognised what they didn't want to put into words.

They were afraid that she had been promiscuous, that she might not even know for sure who had actually got her pregnant. And she had been very upset to realise that her parents could harbour such sordid suspicions about a life she could no longer remember.

'The father of my baby might love me…might be looking for me right now!' she had sobbed in distraught self-defence.

'If he loved you, why were you on your own?'

'If you disappeared, why hasn't he been in touch with the police?'

'And why hasn't he come here looking for you? Surely he would at least have known where your parents lived? Even though you hadn't been in touch with us recently, wouldn't he have arrived here to check us out as a last resort?'

Faced with those unanswerable questions, Faith had finally let go of the idea that she might have conceived her baby in a caring relationship. And from that moment on she had begun suppressing her own curiosity, shrinking from the idea that Connor might be the result of some casual sexual encounter. Yet those suspicions had only fronted worse fears, she conceded now, a hysterical laugh lodging like a giant stone in her throat. These days you read so many horror stories about the level penniless and homeless teenagers could be reduced to just to survive…

'Milly…' Gianni tugged her upright.

'That's n-not my name,' she stated through chattering teeth.

He raised his hands to capture her taut cheekbones and she shivered because he was so very close. 'That's the name I knew you by,' he murmured softly.

'Please let go of me…'

'You're shaking like a jerry-built building in an earthquake,' Gianni countered drily.

She realised that she was. Involuntarily, she braced her hands on his chest. Instantly the heat of him sprang out at her and she swiftly removed her hands again, almost off-balancing in her eagerness to put some distance between them. But the distinctive scent of him still flared in her nostrils. Clean, warm, intrinsically male and somehow earthy in a way Edward was not. Edward always smelt of soap. *Oh, my God, Edward,* a voice screamed inside her pounding head.

Another moan was dredged from her. She covered her distraught face with trembling hands in growing desperation. Connor, whom she loved beyond life itself. Connor's father was here to stake a claim in his son's life. What else could he be here for? Why else had he searched for them?

'Let me tell you something...' Gianni breathed in a charged undertone that reeked of menace but somehow didn't frighten her. 'Three years without me has turned you into a basket case! I'm taking you back to my hotel and getting a doctor to look you over!'

By sheer force of will he got her down the path and out onto the pavement. She wasn't capable of matching the speed of his reactions, but she dimly registered that what he thought he acted on simultaneously, with terrifying decisiveness. She gawped at the sight of the long silver limousine waiting, not to mention the chauffeur surging round the bonnet as if he was running a race to get the passenger door open in time.

'Your hotel...?' she repeated belatedly, her brain functioning only in tiny, cripplingly slow bursts of activity. 'I can't go to your *hotel*!'

Gianni ducked her head down as carefully as an officer of the law tucking a suspect into a police car and settled her onto the rich leather-backed seat. He swung in beside her, forcing her to move deeper into the opulent car, and a split second later the door slammed on them both.

'I'm not going anywhere with you!' Faith protested frantically. 'I've got to get back to the shop—'

'I'm sure your partner will manage without you for a couple of hours.'

'I have to pick up Connor from the nursery...no, I don't...I *forgot*,' she lied jerkily. 'The kids are out on a trip today and they won't be back until—'

Gianni subjected her to a derisive appraisal. 'Wise up,' he

breathed in cool interruption. 'You can't hide Connor or keep him from me. When I want to meet my son, I will, but I'm unlikely to stage that meeting when you're on the edge of hysteria.'

He had seen right through her, and that terrified her. 'I'm not on the edge of hysteria...my car...the house...it wasn't locked up—'

Gianni held up the keys. 'I pulled the door shut behind us. If you give me your car keys, your car will be picked up and driven over to the hotel. You're in no condition to drive.'

Faith surveyed him with huge haunted eyes. She passed over her car keys. He was like a tank, rolling over her to crush her deeper and deeper into the dust. And so cold, so very, very cold, she sensed with a shiver. He had tried to calm her, gripped her hands, made an effort to show that he understood why she was so distressed. But none of that had worked. Why? There was no human warmth in him. His brilliant, beautiful dark eyes now chilled her to ice.

Connor's eyes were lighter in shade, but his skin always had that same golden tint even in winter, she reflected numbly. Maybe he was lying about Connor being his child! Even as her head pounded unmercifully into what felt like the onset of a migraine attack she discarded that faint hope. Gianni D'Angelo wouldn't be wasting his time tracking down a child he didn't know to be his.

Stray, unconnected thoughts kept on hitting her from all directions. She had shared his bed. She shifted on the seat, totally unable to look at him any more. She had bathed in his bath. It had to have been *his* bath. Nothing would convince her that she had ever been in the bracket of owning so luxurious a bath. But he had avoided the usual word 're-lationship' to describe their former intimacy. 'A certain bond'. That was the phrase he had used. Such an odd choice to describe their...their what?

Not an affair, not a relationship? Oh, dear heaven, had she been a one-night stand? Or worse? And she knew what was worse. No, no. She discarded that melodramatic suspicion. If she'd been a hooker, he would hardly be so sure her son was his. Dear heaven, what was she thinking? It was as if her brain had just been unhinged, torn open to let all her most deep-seated anxieties flood out.

In silence, Gianni reached into the built-in bar and withdrew a glass. He poured another brandy and settled it meaningfully into her trembling fingers.

Had she drunk a lot when he knew her? Been a real boozer with a strong head? She raised the glass to her lips, the rim rattling against her teeth. The nightmare just went on and on. What did he want from her? She was too terrified to ask, was in a state of complete panic, incapable of rational dialogue.

She didn't even notice where the limo had been going until he helped her out of the car. It was a big country house hotel about three miles out of town. Faith had dined there on her twenty-sixth birthday. Even her father, who liked to make a show of sophistication, had winced at the cost of that meal.

'I don't want to go in here...just take me home,' she mumbled. 'I'm not feeling very well.'

'You can lie down for a while,' Gianni assured her. 'Get your head together.'

'You're not listening to me—'

'You're not saying anything I want to hear.'

'Did I ever?' she heard herself whisper as he pressed her into the lift and the doors slid shut on them.

His superb bone structure tautened. 'I don't remember,' he said flatly.

Her tummy twisted. Was he making fun of her?

Gianni stared down at her from his imposing height. His mouth curled. 'I guess you could say I don't *want* to remember. It's irrelevant now.'

Her head felt woozy, her legs weak and wobbly. As the lift disgorged them into a smoothly carpeted reception area containing only one door, he settled a bracing hand on her spine. 'I don't want to be here,' she told him afresh.

'I know, but I have a habit of getting what I want.' He made her precede him into an incredibly spacious and luxurious suite. Closing the door, he bent, and without the slightest hesitation scooped her off her feet.

'What are you doing?' she gasped.

'You should've said no to that second drink. But possibly I did you a favour. The alcohol has acted on you like a tranquilliser.' Thrusting open another door, he crossed the room beyond and laid her down on a big bed. 'The doctor will check you out in a few minutes. I brought him down from London with me.'

'I don't need a doctor.'

Gianni studied her without any expression at all and strode back out of the room, leaving the door slightly ajar.

A doctor did come. He was middle-aged and suave. If he gave her his name, she didn't catch it. She was finding it impossible to concentrate, and she was so tired, so unbelievably tired, it took almost incalculable effort to respond to his questions...

Gianni watched Milly sleep. Grudging pity stirred in him. She looked so fragile, and it wasn't an illusion. Right now, Milly was like a delicate porcelain cup with a hair-fine crack. If he wasn't very careful, she would break in half, and he might never get her glued back together again. Connor needed his mother. Connor did not need a mother having a nervous breakdown over the identity crisis that was soon to engulf her.

Porca miseria, Gianni swore inwardly. He wanted to wipe Robin and Davina Jennings from the face of the earth for screwing Milly up. She wasn't the same person any more. She was a shadow imprint. Anxious, nervous as a cat, apologetic, scared. She didn't know him from Adam and yet she had just let him bring her back to his hotel suite. In her current condition she was as foolishly trusting as a very young child.

But there was nothing immature about Gianni's response to her. He wanted to rip her out of that buttoned-up white blouse and gathered floral skirt she wore and free her glorious hair from that ugly plait. And then he wanted to jump her like an animal and keep her in bed for at least twenty-four hours, he acknowledged, with grim acceptance of his own predictability.

He had really hoped she would leave him cold. But she didn't. Sooner or later she would. She was a woman, like other women, and eventually all women bored him. Only she never had in the past, he conceded reluctantly. And if he hadn't caught her with Stefano he would have married her. His dirt-poor Sicilian background of traditional values had surfaced when he'd got her pregnant. He had been ready to buy into the whole dream. The wife, the child, the family hearth. And this tiny, fragile woman, who would only reach his heart now if she stood on literal tiptoes, had exploded the dream and destroyed his relationship with his brother.

He had wanted revenge so badly he could still taste it even now. He had come down to Oxfordshire intending to let revenge simply take its natural course. He emitted a humourless laugh. He hated her, but he craved the oblivion of her sweet body like a drug addict craved a fix. He hated her, but he couldn't bring himself to hurt her. He hated the Jenningses for making him the weapon that had to hurt. He had no choice but to blow Milly's cosy little fake world away. She had to take her own life back, and she couldn't do that without him...

A slight, slanting smile eased the ferocious tension stamped on Gianni's features. She was *his*. He cursed the rampant stirring in his loins. He had been in a state of near constant arousal ever since the airport. Only rigid self-discipline and cold intellect restrained him. For the foreseeable future, she was untouchable. He had waited three years; he could wait a little longer. The fiancé had to be seen off.

How *was* Mr Square and Upwardly Mobile likely to react to the news that Milly wasn't really the boss's daughter?

Milly shifted in her sleep and turned over. The plait lay temptingly exposed on the pillow. Gianni moved forward, and before he even knew what he was doing he was unclasping the stiff black bow, loosening the strands, running his long fingers through her beautiful silky hair. His hands weren't quite steady. Instantly he withdrew them, studied them broodingly, clenched them into defensive fists.

When she had her memory back and he had enjoyed her for a while, he would dump her again. But he would retain a lot of visiting privileges. Purely for his son's benefit, of course. The cascade of half-unravelled wavy golden hair hung over the side of the bed like a lethal lure. It might be quite a while until he dumped her. So what? He asked himself. You couldn't put a price on pleasure.

But how did he tell her the truth about herself in a way that didn't make her hate him? How did you wrap up the fact that at heart she was a gold-digging, cheating tramp who had fooled him right to the bitter end? And if she got her memory back she was going to remember that she had run rings round him right from the minute she'd jumped out of that birthday cake. She was his one weakness, but he could afford to indulge himself just one more time. As long as he never let himself forget for a second what she was *really* like…

'Angel…?'

Somebody was shaking her awake. Faith began to sit up, opening her eyes, only to freeze into immobility.

Gianni D'Angelo stood over her. So very tall, so exotically dark.

'What did you call me?' she mumbled, remembering everything, attempting to block it back out again until she felt better equipped to deal with it.

Faint colour scored his hard cheekbones. 'Milly…I called you Milly.'

'My name's Faith,' she told him flatly, refusing to consider his assurance that he had known her by that other name because such an astonishing claim raised questions about her past she could not yet bring herself to ask. 'Why on earth did you bring me here?'

'You needed time out.'

With a sudden start of dismay, Faith checked her watch. It was almost one. She began to scramble off the bed with alacrity. 'I need to pick up Connor—'

'Call Mrs Jennings. You should eat before you get back behind a steering wheel.'

Mrs Jennings? What an odd way to refer to her mother! Struggling to regain her equilibrium, Faith was even more disconcerted by the untidy cascade of hair now falling round her face. The clasp must have fallen off while she slept. Thrusting the waving mass back behind one small ear, she frowned in Gianni's general direction. 'Eat? I have to pick up Connor—'

He extended a mobile phone to her. 'Ask Mrs Jennings to do it today. We need to talk.'

'No, I—'

'You can't run away from this.'

You can't run away from this. That blunt statement unnerved her. Her lower lip trembled, and then firmed. She twisted her golden head away and snatched in a shuddering breath. Once again Gianni D'Angelo had seen right through her. Her parents and Edward had always been content to accept what they saw on the surface.

And how *was* her fiancé likely to react to the sudden appearance of Connor's natural father? Badly—probably very badly, Faith acknowledged dully. Edward was a very conservative man. And he had once admitted that the very fact he was the only man involved in Connor's life had made it easier for him to accept her son.

The mobile phone was pressed into her tense fingers.

'You think you can just tell me what to do—' she began accusingly.

'Right now, you'd seize on any excuse to walk out of here again!'

Reddening at the accuracy of that stab, Faith turned back reluctantly to look at Gianni D'Angelo.

And, like a slap in the face, she saw all the cool control she craved etched into the arrogant angle of his dark head and the steadiness of his burnished dark gaze. He had complete dominion over himself.

'When you've made your call, we'll have lunch.'

Her teeth ground together. She couldn't hold back her hostility any longer. 'I really don't like you.'

Gianni stilled with one brown hand on the door. 'I know... The Sleeping Beauty woke up to a kiss—'

'She also woke up to a prince!' Faith heard herself interrupt, and then she stiffened, disturbed by the speed of her own retaliation. She never argued with anybody. She was far better known as a peacemaker.

'If I'd kissed you, you might have screamed assault...although possibly that's only what you'd prefer me to believe.' Gianni surveyed her, a sardonic slant to his expressive mouth. 'I think your body remembers me better than your brain does.'

Faith was aghast at that suggestion. 'How *dare* you?'

Gianni gave an exaggerated wince. 'Tell me, how do you square the outraged prudish virgin act with the reality that you're a single mother?'

Beneath his coolly enquiring gaze, Faith's soft mouth opened and closed again. Colour flooded her complexion.

'When something irritates the hell out of me, I usually mention it,' Gianni shared, before he turned on his heel and left her alone.

In his wake, a combustible mix of anger and chagrin engulfed Faith. She punched out her home phone number with a stabbing finger. Her mother answered.

'It's Faith. I'm sorry, but I won't be home for lunch...and I hate to ask you at such short notice but could you pick up Connor from nursery for me?' Faith asked tautly.

'Of course I can, darling,' Davina Jennings responded instantly. 'You sound flustered. Is the shop very busy or is Louise away? Never mind. I'd better get a move on if I'm to collect my grandson *and* still have lunch ready for your father!'

'Thanks, Mum.'

Faith laid down the mobile. As she did so she caught a glimpse of herself in a mirror. *Outraged virgin?* Her cheeks burned afresh. Was that really how she came across?

During her convalescence her mother had warned her that she had a reputation to rebuild, that folk would be quick to pass final judgement on an unmarried mother. Already the target of considerable local curiosity, Faith had been painfully aware of her parents' concern about how she might behave. Her parents were very private people, but they were pillars of both church and community. So Faith had followed her mother's guidance when it came to her wardrobe and had worked hard at cultivating an acceptably low profile.

Distractedly, Faith lifted one of the silver brushes on the dresser to try and tidy her hair as she couldn't find her clasp anywhere. There had been nothing prudish about that blonde in the bath…and, whether she liked it or not, that blonde *had* been her! Yet she still found that so hugely hard to accept. It was like the sudden discovery of an identical twin, who was her exact opposite in personality and behaviour.

After all, in three long years Faith had never had the slightest urge to go to bed with anybody! Quite a few men had asked her out. Unfortunately most had had definite expectations of how the evening should end. Repulsed by those pushy advances, Faith had come to believe that she had a pretty low sex drive, and had occasionally marvelled at Connor's very existence.

Edward had been a family friend long before they had started seeing each other, and she had been grateful that he seemed so ideally suited to her. Her fiancé was neither physically demonstrative nor sexually demanding. He had informed her that he preferred to save intimacy for marriage.

He had even told her that he would respect her more on those terms, particularly when she had made what he called 'a youthful mistake'. When it had dawned on her that the 'mistake' Edward was referring to was Connor, she had been mortified and hurt.

When Faith walked back into the beautifully furnished reception room next door, she saw a waiter standing by a trolley in the elegant dining area. Gianni was poised by the window. He watched her approach with unfathomable eyes. Her tummy flipped and her breathing quickened.

'Let's eat,' he suggested smoothly.

She was surprised to discover how hungry she was, and was grateful for the restraining presence of the waiter. Gianni embarked on an impersonal conversation. He questioned her about local businesses and the recent bankruptcies on the industrial estate. His razor-sharp intellect swiftly outran the depths of her economic knowledge. Where another man might have centred his interest on local history, or the sights to be seen, Gianni functioned on an entirely different level.

Involuntarily, Faith was fascinated. In the midst of her nightmare, Gianni D'Angelo could behave as if nothing remotely abnormal was happening. It was intimidating proof of a very resourceful and clever male in absolute control of a difficult situation.

When the waiter departed after serving them, Faith tensed up again. Gianni surveyed her with slumbrous dark golden eyes and her throat tightened, her heartbeat speeding up.

'Now it's time to talk about Connor,' he told her with immovable cool.

'Connor? How can we?' Faith protested without hesitation. 'As it is, I can hardly get my mind around the idea that you *could* be his father!'

'Not could be, *am*,' Gianni countered with level emphasis. 'You had a test shortly before your disappearance for the child's DNA. I am, without a single shadow of a doubt, Connor's father.'

Faith's knife and fork fell from her loosening hold to rattle jarringly down on her plate. She stared back at him, appalled by that revealing admission. 'You weren't sure that...well, that... You mean you didn't trust me...you suspected there might've been room for doubt?' She struggled valiantly to frame that horribly humiliating question, and her strained voice shook.

Gianni's lean, dark devastating face was now as still as a woodland pool. He cursed his error in referring to the DNA tests to convince her that Connor was his son and murmured evenly, 'I'm a very rich man. The DNA testing was a necessary precaution.'

'A n-necessary precaution...?' Faith stammered.

'A legal safeguard,' Gianni extended with a slight shift of one broad shoulder. 'Once Connor was proven to be my child I could be sure that if anything happened to me his inheritance rights would not be easily contested.'

Faith nodded uncertainly, thoroughly taken aback by the obvious fact that Gianni D'Angelo had already thought to make provision for her son in his will. She also registered that she herself had already moved on in terms of acceptance and expectation. Only three hours ago she had wanted Gianni to vanish, had denied any need to know what ties they might once have had. But now she badly needed to be reassured that they had had a stable relationship which would *not* have entailed DNA testing simply to confirm the paternity of her child.

'You said I was trying to run away from all this,' she reminded him tautly, her clear blue eyes pinned anxiously to his hard bronzed features. 'At first, yes, I was. I was so shocked. But now I have a whole lot of questions I need to ask.'

'About us,' Gianni slotted in softly. 'Unfortunately it would be a bad idea for me to unload too many facts on you right now.'

Faith frowned in complete confusion. 'Why?'

His stunning eyes veiling, Gianni pushed away his plate

and lounged back fluidly in his chair to study her. 'I talked to a psychologist before I came down here.'

'A psychologist?' Disconcerted pink surged up beneath her skin at that admission. The embarrassed distaste with which her parents had regarded all such personnel had left its mark on her.

'It was his view that wherever possible you should only be expected to deal with one thing at a time. That's why we're concentrating on Connor,' Gianni explained, with the slow quiet diction of someone dealing with a child on the brink of a tantrum. 'At this moment, that's enough for you to handle.'

'Let me get this straight,' Faith muttered unevenly. 'You are telling me that you are not prepared to—'

'Muddy the water and confuse you with what is currently extraneous information,' Gianni confirmed, watching her eyes darken and flare with incredulous anger.

Abruptly thrusting back her chair, Faith rose to her feet. 'Who the heck do you think you are to tell me that?'

'Sit down and finish your meal,' Gianni drawled.

Faith trembled. 'I have the right to know what role I played in your life. That is *not* extraneous information!'

'I think it is. I want to talk about my son because I've waited three years to find him and now I would very much like to meet him.' Gianni's measured gaze challenged her.

'You're not meeting Connor until you tell me what I need to know!' Faith's head was starting to pound, not least because a temper she had never known she had was tightening its grip on her, no matter how hard she strove to contain it. 'What was I to you? A one-night stand? *A hooker?*' she slung furiously. 'Or a girlfriend?'

With pronounced cool, Gianni came upright to face her. Even in the overwrought state she was in, his striking grace of movement caught her eye as he stepped out from behind the table. 'No to all of the above. Leave this for another day, *cara*,' he advised very quietly, incisive dark-as-night eyes resting on the revealing clenching and unclenching of her hands. 'When the time's right, I'll tell you everything you want to know.'

'Stop treating me like I'm mentally unfit to deal with my *own* life!' Faith launched back at him in furious condemnation. 'I'll ask you one more time before I walk out of here…what was I to you?'

Gianni expelled his breath in a slow hiss. 'You were my mistress.'

Faith stared back at him, eyes widening and widening, soft mouth rounding but no sound emerging. The angry tension evaporated from her. Sheer shock stilled her, leaving her looking vulnerable and lost. Then she sealed her lips, forced her feet to turn her around and walked to the door. There she hesitated, wheeled back, and hurried across the room again to retrieve her handbag. Not once did she allow her attention to roam back in Gianni's direction.

'Are my car keys in here?' she asked woodenly.

'Yes. This is ridiculous,' Gianni murmured drily.

'How long was I…your mistress?' Faith squeezed out that designation as if her mouth was a clothes-wringer.

'Two years…'

Faith flinched as though he had struck her a second body blow. Then, pushing up her chin and straightening her slight shoulders, she moved back to the door and paused there. 'I hope you paid me well to prostitute myself,' she breathed through painfully compressed lips.

In the thunderous silence that greeted that stinging retaliation Faith turned her head. Gianni gazed back at her, not a muscle moving on his darkly handsome features. But for once she could read him like an open book. His golden eyes blazed his fury. Oddly soothed by that reaction, Faith stalked rigid-backed out of the suite and headed for the lift.

CHAPTER THREE

FAITH'S tenuous control crumpled and fell apart the instant she reached the sanctuary of her car.

Snatching in a gasping breath in an effort to calm herself, Faith stared blindly through the windscreen. *His mistress!* It made a horrible kind of sense. He was filthy rich. She wasn't from the same world. So of course she hadn't been his girl-friend, his *equal*, she reflected bitterly. Now she knew why he had been challenged to quantify their relationship. The commercial element had figured. For two years. *Two years*, an agonised inner voice screeched in condemnation. It had taken her an inexcusably long time to wake up and see the error of her ways.

For two years, two of her missing years, she had been a kept woman. In exchange for sex he had probably paid for the roof over her head, her clothing, all her bills. Faith shuddered, mortified by the self she had clearly been before she'd lost her memory. What kind of woman could she have been? This woman who had called herself Milly? What further humiliating discoveries still awaited her?

Striving hard to get a grip on her wildly seesawing emotions, Faith started the car and drove away from the hotel. Gianni had said she had disappeared. OK, she told herself, it might have taken her a long time but at least she had finally decided to leave him. She must have planned to make a fresh start. And a fresh start was exactly what she had made, she reminded herself doggedly.

Then, just as she came off the roundabout on the outskirts of town, her searing headache became suddenly so much worse that her vision began to blur. Immediately she pulled off the road and parked. Perspiration beaded her short upper lip.

And then it happened. As if somebody was staging a sudden slideshow inside her head. A picture slotted into her mind. She saw herself clutching a phone like a lifeline, and then her awareness shifted and she was suddenly inside that self.

'Gianni...I haven't seen you in three weeks,' she was saying, and tears were stinging her eyes, but she was working really hard at keeping her voice light and teasing because like any workaholic Gianni hated it when she nagged.

'Book yourself a seat on Concorde.'

'OK...' she agreed with studied casualness, furiously blinking back the tears.

'I didn't realise it had been three weeks.' Gianni paused, and then continued with innate superiority and instinctive attention to detail. 'No, it hasn't been three weeks, *cara*. Don't you remember I stopped over one night before I went to Rio?'

'Gianni, much as I love you,' she groaned, 'there are times when I just want to reach down this phone line and *hit* you! You were here for less than five hours!'

And then, just as quickly as it had come, the picture vanished and Faith was left sitting behind the steering wheel of her car in complete shock. But every emotion she had experienced during that slide back into the past had stayed with her, and the revelation of those powerful emotions now took her by storm.

Winding down the window with a shaking hand, Faith drank in great gulps of fresh air. It had happened, this time it had really, definitely happened, and she had genuinely remembered something. But that tiny slice of the past she had relived had been incredibly disturbing.

She had loved him. She had *loved* Gianni D'Angelo! She had had a capacity for emotion then that had virtually eaten her alive. Until now Faith had never dreamt that at any stage of her life she could have experienced such strong feelings.

And it was even more devastating to be forced to accept that once she had adored Gianni D'Angelo, lived from one day to the next on that love, needed him as she needed air to breathe, felt she was barely existing when he wasn't around…

Emerging from that shattering new awareness, Faith tried to block it out again. It had already been a hell of a day. Tomorrow she would take it all out again and deal with it. Not now.

She drove through town and parked at the rear of Petals, the flowershop she ran with Louise.

Gianni D'Angelo's mistress. If she had once been *that* crazy about him, she could even begin to see how she might have ended up trapped in such a relationship. Love had made a fool of her. Love, she told herself urgently, was a lot more presentable an excuse than avarice.

But how was she to tell Edward? Edward was such a conventional man. Faith's heart sank. Edward had chosen to assume that some flash young man had seduced her and then abandoned her when she fell pregnant. That was how Edward had dealt with getting engaged to an unwed mother. He had effectively excused her from all real responsibility and decided to view her as an innocent victim.

But being kept by Gianni D'Angelo as a mistress was a very different kettle of fish. And how could she not tell Edward, when Gianni was here in the flesh demanding to meet his son? It was *all* going to come out. Nothing she could do could prevent that. Gianni D'Angelo's mistress. It was sordid. Why had she tried briefly to persuade herself otherwise? Edward and her parents would be extremely shocked. And Gianni wasn't likely to sink back into the woodwork again. Climbing out of her car, Faith paled at that awareness.

The shop was empty of customers. Louise was dusting shelves and humming to herself. Her partner turned round, and as Faith moved into the light she frowned. 'Heck, what's happened to you?'

Faith stiffened defensively like a hedgehog under sudden attack. 'Nothing...nothing's happened to me.'

'What have you done with your hair?' Louise demanded. 'My goodness, I never realised you had that much of it!'

'I had a headache...have a headache,' Faith corrected awkwardly. 'I'm sorry. I should've called you to tell you that I would be out for so long.'

'Nonsense. Go back home this minute. You look awful,' Louise told her bluntly.

Relieved by that advice, Faith went back out to her car and drove slowly home to the rambling old farmhouse her parents had bought and renovated when she was a child. In the cosy front hall, the scent of beeswax polish and the ticking of the old grandfather clock enveloped her like a healing blanket.

Connor ran out of the kitchen, loosed a noisy whoop of welcome and flung himself at her. 'Mummy!' he carolled.

Faith reached down and lifted her son. She hugged him so tightly he gave a yelp of protest. Instantly she loosened her grip and pressed an apologetic kiss to his smooth brow. A great gush of love had just engulfed her, but for the first time there was a piercing arrow of fearful insecurity inside that love.

He was a gorgeous little boy. The combination of her blonde hair with his dark brows, sparkling brown eyes and golden skin tone was unusual. But all of a sudden Connor wasn't exclusively her little boy any more. He was the son of a very rich man, who wanted a share of him. How much of a share?

Her mother emerged from the kitchen. 'Are you taking the rest of the afternoon off?' she asked, and then frowned. 'Oh dear, what's happened to your hair?'

'I lost the clasp.'

Davina Jennings, a small, comfortably rounded woman with short greying fair hair and an air of bustling activity, sighed. 'You should take time off more often. You do look tired, darling.'

'Do I?'' Averting her head, Faith lowered Connor to the floor.

She would talk to her parents tonight after dinner. There was no point putting it off. Gianni might just arrive on the doorstep. Possibly storming out on him hadn't been the wisest move. It might have made her feel better but it would have increased his hostility. And how could she blame *him* for the reality that she had been his mistress? She had been an adult when she had made that choice, not a helpless little girl.

'Since you're home, I think I'll just pop down to the church hall and check that everything's ready for that choral do this evening,' Davina Jennings continued. 'I know Janet Markham said she would see to it, but I'm afraid the younger women on the ladies' committee aren't always as reliable as they like to think.'

Faith knew that her mother would be out for the rest of the afternoon. Davina loved to be busy. She would go down to the church hall, seize with alacrity on the idea that the floor wasn't quite clean enough or the kitchen looked a little dingy and roll up her sleeves.

Faith went upstairs to her bedroom. Connor got down on his knees to run a toy car along the skirting board, making phroom-phroom noises while she got changed. She pulled on a sweater and a comfy denim skirt and took Connor out to the garden.

It was a lovely mild winter day. But the sense of tranquillity that usually enveloped her outdoors refused to come. What would Gianni do next? She was just sitting here on pins waiting to find out, wasn't she? Suddenly ashamed of her own passiveness, Faith walked into the kitchen and reached for the phone. It made sense that she should contact Gianni to arrange to meet up with him. The last thing she wanted was for him to arrive unannounced at her home...

But the receptionist at the hotel didn't seem to know whether they had a Gianni D'Angelo staying or not. Yet she still requested Faith's name and address before she might condescend to pass on such privileged information. Exasperated, because she was afraid she might lose her nerve, Faith decided to leave a message instead.

'Tell him Milly would like to see him. I'll be...I'll be in the park at four,' she dictated tautly, and hurriedly replaced the receiver.

Cloak and dagger stuff, but why give her own name when it wasn't necessary? And this way she would get the worst over with, she told herself bracingly. She would let him see Connor and find out exactly what he wanted. She was dealing with a very rich and powerful male, who was already hostile towards her. At this point, antagonising him without good reason would be foolish.

An hour later, Faith drew into the car park. There was no limo, so Gianni hadn't arrived yet. In fact there were no other cars parked at all. With Connor holding her hand, Faith walked down the sloping path that ran between the steeply banked wildflower meadows towards the playground and the artificial lake. Her heart was now beating so fast she pressed a hand against her breast.

She rounded a corner and saw a man in a dark suit talking into a radio. She tensed, wondering what he was doing, suddenly appreciating that she had come to a very lonely place at an hour when it was likely to be deserted. The man fell silent as she moved past. Connor pulled free of her hold and ran ahead into the playground, his sturdy little legs carrying him towards the slide he loved at a steady rate of knots.

'See me, Mummy!' he shouted breathlessly as he reached the final step, his face ablaze with achievement.

And at that exact moment Gianni appeared, striding down the path she had just emerged from. Something disturbingly akin to excitement flashed through Faith, freezing her in her tracks. The man with the radio spoke to him, but Gianni slashed a silencing hand through the air. Gianni's entire attention was already fixed on the little boy carefully settling himself to the top of the slide, tiny hands holding the toddler grips tight.

The whole atmosphere seemed to charge up. Faith couldn't take her eyes off Gianni. She watched him swallow, slowly shake his gleaming dark head in an almost vulnerable movement, and suddenly ram his hands into the pockets of his exquisitely tailored trousers. He stared at Connor as if he was the Holy Grail, and he did it with a raw intensity of emotional response that shook Faith to her innermost depths.

Did he ever look at *me* like that? she found herself wondering. She wouldn't have credited that Gianni D'Angelo had that much emotion in him. But the stark prominence of his superb bone structure, the shimmering brilliance of his ferociously intent eyes and the hands that he didn't seem to know what to do with any more as he jerked them back out of his pockets again all spoke for him.

Her throat thickened. Suddenly she felt on the outside, looking in. She had picked a guy who loved children but she had run away with his child. Why had she done that? He had known she was pregnant before she left him. Why *had* she left him? Hadn't she realised that he might feel like this about their baby?

Without the slightest warning or expectation, Faith was beginning to feel guilty.

He had known her by another name. Clearly she had lied to him and given him that false name. Why had she done that? Had she been ashamed of the life she was leading with him? Had she been trying to ensure that nobody could ever connect Faith Jennings with Gianni D'Angelo's mistress? Well, her lies must have hampered his every attempt to find them again. He couldn't possibly have known where her parents lived, or indeed anything about them.

'Whee!' Connor screeched as he whooshed down the slide, scrambling off at the foot to race back round to the steps to do it again, totally uninterested in the adults watching him.

'He's blond...' Gianni breathed gruffly from his stance several feet away, still not sparing her an actual glance. 'Somehow I never thought of that.'

Faith's breath feathered in her tightening throat. 'He has dark eyes and dark brows and he takes a tremendous tan,' she squeezed out unevenly. 'And he's pretty tall for his age, which he certainly didn't get from me—'

'He's just tremendous,' Gianni incised almost roughly, his foreign accent far more noticeable than it had been earlier in the day.

One day, in fact considerably less than twelve hours, Faith acknowledged. But today, in the space of those few hours, Gianni D'Angelo had changed her whole life.

Suddenly he turned his proud head, cold, dark flashing eyes seeking out hers in a look as physical as a blow. 'I've missed out on two and a half years of my son's life. You owe me...' he murmured in sibilant condemnation.

Faith went pale and crossed her arms jerkily. 'I didn't know...I didn't remember.'

'You knew when you did your vanishing act,' Gianni reminded her darkly. 'Now go and get Connor and tell him who I am!'

Faith blinked in disconcertion. 'I can't do that—'

'Why not?' Gianni shot back at her.

'I mean, he doesn't know you...it's far too soon,' she argued.

'I won't allow you to introduce me to my own child as some passing stranger,' Gianni spelt out. 'I'm his father. At his age, he's hardly likely to be traumatised by the news!'

Put squarely on the spot, Faith studied him with strained eyes. She hadn't been prepared for that demand. Foolishly, she hadn't thought beyond letting him see Connor, and even that decision, she recognised now with sudden shame, hadn't been made for the right reasons. Playing for time, she had dangled Connor like a carrot, in an effort to soothe Gianni and prevent him from taking any other form of action.

'*Porca miseria!*' Gianni suddenly gritted in a fierce undertone, striding forward, dark eyes flaming threat. 'Does he call your fiancé Daddy?'

Faith backed off a startled step and trembled. 'No, of course not!' she gasped.

Equally as suddenly, Gianni stilled. Dark, feverish colour had sprung up over his spectacular cheekbones as he surveyed her: a slight, shivering figure with replaited hair, drawn features and frightened confused eyes. Now clad in an ugly mud-coloured jacket, flat walking shoes and a shapeless denim skirt, she looked like a waif. The bitter anger sparked by his first emotive sight of a son who didn't know him drained away. One thing hadn't changed, he acknowledged ruefully. Without him around she was still a fashion disaster, choosing comfort and practicality over style.

'It's all right, *cara*,' Gianni murmured quietly. 'Really, it's all right.'

'I don't know what I'm doing here,' Faith whispered truthfully, her vision blurring with sudden tears.

'I don't know about the location, but this meeting was definitely a step in the right direction,' Gianni told her bracingly, checking that Connor was still wholly entranced by the slide before extending a supportive arm around her. 'Take a deep breath and let it out again...'

'I might fall over...' She tried to joke, but her taut voice emerged flat as a pancake. As he eased her into the shelter of his lean body she was alarmingly conscious of his male warmth and his intimate scent. Her tummy flipped, leaving her feeling desperately ill at ease.

'Not when I'm around.'

'I really don't know why I gave you a false name,' Faith heard herself confide. 'It seems such a strange thing to have done, and I've always thought I was an honest person...I really did think that.'

Gianni tensed and suppressed a groan. The plot thickens, he conceded grimly. Of course she was going to assume that her real name was the false one. What else was she to think while she still fondly imagined that the Jenningses were her parents? But by the end of the day he would have dealt with that problem as well, he reminded himself grimly. Handling one problem at a time had become an impossible challenge.

'Take me over to Connor,' he urged.

His lack of comment surprised Faith. But then it had hardly been the right moment for that confession, she decided dully. His sole interest right now was naturally his son.

As she headed for Connor, Gianni let his arm slide from her. It felt oddly like being pushed away. Confusion assailed her. She was uneasily conscious of the change within herself. Since she had had that flashback Gianni no longer felt like a stranger. Now she was hugely aware that she had once loved him. A terrifying, all-or-nothing, no-sacrifice-too-great love, which she had apparently offered freely. But she didn't think he had ever loved her. She had sensed her own insecurity during that phone call, relived her own determined attempt to conceal that insecurity.

When he saw them coming towards him, Connor perched on the end of the slide, restlessly swinging his legs, only curiosity in his eyes as he studied Gianni. He was a friendly, confident child, who had never been shy.

'You're *big*!' he said to Gianni, his blond head falling back to take in the height of a male at least six feet three inches tall, big brown eyes wide as the sky above and openly impressed.

Gianni laughed, and immediately hunkered down to his son's level. 'I think you're going to be big too,' he commented, half to himself.

'This is...' Faith had to stop and start again as Connor gazed up at her with innocently enquiring eyes. 'This is your father, Connor.'

Connor looked blank.

'Your daddy,' Faith rephrased in a taut undertone.

He recognised that word. 'Daddy?' he repeated, small legs falling still, a puzzled look on his face. Then his dark eyes rounded and he studied Gianni with dawning wonderment. 'Peter daddy?'

As Gianni tensed, Faith crouched down beside him. 'Yes, that's right…like Peter has a daddy. This is your daddy,' she explained.

'Who's Peter?' Gianni enquired out of the corner of his mouth.

'His friend at nursery,' Faith whispered back. 'He's been to his house to play.'

'Play ball?' Connor demanded, suddenly bouncing upright in excitement. 'Daddy play ball?'

Gianni released his pent-up breath. 'Not for a long time, but willing to learn,' he muttered not quite steadily. 'Why didn't I think of bringing something like that?'

Connor danced on the spot. Peter's daddy was more of a favourite than even Faith had appreciated. 'Play cars? Phroom-phroom?' he carolled hopefully, withdrawing a tiny toy car from his pocket.

'Phroom…phroom,' Gianni sounded obediently. 'I *love* playing cars!'

Connor grinned and raised his arms to be lifted. 'Phroom…phroom…phroom!' he said exuberantly.

Gianni reached out and eased his son into his arms and then slowly came upright, a slightly stunned light in his usually keen dark eyes. He held Connor awkwardly, at a slight distance from him, visibly afraid of taking too many liberties too soon and spoiling the moment.

Reacting to the amount of attention he was receiving, Connor spread his arms and proceeded to noisily intimate an aeroplane going into freefall.

'Connor, behave!' Faith scolded in dismay, but Gianni saw his mistake and hauled his son closer before he could divebomb out of his arms.

'Daddy!' Connor exclaimed, and wound his arms round Gianni's neck to plant a big kiss on his cheek. 'My Daddy…*mine*!' he stressed, with all the satisfaction of ownership.

Faith's eyes smarted. Even at this age, her son had clearly felt the difference between himself and his friend Peter. She would never have suspected that. She had thought he was too young to appreciate the absence of a father in his life, had once assumed that the presence of her own father would fill that gap. Unfortunately, Robin Jennings worked long hours, and Connor was invariably in bed when his grandfather was at home. And Edward found the high-octane energy of a toddler difficult to handle, had frankly admitted that he would feel more at home with Connor when he was a little older.

Yet Gianni's damp eyes shone. Edward had never looked at her son with such pride and emotion and fascination. And why should he have done? Edward was not Connor's father.

'Down!' Connor demanded.

Gianni lowered him to the thick carpet of bark on the ground. Connor got cheerfully down on all fours, stuck his bottom in the air and cried, 'Woof! Woof!'

'He's doing his dog impression. You're getting his whole repertoire,' Faith explained tightly. 'He's showing off like mad.'

'He's so full of life...so sweet,' Gianni murmured huskily, hunkering down again, careless of the muddy bark welling round his superb Italian leather shoes, to stay close to his son.

Connor got bored with being a dog very quickly. 'Ducks!' he reminded his mother.

Gianni regarded Faith enquiringly.

'On the lake. He likes to see them.'

Connor had already scampered off in the direction of the lake path and Faith hurried after him. The light was fast beginning to fade. Gianni fell into step beside her. The mature trees on the woodland trail cast dark shadows. When a man suddenly stepped into view several feet ahead of them, Faith gave a start of dismay.

Gianni spoke to him in Italian, and only then did she recall the other man who had been standing above the playground.

'What's going on?' she questioned nervously as they moved on. 'Who are those men?'

'I was really surprised when I got your message earlier, particularly when you styled yourself "Milly",' Gianni admitted.

Faith coloured. 'It seemed more discreet to do that.'

'Unfortunately my security staff were convinced the message was a set-up.'

'Security staff?' Those men worked for him?

'The park is swarming with them. They've had the time of their lives staking out this place over the past hour. They love stuff like this,' Gianni conceded with wry amusement.

'Why a set-up?' she queried. 'Why would anybody think that?'

'People don't, as a rule, ask me to meet them in such public places. I did wonder if the press had finally got on to us and whether you might have received a similar message purporting to be from me. The tabloids would pay a fortune for a photo of us all together—'

'Tabloids?' she exclaimed, thoroughly taken aback.

'Wake up, *cara*. The news that I have a child will be a major scoop. And sooner or later it *will* come out,' Gianni informed her. 'I could only protect you from that exposure by staying away from my son, and I'm not prepared to do that. I won't behave as if Connor is some grubby secret in my life.'

Faith was horrified by what he was telling her. His very arrival had already exploded her quiet life out of existence. Now he was calmly admitting that there would be worse to come. Naturally the press would have an interest in the private life of a male as wealthy and powerful as Gianni. But threat of such public exposure made Faith feel ill. If it happened, her parents would be devastated, and once again she would be responsible for hurting them.

Since Connor had got down on the grass verge to play with the gravel on the path, Faith came to a halt and rested back weakly against the trunk of a tall beech tree. 'You don't give a damn, do you?' she muttered shakily. 'No matter how it affects me and my family, you'll still go ahead and demand access to Connor.'

'Guilty as charged,' Gianni said drily. 'I've been excluded from my son's life long enough.'

In the twilight, Faith focused on his lean bronzed features with a heart that was chilled even as its beat involuntarily quickened. His dark, deep-set eyes had an aggressive golden glimmer that challenged. He was tougher than titanium and he wasn't going to quit. 'You're so unfeeling,' she condemned unevenly.

Moving fluidly forward, Gianni braced one lean hand against the trunk and stared down at her, spiky black lashes low over his slumbrous gaze. 'Am I?' he questioned in a lazy undertone as smooth as black silk.

That deep, dark drawl sent tiny little shivers running down her taut spinal cord. Her bemused eyes locked to his and feverish tension snaked through her. For the space of a heartbeat she wanted to move away, and then she wasn't sure what she had wanted or even why she might have wanted it. As rational thought blurred, other more intrusive physical sensations took precedence.

That close, Gianni truly mesmerized her. Her breathing quickened, her mouth running dry. Dark excitement flowcred into being inside her. Her muscles tightened on a delicious thrilling edge. The sudden aching fullness of her breasts and the urgent sensitivity of her nipples made her tremble, every pulse racing at fevered speed.

She could hardly breathe as Gianni watched her with the still golden eyes of a hunter. He brought up his other hand and let his thumb slowly graze the full curve of her lower lip. At the first touch of his hand, heat burst into being low in her pelvis, and she was betrayed into a tiny startled gasp. As Connor played at their feet, Gianni let long fingers curve to her flushed cheekbone and slowly he smiled. Faith braced herself against the tree to stay upright. That smile dazzled her, knocked her sideways, and filled her with an elemental hunger so powerful it hurt.

'Poor Edward...' Gianni husked with indolent satisfaction as he withdrew his hand and straightened again with innate grace. 'This is all about to blow up in his face. Let him go before it gets dirty, *cara*.'

Only slowly emerging from what felt vaguely like a partial black-out, Faith stared with darkened eyes up at the tall, dark male towering over her as if he had suddenly become the devil incarnate. Now she recognised the studied insolence of that smile. The frantic heat that had filled her with such mindless yearning seconds earlier now engulfed her in shame. How could she be attracted to him like this? How *could* she be? Maybe it was the disorientating sense of having one foot lodge in the past and the other foot threatening to buckle in the present. All of a sudden it was so difficult to know what she was really feeling.

'Leave Edward out of this!' she told him, with all the fierceness of her own guilty mortification.

'But he's right in the middle,' Gianni responded with supreme cool. 'So why drag out his demise? There's no contest, is there?'

'I don't know wh-what you're talking about,' Faith stammered, although she was dreadfully afraid that she did, and what he was now suggesting terrified her.

Gianni dealt her a long, slow, sardonic look. 'I don't have much compassion to spare in Benson's direction, but I'm fair enough to concede that he didn't know he was poaching on my territory...so let him go now.'

'Your territory?' Faith parroted, scarcely believing her ears.

Gianni ran a mocking fingertip down the exposed line of her extended throat and watched her jerk and instinctively lean closer. 'You're still mine, *cara*. You don't have any resistance to me at all. But then you never did have... I want you back, Milly.'

'You couldn't possibly! You're nothing to do with me any more. Our only connection now is Connor!' Faith asserted in a feverish rush of protest. Hurrying forward, she stooped to grab her son's hand and turn back the way they had come. 'It's getting dark…it's time I went home.'

'Ducks?' Connor cried in plaintive surprise.

'The ducks have gone to bed,' Faith told him with desperate urgency.

And the last sound she heard was Gianni's husky appreciative laughter.

CHAPTER FOUR

AFTER buckling a squirming complaining Connor into his car seat, Faith ruefully acknowledged that she had done it again. She had reached saturation point and fled when she could take no more. Once more Gianni D'Angelo had breached the boundaries of her expectations and forced her into uncharted waters.

His territory. She recalled that assertion with a shiver. *Gianni wanted her back.* And with that shattering statement of intent Gianni D'Angelo had plunged her into shock again. Just as she was struggling to regard and accept him as Connor's father, Gianni had revealed a motivation she had never dreamt might exist.

He had been so casual about it too, but in the cool fatalistic fashion of a male referring to an inevitable event. And he had totally unnerved her when he had urged her to let Edward go. Edward was the man she *loved*, the man she was to marry in a few months' time! Yet with frightening confidence Gianni had talked as though her fiancé was already on the way out of her life.

But mightn't she herself have unwittingly encouraged that attitude? Faith squirmed, steeped in shame over behaviour which had merely increased her emotional turmoil. Gianni was incredibly attractive, but he had one trait more disturbing and more dangerous than all the rest put together, and that was a high-voltage aura of pure sex.

She had never recognised that in a man before. But she had been susceptible, indeed had found it quite impossible to control her own intense awareness of him. But then, around Gianni she was steadily becoming a person she didn't know...

Edward hadn't come into her mind once while her wretched body had come alive like an insidious enemy. And then, as she sat there fighting to understand what was happening to her, Faith suddenly found an escape route from the daunting conviction that in responding in any way to Gianni she had betrayed Edward.

Why was she being so tough on herself? What a fool she was being! That flashback about that long-ago phone call had destabilised her. The instant she'd realised that she had once loved Gianni it had become a huge challenge to deal with him as a stranger. So for a few minutes her barriers had slipped. The line between the past and the present had blurred. And in the enervated state she was in, she had reacted in a way she would never normally have reacted...

Now that she knew the problem it wouldn't ever happen again, she told herself urgently. She had behaved as if she was still the woman making that phone call, hadn't she? She had behaved as if Gianni was her lover. So she wasn't *really* still attracted to Gianni. Involuntarily, she had responded to an eerie sense of familiarity.

Since Faith hadn't heard the limousine pulling into the car park, and certainly hadn't seen it, she almost leapt from her seat in fright when a hand gently rapped on the windscreen to attract her attention. Her head twisted round. She recognised Gianni's burgundy silk tie and it was like an instant shot of adrenalin.

Gianni opened the car door to subject her to a fulminating appraisal.

'What are you doing?' Faith demanded defensively.

'You're sitting in the dark in an unlocked car in a deserted park. You've got a lot on your mind. Let me run you home,' Gianni urged, his dark, deep drawl sending an odd little shiver through her.

'If I've got a lot on my mind, whose fault is it?' she condemned tautly. 'Why can't you give me five minutes of peace?'

'You shouldn't be on your own here.' Delivering that assurance with the supreme confidence of a male making an unarguable statement, Gianni lowered his arrogant dark head to glance into the back of the car. His brilliant dark eyes connected with hers again. 'Connor looks pretty miserable too.'

'Daddy!' Connor squealed in sudden excitement.

Flinching from that cry of recognition, Faith bowed her forehead down against the steering wheel and fought off an urge to bang it hard. But she had seen the reproof in his gaze. He hadn't needed to say anything. 'Go away, Gianni...'

'Only if you go straight home and go to bed. You're exhausted.

Faith tensed even more. She didn't *want* to go home. No longer did she feel up to dealing with her parents, who were likely to be very upset by the news that Connor's father had surfaced. Her past had caught up with her with a vengeance, and nobody was going to escape the fall-out, she acknowledged guiltily.

Lifting her head again, Faith turned the ignition key. 'I'll phone you tomorrow. I'm taking Connor to a fast-food restaurant for tea,' she announced defiantly, and, reaching out, she slammed the door loudly on Gianni.

Connor sobbed when she drove off, which really bothered her. Had he already taken that much of a liking to Gianni? Half a mile down the road, she stopped at a callbox to ring home and yet again excuse herself from a family meal. The phone rang a long time before it was answered by her father.

After she'd explained why she wouldn't be home, her father said in a curiously quiet voice. 'That's fine. Actually, we're dining out ourselves, and we'll probably be late back, so don't wait up for us. By the way, Edward's home.'

'He is?' Faith exclaimed in surprise.

'He caught an earlier flight and called in at the plant just as I was leaving,' Robin Jennings told her.

Faith drove to the restaurant. Connor ate with gusto. Faith nibbled at the odd chip and surveyed her son with her an-

guished heart in her eyes. Gianni had rights she couldn't
deny. Gianni had had a tough deal. At lot of men who fathered children outside marriage sought to evade their responsibilities, but her son had a father who had spent three
years trying to track him down. A father who showed every
sign of wanting to be very much a part of Connor's life. But
a father whose very existence was likely to cause Connor's
mother endless hassle and grief.

Edward was home, so she knew where she was heading
next. More than anybody else, her fiancé deserved to hear
her news first. Edward was always calm, she reminded herself. He certainly wouldn't be happy, but surely he would
ultimately take this unexpected development in his stride?

Beginning to feel like a traveller who had no place to lay
her head, Faith wearily parked outside the Edwardian villa
where Edward still lived with his mother. She thanked
heaven that it was one of Mrs Benson's bridge nights.
Connor was half asleep, and she carried him up the steps
feeling like the worst of mothers for keeping him out beyond
his bedtime.

Edward opened the front door and studied her in surprise.
'Faith?'

Faith chewed at her lower lip. 'Dad told me you'd got
back early and I needed to see you…so here I am.'

'But why didn't you leave Connor at home?' Edward enquired.

'Mum and Dad are dining out.'

'Are you sure of that? Your father's with your mother?
When I walked into Robin's office this afternoon, he was
cancelling the business dinner he had arranged for tonight.'
Her fiancé continued with pronounced disapproval, 'And,
believe me, Bill Smith is too valuable a customer to cancel
at such short notice!'

Engaged in settling Connor's limp little body into a corner
of the sofa in the chilly lounge, Faith made no response. She
was too worked up about what she had to tell Edward.

'Something rather unexpected has happened,' she said stiltedly.

'Everybody does seem to be acting in a very unexpected way today. Your father's evasive manner with me was distinctly odd,' Edward informed her flatly, his pale blue eyes reflecting his annoyance at what he had clearly taken as a snub.

'Look, this is *really* important, Edward,' Faith stressed.

Edward planted himself by the fireplace, a rather irritating air of indulgence in his scrutiny. 'What's up? Wedding stationery not up to scratch?'

'Something I never, ever thought was likely to happen. Connor's father, Gianni D'Angelo, has turned up!' Faith shared in a driven rush.

Edward stiffened. She certainly had his attention now. He began shooting questions at her as if she was in the witness box, charged with some kind of crime.

'Gianni D'Angelo...' Edward repeated incredulously. 'Let me get this straight. You are telling me that the electronics tycoon Gianni D'Angelo is Connor's *father*?'

'Yes, I was pretty shocked too,' Faith admitted heavily.

'Stop talking as if when all this took place it happened to somebody else!' Edward suddenly snapped accusingly. 'Believe me, I'm not too happy with the sound of all this. It's hardly what I expected, is it? Gianni D'Angelo! How on earth did you meet a man like that?'

'I don't remember, Edward—'

'Did you work for him?'

'No...' Faith began pleating a fold in her shirt with tense fingers.

'I'm starting to suspect your loss of memory might be based on a very sound instinct to bury a less than presentable past,' Edward told her in a derisive undertone.

'That's a horrible thing to say. It's not like it's something I can help,' Faith whispered painfully.

'Gianni D'Angelo...so once you moved in distinctly rarefied circles,' Edward remarked snidely, and she winced. 'What sort of relationship did you have with him?'

Stress made Faith's stomach twist. Edward's anger was already greater than she had naively anticipated, and his contempt was an equally unpleasant surprise. I can't tell him the whole truth now. I *can't*, she thought in desperation.

'As your future husband, I have the right to know, and if you don't tell me I have every intention of asking him!'

'He said...he said I was his mistress,' Faith admitted in a deadened voice. She was too exhausted to withstand any more pressure.

The silence went on and on and on. Finally she raised enough courage to look up.

Edward had gone all red in the face. He was also surveying her as if she had turned into an alien before his eyes.

'I'm very ashamed of it,' she told him unevenly.

'So that's who I'm about to marry...Gianni D'Angelo's slut.' Edward labelled her with cold venom. 'Thanks for telling me.'

Pale as milk, Faith got up and bent down to lift her son back into her arms. 'There's not much point continuing this conversation,' she replied tightly. 'You're shocked, and I understand that, but it's my past, *not* my present, Edward.'

'*Shocked* barely covers it...a sleazy association of that nature!' Edward fired back in furious disgust. 'If this gets out locally, I'll be a laughing stock!'

'Gianni's not likely to go around telling people. I only told you because it's not something I felt I could keep to myself.' Only now, she acknowledged, she very much wished she had.

Edward vented a humourless laugh. 'My mother once said I didn't know what I might be taking on with you. Clearly I should have listened!'

'Do you want your ring back?' Faith heard herself ask, without any expression at all.

Edward went rigid, bitter resentment showing in his eyes.

'Of course I don't! My God, can't I let off a little steam without you asking me that?'

'Calling me a slut is more than "a little steam",' Faith countered jaggedly, already wondering if, after their marriage, Edward would throw her past in her teeth every time she annoyed or disappointed him. 'You might as well know the lot. I was Gianni's mistress for two years...and I loved him.'

Edward surveyed her in near disbelief. Whether Faith realised it or not there had been a decided edge of defiance in that final announcement.

'Faith—' he began brusquely.

'I just want to go home, Edward. Could you open the door, please?' she asked woodenly.

Connor restored to his car seat, Faith drove off. Edward was never likely to see her in the same light again. Could she blame him for that? Edward was always very conscious of what others might think. A lot of people had seemed surprised that he should ask a single mother to be his wife. Now Edward was questioning that decision. Were his feelings for her strong enough to withstand such damaging revelations?

Arriving home to find all lights blazing, Faith carried her son straight upstairs and quickly put him to bed. Only when she went downstairs again did it occur to her that the house had the strangest air of being like the *Marie Celeste*. The kitchen even showed every sign of her mother's initial preparations for an evening meal. Faith began to tidy up, amazed that the older woman had gone out leaving potatoes half-unpeeled and the radio still playing.

Where had her parents gone in such a hurry? Her father had cancelled a business dinner and her mother should have been attending the choral evening in the church hall. It wasn't their anniversary or either of their birthdays. Their behaviour didn't make sense, but Faith was already so tired that she fell into bed, determined to suppress every anxiety and every thought.

Once she had caught up on her sleep nothing would look so bad, she assured herself. Edward would have had time to come to terms with her bombshell. He had hurt her, but possibly she had expected too much from him. After all, she too had been upset by what she had learnt about her own past today. Let the dust settle, she urged herself wearily. Tomorrow would be a whole new day.

Accustomed to being rudely awakened by Connor bouncing on her bed, Faith woke the next morning to a curious silence. Glancing drowsily at her alarm clock, she stiffened and then leapt out of bed in dismay. It was just after ten! For goodness' sake, why hadn't her mother roused her?

On her way into the bathroom Faith registered that her son's bed was already neatly made. After washing at speed, she pulled on a brown skirt and a burgundy sweater. This morning it had been her turn to open the shop early for the deliveries. A perplexed frown on her face, she hurried downstairs.

She stilled at the sight of her parents sitting together in silence in the lounge. They looked odd: stiff and strained, and somehow aged.

Robin Jennings rose heavily upright, a stocky well-built man with grey hair. 'We thought we should let you sleep in, so I called Louise first thing and said that you weren't well,' he explained. 'Then I took Connor to the nursery as usual. We need to have a serious talk with you and we felt—well, Mr D'Angelo felt it would be wiser to keep the child away from all this.'

'Mr…? Gianni…?' Faith echoed in growing confusion. 'How…I mean…oh, so you *know* about Gianni?' she suddenly gasped.

'Please sit down,' her father urged.

A hectic flush on her cheeks, Faith was instantly convinced that she knew what was happening. At that moment she absolutely loathed Gianni D'Angelo. Obviously he had gone over her head and contacted her parents. That was probably where they had been last night. *With him.* And her poor parents looked very much as if they had been completely crushed by what they had learnt about her.

'Gianni had no right to interfere!' she exclaimed furiously.

Her father grimaced. 'Faith, Mr D'Angelo—'

A slight movement at the edge of her vision made Faith spin round. She stared, dumbstruck. Gianni now stood in the archway between the lounge and the dining room. She shook her head in urgent negative. Bewildered anger and resentment burned in her questioning gaze. 'What are *you* doing here? How dare you interfere like this? How dare you go behind my back and talk to my parents?'

'That's enough, Faith,' Robin Jennings said stiffly.

'Why did you let him into this house?' Faith demanded fiercely.

Gianni strolled forward with measured steps. 'Keep quiet and sit down,' he told her, his stunning dark features stamped with gravity, his eyes impenetrable. 'I asked to be present. Robin and Davina have a rather disturbing confession to make and they need you to listen to them.'

A confession? A confession about what? Complete confusion made Faith sink slowly down into an armchair. Her accusing stare stayed on Gianni. He dominated the low-ceilinged room, with his height and presence, as alien against the backdrop of the cosy décor as a tiger prowling a busy city street. He didn't belong here, she thought bitterly, and she couldn't credit that her parents could have been influenced by any request of his.

He wore a silver-grey suit, fabulously well cut to his lithe, lean and powerful frame. The fabric had the smooth gleam of wildly expensive cloth, his shirt the sheen of silk. She clashed with dark, deep-set eyes, and suddenly it was an effort to summon up a single connected thought.

'Faith...' her father breathed curtly.

Faith looked back to her parents with some embarrassment. 'What's going on?'

'When we identified you at the hospital three years ago,

we didn't have the smallest doubt that you were our child,' the older man told her flatly. 'You were wearing the bracelet we gave our daughter on her sixteenth birthday. You were blonde, blue-eyed, about an inch taller than you had been when you left. You were a lot thinner, but then why not? Seven years is a long time.'

'Why are you talking about this?' Faith frowned.

Her mother crammed a tissue to her lips and twisted her head away with a stifled gasp. 'I can't bear this—'

'What Robin is trying to tell you is that he and his wife made a very unfortunate mistake.' Gianni advanced, sounding every word with precision.

'We were so overjoyed at getting you back,' Davina Jennings confided jerkily. 'It was over a year before I even admitted to myself that there might be room for doubt about your identity…'

Faith was now as still as a statue, her shaken eyes the only life in her taut face. 'I don't understand what you're trying to say…'

'At the start you were very ill. Then you came round and you had no memories,' Robin Jennings reminded her tensely. 'Our daughter had no distinguishing marks that we could go on. Nothing jarred at that stage. You had grown up. Naturally you had to have matured and changed.'

Gianni shot Faith's perplexed expression a perceptive glance and murmured levelly, 'They're trying to tell you that they are *not* your parents.'

'Not my parents,' Faith repeated like an obedient child. She couldn't believe that, she just couldn't believe it, couldn't even take such a gigantic concept on board long enough to consider it. 'This is crazy…why are you telling me this stuff?'

'We came to love you very much,' her father—who, according to Gianni, was *not* her father—explained almost eagerly. 'In fact as we got to know the person we believed you had become we couldn't have been happier.'

'But eventually we began making discoveries about you

that we couldn't just ignore or explain away,' Davina continued reluctantly. 'You have a lovely singing voice. Our daughter couldn't even sing in tune. You speak French like a native...our daughter failed French at GCSE. She was hopeless at languages.'

Locked suddenly into a world of her own, Faith remembered the evening her father had brought a French client home for dinner. The instant the man had uttered a French phrase she had turned without hesitation to address him in the same language. Dimly she recalled how astonished her parents had been. But at the time she hadn't thought anything of that. In fact she'd been delighted when the Frenchman had told her that she had a remarkable idiomatic grasp of his language. In those days it had seemed to her that she had no useful talents, and it had felt good to discover she had at least one.

'All the little discrepancies we'd so easily explained away at the beginning came back to haunt us. Your handwriting is so different.' Robin Jennings sighed. 'You like cats. Faith was allergic to cats. It wasn't really very likely that you'd grown out of that. We began to look rather desperately for you to remind us in some way of the daughter we remembered, but there was nothing.'

Faith sat there in the kind of shock that felt like a great weight squeezing the life force from her. 'But the bracelet...I was wearing Granny's bracelet—'

'Our daughter must've sold it. Although she took it with her when she went, she wasn't that fond of it. Perhaps you bought the bracelet, or somebody else gave it to you. We were foolish to rely so much on a piece of jewellery,' Davina conceded curtly.

'This isn't possible,' Faith said very carefully, but as the bracelet that she had long regarded as a kind of talisman was dismissed her voice sank to a mere thread of its usual volume.

Gianni released his breath in a charged hiss.

'If she doesn't want to believe it, I'm quite content,'

Davina Jennings announced, shooting a glance of bitter dislike at Gianni. 'In every way that matters she is our daughter and we love her and we don't want to lose her. Neither Robin nor I want anything to change. We told you that last night—'

'And I asked you what you intended to do if the *real* Faith showed up,' Gianni reminded the older woman without hesitation.

Davina stiffened defensively. 'Not very likely after ten years.'

'This is really happening,' Faith registered finally. 'You're telling me that I'm not really your child, that I was never your child…that this life I'm living actually belongs to another woman.'

'Your name is Milly Henner and you're twenty-four years old,' Gianni delivered. 'And while I'm here there is nothing to be afraid of.'

Milly, she thought numbly. My name *is* Milly. She fought to concentrate on thoughts that were whirling like tangled spaghetti inside her blitzed brain. She studied the people whom she had believed were her parents with a deep sense of pain and dislocation. 'How long have you known that I wasn't your daughter?'

The silence thundered. Seemingly neither wished to discuss that point.

Gianni had no such inhibition. 'They've known for about eighteen months. They only admitted their suspicions to each other then—'

'We sat up all night talking,' Robin Jennings cut in heavily. 'We just didn't know what to do. You'd accepted us. We loved you and Connor. We'd introduced you everywhere as our daughter—'

'You kept quiet sooner than face the embarrassment of admitting that you could make such an appalling mistake,' Milly, who still so desperately wanted to be Faith, condemned, at that instant hating everybody in the room. They all knew who they were and where they belonged. But she was an outsider.

'We were happy with the way things were,' Davina argued vehemently. 'Nor do we see why anything should change!'

Milly surveyed her dully.

'I will make every possible effort to trace your real daughter,' Gianni promised the older couple. 'But Milly can't stay here any longer.'

'She can if she wants to,' Robin Jennings asserted curtly.

'She can stay in touch with you. She can even visit. But as who she really is, *not* as who you'd like her to be!' Gianni's attention was on Milly's stark white face and the blank horror growing in her eyes. 'She had another life, and she needs to see that life before she makes any decisions.'

'For heaven's sake, she's engaged…she's getting married!' Davina exclaimed.

'And how do you think Edward is likely to react to this fiasco?' her husband groaned. 'I'll deal with that. I'll see him this morning and explain everything.'

With a sense of numb disbelief, Milly studied them all. Gianni stood apart, his self-discipline absolute. His dark, deep flashing eyes held hers, and she saw the pity he couldn't hide and just wanted to die. She stood up, and walked out of the room.

As Davina leapt up to follow her Gianni planted a staying hand on her arm. 'You can't help Milly with this, Mrs Jennings. Not right now, you can't,' he asserted. 'She feels betrayed by the two people she relied on most. She needs time to come to terms with this.'

'And what exactly are your plans for her, Mr D'Angelo?' the older woman demanded bitterly.

Gianni viewed his companions with concealed hostility. They might love Milly, but they had damaged her. Three years ago they had denied her the further professional help she'd needed. They had done nothing to help her regain her memory. And, unforgivably, when they had realized their mistake they had selfishly refused to put it right. They had ignored the reality that the unknown woman they had erroneously identified as their daughter must have had a life elsewhere.

They also acted as if they owned Milly, and as if she couldn't speak or think for herself. It was an attitude which filled Gianni with violent antipathy. After all, if Milly belonged to anybody, she belonged to him!

She was the mother of his son. He knew her better than anybody alive. He could put her back into the world she had left behind. Leaving Milly anywhere within reach of the Jennings would hamper her recovery. They didn't want to let go even briefly. They wanted her to go on living a fake life while he could not wait to free her from an existence that struck him as suffocating. Milly was very much a free spirit...

The free spirit stared at herself in the bedroom mirror.

Who am I? Who is Milly Henner?

This was not her home. This was not where she had grown up. Those people downstairs were not her parents. Nothing that she had believed was hers was really hers. Not the share of the shop her supposed father had insisted on buying for her, not her car, which had been a birthday present—presented on a day that probably wasn't really her birthday. Only Connor was *really* hers...

As the world she had innocently believed and trusted in caved in around her, Milly experienced an instant of pure terror that threatened to wipe her out entirely.

'Milly...come back to the hotel with me.'

She spun round and focused on Gianni. Naked loathing rippled through her. *He* had done this to her. *He* had ripped her life apart. 'I hate you...' she framed, trembling with the force of her emotions.

'You'll get over that,' Gianni informed her, without an ounce of uncertainty.

'I want Edward,' she admitted shakily, and turned away again.

'You'll get over that too,' Gianni asserted harshly.

'You can't take *him* away from me!'' Milly suddenly slung wildly. 'You can take everything else but not Edward!'

'You can't love him.' Gianni's gaze was black as a stormy night, his tone pure derision. 'You can't. He's nobody; he's nothing!'

Milly's teeth gritted. 'He's the man I love!'

Gianni breathed in deep, his eyes flashing gold with raw menace. 'You couldn't possibly love a calculating little creep like that!'

'Edward is none of your business! Haven't you done enough damage?'

Gianni studied her with shimmering eyes, and then he reached for her without any warning at all. He pulled her into his powerful arms and brought his mouth down on hers. Suddenly she was on fire, her breath rasping in her throat, her slim body burning at every point of contact with his. The heated onslaught of that wide, sensual mouth was a revelation. Nothing had ever felt so necessary. Hunger clawed up through her with such greedy force that her head spun, her senses reeled. Riven with wild excitement, she pressed herself into his hard male frame with a shaken moan of surrender.

'Faith!' Davina intervened, shrill with condemnation.

As Gianni held Milly back from him she trembled in a daze of shock. She focused in startled embarrassment on the older woman lodged in the bedroom doorway.

'I'm not Faith,' she heard herself say unevenly, for she could hardly get air back into her lungs. 'I'm Milly.'

'You're still an engaged woman!' Davina turned to address Gianni. 'She's upset and confused. Why can't you leave her alone?'

Momentarily, Milly was in a world of her own. She could not credit the terrifying intensity of what Gianni had made her feel. She had behaved like a wanton, pushing closer to him and clinging. If she was mortified now, she deserved to be. But then, as the older woman had pointed out, she was upset and in no state to know what she was really feeling...

'I think it's time you told Milly the truth about her engagement,' Gianni murmured silkily.

'I haven't a clue what you're trying to imply,' Davina said thinly.

Gianni gazed down at Milly. His expressive mouth twisted. 'On your wedding day, Edward becomes a fully-fledged partner in the family firm.'

Stunned by that statement, Milly stared back at him. 'That's not true-'

'That news was to have been our wedding present to both you and Edward.' Davina tilted her chin, defying further comment.

Gianni loosed a sardonic laugh. 'Why don't you tell her the truth, Mrs Jennings? Benson got that promise before he even *asked* her to marry him!'

'That's a lie!' Milly's hands curled into tight fists by her sides as she gazed expectantly at the older woman, willing her to shoot Gianni's humiliating aspersions down in flames.

Coins of colour now embellished Davina's cheeks. 'It was a simple business agreement, Mr D'Angelo. Edward is my husband's natural successor.'

'Free partnerships are not the norm in the business world, Mrs Jennings. And you should've warned Benson to keep the news from his mother. She's ensured that half the town knows why her son is prepared to take on another man's child. You made it well worth his while,' Gianni countered very drily.

Tell me it wasn't like that, Milly wanted to beg the older woman strickenly, but she bit back the plea and straightened her shoulders to walk to the door. Only Edward could tell her what it had been like. Only Edward could convince her that he hadn't needed the bribe of a partnership in the firm to persuade him to propose.

'Where on earth are you going?' Davina demanded.

'To see Edward,' Milly looked at Gianni D'Angelo, and, try as she could, she could not suppress the sheer loathing raging through her. 'You are a complete and utter bastard!' she raked at him, heedless of the other woman's shocked gasp. 'And I don't need a memory to tell me why I left you!'

CHAPTER FIVE

REFUSING to be turned from her purpose, Milly snatched her car keys from the hall table and drove over to Jennings Engineering. On the way, she thought back over the months since she had started seeing Edward.

Right from the start he had been attentive and caring. The *dream* boyfriend for an unwed mother? a more cynical voice enquired. Certainly her pseudo-parents had heavily encouraged the relationship, but why not? As a family friend and a trusted employee, Edward had naturally impressed them as being ideal.

But Milly had been more impressed by Edward's apparent indifference to her amnesia. She had relaxed in his company. Other men she had dated had assumed that she was promiscuous just because she already had a child; Edward's respectful attitude had come as a very welcome relief. It was hardly surprising that she had fallen in love with him.

So what if it was a different kind of love from that which she had once felt for Gianni D'Angelo? From what she recalled of those emotions she imagined a lowering form of enslavement, made all the more dangerous and destructive by the strength of her sexual craving for him. There, it was out at last, she acknowledged angrily. An admission of the physical weakness which had probably got her involved with Gianni in the first place.

Yet sex barely figured in her relationship with Edward. But then what she felt for Edward was a more mature and lasting love. So cymbals didn't clash and fireworks didn't go off when Edward kissed her. But where had the cymbals and the fireworks got her before? Down and out and preg-

nant by a male so frighteningly ruthless she could only admire herself for walking out on him three years earlier.

Milly parked the car outside the small office block beside
the engineering plant. She was relieved that Robin Jennings
was still at home. She had had enough of other people's
interference.

A nightmare mistake had been made, but she was OK,
she told herself bracingly; she was coping. Gianni had tried
to destroy everything, but as long as she still had Edward
she would manage to come to terms with all the rest. She
blocked out the little voice that warned that she was hanging
by her fingernails onto her last shred of control.

Edward was in his office. Her unannounced entrance
made him rise from behind his desk in surprise. Strain from
their contentious meeting the night before showed in the
stiffness of his greeting.

'I was going to call you this afternoon,' he told her rather
defensively.

'I needed to see you to talk. This morning I found out
something that I wish you'd thought to share openly with
me,' Milly admitted tautly.

'Unlike your life, mine is an open book,' Edward retorted
crisply. 'I've kept nothing from you.'

'What about the partnership you get the day you marry
me?' Milly enquired, wanting him to tell her that that was
a very twisted version of the truth.

Edward stiffened. 'Your parents told me they wanted that
news to be a surprise. Naturally I didn't discuss it with you.'

Her knees now unreliable supports, Milly dropped down
on the arm of a chair. 'Would you have asked me to marry
you without that partnership, Edward?' she asked tightly.
'Please be honest.'

Edward's fair complexion reddened. 'That is a very unfair
question.'

'But you're not denying that the partnership was put on
the table *before* you decided to propose, are you?'

Edward studied her with unconcealed resentment. 'I don't

see why you should have a problem with that. Your father's generous offer meant that we could have a financially secure future together. Of course it made a difference.'

Nausea pooled in Milly's stomach. 'What about love?'

'I'm very fond of you. But I'd be a liar if I didn't admit that I was also very concerned about the risks of forming a lasting relationship with you.'

'Risks?'

'Do I have to spell it out? That bombshell you dropped on me last night wouldn't have occurred in a *normal* relationship!' he reminded her with derision. 'Like any other man, I want to feel confident that I know everything there is to know about my wife's past. You can't give me that confidence.'

'But the assurance of a financially secure future persuaded you to overlook those drawbacks,' Milly gathered, struggling to keep her voice level. 'Yet you *said* you loved me.'

'For pity's sake, you're talking like a silly teenager-'

'I think maybe I still am just a teenager inside, Edward. If I had had any idea how many reservations you had about me, I'd never have agreed to marry you.' Tugging the solitaire from her finger, Milly stood up to place it on the edge of his desk.

Edward was outraged. 'You *asked* me to be honest!'

But he had been cruelly belittling her from the minute she started speaking, Milly reflected painfully. 'When you hear what your boss has to tell you, I think you'll be relieved to have that ring back. I imagine he'll offer you the partnership anyway. I do wish you well, Edward.'

Striding forward, he snapped bruising fingers round her slender wrist to prevent her departure. 'Who do you think you are to talk to me like this?' he demanded contemptuously.

Milly was shaken. 'Let go of me…you're hurting me—'

'I found your attitude equally offensive last night,' Edward snapped furiously. 'It seems to me that the minute you discovered that Connor's father was a rich man, you got too big for your boots! Now put that ring back on and we'll say no more about this nonsense!'

Taken aback as she was by his aggression, Milly was relieved when a knock sounded on the door and his secretary interrupted them. Edward released her immediately. Milly hurried down the corridor, ignoring his call in his wake. And then, out at Reception, she hesitated and looked at the car keys still clutched in her hand. She left them with the receptionist for Robin Jennings to collect. Suddenly she wanted *nothing* that had belonged to Faith Jennings...

Edward had never loved her. Indeed, right from the start Edward had had serious reservations about a woman with a past she couldn't remember. Without the partnership deal he would never have proposed. And why had she never noticed what a bad-tempered bully Edward could be if he was crossed? The answer was that until last night she had never crossed or challenged Edward. She had been a doormat, ashamed of her unwed mother status, thinking herself very fortunate to be the intended wife of a respectable professional man. And who had given her such low expectations and such a poor self-image? Her fake parents, who had packaged her up with a lucrative partnership to persuade Edward to marry her.

There was a stiff breeze blowing and it was cold. Milly had left her jacket locked in the car, but she still hurried away from the engineering plant. When she found herself on the main road she just kept on walking, insensibly soothed by the noise of the anonymous traffic. All the shocks she had withstood over the past twenty-four hours were hitting her now full force. Edward had seemed like a safe and sturdy post to clutch in the storm, but the post had toppled when she had reached for its support. The oddest thing was that she couldn't yet feel a single shard of grief. But then, she acknowledged dully, she wasn't really feeling anything...

'*Where the hell is she?*' Gianni raked into the phone.

'We've found her. She's OK. She's sitting on a bench by

the lake in that park.'

'*Madre di Dio!*' Gianni launched, paling at that information. 'I want two of you within six feet of her until I get
there!'

After telling his driver to go as fast as the speed limit
would allow, Gianni threw back a brandy to steady himself.
He was furious with himself. He had known he had to go
slowly with Milly. The psychologist had warned him to be
careful. But from the first moment he had wildly overplayed
his hand.

He should have kept quiet about Benson and the partnership. He had planned to hold that in reserve for a few days.
Yet he, who had the reputation for being a brilliant tactician
with a superb sense of timing, had ploughed in like a bull
in a china shop. The prospect of reaping his own just deserts
didn't bother him. But he went into a cold sweat at the threat
of Milly reaping them for him...

Milly knew she was being watched at the lake. The instant
she recognised the dark-suited men trying not to draw attention to themselves and failing abysmally in their efforts to
lurk behind winter-bare trees she almost smiled. Gianni's
employees. He must have had her followed. As long as they
left her alone, it was almost comforting to think that somebody was looking out for her.

That sound of brisk footsteps made her lift her head.
Gianni was bearing down on her, his hard, bronzed features
set in grim lines which detracted not one iota from his devastating good looks, she conceded absently. A light grey
cashmere overcoat protected him from the chilly breeze ruf-
fling his luxuriant black hair.

'This is a very dreary place.' Both disapproval and impatience rang from every syllable. Gianni slung a deeply
unappreciative glance over his surroundings. '*And* it's freezing. Why haven't you got a coat on?'

Even before he peeled off his overcoat and dropped it
round her with the pronounced casualness of a male who

didn't want to make a production out of doing it, Milly's sense of isolation lessened. Gianni was exasperated and he was letting her see the fact.

'What the hell are you smiling at?' Gianni demanded, thrown by that slight undeniable tilt to her formerly tense mouth.

Almost drowning in the heavy, enveloping folds of his overcoat, and curiously soothed by the warm scent of him that still clung to the silk-lined garment, Milly gazed up at him with rueful blue eyes. 'I don't know.'

'Why did you leave your car behind at the engineering plant? Did it break down?'

'It's not my car. The Jenningses bought it when they still thought I was their daughter. I guess I'm not in a very practical mood,' Milly conceded.

As she lifted her hand to prevent his overcoat lurching off her shoulder, Gianni muttered something raw in his own language and caught her fingers in his. Milly stiffened as he scrutinised the blue-black bruising encircling her wrist.

'You damned well didn't do that to yourself!' Gianni bit out wrathfully.

Milly tugged her hand free and hurriedly curved it out of sight again.

'*Per meraviglia!* The cowardly little bastard,' he growled, well-nigh incredulous, it seemed, that anybody should have dared to lay a rough hand on her. 'I'll make him pay for hurting you!'

'No, you won't,' Milly whispered flatly. 'Those bruises came cheap at the price of what they taught me. Maybe I'm wronging Edward, but I suspect he would have lashed out in temper again once we were married. He really did feel that he was marrying beneath himself. He could never have accepted me as I am.'

Gianni glanced at her other hand, only now noticing the absence of the diamond engagement ring. Milly watched his eloquent dark eyes shimmer with unadulterated satisfaction. On the most basic level, she was beginning to understand

Gianni. He was delighted that her engagement was broken. He wouldn't waste his breath uttering empty conventional regrets.

'I don't have *any* close relatives, do I?' Milly prompted abruptly.

Gianni frowned.

That frown was answer enough for Milly. She averted her head, determined not to betray that a foolish glimmer of hope had just been extinguished.

'How did you work that out for yourself?' It was the tone of a very clever male unaccustomed to being second-guessed.

'If I'd had a genuine suffering close relation waiting somewhere for word of me, you'd have been sure to tell Robin and Davina so that they could feel even worse.'

A laugh of reluctant appreciation was torn from Gianni.

'So, since everybody starts out with parents,' Milly continued doggedly, 'I presume mine are long gone.'

'Your mother when you were eight, your father shortly before we met,' Gianni confirmed unemotionally. 'You were an only child. As far as I'm aware there were no other relatives.'

So, but for Connor, she really was alone.

'Let's go,' Gianni reached down, closed his hand firmly over hers and tugged her upright to walk her back along the path. 'Why did you come here anyway?'

'I've spent a lot of happy times here with Connor…but today I felt lost,' she admitted reluctantly.

'Even the worst situations have at least one positive aspect. You've had an extraordinary experience,' Gianni told her. 'How many people get the chance to live more than one life?'

Disconcerted, Milly blinked. That reality hadn't crossed her mind once.

'Right now you're between lives, but no way are you lost. You've got me,' Gianni delivered with supreme cool.

'You make it all sound so simple.'

'It is. You don't belong here. That's why you feel strange. I know you care about the Jenningses, but they didn't do you any favours. If they hadn't claimed you, I'd have found you ages ago,' Gianni reminded her grimly.

'Did you list me as missing?'

'Of course I did!' Gianni growled, as if he was insulted by the idea that she could think otherwise.

'I *so* wish you'd found me first…' That thought had translated itself into charged admission before she could think better of it. She tensed. All the barriers she had tried to put up against Gianni had somehow tumbled down. It made her feel very vulnerable.

'Luck wasn't on my side. You walked out of the apartment of your own free will. There were no suspicious circumstances, so the police weren't interested. Adults have the right to lose themselves if they want to,' Gianni informed her wryly.

As they reached the park exit the limousine drew up, and Milly climbed in without protest.

Only a couple of hours ago she had hated Gianni D'Angelo like poison. He had been the destroyer. He had been the target of all her furious disbelief and bitter resentment. But now, as he used the car phone and talked in fluid Italian, she studied him with helpless intensity. The strong bone structure, the straight, arrogant nose, the firmly chiselled mouth. The dangerous dark eyes that knew too much, saw too much, and which he could turn on her like a weapon to express more than most people could say in five minutes. Those eyes were spectacular in the frame of that lean, dark face.

His gaze narrowed slumbrously, his arrogant dark head tilting back almost as if he was inviting her appraisal to continue. The elegant, sexily indolent sprawl of his long, lean, powerful body made her breath shorten in her throat, her heart thump against her breastbone. He really was *so* beautiful…

Colour ran up beneath her complexion and she tore her

attention from him, dismay and embarrassment darting through her. How could she be thinking such thoughts now? And she could feel herself wanting to trust him, but how could she trust him when she couldn't even trust herself? If she had learned anything over the past hours, it was that every single thing came at a price.

'Did you say you wanted me back because of Connor?' She got even redder as she spoke, knowing that she was being too blunt.

'No,' Gianni drawled, with all the cool she lacked. 'I wouldn't pretend even for the sake of my son. If you tried to deny me access to him, I would fight you through legal channels, but I believe you already accept that Connor has a right to get to know his father.'

'Yes.' Milly was impressed by that clear-minded reading of the situation. Succinct, realistic, fair.

On the drive through town, the limo pulled up on the main street. Gianni buzzed a window down. One of his security men passed in a large shallow box stamped with the logo of a newly opened pizza parlour. Seconds later, the limo re-joined the traffic.

Gianni settled the box on her lap without ceremony. 'You're crazy about pizza.'

'Am I?' Pizza wasn't something that featured on the menu in the Jenningses' home, and Edward despised all fast food.

'You didn't even have breakfast this morning. You need to eat something before we go and collect Connor.' Gianni poured her a soft drink from the built-in bar. 'Why are you staring at me?'

'No reason…' Possibly it was the combination of the vast, opulent limo, the humble pizza box and Gianni's total lack of snobbery. Or possibly it was the regularity with which he seemed to act to ensure her well-being. And always without comment or fanfare, as if it was the most natural thing in the world that he should take care of her.

Touched by that comforting thought, after the lack of caring Edward had demonstrated when the chips were down,

Milly opened the box. She lifted out a warm, flavoursome wedge and was surprised to feel her tastebuds water. 'Aren't you having any?'

'I'm not hungry.'

But Milly was ravenous, and nothing had ever tasted so good as that pizza. When she could eat no more, she sat unselfconsciously licking her fingers clean until some sixth sense made her lift her head. Gianni's burnished gaze roamed intently from her wet fingertip to her moist pink rounded mouth and flashed a message of very masculine hunger straight into her widening eyes. The atmosphere was electric.

Her breathing fracturing, Milly shifted on the seat. A starburst of heat blossomed between her thighs, making her flush with discomfiture. Shaken by a response that she couldn't control, she shivered. All of a sudden she was painfully conscious of the ripe fullness of her breasts and the swollen tightness of her nipples. The sexual sizzle in the air unnerved her. And Gianni's tension was patent. Feverish colour lay in a hard line over his taut cheekbones. Her pupils dilating, she stared wordlessly back at him, torn by a bewildering mixture of excitement, fear and fascination.

'I know I can't touch you. Don't tease me, ' Gianni breathed in charged reproof.

In sudden embarrassment, Milly closed her eyes to shut him out. 'I'm not like that…like *this*!' she stressed in denial.

'Stretch your imagination. Once you regarded a healthy desire to rip my clothes off as the most natural thing in the world.' His deep-pitched drawl was as abrasive as sand sliding over silk. 'It was the same for both of us. I once withstood a flight of sixteen hours just to spend two hours with you and then fly right back again.'

That deep, dark drawl scent erotic images that made her squirm skimming into her mind's eye. He had flown halfway across the world just to spend two hours with her? She was stunned by that knowledge. And was there a woman alive who wouldn't feel her self-esteem enhanced by such an extravagant gesture?

'Every time we made love felt like the first time. Endless variations on the same glorious theme. The hunger was never satisfied. I don't like anything that comes between me and control,' Gianni confessed huskily. 'But nobody else has ever made me feel the way you can make me feel. So if I'm not ashamed of it, why should you be?'

And Milly listened, *of course* she listened, drinking in every word, taken aback and then impressed by his honesty. It no longer felt quite so indecent to experience a sudden violent longing to be in his arms. Past chemistry had to be operating on her, a powerful physical sense of familiarity. And at least Gianni really genuinely wanted her, she found herself thinking helplessly. Edward hadn't, not really.

And Gianni had nothing to gain and no reason to lie to her. She respected his need to forge a relationship with his son. He already knew she wouldn't try to keep them apart. He was being so kind today. So why had he seemed so very cold and hostile to her yesterday?

Perhaps he had just felt awkward. Perhaps he had been apprehensive of her reaction to the idea of having to share her son. She had been overwrought, confused and angry. Her initial reactions to him would have been far from reassuring, she decided.

'I've booked the suite above mine for you and Connor,' Gianni divulged lazily as the limo pulled up outside Connor's nursery.

Milly glanced up and met his eyes in dismay. 'I—'

'You have to make that break. It's up to you whether you do it now or later. But if you stay with the Jenningses you're likely to find yourself being put under more pressure, and you have enough to cope with right now. They're not ready to accept that things have changed.'

Things have changed. Such a bland description of the shattering new knowledge that had virtually wiped out the past three years of her life. But to move straight out into a hotel? Gianni's hotel? She needed to stand on her own feet, no matter how difficult it was. But Gianni *was* Connor's father. Surely she could trust him that far? She badly needed a quiet corner where she could lick her wounds, pull herself together and decide what to do next.

'Would you leave me alone?'

'If that's what you want.'

She wasn't at all sure it was, but somehow it had seemed safer to give him that impression.

'But I'd like to spend time with Connor,' Gianni completed.

'I'd have gone to my friend, Louise...but she wouldn't have room for us.'

She went to collect Connor. He did an excited dance on the pavement when he saw the big car. One look at Gianni and his whole face lit up. Connor scrambled into the back seat and wedged himself cheerfully as close as he could get to Gianni.

'Phroom-phroom!' he urged with a grin, impatient for the limo to move off again.

Milly's heart clenched when she saw Gianni meet that satisfied grin with one of his own. A startlingly easy, natural smile such as he had never shown her. It wiped every scrap of reserve from his lean bronzed features and was, she sensed, a rare event. Can I trust him...dare I trust him? What have I got to lose?

Gianni watched Milly pace restively round the dimly lit and spacious reception room, her slender body rigid as a bowstring.

So far her control had been too good to be true. A return visit to the Jenningses' home had been yet another distressing experience for her. She had been greeted with recriminations about her treatment of Edward and shocked reproaches at the speed with which she was moving out. And Gianni had been as welcome as the Grim Reaper calling in at a christening.

However, Milly had still sat down with Robin and Davina

Jennings to tell them how truly grateful she was for all they had done for her. In fact, Milly had shone like a star. She had said and done all the right things. She had come across as loyal, compassionate and forgiving. It had been a hell of an impressive show. But Gianni had watched her like a hawk, waiting for a fleeting expression to reveal to his cynical eyes at least that it was all just a clever act.

Yet once Gianni had fully believed that what you saw *was* what you got with Milly. But no decent woman would have betrayed him with his own brother for the sake of a quick sexual fix. He had realised then that Milly had to have a really shallow core which she was outstandingly good at keeping hidden. Bitter anger lanced through Gianni at that knowledge. No way was he about to allow her to suck him in with that I'm-so-nice act again!

So why *was* he still hanging about, holding her hand and being supportive? She didn't deserve that sort of stuff any more. She was playing him like a little lapdog on a lead! Just because she looked all fragile and forlorn, so touchingly brave in the face of adversity! Gianni slung her a brooding appraisal and then stiffened. What a total idiot he was being! A billionaire turning up to reclaim her had to be of considerable comfort! No wonder she wasn't coming apart at the seams! Suddenly he wished he had shown up in a battered old car and pretended to be poor...

His lean, strong face grim, Gianni strode rigid-backed towards the door. 'Call Room Service when you want to eat,' he told Milly.

Milly stopped pacing, shadowed blue eyes flying to him in unconcealed dismay. 'Where are you going?'

'Look, all this stuff is taking a large chunk out of my work schedule,' Gianni informed her flatly. 'Just thought I'd mention it.'

Milly's lower lip trembled. He sounded so fed up with her, but when she thought about what he had had to put up with over the past day or so, suddenly she wasn't the least bit surprised by the way he was behaving. Her wobbly mouth made a determined stab at an apologetic smile. 'I'm really sorry, Gianni.'

Gianni shifted one broad shoulder in an infinitesimal and very Latin shrug. 'What for?'

'Because I've been really selfish,' Milly acknowledged guiltily. 'You've been dragged into the midst of all my problems and this morning I was even calling you names! If it wasn't for you, I'd still be thinking I was Faith Jennings. But not once have I stopped to say thank you—'

'I don't want gratitude.'

Milly looked uncertainly at him. Sensing his eagerness to be gone, she suppressed the awareness that she didn't want to be alone with only her own thoughts to keep her company. She wasn't a baby. She had to manage.

'Could you bring your work up here?' she nonetheless heard herself ask.

'I have half a dozen staff working flat out. I doubt if Connor would sleep through the racket.'

Milly nodded slowly, forced an understanding smile and turned away.

Gianni opened the door.

'How do I get in touch with you if I need to?' she suddenly spun back to demand.

Gianni stilled. 'I'm only one floor below you,' he pointed out drily.

'So what's the number of your suite?' she prompted anxiously.

Gianni studied her for a long, tense moment, brilliant dark eyes veiled. 'I'll send a mobile phone up…OK?'

Her throat thickening, she nodded again.

He compressed his expressive mouth even more. 'You can call me as much as you want…all right?'

Milly kept on nodding like a puppet.

She wouldn't call. He wouldn't want to be interrupted. But didn't he realise that she needed to talk? She stopped herself dead on that censorious thought. Exactly when had she begun pinning so many expectations on Gianni? Maybe right at this moment she badly needed to believe that Gianni really cared about what happened to her, but that didn't give her an excuse to cling to him.

Yet Gianni was the only person who *knew* Milly Henner, her one connection, her sole link to twenty-three years of her life. Everything she had ever told him about herself was locked inside that proud dark head of his. But he wasn't parting with any of it in a hurry, was he? He was sitting on all that information like a miser on a gold mountain!

With Gianni gone, Milly made herself order a meal. Connor was fast asleep in one of the two bedrooms. He had had tea before she'd left her former home. After the fastest bath on record, she had changed him into his pyjamas and tucked him into bed. Already overtired, he had slept within minutes.

Milly took her time eating, but tasted nothing. Then she went for a long shower, donned a pale blue cotton nightdress and carefully dried her hair. When she emerged from the bedroom, the mobile phone Gianni had sent up was buzzing like an angry wasp on the coffee table.

She picked it up. 'Yes?'

'Why the blazes haven't you called me?' Gianni demanded rawly.

'I didn't want to bother you.'

'How am I supposed to work when I'm worrying about why you haven't called?' Gianni gritted.

'I'm sorry. I didn't realise you were worrying.' Milly sank down on the nearest sofa, much of her extreme tension evaporating under that comforting assurance. 'Gianni, can I ask you some questions now about us?'

'You're limited to three.'

'How did we meet?'

'You jumped out of my birthday cake. Next question.'

'I…I did *what*?' Milly gasped, thunderstruck. 'Honestly?'

'Honestly, and only two more questions to go,' Gianni reminded her.

'Why…why did I leave you?' she asked awkwardly.

Silence thundered on the line.

'That one's on the forbidden list,' Gianni responded flatly.

'That's not fair,' Milly protested. 'I mean, obviously I want to know that!'

'I'm not telling you. When you've come up with a replacement question, call me back,' Gianni suggested drily.

The line went dead.

Had Gianni done something dreadful to make her walk out? Had she done something dreadful? Or had they had a foolish argument in which one of them or both of them had said too much? An argument which struck Gianni as so stupid in retrospect that it really galled him to even think of it now?

She waited ten minutes and then she punched out the number that had arrived with the phone.

'It's me,' she announced.

'I know it's you,' Gianni breathed wryly.

'Second question,' she began rather tautly after his last response. 'Was I happy with you?'

'I thought you were deliriously happy, but that's not really a question I can answer for you.'

In the last three years, Milly had known not one minute of what she could have termed *delirious* happiness. The concept of such an extreme couldn't help but impress her to death.

'Gianni...what was I like then?'

'Stubborn, quick-tempered, full of life, unconventional...hell, this isn't a safe subject!'

Milly snatched in a ragged breath, still reeling in astonishment from that disturbing flood of adjectives.

'Are you OK?'

A choked sob was lodged in her throat. 'Fine,' she managed. 'I think I'll go to bed now.'

Milly Henner, it seemed, had been another woman entirely. A definite individual. Lively, strong...*unconventional*? A humourless laugh escaped Milly as she climbed into bed. Gianni's description had knocked her for six.

She had judged their past relationship on the basis of the narrow outlook she had developed over the past three years. His mistress. She had been shocked, ashamed. She had immediately seen herself as a victim. But Gianni hadn't described a woman who was a victim; Gianni had described an equal. Where had that stronger and more confident woman gone? And was she ever going to find her again?

Exhaustion sent Milly to sleep quickly, but dreams full of disturbing and increasingly frightening images kept her tossing and turning. Terror began to rise notch by notch until finally she came awake in a complete panic, shaking like a leaf and sobbing out loud, so confused she didn't even know where she was.

'*Dio mio, cara*…calm down!'

The instant she heard Gianni's voice she froze, and then just crumpled into the shelter of his arms, sick with relief that he was there.

CHAPTER SIX

A SOB catching in her throat, Milly pressed her damp face into Gianni's shoulder. The faint tang of expensive cologne underlying his own distinctive male scent made her nostrils flare. She breathed him in deep, like a drug.

'That must have been some nightmare, *cara*.' Gianni held her back from him.

Her eyes were huge and shadowed in the stark white triangle of her face. 'I was struggling with someone in the dark…it felt so *real*!'

'But it couldn't have been. Nothing like that ever happened to you, at least not when I knew you.' Gianni spread long fingers across her taut cheekbones, dark, deep flashing eyes scanning her still frightened face.

Some of her tension drained away at that comforting assurance, but not all of it. She had never had a dream like that before, could not help suspecting that something she had once experienced had summoned it up.

'Before you woke up, you called my name at the top of your voice,' Gianni imparted softly, mesmeric dark eyes glinting.

'Did I?' Milly didn't want to talk about the dream any more. It had scared her too much. Her brows drew together. 'How did you hear me…I mean, where on earth did you come from?' she belatedly thought to ask.

'About thirty feet away,' Gianni told her. 'I'd moved to work in the room next door. I didn't think you should be alone tonight, so I came up about an hour ago. If you hadn't wakened, you'd never have known I was there.'

In the dim light, Milly studied him properly for the first time. Shorn of his jacket and tie, his white silk shirt open at his strong brown throat and his black hair slightly tousled, he looked infinitely more approachable than he usually did. A faint blue-black shadow had already darkened his aggressive jawline. Even stubble, she thought guiltily, added to his appeal. Hurriedly she turned her head away and made herself rest back against the pillows.

'I'll get back to work.' Gianni began to stand up.

Milly tensed in dismay. 'Do you have to?'

'You want me to stay?'

Milly nodded agreement. 'And talk about something cheerful. You could tell me about my parents, if you like.'

Gianni folded down on the bed, stretched his long, lean frame out with intrinsic grace and sent her a winging glance from beneath heavily lidded eyes. 'You know what's going to happen, don't you?' he murmured, like an indolent tiger.

'Nothing's going to happen.' Milly reddened. 'Think of the bed as a sofa.'

Gianni loosed a low-pitched laugh and tilted his arrogant dark head back against the white pillows. 'Your parents...you told me they were crazy about each other. Your father was called Leo and he was a Londoner. Your mother, Suzanne, was French—'

'French?' Milly rolled over in surprise to stare at him.

'You're practically bilingual. Didn't you find that out yet? You spent the first eight years of your life in Paris.'

'You're supposed to start at the beginning. Do you know when my parents got married?'

'They didn't...they weren't into matrimony.'

Milly was stunned. 'You mean, I'm...?'

'Yes.'

She slowly shook her head. Her throat tickled, and then the laughter just bubbled out of her.

Gianni leant down, curved his hands to her shaking shoulders and tugged her up to his level. 'What's so funny?'

Struggling to get a grip on herself again, Milly released a rueful groan. 'It's just so ironic. In the world I've been living in for the past three years illegitimacy is a very serious issue, and now I find out that *I* was born out of wedlock too! Tell me about Leo and Suzanne,' she urged.

'They were pavement artists.'

'Pavement artists,' Milly repeated weakly, and then she smiled. 'I like that.'

'Suzanne was knocked down and killed by a drunk driver in Paris. Your father never really got over it, and that was the end of your settled home life. He took you roving all over Europe with him. You didn't see the inside of too many schools, but you adored your father and you always talked as if you'd had a wonderful childhood.'

Milly gazed up into Gianni's lean bronzed face like a child listening to an enthralling bedtime story. 'I'm glad.'

'But then you always were a sunny optimist.' Gianni skimmed a lazy forefinger lightly through the glossy strands of blonde hair tumbling across his forearm and stared down at her with glittering dark golden eyes.

Her heart skipped a beat and then began to thud heavily. Her stomach clenched. The silence lingered and Gianni's eloquent mouth tipped into an indolent smile that welded her attention to him.

'I'm a real pessimist about most things,' Gianni shared softly. 'But in one field I'm rarely disappointed...'

A curious languor had crept over Milly. Her body felt weighted, yet incredibly alive, every sense feeling somehow keener, sharper. What a wonderful voice he had, she thought absently, as a little tremor ran down her taut spinal cord. Like sinfully rich chocolate. *Sin*... Her abstracted brain began to play with the word. *Sin*fully stunning, *sin*fully sexy...

Hot pink staining her cheekbones, she attempted to concentrate on what he was saying—which was a little difficult, she discovered, when he wasn't actually saying anything!

Slumbrous golden eyes framed with lush ebony lashes rested on her. And, like a tidal wave, Milly felt an enormous rush of yearning well up inside her. She remembered that sensational kiss. The cymbals...the fireworks. Unwittingly, she began to lift her head, push up on one elbow, soft lips tremulously parted, her slim length beginning to curve towards him as if he was a magnet and she was a nail.

'And you have never once disappointed me in that field,' Gianni informed her huskily.

Milly hadn't a clue what he was talking about, and couldn't have strung two rational thoughts together. 'Didn't I?' she managed breathlessly.

'In that one corner of our relationship I had total and absolute control.' Gianni's wide, sensual mouth curved into a wickedly charismatic smile that squeezed her heart in a sneak attack.

The dim light accentuated the smooth dark planes and hollows of his chiselled features. His bronzed skin was vibrant against the pristine whiteness of his shirt. With one long, lean and powerful thigh raised in a very masculine attitude of relaxation, Gianni was so physically arresting he just took her breath away.

In fact, she was so tense her muscles hurt. Yet she couldn't make herself move, couldn't drag her eyes from him, couldn't suppress the increasingly desperate craving holding her so still. Gianni bent his dark head slowly. His breath fanned her cheek. He let his tongue dart between her parted lips and she jerked and moaned and reached up for him, her hands spearing fiercely into his silky black hair.

He did it again, and her whole body leapt, electrified. Just one kiss, just one kiss, she promised herself, like an alcoholic craving what she knew she shouldn't have.

'Oh Gi-anni...' she gasped on the back of an aching sigh.

He pressed his mouth to her cheek, her brow, her lowered eyelids, teasing her with feather-light kisses until she strained up to him even more. 'Any time, any place, any way I want,' Gianni murmured thickly. 'I don't have to say anything, I don't have to do anything. I just start thinking about sex and you are so tuned in to me you just *melt*...'

He kissed her, and it was like being shot to heaven on a rocket. She melted to boiling point in seconds. He made love to her mouth with an intimacy that shook her. He delved and tasted and skimmed until she was burning up, clutching at him, living from one second to the next on the single terrifying thought that he might stop.

Peeling her hands from him, Gianni lowered her back to the bed. He sat up and ripped off his shirt in one impatient movement. Struggling to get air back into her constricted lungs, Milly was totally transfixed. He had a torso like a Greek god. Wide brown shoulders, rippling pectoral muscles roughened by a triangle of black curling hair and a stomach as flat as a washboard.

A tiny pinching sensation attacked low in her pelvis. She felt light-headed, but her body was so tense it screamed at her, every sense recognising Gianni as her lover. The scent of him, the touch of him, the very taste of him. She couldn't believe what was happening to her. She shivered in shock laced with a kind of death-defying excitement.

'Gianni…' she whispered jaggedly, struggling to reinstate some form of control, some sense of reality to her own mounting disorientation. 'I…*we*—'

Gianni came back down to her, dark eyes now bright as flames, his feverish tension as marked as her own. She saw a hunger in him that twisted something painfully inside her, and with a muffled little sound of surrender she reached up instinctively and opened her lips to him again.

With a dark, driven groan of satisfaction, Gianni lifted her up to him with two powerful hands and ravaged the tender interior of her mouth with a raw, demanding passion that overwhelmed her.

'We both need this,' he said thickly. 'You want me; you *always* want me…'

She looked at him, her heart pounding like crazy. She raised a trembling hand and touched his beautiful mouth with tender caressing fingertips, controlled by instincts that filled her with almost unbearably powerful feelings. 'Like I need air to breathe,' she whispered shakily.

Gianni raised her up and divested her of her nightdress

with an easy expertise that somehow shocked her. And suddenly that wholly inborn feeling of security abandoned Milly. She stared in dismay down at the ripe swell of her bare breasts, her face hot with colour. She felt wanton, and then very, very shy as Gianni's gaze burned over her exposed flesh like the kiss of fire.

'*Dio…*' he growled, raising an unsteady hand to cup a pale, pouting breast adorned by a straining pink nipple, lingering to rub a thumb and forefinger over that stiffened peak.

The violence of her own response tore a startled moan from Milly. Her mind closed in on itself again, stripping away that brief awareness of anything beyond the physical. She shut her eyes tight, letting her head fall back. As he toyed with the achingly sensitive bud her own heartbeat thrummed in her eardrums.

'I always adored your breasts. You're exquisite,' Gianni groaned, knotting one possessive hand into her cascading mane of golden hair and letting his mouth swoop down to replace his fingers.

Excitement took hold of her like a bushfire, blazing out of her control. The erotic mastery he unleashed with the tug of his teeth and the wet rasp of his tongue dragged her down so fast into a world of pure sensation that she was lost. She moaned and twisted, suddenly hotter than she could bear. She was wildly aware now of the maddening burn at the very core of her body, the pulse of damp warmth beginning to beat and ache between her thighs.

Gianni wrenched back from her to dispose of the remainder of his clothing. Milly opened passion-glazed eyes. She was trembling, her whole body just one gigantic pleading ache. 'Gianni…*please…*' She didn't even know where the words came from.

'It hurts to want this much, doesn't it?' Gianni leant over her, his long, lean body golden and tight with leashed power in the lamplight. His brilliant eyes savoured her quivering tension, watched her look at him with wonder.

'Yes…' It hurt like a knot tightening and tightening inside

her. Her spellbound gaze roamed down over his powerful frame, lingering in sensual shock on the aggressive masculine thrust of his virility. Her mouth ran dry and it was like something unlocked inside her, loosing a hot flood of honey to pool heavily at the very heart of her.

All conquering male, Gianni pulled her close. Then he stared down into her hectically flushed face, his spectacular bone structure ferociously taut, his bright eyes curiously chilling, his beautiful shaped mouth hardening. 'We always connected best at this level, *cara mia.*'

Something in that dark sardonic drawl spooked her, but before she could try to identify that apprehensive dart of unease Gianni eased her slender thighs apart and began to explore her wildly sensitive flesh. Her body jack-knifed under that surge of almost intolerable pleasure. It was mindless, all-encompassing, and she craved its continuance with every tortured and sobbing breath she drew.

But it was still a surprise when Gianni came over her, sinking rough, impatient hands beneath her squirming hips. And suddenly he was there, where the ache was worst, entering her in one powerful thrust that made her cry out.

Excited beyond belief by him, Milly clashed with the charged darkness of his eyes. 'Gianni…?' she gasped.

'*Madre di Dio…*I have to black out *my* memory to do this!' Gianni gritted savagely, driving into her again, making her tender flesh yield more fully to enclose him.

And even as she struggled to comprehend what was wrong, what he meant, the primitive rhythm of his possession engulfed a body too long starved of such sensation. Her confusion was not equal to the overpowering hunger he had awakened. With every driving invasion Gianni sent excitement hurtling through her at storm-force potency. Hot, aching pleasure took her over. Release came in a shattering ecstatic surge that jolted and freed what felt like every fibre of her being.

Within seconds, Gianni hit that same peak with a shuddering groan. Her arms came round him, tears flooding her eyes. That didn't surprise her. It always happened. Sometimes she loved Gianni so much she wanted to scream it from the rooftops, she thought helplessly. She pressed her lips adoringly to a satin-smooth shoulder damp with sweat and whispered it instead.

With startling abruptness he pulled back from her. With a bitten-off Italian curse, he shoved himself away from her. Then he surveyed her with blazing anger and condemnation. 'Bye-bye, Edward, hello, Gianni—all in the space of one day?' he ground out raggedly, strikingly pale beneath his naturally dark skin. 'What sort of a fool do you take me for?'

And Milly went into deep shock then. The cloaking, blinding veil of physical satiation was torn from her mind and dissipated as though it had never been. Every scrap of colour drained from her stricken face as she stared at Gianni, and she stared at him and registered that both past and present now existed in a seamless joining inside her head.

Gianni snatched in a shuddering breath. 'OK…you didn't mean to say it and I overreacted,' he conceded, a slight tremor interfering with his usually even diction, his Sicilian accent very strong.

Sicilian to the backbone, Milly recalled absently, locked into the terrifying enormity of the memories hitting her now from all sides.

'Stop looking at me like that,' Gianni told her.

He thinks he's going to have to apologise, and he hates apologising, so he's digging himself into a deeper hole because when he's really upset about anything he will go to enormous lengths not to confront that reality. All the strength in Milly's body just seeped away as she completed that instant appraisal. She was immobilised by what had happened inside her own head. She had finally got her memory back. Now the shock was telling.

'Milly…' Gianni sat up, dark, deep flashing eyes narrowing on her anguished face and the distance in her eyes. A distance which suggested that though she might appear to be looking at him, for some reason he wasn't really registering.

Gianni, the love of her life, Milly labelled him, in a growing haze of emotional agony. Walking away, acknowledging defeat, had been like driving a knife into her own heart.

'You *hate* me...' she framed sickly, shaking her head back and forth on the pillow in urgent negative, soundless tears beginning to track down her cheeks. 'You *touched* me, hating me!'

Gianni was stunned.

'And how do I know that?' Milly gulped strickenly. 'I know that because I can remember *everything*—but I don't want to...I don't want to remember!' she lashed at him in passionate pain.

Gianni laid Milly down on the great canopied bed in the master suite of his country house—which he had yet to spend a single night in. Back at the hotel, the doctor had given her a sedative, and had then told Gianni in no uncertain terms exactly what he thought of him.

There had been no hiding the fact that that hotel bed had harboured more than one body. With a humility that would have astounded all who knew him, Gianni had withstood being called a selfish swine. At that instant, hovering while Milly shivered and shook with those horrible silent tears, Gianni would have welcomed far stronger censure if it had in any way lessened his own appalling sense of guilt.

He had traumatised her. *Him*. Nobody else. The Jenningses had loved her, and would have protected her while she tried to come to terms with what was happening to her. But he had deliberately severed every tie she had and then quite ruthlessly seduced her back into sexual intimacy. She hadn't been ready for that. She might never have been ready for that again. He had hit on her like a stud when she was weak and confused and scared. She had trustingly turned to him for comfort and he had let his driving need to re-establish a hold on her triumph. He had never sunk so low in his life…

And it was no consolation to know *why* he had done it. Jealousy, bitter and angry, seething up inside him like hot, destructive lava. The thought of Milly loving Benson, wanting him, sleeping with him. Thinking about her with Stefano had been bad enough, but he had learned to block that out. Iron self-discipline had worked for three years. Only it had come apart at the seams the instant he'd tried to make love to her again, suddenly terrified for the first time in his life that he might not be able to do it and then acting like an animal in rut. Great footnote, Gianni. The one and only thing that was ever perfect, you blew!

'Not sleeping?' Connor asked, his little face full of hope.

'Not sleeping,' Milly confirmed gruffly as she set aside her breakfast tray and dragged her son down into her arms to tickle him, listening to his delighted chortles with a sudden lightening of her heart. She kissed his soft cheek and ran a fingertip lovingly down over his small nose. 'I gather I've been sleeping *too* long.'

Connor scrambled down off the bed at speed. Retrieving something from the floor, he clambered back up to show it to her. It was a child's board book. He pointed to the golden-haired princess sleeping on the front cover and said with tremendous pride, 'My mummy!'

As she noted the title, Milly breathed in very deep. *The Sleeping Beauty.* Gianni was very creative in tight corners, and explaining Mummy's sudden need to sleep the clock round and more had evidently not over-taxed his agile brain. Gianni, she reflected tautly, for so long never more than a heartbeat away from her next thought.

Why, oh, why hadn't he just let her stay lost? Connor. But not *only* Connor. Revenge, she decided with a helpless shiver. Revenge as only a Sicilian could enact it. In a reckless drunken attack of lust, Stefano had destroyed them. On his deathbed Gianni wouldn't forgive her for what he be-

lieved she'd done to him. And at his coldest Gianni was at
his most dangerous. If only she had been armoured with the
knowledge that she was dealing with a male who hated and
despised her when they'd first met again...

But then how many 'if onlys' already littered her history
with Gianni? So she had ended up in bed with him again.
So she had had a fantastic time. That was the painful crux
of the matter, wasn't it? That she had sobbed with ecstasy
and clung to a guy who had invaded her eager body with
all the rampaging finesse of a stud on a one-night stand!

Gianni, who had taught her that making love could be an
art form, Gianni, who was endlessly creative in the bedroom
but never, ever rough. Quite deliberately he had set out to
use and humiliate her. But it had been the shatteringly sudden return of her memory which had torn her apart. And
Gianni was in for a very big surprise if he fondly imagined
she was about to greet him with shamed eyes and streaming
tears at their next meeting!

But life went on no matter what, Milly told herself with
feverish urgency. Gianni was Connor's father now. Nothing
more. Her problem was that she needed to learn a whole
new way of thinking. Time hadn't passed for her in quite
the same way as it had passed for Gianni. Three years ago
she had still been hopelessly in love with him. At the instant
her memories came alive again she had been engulfed in a
devastatingly intense storm of emotion, the most bitter sense
of betrayal, loss and anguished pain. Because the man she
loved had turned his back on her and walked away. It was
those feelings she had to deal with now, and then she had
to put them all away again, back where they *really* belonged—in the past.

From her magnificent bed, she surveyed her imposing new
surroundings with grudging curiosity, and then, pushing
back the fine linen sheet, she got up. When she'd arrived,
she had used the bathroom, which had been left helpfully lit
with the door ajar. Now that she registered that there were
three other doors to choose between she knew why.

Wandering over to one of the tall windows to glance out, she almost tripped over Connor in surprise. Beautiful gardens gave way to rolling fields and distant woodland. She had dimly assumed that she was in a townhouse, hadn't thought to question the lack of traffic noise. Gianni now owned a country home? Gianni, who had once regarded the countryside as the long, boring bit between cities? But then what did she know about Gianni's life these days?

Tensing, she instantly reminded herself that she didn't *want* to know anything! With Connor tagging in her wake she went for a shower, and was drying her hair when a brisk knock sounded on the bedroom door. A youthful brunette peered in, and then flushed when she saw Milly in her bathrobe. 'I'm sorry, Miss Henner. I didn't realise you were up and about. My name's Barbara Withers—'

Connor interrupted her with an exuberant cry of recognition. 'Barb!'

'I'm Connor's temporary nanny. Mr D'Angelo did stress that a permanent appointment would be subject to your approval,' she advanced anxiously.

'Yes...' Conscious of the younger woman's discomfiture, Milly concealed her own disconcertion.

'I was about to offer to take Connor outside to play. Since Mr D'Angelo left him with you after breakfast, I thought you might be tired now,' Barbara explained.

So Connor hadn't wandered into her bedroom under his own steam. Milly had been concerned that no adult appeared to be in charge of him. But it seemed that Gianni had sneakily fed their son in through the door without making a personal appearance. But then with Connor around perhaps that had been a wise decision, and she didn't want him present when she saw Gianni again.

'I'm sure Connor would enjoy that.' Milly's smile was strained by the thought of what lay ahead of her. And that was facing up to the male who, after that dreadful night three years ago, had refused to meet her again, accept her phone calls or answer her letters. Closure had not been a problem for Gianni. He had judged her, dumped her, and replaced her at spectacular speed.

Suddenly cold inside herself, Milly leafed through the garments she had found unpacked in the adjoining dressing room. She had a curious aversion to wearing the clothes she had worn as Faith Jennings, but she had nothing else available. With regret she recalled the wonderful wardrobe she had loftily chosen to leave behind when she had left Paris three years earlier.

In the end she pulled on a pair of faded jeans she had used for gardening and a long-sleeved black polo shirt. Leaving her tumbling mass of golden hair loose round her shoulders, she set off in search of Gianni.

She emerged onto a huge galleried landing dominated by superb oil paintings. For 'country house' she now substituted 'stately home'. The stamp of Gianni's ownership was everywhere. The most magnificent furniture, the most exquisite artwork. He surrounded himself with beautiful possessions and he had fabulous taste and considerable knowledge, all acquired as an adult.

An extraordinary man, she conceded reluctantly. Always a target for the paparazzi, rarely out of the newspapers, inevitably a focus of fascination for others. Precious few men rose to Gianni's level from a deprived and brutalised childhood. A drunken, abusive father, a prostitute mother who had abandoned him, followed by a stepmother who had fed him alongside the dog and chucked him out on the streets of Palermo to fend for himself at the age of ten. Why was she remembering all that? she asked herself angrily.

But all of a sudden it was as if a dam had broken its banks inside Milly's subconscious: memories gushed out against her volition, demanding her attention, refusing to go away...

The year Milly had turned nineteen her life had changed out of all recognition. Leo, her feckless but very charming father, had died of a sudden heart attack in Spain.

After eleven years of sharing her father's gypsy lifestyle,

Milly had wanted to put down roots and make plans. She had applied for a place on a two-year horticultural course at a London college. With not a single educational qualification to her name it had taken courage to put herself forward, and she had been overjoyed when she'd been accepted as a full-time student.

She had lived on a shoestring in a dingy bedsit, working part-time in a supermarket to supplement her tiny grant. Her first real friend had been the bubbly blonde who'd lived across the landing. Lisa had worked for a strippergram agency and had lived in considerably greater comfort than Milly.

One afternoon, Lisa had come to her door in a real state. 'I have to do a booking in the City tonight and I can't make it,' she groaned. 'Stevie's just called to ask me out to dinner and you *know* what he's like! If I'm not available, he'll ask someone else!'

Lisa had given her heart to a real creep. The saga of her sufferings at Stevie's ruthlessly selfish hands could have filled a book the size of the Bible. Yet when Stevie called Lisa still dropped everything and ran, because he had trained her that way.

'Please do this booking for me,' Lisa pleaded frantically. 'You don't have to take *anything* off. All you've got to do is jump out of this stupid fake cake dressed as an angel and smile!'

Milly grimaced. Lisa raced back to her bedsit and returned with an armful of celestial white robes and a small gilded harp. 'It's a really dated stunt, but these executive-types want something tasteful because they're scared witless of offending the big boss. It's his birthday and his name is D'Angelo...*angel*—get it?'

So that was how Milly had ended up jumping out of Gianni's birthday cake. She had thrown herself upright and found herself looking straight down into dark eyes that flashed to the most amazing shade of gold. Those eyes had spooked her. Tripping in her oversized robes, she had lurched off the trolley, careened into the board table beside it to send half the drinks flying and had finally landed in a tumbled heap at Gianni's feet. The ghastly silence her clumsiness had evoked remained with her even now.

'Happy birthday, Mr D'Angelo,' she had muttered doggedly.

'What do you do for an encore?' Gianni enquired in silken enquiry. 'Level the building?'

Severe embarrassment flipped into sudden fury at that sarcastic sally. 'Don't be such an insensitive prat!' Milly hissed in angry reproach. 'Go on—help me up...don't you have any manners at all?'

A swelling tide of gasps, sharp, indrawn breaths and muted groans rose from the executives still glued to their seats round the board table.

Gianni looked stunned. Then, disorientatingly, he threw back his arrogant dark head and laughed. 'For a little titchy thing, you've got quite a tongue, haven't you?'

'You are one ignorant pig!' Milly told him, even as he extended a lean hand to help her upright. She pushed his hand away and sat carefully untangling the robes from her legs so that she could rise without assistance and take a step back to impose some distance between them.

Gianni then helpfully extended the harp she had dropped on him. 'What do you do next?' he asked, lounging back in his imposing chair with an air of sardonic anticipation.

Milly snatched the harp back. 'If you're hoping I'm about to start stripping, it's not your day! I keep all my clothes on.'

Gianni studied her with even greater amusement. 'Aren't you supposed to at least *sing* many happy returns?'

At that reminder, Milly stiffened resentfully. 'I couldn't hold a tune in a bucket.'

'You...are...priceless.' Gianni savoured her, brilliant eyes fixed like lasers to her expressive face.

Rising from his chair to his full intimidating height, Gianni closed one hand over hers and turned to address their gaping audience. 'Check the Health and Safety rules next time you decide to give me a surprise. This particular angel could have sued the pants off us if she'd been hurt!'

'Let go of my hand,' Milly urged as he carried her across the room with him.

He thrust open the door that led back into the corridor. 'Was this your last booking?'

'My only one—'

'Then I'll take you home.'

'No thanks.' Pulling free of his hold, Milly hurried back to the cloakroom in which she had earlier changed out of her own clothes.

When she emerged, clad in jeans and a sweater, Gianni was still waiting for her.

'You're a bit like a dog with a bone, aren't you?'

'You're very beautiful. Don't act so surprised when I tell you that. It doesn't wash with looks like yours,' Gianni drawled with a cynical smile. 'I'll take you home. You can get dressed up. We'll go out to dinner.'

'No, thanks,' she said tautly, annoyed that temptation was flickering when he was so screamingly unsuitable. Dressed up? Dressed up in *what*? Did he think she had a designer wardrobe to fall back on?

'Why not?'

'How many reasons do you need?'

'This is very entertaining. Feel free to speak your mind.'

'All right. One, you're too slick for me. Two, you look filthy rich. Three, you have to be at least ten years older than me, and I can't imagine that we'd have a single thing in common.'

'Are you always this…sharp-tongued?'

She picked up on the deliberate hesitation, recognised the coolness that had quenched the vibrancy in his extraordinary eyes and felt herself shrivel up inside, but still she said, 'No, you bring out the best in me.'

'Instant loathing?'

She shivered, and then, ashamed of her disturbingly unfamiliar need to continually attack him, she decided to be honest. 'No, I fancied you like mad the minute I laid eyes on you, but it's not something I want to follow up,' she admitted, suddenly finding herself alarmingly short of breath. 'Bye. Have a nice birthday!'

The following afternoon, Gianni was waiting for her to come home from college. Having tripped over him on the landing, Lisa was bending over backwards to entertain him in Milly's absence.

'How on earth did you find out where I lived?'

'Bribed the sleazebag who owns the strippergram agency. He told me your name was Lisa. Then I met Lisa and she explained who you *really* were.' Gianni angled a slanting smile over her—a smile that had megawatt charisma.

'You shouldn't have come here—'

'*Dio mio*…what did you expect? You think I'm about to walk in the opposite direction when you're feeling the same way I feel?'

'Tell me one thing we have in common?' Milly invited.

'Sex.'

'When you think of something else, I'll have dinner with you,' Milly told him, hot-cheeked.

Gianni stuck a swift foot in the door she was trying to close on him. 'Quick tempers.'

'You are *so* persistent!'

'OK.' Strong jawline squaring, he shrugged with eye-catching elegance. 'I'm out of here.'

She let him get as far as the floor below, and then, stabbed by the sudden realisation that she would never see him again, she darted back out to the landing and hung over the banister to call, 'Just dinner…all right?'

'What about breakfast?' Gianni asked without hesitation.

'No chance, but I appreciate you being this honest about your intentions. Honesty is very important to me, even if the truth isn't always welcome. So I should tell you now that I'm not into casual sex and I'm very romantic.'

Gianni sighed softly. 'One of us is set to crash into a solid brick wall.'

'It won't be me,' Milly told him gently. 'I couldn't possibly fall in love with someone like you.'

'*Accidenti*…why would I *want* you to fall in love with me?' Gianni demanded incredulously. 'My sole interest in you is—'

'Shut up before you talk yourself out of a dinner date,' Milly advised.

Emerging from the frighteningly fresh hold of those memories back into the present, Milly blinked and looked around herself. She was still standing on the gallery. Breathing in deep, shaken by the tremendous pull of the past, she walked slowly towards the stairs.

As she descended the sweeping staircase Gianni strode out into the wonderful Georgian hall below. Instantly she felt her tender heart quake like a stupid jelly, as if three years hadn't passed, as if her brain was forever locked in time, incapable of moving on and healing. As she stilled two steps up from the foot of the stairs, so that for once she was at his level, her hands closed into defensive fists by her sides.

CHAPTER SEVEN

'GIANNI...' Milly breathed, and she could hardly get his name past her dry lips.

'You don't look at all well,' Gianni drawled with measured cool, incisive dark eyes resting on her without any perceptible expression. 'You really should have stayed in bed.'

Yes, he could have handled her best as a total invalid, Milly decided. Then she would have been an object of pity, too weak and pathetic to require confrontation. Gianni went to quite incredible lengths to avoid emotional scenes. He could not bear to be vulnerable. He could not tolerate any loss of control. So he attached himself to objects, not to people. Perhaps Connor would teach him to love. She had failed—oh, boy, had she failed...

'I'm fine,' she lied, terrified that he was registering just how much he could still affect her.

Gianni looked back at her. She was so small, so slender, so pale, haunted eyes fixed to him as if he was about to unfurl a set of cloven hooves and a toasting fork. *Fine?* The fear she couldn't hide filled him with seething bitterness.

Suddenly he wished her memory had stayed lost. Memories were bloody painful afflictions! That night in the hotel she had been so sweet. Trusting, open, just as he remembered her. The only person alive who had ever treated him as if he was just an ordinary guy. Nagging him when he was late, complaining when he was preoccupied, yawning through the business news and totally forgetting about him when she was out in her precious garden. In every way she had been different from every other woman he had had, either before or since.

110

Once she would have filled this awful silence, instinctively understanding that he couldn't, that when he was wound up about something he turned cold and aggressive and silent in self-defence. Then he reminded himself that this bit would be over soon. Not for nothing had he spent the past twenty-four hours seeking a rational solution to the mess they were in. And around dawn, he had come up with the answer.

Not perfect, but simple. And the instant he made that proposal Milly would go back to normal—well, maybe not immediately, he conceded grudgingly, but *obviously* she'd be over the moon. He'd also have the tactical advantage of surprise. She'd appreciate that he was making a really huge and stupendously generous effort for Connor's sake. And naturally she'd be grateful. Grateful enough to go back upstairs with him and consolidate their new understanding in the most logical way of all?

Milly knew she was gaping at Gianni like a pheasant looking up the barrel of a shotgun. But the lurch of her heart had appalled her. Feeling that sensitive to dark, deep flashing eyes as chilly as a winter's day was not a good sign. Noticing that he looked shockingly spectacular in a casual designer suit the colour of caramel was an even worse sign. Say something, a voice in her head screeched, for heaven's sake, *say* something. But her mind was a complete blank. She didn't know where to start or how she would ever stop if she did start. Silence seemed a lot safer.

Milly stiffened as Gianni extended a hand to her. It was the very last gesture she had expected from him. Uncurling her fingers, she lifted her arm in slow motion. He got tired waiting. He brought up his other hand, closed both round her waist and lifted her down to the marble-tiled floor.

A slight gasp of disconcertion escaped her. However, the sudden shrinkage in stature she suffered helped. Suddenly her strained eyes were mercifully level with Gianni's chest.

'We've got some talking to do,' Gianni informed her next.

Milly was poleaxed. Only a woman who had been intimately involved with Gianni could have understood that acknowledgement to be ground-breaking and incredible. Whenever she had wanted to talk, seriously talk about personal things, Gianni had had a hundred evasive techniques. 'Later' had been a particular favourite, followed by a sudden rampant desire for her body or a pressing appointment. It had taken her a very long time to appreciate that 'later' meant never.

'A lot…' Milly agreed breathlessly, suddenly experiencing a stark, shameful stab of pained resentment. What had changed Gianni? *Who* had changed him? Who had finally persuaded him that honest communication was the only option when the going got tough? It was what they had once so badly needed, but the offer was coming way too late for her to benefit.

He showed her into a library, where a log fire was burning in the grate. He strode over to the desk, lifted the phone and ordered coffee. Stilling by the hearth, Milly stretched her unsteady hands out to the heat and let her gaze travel around the magnificent room with its warm red décor.

'What do you think of Heywood House?' Gianni asked.

'It's beautiful.' She resisted the urge to admit that it wasn't at all what she had expected. She didn't want to stray onto impersonal topics and deflect him from anything he might want to say to her.

'The gardens are famous. I've ensured that they've been maintained to the highest standards,' Gianni advanced smoothly.

Milly wandered over to the nearest window. She adored gardens, but right now she was so enervated she couldn't even appreciate the wonderful view. 'It looks tremendous.'

'There's a rare plant centre attached to the estate. I rebuilt it,' Gianni continued. 'It doesn't exactly do a roaring trade, but the manager tells me it's a real haunt for the connoisseur.

Bewildered by this flood of extraneous information from a male who barely knew the difference between a rose and a daisy and was content to remain in a state of blissful ignorance, Milly suddenly frowned as her mind homed in on something else entirely, and she exclaimed, 'For goodness' sake, Gianni...I haven't even spoken to Louise! What on earth must she be thinking? She's my partner and my best friend and I didn't even *phone* her!'

The silence spread and spread.

Gianni dealt her a fulminating look. 'I phoned her. She was very concerned. I said you'd be in touch when you were well enough...OK?'

Milly released her breath, relieved by that assurance. But she wondered why he had delivered the news with such an air of impatience. It wasn't as if she had interrupted him when he'd been talking about anything important. The door opened and a maid entered with a tray of coffee. It was a welcome diversion.

She sat down in a leather wing-back armchair and poured the coffee. Without hesitation she added three sugars to Gianni's cup.

'We'll deal with practicalities first, get them out of the way,' Gianni announced with decisive cool. 'And naturally the first thing I want to know is, have you any idea who left you lying badly injured on that road in Cornwall? And how did it happen?'

Milly jerked and froze, her heartbeat thudding loudly in her ears. Such obvious questions. Why hadn't she been prepared for them?

'It must be distressing for you to have to remember that night. But it has to be dealt with.' Gianni watched her with keen, dark expectant eyes.

Milly was shot right back to that night, forced to recall things she would have preferred to leave buried, things that had nothing whatsoever to do with the accident. She lost colour. Her hand began to shake. She set down her coffee again with a clatter. She hoped to heaven Gianni didn't ask her what she had been *doing* in Cornwall in the first place, because if he did ask, she certainly didn't feel like telling him the truth.

'Milly…?' Gianni pressed, more gently. 'Do you remember what happened now?'

'M-mostly…not very clearly.' A taxi had dropped her off at the cottage where Stefano had been staying with his girlfriend. She had forgotten to ask the taxi driver to wait for her: a very foolish oversight. But it had taken a lot of courage to seek out and confront Stefano. And when she had walked back out of that cottage she had felt dead inside and she really hadn't cared about anything. Not the darkness, not the wind, not the rain. She had just started walking away as fast as she could.

'I got lost,' Milly muttered tightly.

'Where was this? Why were you were on foot?'

'I'd gone visiting…and, coming back, I messed up my transport arrangements. So was walking,' she began afresh, staring blindly at the silver sugar bowl, determined not to tell him any actual lies. 'It was a horrible wet night.'

Gianni bent down, closed a hand over her knotted fingers and eased her slowly upright into the circle of his arms. 'It was also a long time ago, *cara*. It can't hurt you now.'

Helplessly, Milly leant into him for support, but she felt like a fraud. 'There really isn't much to remember, Gianni. I *think* I may have heard the car that hit me approaching but that's it. There's nothing else. I don't recall seeing a car or being hit.' She bowed her damp brow against his chest. 'What has always given me the creeps is the knowledge that somebody robbed me while I was lying there hurt. I had an overnight bag with me.'

'The hit-and-run driver and the thief may well have been the same person,' Gianni ground out, and she could feel the massive restraint he was exerting over his anger on her behalf. The knowledge of that anger comforted her. 'I'm afraid the police will be hoping for more details than you've been able to give me.'

'The police?' Milly echoed in surprise.

'Some bastard left you lying by the side of that road like a piece of rubbish!' Gianni reminded her with barely suppressed savagery. 'You'd be dead if a passing motorist hadn't seen you and contacted the emergency services. It's a complete miracle that you didn't have a miscarriage!'

Milly sighed. 'I don't really want to talk to the police about this again.'

Gianni veiled his gaze. 'You'll have to make a new statement, but I can understand that you don't like the idea of it all being raked up again,' he conceded soothingly as he settled her back into the wing-back chair. 'I've still got a few questions I'd like answered, but we'll leave them for now.'

'Yes...' Milly averted her pounding head, stomach still churning. She really didn't want Gianni to know she'd gone to see Stefano. She knew what interpretation he would put on that revelation. And Stefano had clearly known better than to ever mention her visit. That was no surprise to her. Gianni's kid brother had treated her like Typhoid Mary that night. With great difficulty, Milly put away that memory.

'Right,' Gianni breathed in a next-on-the-agenda tone, as if he was chairing a board meeting. 'I imagine you'd like to know where we're heading now.'

Considering that in two entire years with her Gianni had not once even hinted that they might be heading anywhere beyond his next flying visit, Milly was taken aback by that concise assurance. She looked up, sapphire-blue eyes very wide and wary.

Gianni leant back against his desk, looking incredibly sophisticated and elegant in his unstructured caramel suit and black T-shirt. Milly averted her head again and rubbed at a worn seam on her jeans with restive fingers.

'To start with I should tell you why I bought this place two years ago.'

Milly frowned, not understanding why that should be of interest to her.

'Heywood House is convenient both to the airport and the City of London. I hoped that once I found you both, you would move in here—'

'Move in here?' Milly glanced up in frank bewilderment. *'Why?'*

Gianni sighed, as if she was being incredibly slow on the uptake. 'Naturally I want you to live at a location where I can easily maintain regular contact with Connor. Heywood House fits the bill very well.'

'Two years ago, you purchased this property for *me*?' Milly was thinking out loud, and she flushed with embarrassment when reality sank in a split second later.

Gianni had bought a stately home and turned it into a treasure house. Naturally *not* for her benefit but for his child's! Even that far back Gianni had been making plans. Selecting the kind of home he wanted his child to grow up in, filling it with priceless artwork and furniture to create a gilded cocoon of wealth and privilege. Could she ever have dreamt three years ago that he would warm to the concept of being a father to such an extent? With an effort, she forced her attention back to him.

'To all intents and purposes Heywood House *will* be yours, until Connor reaches his twenty-fifth birthday.' Gianni made that distinction with complete cool. 'I intend to sign all the documentation to that effect and this is now your home. I want you to feel secure here.'

Everything to be tied up all nice and tight and legal. Very much Gianni's stamp. Gianni had already worked out how best to control her and, through her, his child. Where they lived, *how* they lived. And, to that end, Heywood House would be put in trust for their son. Milly stared down into her untouched coffee, feeling incredibly hurt and humiliated. He didn't trust her as far as he could throw her now—but then had he ever?

For the first time since she had recovered her memory, Milly recalled the DNA testing Gianni had mentioned. A shudder of very real repulsion ran through her in response. One glimpse of her with Stefano and that had been that. Instantly Gianni had been willing to believe her capable of any evil. Two years of her loving faith had been eradicated in a nano-second. Now, it seemed, he didn't even trust her not to try and make a claim for a share of this house at some time in the future.

'I thought you'd be pleased about the gardens and the plant centre.' Gianni regarded her like a generous benefactor, still awaiting the gratitude he saw as his due and keen to give her a helpful nudge in the right direction. 'Obviously those factors influenced my choice of this particular property.'

Unable to credit that, hating her as he did, he could have been influenced by any desire to please her, Milly swallowed hard. 'Didn't it occur to you that I might want to live somewhere of my *own* choosing?'

'Within certain parameters,' Gianni qualified without hesitation. 'This is my son we're talking about, but let's put that issue aside for now. I have something far more important I want to discuss with you…'

A slightly jagged laugh escaped Milly's tight, dry throat. Her nerves were already stretched tight as piano wires.

'What's so funny?' Gianni asked.

'Once, whenever I said anything like that to you, it really used to spook you,' Milly reminded him helplessly.

His lean, dark features clenched hard, the dark, deep flashing eyes chilling to polar ice. '"Once" is not a barrier we want to cross. I don't want to rake over the past.'

The sudden freeze in the atmosphere raised goosebumps on Milly's over-sensitive skin. She tore her strained and shadowed gaze away. She got the message. Three years ago he had denied her the chance to give her version of what happened the night he had found her with Stefano. And now he was telling her that she would never get that chance. *Never, ever.* Only Gianni, so practised at keeping unpleasant or awkward things in tight little separate compartments, could fondly imagine it possible for her to respect such an embargo.

'For Connor's sake, we *need* to move on,' Gianni added with cool emphasis.

Honest communication? Why on earth had she got her hopes up? They were to move on without ever having paused to consider. Gianni hadn't changed one iota. And Gianni was far too proud to confront an episode that had undoubtedly savaged his ego. So their entire past had now become a conversational no-go area. *For Connor's sake.* That phrase had an almost pious ring of superiority. Naturally it did. Gianni thought Connor's mother was the immoral slut who had lured his kid brother into bed with her.

'I'd like my son to have my name,' Gianni admitted.

Milly raised dulled eyes, wishing he could look ugly to her just once, wishing his flaws would shriek at her loud enough to destroy the dangerous emotions swilling about inside her. But, no, Gianni lounged back against that desk looking drop-dead gorgeous, relaxed and in spectacular control of the situation.

Milly rose to her feet. She parted her lips, and with a defiance she could not withstand breathed raggedly, 'Your brother assaulted me.'

Gianni froze. A kind of incredulous outrage laced with black fury flared in his brilliant eyes.

'Just thought you should know,' Milly completed shakily.

'Keep quiet…' All cool ditched, Gianni studied her with glittering rage and derision, every line of his big, powerful body poised like a predator about to spring. 'I won't listen to your lies. I will not discuss this with you, *capisce*? One more word and I walk out of this room—'

'Go ahead.' Milly stood her ground. Indeed, all of a sudden she felt as if she was wedged in concrete, ready to hold steady through any storm.

'And I head straight for my lawyers and I throw everything I've got at you and fight for custody of Connor!'

Milly's stomach lurched as suddenly as if Gianni had thrown her off a cliff. White as milk, she gazed back at him in horror.

'Now you've got the message,' Gianni murmured grittily, his anger back under lock and key as he recognised her response.

The shock of that unashamed threat savaged Milly. And suddenly she couldn't bear to look at him any longer. She was too damned scared of him. Scared of Gianni for the first time in her life. Before, she had only feared his hold on her emotions. Now she feared a whole lot of other things as well. His innate ruthlessness, his enormous wealth, the dangerous power and influence he had at his fingertips.

She was shaking, and she hated that he should see that. But she didn't need a crystal ball to guess the sort of weapons which might be used against her in any custody battle. A woman capable of spending three years living another woman's life might well fail to impress a judge as a stable mother figure. In fact, her recent past would put her at a distinct disadvantage, Milly reflected bitterly.

'But I wouldn't do that, to you *or* Connor. I think you're a great mother. I have no intention of trying to take him away from you. OK?' Gianni breathed tautly.

Her arms protectively wrapped around herself and her back turned to him, Milly continued to stare blindly out of the window. His words meant nothing to her. She knew she would never forget the way Gianni had just turned on her. His façade of civilised cool and control had dropped to let her see the cold menace that still lay beneath. Why was she so shocked? Hadn't she always known that Gianni was totally incapable of forgiving her for what he believed she had done?

'I suppose I should've expected you to come out with that sort of stuff today,' Gianni continued flatly. 'But you have to accept that I've put all that behind me.'

Her supposed betrayal. Like a gun he concealed behind his back, always primed to shoot.

'To the extent...' Unusually, Gianni hesitated. 'You've really messed this moment up, Milly.'

'What moment?' she muttered in confusion.

'I was about to ask you to marry me. *Accidenti*, I *am* asking you to marry me!' Gianni rephrased, with more than a suggestion of gritted teeth.

Milly went from shock into bigger, deeper shock. She had to consciously will her feet to turn around so that she could look at him again. She *had* to look at him to believe the evidence of her own ears.

A dark line of colour accentuating his stunning cheekbones, Gianni subjected her to a grim, glittering appraisal. 'In spite of everything you've done, I'm willing to give you another chance and make you my wife.'

'Wife...' Milly could hardly get her tongue round that astounding word. 'But you hate me...'

Gianni raised two lean brown hands and spread them at truly impressive speed to indicate his distaste for that subject. 'I don't want to get into emotions here. They're quite irrelevant.'

'Irrelevant...' Milly stared at him with huge wondering eyes.

'All that really matters is that you're the mother of my son. Connor deserves a proper family life and he's not going to get that if I'm just the guy who flies in to visit every week,' Gianni pointed out levelly. 'I want to be a real father. I don't want him turning round and asking me as a teenager why I never thought enough of him to marry his mother and be a genuine part of his life.'

Milly nodded in slow motion.

'Then there's us,' Gianni added in an obvious afterthought. 'Let's be frank, *cara*. You wouldn't kick me out of bed.'

Hot, humiliated colour drenching her former pallor, Milly discovered that she wanted to kick him to kingdom come.

'I don't see any reason why things shouldn't go right back to the way they were,' Gianni told her with complete conviction. 'I still find it a real challenge to keep my hands off you.''

'That's a...a compliment?' Milly prompted unevenly.

Gianni slanted an ebony brow. 'I'm asking you to marry me. I can understand that you're pretty surprised by this development, but you should be really pleased.'

'Why?'

'Why?' Gianni repeated with unconcealed incredulity. 'It's what you always secretly wanted. Do you think I didn't realise that?'

Kicking him to kingdom come wouldn't be enough. It would be too quick, too clean. Milly wanted him stretched on a rack and tortured. How could a male so very clever make a marriage proposal sound so deeply offensive? It *had* to be deliberate. He had decided he had to marry her for Connor's sake, but he was making it brutally clear that his sole use for her would be sexual. Connor deserved a relationship; she didn't.

Gianni surveyed Milly's frozen little face with mounting tension. He could feel his temper rising again, no matter how hard he tried to ram it down. Wasn't she capable of a logical reaction? First she had wrecked everything by actually daring to refer to that disgusting episode with Stefano. Next she had told stupid lies. And now she was reacting to his extraordinarily generous proposal as if he had insulted her beyond belief!

Here he was, striving in the only way he could to make amends for his own errors of judgement over the past few days! He was giving her what she must always have wanted when she least deserved it, but not one ounce of appreciation was he receiving for his impressive ability to rise above *her* unforgivable act of betrayal three years ago! And, finally, he had been *honest* with her, Gianni reflected with smouldering resentment. Right from the instant he had first met her, she had stressed how important it was that he should always be honest with her. So he had been honest. Only somehow honesty wasn't working like any magic charm!

'You said that to all intents and purposes this is my home,' Milly reminded him tightly.

'What's that got to do with anything?' Gianni demanded with stark impatience, brilliant eyes glittering like ice shards.

'If this *is* my home, I can ask you to get out of it,' Milly informed him, her breath catching audibly in her throat. 'So I'm asking…'

Gianni frowned at her. 'Run that by me again.'

Milly thrust up her chin. 'In fact, I'm not asking. I'm *telling* you to get out!'

Wrathful incredulity emanated from Gianni in powerful waves. His eyes flashed shimmering gold. 'How *dare* you talk to me like that?'

Milly's temper rose hot enough to equal his own. She took a step forward. 'You're complaining about how *I'm* talking to *you*? You dragged me back into bed at the hotel just so that you could satisfy yourself that you could still pull me like a Christmas cracker!'

'*Dio*…how can you be so vulgar?' Gianni shot at her thunderously.

'Vulgar? *Me?*' Milly gasped in disbelief. 'Would you listen to yourself? You're the cockroach who had to boast about the fact that I *didn't* have the wit to kick you out of bed! Well, now that I've got my memory back, I know I'd sooner be dead than let you touch me again!'

'Is that a fact?' Before she could even guess his intention, Gianni reached out and simply lifted her up into his powerful arms as if she were a doll.

'Put me down this minute!' Milly shrieked at him furiously.

His mouth slammed down on hers like a silencer. Rage hurtled up inside her, only to be transformed into a blaze of white-hot hunger so intense it literally hurt. It physically hurt to want, to need, to crave to such an extent, for nothing he could do could ever be enough. She always wanted more. The drugging heat of his mouth, the provocative stab of his tongue driving her wild only made her ache unbearably for the fulfilment that he alone could give. Heartbeat pounding, pulses racing, she dug her fingers into his luxuriant hair and kissed him back so frantically she couldn't even stop to breathe.

Gianni dragged his mouth off hers. He was breathing heavily, but his dark golden eyes shimmered with un-ashamed satisfaction. 'Somehow I don't think death before dishonour is likely to figure in this reconciliation, *cara mia.*'

The raging fire within Milly shrank to a tiny mortified flicker and was doused entirely by an all-consuming ache of regret. Her cheeks a hectic pink, she removed her fingers shakily from his hair, tormented by her own weakness.

Gianni lowered her to the carpet again with exaggerated care.

Immediately she spun away in a jerky movement. 'Go, Gianni,' she urged in desperation.

'Call me when you've thought things over,' he murmured silkily, all cool now restored.

Milly listened to the quiet thud of the door closing on his exit and slumped, bitterly ashamed of her own behaviour. He had levelled the score. He had had the last word. Although, as usual, language hadn't played much part in her defeat. But it hadn't always been like that between them, she reminded herself fiercely. Once she *had* been strong enough to hang onto her pride and independence and protect herself from a male determined not to commit himself...

Five years ago, on the very first day they met and admitted to diametrically opposed expectations, Gianni had accurately forecast that *one* of them was set to crash into a solid brick wall.

Gianni had wanted a no-strings-attached affair, but Milly had wanted and needed something much deeper. Within the first week, she had recognised the disturbing intensity of her own emotional response to him. And the discovery that one kiss could set a bushfire burning inside her had been no more welcome.

Milly had tried to back off and protect herself by making loads of rules to ensure that she never emulated poor Lisa with Stevie. No man was going to turn *her* into a puppet on a string! So, if Gianni hadn't called far enough in advance, she'd always been busy. If Gianni had just turned up without calling, she'd always been on the way out of the door to a pressing engagement. If Gianni had been late, she'd gone out and stayed out. And she had never, ever called him.

But then Gianni had gone over to New York for three weeks, and her whole world had turned gloomy grey. She'd begun marking off days on the calendar, hanging over the phone anxiously, and driving herself crazy with the suspicion that he might have other women in his life.

'Have you?' Milly had asked baldly, the first time she'd seen him again.

'Of course I have,' Gianni admitted without hesitation. 'I travel a great deal. Anything else would be impractical.'

Feeling as if she had been slugged by a sack of coal, Milly cleared her throat. 'But if we have an affair, that would change...wouldn't it?' she almost whispered.

Gianni lifted one broad shoulder in an infinitesimal shrug, too slick an operator to be entrapped by a verbal response.

But Milly had got her answer in that silence. And, having naively assumed that even Gianni would concede that intimacy should be accompanied by total fidelity, she was shocked and furious. 'All I can say is, thank heaven I found this out before I slept with you!' she slung as she rose from her seat and stalked out of the restaurant.

'I don't like public scenes. Nor do I admire jealous, possessive women,' Gianni imparted chillingly, outside on the pavement.

'Then what are you doing with me?' Milly demanded. 'I'm jealous and I'm *very* possessive, so get out of my life now and don't come back!'

Gianni stayed away another full month.

Milly lost a stone in weight, but she didn't wait by the phone; she didn't ever expect to see him again. But Gianni was waiting for her to come home one evening when she finished her supermarket shift.

One look and she was sick with simultaneous nerves and sheer, undiluted joy. Gianni took her back to his Park Lane apartment. He dropped the news that she no longer had competition. She asked him how she could be sure of that. Gianni could freely admit that *he* didn't trust anybody, but, faced with her lack of faith in *him*, he was outraged. They almost had another fight.

She was in tears, and then he kissed her—a standard Gianni response when things got too emotional. And the wild passion just blazed up so powerfully inside her she finally surrendered. He was astonished when he realised he was her first lover.

Making love with Gianni was glorious; staying for breakfast feeling totally superfluous while he made calls and read stockmarket reports was something less than glorious.

So Milly drew up a new set of rules. No staying overnight. No asking when she would see him again. Always saying goodbye with a breezy smile. By then, she knew she was in love with him, but she was well aware that he didn't love her. He found her good company. She made him laugh. He couldn't get enough of her in bed. But never once did he do or say anything that gave her any hope that their affair might last.

As part of her college course that year Milly had to spend two months gaining practical experience of working in a large garden or park. She was allotted a place on a big private estate far from London. When she informed Gianni that she would be going away, they had a blistering row.

'How the hell am I supposed to see you up there?' he demanded incredulously.

'You're out of the country at least two weeks out of every four,' she reminded him.

'*Porca miseria*…you can't make a comparison like that!'

'Don't say what you're dying to say,' she warned him tautly. 'It'll make me very angry.'

'I don't know what you're talking about.'

So she said it for him. 'You think your life and your

business empire are one hundred times more important than anything in mine.'

'Obviously they are,' Gianni stated without flinching. 'And, while we're on the subject, I can think of a thousand more suitable career choices than a peculiar desire to go grubbing about in the dirt of somebody else's garden!'

'It's what I want to do. It's what I'll be doing a long, long time after you're gone. So really, in every way, it has to take precedence,' Milly retorted shakily.

'Over *me*?' Gianni breathed chillingly. 'Haven't I offered to find you a decent job?'

'I'm happy with the career choice I'm training for.'

'Fine. Just don't expect me to follow you north to the rural wastes!'

'I never did expect you to. You're far too used to people doing the running for you. You never, ever put yourself out for anybody,' Milly pointed out with quiet dignity. 'So that's that, then. We're at the end of the road.'

'Spare me the clichés at least,' Gianni ground out as she walked straight-backed to the door. 'Tell me, am I being dumped *again*?'

Milly thought about it, and nodded.

'This is a wind-up,' Gianni drawled in icy condemnation. 'This is a power-play.'

'Goodbye,' she said gruffly.

He did come up north. His limo got bogged down in a country lane. He was fit to be tied when he ended up lodged in a very small and far from luxurious hotel. And he was furious when she wouldn't let him come to the estate to pick her up for the weekend. He didn't appreciate being told that she didn't want to shock the head gardener and his wife, who were letting her stay in their guest-room. By the time she had finished explaining that a humble student trainee couldn't have a very rich, flash older boyfriend without her reputation taking a nosedive, and the all too human effect that might have on her receiving a fair assessment of her work, Gianni was not in a very good mood.

'So I'll buy you a big garden of your own,' he announced, in the dark of the night.

'Don't be silly.'

'Then I'll buy the garden for myself. I'll pay you to look after it for me!'

'You're embarrassing me,' she groaned. 'Stop living in fantasy land.'

'When I've got free time, I'd like you to be available *occasionally*.'

'I know how that feels. You're away much more than I am,' she complained sleepily, looking forward to spending two entire nights with him, snuggling up to him with a euphoric smile in the darkness.

'Do you think the head gardener and his wife would be shocked if I delivered you back strangled?' Gianni mused reflectively. 'What am I *doing* here in this lousy dump with you?'

Sex, she reflected. Sex and only sex—and it was an ongoing source of amazement to her that her body could possibly have such a hold on him. It was a perfectly ordinary body. Slender, well-honed, but far from being centrefold material. Yet he kept on coming back to her. She was developing expectations on that basis. That worried her terribly After all, some day soon he would lose interest and vanish for good.

He came up north three more weekends. She was so happy she couldn't hide it from him. It was getting harder and harder to obey her own rules. It was as if he knew her rules and worked overtime to try and get her to compromise them. That next summer he was away a lot, and she pined, went off her food, couldn't sleep. He gave her a mobile phone and she accepted it, and used it much more than she felt she should.

Then they had their six-month anniversary, and she was stupid enough to mention it. He frowned. 'That long?' he questioned with brooding coolness, and went silent on her for the rest of the evening.

He didn't call her for a week after that. So she called him in a temper and told him he was history and that she was going to find a man who would treat her with the respect she deserved.

'Tell him in advance how demanding you are,' Gianni advised helpfully. 'That you have a very hot temper, a habit of saying things you don't mean and a stubborn streak a mile wide.'

'I'm finished with you—'

'I'll pick you up for dinner at eight, and if you're not there, I'm not waiting. It's time to join the grown-ups and stop playing hard to get.'

Just before she started back at college, she suffered what appeared to be a really bad bout of tonsillitis, and instead of getting better she lost her energy and her appetite. Gianni was in South America. She told him that she thought she had the flu and soldiered on, exhausted, to her classes and her part-time job. By the time Gianni flew back to London she was so weak that walking from the bed to the door was enough to reduce her to a perspiring wreck.

Gianni was furious with her. He got another doctor. Acute glandular fever was diagnosed. She was told she would have to rest for weeks. She wouldn't be fit for her classes or for any other form of work—and by the way, the doctor added, physical intimacy was out for the foreseeable future too. That quickly, her whole world fell apart. At the time she just could not comprehend why Gianni, threatened by weeks of celibacy, should still seem so incredibly supportive.

Forty-eight hours later, she was flown to Paris in Gianni's private jet and installed in a fabulous townhouse with a garden. When she was least able to oppose him Gianni made his move, at supersonic speed.

His every argument had been unanswerable. Who would look after her in London? How could he take care of her from a distance? And she loved Paris, didn't she? If she couldn't study and she couldn't work, she might as well regard her lengthy convalescence as a vacation. And the sad truth was that she was so desperately grateful that Gianni wasn't abandoning her she didn't protest that much.

He was really wonderful when she was ill. She learnt that he liked to be needed, and that in constantly asserting her independence she had been missing out on probably the very best side of him. From that time on, Gianni became the love of her life, the centre of her existence. She stopped trying to contain her own feelings. The last barriers came down. She told him she loved him. He froze, but he didn't back off. The more she told him, the less he froze, and eventually he even began to smile.

And she decided then that maybe if she absolutely showered him in love and trust and affection, if she gave and gave and gave, with complete honesty and generosity, she might break his barriers down too. Her only goal was that he should return her love. So she never did go back to complete her college course.

Gianni became her full-time occupation. He finally got everything the way he wanted. He got to buy her clothes and jewellery, to switch her between the house in Paris and the apartment in New York, according to what best suited his travelling itinerary. She became his mistress full-time without ever acknowledging what she had become. And he was right; she *was* deliriously happy—right up until the day she discovered she was pregnant.

In the heat of passion, Gianni had on several occasions neglected to take precautions. She knew that. *He* knew that. But, like so much else, they had never discussed the fact that he had taken that risk.

Yet the evening she broke the news Gianni went into shock, like a teenager who had honestly believed it couldn't possibly be that easy to get a girl pregnant.

'You can't be...' he said, turning visibly pale beneath his bronzed skin.

'I *am*...no doubt about it. No mistake,' she stressed, getting more and more apprehensive. 'It was that night we—'

'Let's not get bogged down in details,' Gianni interrupted,

striding across the room to help himself to a very large brandy.

'You don't want to talk about this, do you?' she muttered tightly.

'Not right now, no.' Quick glance at gold watch, apologetic look laced with a hint of near desperation.

'You've got some calls to make?'

'No—'

'You have a business meeting at eleven o'clock at night? Well, some celebration this is turning out to be.'

'Celebration?' Gianni awarded her a truly stunned appraisal. 'You're pregnant and we're not married and you want to *celebrate*?'

'Since you're the one who's been playing Russian roulette with my body, maybe you'd like to tell me what end result you expected?'

'I just didn't *think*!' he ground out, like a caged lion, longing to claw at the bars surrounding him, resisting the urge with visible difficulty.

Yet he thought about everything else…incessantly. He thought rings round her. He planned business manoeuvres in his sleep. He was seriously telling her that he hadn't once acknowledged the likely consequences of making love without contraception?

'I'm not having a termination. You might as well know that now,' she whispered sickly.

'*Madre di Dio*…why do you *always* think you know what's on my mind when you don't?' he slashed back at her rawly. 'I don't believe in abortion!'

Only a little of her tension evaporated. 'I'm tired. I'm going to bed.'

'I'm going out.'

'I know.' She closed the door softly, heard the brandy goblet smash and shivered. He was right. So much of the time she did not have one earthly clue what was going on inside him. But that night she believed she did. He might not believe in abortion, but he still didn't want her to have his baby.

The next development shocked her rigid. Gianni walked out of the Paris apartment that night and vanished into thin air for thirty-six hours. He even switched off his mobile phone—an unheard-of development. His security staff went crazy the next morning, questioning her, checking the hospitals, considering kidnapping. They weren't able to accept that Gianni should choose to deliberately take himself off without cancelling his appointments.

Milly convinced herself that he had gone to some other woman.

But Gianni reappeared, looking pale and grim as death, hiding behind an enormous bunch of flowers. And she didn't say a word, behaved as if he had only stepped out an hour earlier. Patently relieved by that low-key reception, Gianni swept her up into his arms and just held her for the first time in his life, so tightly she could barely breathe.

'You just took me by surprise. My own father...if he *was* my father,' he qualified in a roughened undertone. 'He was abusive. I don't know how to be a father, but I don't want to lose you!'

She had never loved Gianni more than she loved him at that moment. It felt like an emotional breakthrough: Gianni trusting her enough to refer to the childhood he never mentioned and actually admitting to self-doubt. Her heart and her hopes soared as high as the sky. Yet, just two short months later, Gianni had almost destroyed her with his lack of his faith...

Coming back to the present to gaze like a wakening sleeper round the library of Heywood House, Milly found that her cheeks were wet with tears. You've got to stop this, she warned herself angrily. There *is* life after Gianni. Three years ago she hadn't felt able to cope with that challenge. But now she was older, wiser...only still as hopelessly in love with him as she had ever been.

CHAPTER EIGHT

'GIANNI...it's me,' Milly announced tautly, her grip so tight on the phone that her knuckles showed white.

'I'm listening,' Gianni responded softly.

'Connor's asking about you all the time.' Milly's troubled eyes were pinned to where her son sat listlessly swinging his feet. 'When I asked you to leave, I overlooked the fact that he's lost a whole life too. The last thing he needs right now is for you to vanish as well—'

'I can be with you in two hours,' Gianni interposed, smooth as silk, but she sensed the buzz of his satisfaction nonetheless. 'Why did you wait four days to contact me?'

Milly tensed. 'I needed some time to myself.'

Before he could ask her what she had decided to do about the marriage question, she finished the call. Then she breathed in very deep to steady herself.

She had lunch with Connor, who could hardly eat for excitement. Leaving him in Barbara's care, she then took herself off outdoors, keen to be elsewhere when Gianni arrived to spend time with their son.

An afternoon spent energetically digging in the walled kitchen garden which had been abandoned to the forces of nature for a good twenty years proved therapeutic. She was going to marry Gianni. *Of course* she was. If he married her, he could hardly use her recent past as a weapon against her in any custody battle. As a wife she would be safer. That way, and only that way, could she ensure that Gianni would find it extremely difficult to try and remove their son from her care.

And if she didn't marry him mightn't he eventually marry someone else? With sudden violence, Milly slashed a bramble out of her path. Once she would not have believed that possible. Once she would have sworn that Gianni would die single. But that conviction had died when Gianni had stunned her by proposing. Even if it was only for his son's benefit, Gianni was finally prepared to offer commitment. If Milly turned him down, sooner or later he would end up marrying some other woman.

And that was a development which Milly *knew* she would not be able to bear. She was possessive. She was very possessive. Currently hating and resenting Gianni to the same degree with which she loved him did not blind Milly to her own vulnerability. To stand by on the sidelines and watch Gianni with another woman would be to tear herself to shreds. After all, she reflected painfully, she already knew what that experience felt like. So there was a lot to be said for choosing to be miserable *with* Gianni now that she had faced the fact that she would be even more miserable without him.

'I really love it when you dress up for me like this, *cara...*'

Milly jerked, froze, and then slowly lifted her golden head. Silhouetted against the fading light of the afternoon, Gianni was poised several feet away, a faint smile on his wide, sensual mouth. His navy cashmere coat hung open to reveal a formal pinstripe suit cut to faithfully follow his powerful frame and his long, long legs. He looked spectacular. Her eyes widened, her mouth ran dry, her heart just lurched.

Milly leant on her spade for support. Her tumbled hair was roughly caught back with a piece of twine. She wore ancient jeans, a warm but shapeless sweater and workmanlike boots. Her lack of elegance didn't trouble her. But she could see it was troubling Gianni, who was reading all sorts of deeper messages into her appearance. Women wore make-up in bed with Gianni. Women spent hours dressing to go out with him. He never had known quite how to handle her unconcern at letting him occasionally see her just as she was, bare of both fashion and artifice.

'You lost track of time. You didn't realise I'd arrived,' Gianni decided instantly.

Milly was not in a conciliatory mood. 'I could hardly have missed the helicopter landing, and that was what…two, three hours ago?'

'Your phone is switched off. Barbara Withers told me where to find you.' Gianni couldn't quite conceal his irritation that he had been reduced to asking such a question. 'You shouldn't be working outdoors in this weather.'

'You're annoyed I wasn't waiting for you at the house,' Milly interpreted without the slightest difficulty. 'But why come all the way down here to get an answer you don't need? The last time you were here you made it clear that you saw my answer as a foregone conclusion.'

His lean, strong face darkened, brilliant eyes veiling to reveal only a watchful glimmer of gold.

'*And,*' Milly continued flatly, aiming a particularly vicious jab of the spade at the undergrowth surrounding her, 'as usual you were right. How *can* I say no?'

'You're going to marry me.' Ignoring the hostile undertones with the practised ease of a male who never looked for trouble with a woman unless it rose up and slapped him smack in the face, Gianni surveyed her with a slow smile curling his expressive mouth. He retained his cool like a cloaking device, but his eyes glittered like the heart of a fire.

'But I have certain conditions,' Milly extended gently.

Caught off guard, Gianni strode closer, stepping off the path to mire his polished Italian leather shoes in mud. '*Conditions?*'

Milly threw back her slight shoulders like a boxer about to enter the ring. 'To start with, I'd like you to have a medical, so that I can be assured that you have a completely clean bill of health.'

His winged brows lifted. 'What are you talking about?'

'Whether you choose to believe it or not, I have *not* been

intimate with anybody but you,' Milly stated, watching his strikingly handsome features freeze, his big, powerful body stiffen. 'However, you can't offer me the same reassurance, and I feel I have the right to ask.'

Gianni drew himself up to his full height, dark eyes blazing derision. '*Porca miseria!* You think that you can make me believe that you didn't sleep with your fiancé?'

'I don't really care what you believe…'

'Then what kind of nonsense is this? I have never been promiscuous…why the hell are you looking at me like that?' he demanded in fierce condemnation.

Milly returned to her digging, thinking with inescapable bitterness and pain of the speed with which he had turned to another woman three years earlier. 'You shouldn't need to be told.'

The tense silence thundered and shouted and snarled. Flailed by pain and anger, Milly hacked at winter-bare brambles. 'I have cause to know that you're not always *careful* with—'

'I have never taken risks like that with anybody but you!' Gianni shot back in a savage undertone.

'Then why with me?' Milly glanced up enquiringly.

His lean brown hands closed into powerful fists. He swung restively away from her. 'That was different…'

'How was it different?'

He didn't answer her. 'A clean bill of health,' he ground out instead, as if he was spitting tacks, apparently choosing to settle for the lesser of two evils. 'OK. I already have that. My most recent medical was less than a month ago.'

But if Gianni thought he was getting off the hook that easily he was mistaken. Milly wasn't finished yet. 'I will also expect total fidelity.'

His eyes shot like flaming golden arrows into hers, his incredulity unfeigned. '*Accidenti*…where do you get the nerve to demand that of *me*?'

'I'm thinking of Connor's need for stability.' Cheeks

burning, because her own needs had risen first and foremost to her mind, Milly focused on the distant wall.

'*Connor?*' Gianni repeated rawly.

'You must set Connor a good example. Our son must be able to respect our marriage. So you can't have a mistress,' Milly informed him, warming to her theme by the second. 'And if I were to discover that you had been unfaithful, I'm afraid I would have to divorce you. I won't have Connor damaged by a destructive relationship.'

All tight-mouthed tolerance now fully breached, Gianni slashed a savage hand through the air. 'You are lecturing me about…*fidelity*?' His Sicilian accent was so thick she had to strain to comprehend that final word.

'I don't think it's a *lecture* to state what I want up front,' Milly responded stubbornly. 'And, after all, you *did* say that you had put the past behind you…'

Sheer rage turned Gianni pale beneath his vibrant bronze skin. In seething silence he studied her, as if he just could not believe that she had dared to remind him of that statement.

'And finally,' Milly added not quite steadily, watching the ice front settle over him like her most dangerous old enemy, 'I'm not prepared to sign a pre-nuptial contract.'

At that provocative announcement Gianni appraised her with eyes that would have chilled a polar bear, aggression emanating from every dangerously still and silent inch of him.

'Not because I have any desire to get my hands on a larger share of your wealth,' Milly explained heavily. 'But because I believe that the absence of a pre-nuptial contract will make it easier for you to respect our marriage. You see, you don't respect me, but I think you *will* respect what a divorce might cost you.'

Gianni stared at her with cold, brooding menace.

Milly shook her head in a sudden helpless gesture of despair. 'Gianni…when I left Paris, I also left everything you ever gave me behind. The clothes, the jewellery, the credit cards. I took nothing. Doesn't that at least prove that I'm not the mercenary type?' Her own voice emerged with a quality of pleading that embarrassed her, and hurriedly she compressed her lips.

Eyes black and reflective as mirrors, Gianni simply swung on his heel and started to walk away.

Milly suppressed a groan.

'Gianni!' she called.

He didn't even pause.

She hurried after him and then forced herself to a halt, watching in frustration as he receded from her with every impossibly long stride. 'Gianni, if you agree to my conditions…I'll try really hard to make everything the way it was!'

Abruptly he stopped dead, but he didn't turn round.

'It's going to be very difficult, but I'll *try* to learn to trust you again,' Milly completed huskily, tears thickening her throat as she thought of what they had once had and had so brutally had taken from them.

Gianni swung back. He sent her a scorching look of rampant disbelief. *You* will try to trust *me* again? Speech wasn't necessary. A split second later, he turned his arrogant dark head away and strode through the crumbling gateway out of sight.

Well, you handled him like a real pro, didn't you? Never had Milly seen a satisfied smile die faster. And her own emotions were all over the place. Until Gianni had appeared, she honestly hadn't appreciated the depth of her own bitterness. But three years ago Gianni had hurt her *so* much. In a blaze of publicity, he had taken off to the Caribbean with a supermodel, infinitely more beautiful than Milly could ever be. And Milly had immediately to her house in Paris, and had sat waiting, torn apart but struggling to understand what he was going through, and still hoping against hope that their unborn child would eventually bring Gianni back within talking distance, even if it only meant he lifted the phone.

With deeply troubled eyes, she watched the helicopter

take off again as she walked back towards the house. She hadn't meant for that to happen. She hadn't meant to drive him away again. Connor would be upset. Oh, for heaven's sake, why didn't she just admit it? *She* was upset!

The following morning Milly's portable phone, switched on since Gianni's departure, buzzed at seven. She had just got out of the bath. She leapt for the phone.

'You drive a hard bargain,' Gianni murmured softly. 'But so do I…'

Sinking down on the carpet, huddled in a towel, Milly nodded without speaking, tension strangling her ability to respond.

'You promise me that the past stays buried—'

'I *can't* do that!'

'And you don't ever tell me you love me again.'

Milly gritted her teeth and bowed her head over her knees.

Gianni loosed a cynical laugh. 'I thought you'd be able to manage that one…'

'I'm damned if I do…and I'm damned if I don't, aren't I?' Milly countered painfully.

'Only a week ago you were madly in love with another man—'

'And then I got my memory back and *everything* changed!' Milly argued vehemently. 'Judging me on that isn't fair… I—'

She snapped her mouth shut in despair, for she knew now that she had never loved Edward. She had wanted to love him and had convinced herself that she did. The illusion had vanished the instant she got her memory back. But even before that point she had been responding to Gianni. Dear heaven, she had gone to bed with him again! Was it any wonder that he saw that wanton surrender as yet more evidence that her emotions ran only skin-deep?

'Gianni…think what you want,' Milly sighed.

'I always do. I also want to celebrate my way,' he murmured silkily. 'I'll need you tonight at the house in Paris—'

She stiffened in astonishment. 'You still *have* the house?'

Aware that Gianni had only bought that house for her occupation, and equally aware of the ruthless efficiency with which he usually cut loose from the past, she was genuinely amazed that he hadn't long since sold it.

'Around seven,' Gianni continued, as if she hadn't spoken. 'You'll be picked up this afternoon and you'll be back with Connor early tomorrow.'

'But I don't have a passport!' Milly was wildly disconcerted by his proposition. 'I lost it three years ago and I never applied for one as Faith Jennings, so if you're thinking that I—'

'You didn't *lose* your passport, *cara*. You left it behind in the townhouse and I eventually took it back to London with me. Fortunately it's still current, and it'll be waiting for you to collect at the airport. How did you contrive to get back into the UK without it?' Gianni enquired drily.

'I was a ferry passenger. I didn't realise I didn't have my passport until just before I got off. I was ready to panic, but in the end I wasn't actually challenged,' Milly recalled ruefully. 'In the crush I managed to slip through. But I've never been so nervous in my life and it's not something I'd ever try again. I felt like a criminal, waiting for a hand to fall on my shoulder.'

'I wish Immigration had picked you up and thrown you in a cell until I caught up with you,' Gianni confided grimly. 'I wasted a lot of time searching France for you!'

'I don't want to come to Paris tonight,' Milly admitted in a taut undertone.

'It's not negotiable. I'll see you later,' Gianni countered, and finished the call.

Celebrating *his* way? In Paris, where they had been happiest? Stefano had never set foot in the townhouse. The moment Gianni's brother came into her mind Milly tried to push him out again, but her bitterness rose simultaneously and it was impossible to evade her memories...

Gianni had kept Milly and Stefano in separate compart-

ments. If Stefano hadn't chosen to breach those boundaries,
Milly believed she would never have met him. Throughout
their entire relationship Gianni had maintained his own
homes in New York and London, and although he had occasionally mentioned Stefano, he had never once suggested
that they should meet.

Stefano was Gianni's half-brother, born of his putative
father's relationship with his stepmother. At the age of
eleven, Stefano had been taken to Sicily and Gianni had
become his legal guardian. Milly had first met Stefano at the
New York apartment which Gianni had purchased for her
use. By then Stefano had been studying at Harvard. He had
just arrived on the doorstep one evening when Gianni was
staying.

'I hardly see Gianni any more. Now I now why!' Stefano
had laughed.

Initially, Gianni had been uneasy about his kid brother's
descent, but, knowing how fond he was of Stefano, Milly
had been pleased. It was so hard now to remember that she
herself had once liked Stefano.

He had been immature, and pretty spoilt by Gianni's indulgence, but he had been easy company. During the final
months of her relationship with Gianni, Stefano had called
in whenever she was over in New York. Sometimes Gianni
had been there; sometimes he hadn't been. Registering that
Gianni had actually been enjoying the fact that he was seeing
more of his brother, Milly had made every effort to be welcoming.

'If my brother really cares about you, he should marry
you,' Stefano had said once, seriously embarrassing her.

But at the time she'd thought little of that comment—
certainly hadn't registered that Stefano's interest in her had
become rather too personal. After all, Stefano had had a live-
in girlfriend of his own. And Milly had been very wrapped
up in Gianni and her own concerns. It had been shortly after
first meeting Stefano that she had discovered that she was
pregnant.

Even after Gianni had told her that he didn't want to lose her, Milly had gone on feeling insecure. He hadn't ever said up front that he wanted their baby. And although he had been more tender and caring in all sorts of quiet ways she had feared that he was simply making the best of a bad situation. She had also waited for Gianni to tell his brother that she was pregnant. When Gianni had stayed silent, Milly had become more and more uneasy about his attitude.

The night that her world had fallen apart, she had been alone when Stefano dropped in to visit. He had been drinking, and for the first time Milly had felt uncomfortable with him, although even at that late stage she hadn't understood why—until he'd spoken, and shattered the casual camaraderie she had believed they'd had.

'You just don't see me, do you?' Stefano launched at her bitterly, his darkly handsome features flushed as the condemnation simply erupted from him. 'I don't exist for you except as Gianni's brother. I come round here to see you and all we ever talk about is *him*.'

'I don't understand…what—?'

'I'm in love with you!' Stefano shot at her accusingly. 'You haven't even noticed, have you?'

Milly was aghast, exploded out of her self-absorption with a vengeance. 'You've had too much to drink…you don't know what you're saying—'

'Don't talk down to me like I'm some little kid!' Stefano rounded on her furiously. 'You're not much older than I am. But Gianni's *years* older. He's almost a different generation! You've got much more in common with me—'

'Let's just forget you ever said this stuff,' Milly cut in tautly. 'You have to know how I feel about your brother—'

'And how does he *feel* about you?' Stefano slammed back, the words slurring. 'He jets in, takes you to bed and jets off again. All he does is *use* you…can't you see that?'

'I won't discuss our relationship with you,' Milly said shakily, seriously stung by that assessment.

'Don't tell me I leave you stone-cold. I won't believe you.

I've never met a girl who didn't think *I* was something special!' Stefano launched at her like a spoilt little boy, needing to blow his own trumpet. 'I'd treat you like a queen, Angel.'

'I've had enough of this, Stefano. I've only ever thought of you as Gianni's brother and I'm going to forget this ever happened, just like you'll want to forget it tomorrow morning,' Milly forecast witheringly. 'Now I'm going to call a taxi so that you can go home.'

'I'll call my own cab when I'm ready to leave,' Stefano informed her truculently. 'This is Gianni's place, not yours. I've got every right to be here if I want to be!'

While he angrily paced the room, his clumsy gait telling her that he was a lot drunker than she had initially appreciated, a wave of sick dizziness ran over Milly. But the look of utter misery in Stefano's brown eyes still hit her hard, making her feel responsible, even though she was well aware that she had never done or said anything which might have encouraged him. 'Look, it's just a crush, Stefano. That's all it is—'

'It's not a crush! I really, *really* love you!'

Nausea stirred in her stomach. 'But I'm not attracted to you—'

'You could be if you'd let yourself,' Stefano had flung stubbornly. 'I may not be the stud Gianni is, but I'm no teenage virgin!'

Milly's nausea grew suddenly worse. 'Look, let yourself out. I'm not feeling well. I'm going to bed!' she gasped as she raced like a maniac for the privacy of the bathroom that adjoined her bedroom.

She was horribly sick. As she slowly recovered from that bout, she heard what she assumed to be the slam of the front door on Stefano's departure. She meant to go and do up the locks and switch out the lights, but she ended up going for a shower instead. She was exhausted, and very upset. And her distress was exacerbated by the conviction that she would have to keep the whole messy episode a secret from Gianni.

How could she confide in him without causing friction between the two brothers? She didn't want to be the source of the smallest conflict between Gianni and his only living relative. And, although she didn't acknowledge it at the time, she was also afraid to add any further stress to their own relationship.

So, although Milly desperately longed to reach for the phone to talk to Gianni about what had happened, she resisted the temptation and staunchly told herself that it would all blow over. Stefano had got drunk to make that foolish declaration. When he sobered up, he would be angry that he had made a fool of himself. He would stay away from her from now on.

She pulled on a nightdress and climbed into bed. The bedroom door was still ajar. The light in the corridor was still on. Too weary even to get out of bed to turn it off, she stuffed her face in a pillow and went to sleep. It didn't once cross her mind that she might *not* be alone in the apartment...

With an angry shiver, Milly sank back to the present. She still found it so hard to credit that the reckless, selfish arrogance of a teenager unable to tolerate rejection could have devastated her life.

CHAPTER NINE

As THE limo which had picked Milly up at Charles de Gaulle airport wafted her through Paris that evening, her every thought was a memory…

Gianni had bought her the finest chocolates, perfume, and taken her to dine at exclusive restaurants. His knowledge of Paris related only to the exclusive haunts of the rich. Milly had returned the favour by making him queue up for ice-cream from her favourite parlour, browse for books, wander through the flea markets, enjoy the jazz festival and watch French plays in the Shakespeare garden in the Bois de Boulogne.

Employing the keys which had been waiting with her passport for her to collect, Milly let herself into the town-house on the Rue de Varenne. As she discarded her coat, her heart was beating very fast. She scolded herself for her nervous tension. Everything would be different. Since Gianni had retained the house for his own use, he would have made sweeping changes. The vibrant colours, exotic throws and comfortable furniture she had favoured would have been superceded by classic shades, cool elegance and superb antiques.

So it was a real shock for Milly to walk into the spacious reception rooms and see everything exactly as she had left it three years earlier. Her steps quickened as she took a tour and finally hurried upstairs to the bedroom they had once shared. The connecting door stood wide on the fabulous marble bathroom.

Milly focused on the giant bath, her breath catching in her throat as she remembered the night she had bathed in bubbles and Gianni had stolen that photograph. Racing after him, clutching a towel, she had cornered him in the bedroom.

'Give me that camera!' she had yelled furiously.

'Come and get it,' Gianni had invited, stunning dark eyes brimming with vibrant amusement as she had dripped all over the carpet.

'*Gianni*...I'm warning you!'

As he had stood there, naked but for a pair of silk boxer shorts, his lithe, bronzed body a powerful enticement, a wolfish grin had slashed his mouth and sent her treacherous pulses racing. '*Dio mio*, you're so sexy when you get aggressive.'

Milly had made a wild grab for the camera, but Gianni had cast it aside and caught her up in his arms to crush her mouth with hungry urgency under his.

'I want that film destroyed,' she had told him breathlessly, a long while later, still trembling from the raw potency of his stormy possession.

Gianni had given her a slow-burning smile and had said nothing.

So intense was that recollection that Milly stared at the bed almost as if she expected to see the ghosts of Gianni and herself *still* lying there. She blinked, and turned around in an uncoordinated circle, and then found herself heading for the fitted units in the dressing room. She stared in frank astonishment at the clothing carefully stored in garment bags and then sped into the bathroom to check cupboards.

Finally, with her legs threatening to buckle, she sank down on the corner of the bed. Unbelievable as it was to her, Gianni had left all her belongings intact. Nothing had been changed, nothing had been dumped. It was eerie. But for the garment bags, the past three years might not have happened. The whole house appeared to be locked in an astonishing time warp.

'You wouldn't believe how often I've pictured you here like this...' That deep, dark sexy drawl slashed through her reverie and sent her head flying up, shining waves of hair tumbling back from her oval face to accentuate troubled eyes as blue as lapis lazuli.

Milly looked fantastic, Gianni acknowledged with satisfaction, long past the stage of questioning why this one small woman should excite him to such an extent. It was sex, just sex. He was content with that explanation. It wasn't something he had to think about; the ache of hot, instantaneous arousal was reassuringly familiar. She was wearing something bright and clingy, which for Milly signified a fairly substantial degree of effort on her behalf. She was also trying to smile, but her eyes were strained. She was just nervous; she *had* to be happier than she looked, Gianni told himself impatiently, discarding that initial impression. He just could not see that she had the smallest thing to be unhappy about.

Milly stared at Gianni with colour steadily mounting in her cheeks. He lounged in the doorway, six feet three inches of stunning dark good looks and lean, lithe elegance, his attitude one of deceptive indolence.

Abruptly, she slid upright, smoothing uncertain hands down over the turquoise dress she wore. 'I didn't hear you arrive…'

Shimmering golden eyes roamed over her, lingering on the generous curve of her soft mouth, the defined thrust of her firm breasts and rounded hips in the sleek silky fabric. 'You've been shopping—'

'No. This was an impulse buy last year. I never wore it.'

'Sexy, *cara mia*,' Gianni told her with husky approval, slowly raising lean brown hands to shrug out of his overcoat and let it fall.

Milly's heart started to beat so fast she thought it might burst from her chest. He removed the jacket of the formal suit he wore beneath. Her breath began to rasp in her throat, making her mouth run dry. Without removing his smouldering attention from her for a second, he tugged loose his gold tie and unbuttoned his shirt.

'Gianni…' she began unevenly, her body reacting invol-

untarily to the wild, hot sexual charge in the atmosphere. As
her breasts swelled with languorous heaviness, and her nipples stiffened to push against the confines of her bra, she
shifted uneasily. 'We really should talk.'

'Never got us anywhere before.'

'Because we never actually *did* it!'

'Everything the way it was,' Gianni reminded her with
scorching golden eyes as he took an almost compulsive step
forward. 'You promised.'

Had she promised? Hadn't she just said she'd *try*? But as
Gianni came closer the question became academic as rational thought blurred and infinitely more basic promptings
took over. Suddenly she couldn't wait to get close. She
merged with his outrageously masculine frame on legs that
already felt weak and hollow, eagerly drawing in the familiar
warm, male scent of his skin.

'You want me...' Long fingers curved to her chin, exerting pressure to turn up her face and see the hunger she
couldn't hide.

Breathless, she gazed up into his spectacular eyes, heat
spearing up almost painfully in her stomach to stretch every
nerve-ending taut. 'Always.'

'That's all I need, *cara mia*,' Gianni asserted with complete conviction.

She reached up to him first, encouraging him to drive her
lips apart in a devouringly hungry kiss. Her head spun and
her senses whirled. He tasted like water in the desert, so
sweet, so precious she felt she would die if she didn't drink
deep. Painful memories fell away from her. She met those
dark, deep flashing eyes with an instinctive sense of coming
home.

Unzipping her dress, Gianni peeled it off. She shivered,
pressed her thighs together, seeking to contain the heat he
had already awakened. But in one easy movement she un-
clasped her own bra. Her face burned, but she revelled in
the sudden blaze of gold in Gianni's appreciative appraisal
as her pouting breasts fell free.

'Witch,' he rasped, tumbling her down backwards on the bed with a thrilling lack of cool.

Her spine curved in wondering pleasure as his expert mouth travelled hungrily between her urgently sensitive nipples. As he sucked on a straining pink bud she gasped, her hands clutching at shoulders still frustratingly sheathed in fabric.

'Take your clothes off,' she urged shakily.

Expelling his breath in a driven hiss, Gianni raised himself. He scrutinised her flushed face and moist parted lips with ravenous desire, his lean, strong features taut with the effort self-control demanded. Beginning to sit up, she arched her back, and his mesmerised gaze welded to the projecting peaks of her exquisite breasts.

'*Dio…* I can't spare that much time,' Gianni groaned raggedly.

He curved a not quite steady hand to her temptingly swollen flesh and then drove her flat again with the onslaught of his passionate mouth on hers. His tongue dipped with slow, skilful intimacy between her parted lips, tasting her with an eroticism that released a startled moan of excitement from her throat.

With a roughened laugh of satisfaction, Gianni lifted his head again and surveyed her. 'I might want to jump you like a starving animal, but tonight is going to be different,' he swore, rubbing a thumb gently along the ripe curve of her full lower lip, and she shivered with helpless anticipation.

'Different?'

'*Special,*' Gianni husked thickly against her mouth, and kissed her again. This time she didn't just see cymbals and fireworks, she saw a whole chamber orchestra illuminated by shooting rockets.

'I love the way you kiss,' she confided feverishly as she tried to wrench him out of his shirt. 'But if you don't take your clothes off I'll scream!'

Gianni finally backed off the bed. The slashing grin of

appreciation lightening his strong dark features squeezed her heart as efficiently as a vice.

Her softened eyes roamed over him. Not even the most perfectly tailored trousers could conceal the bold jut of his erection. A twist of almost shocking excitement slivered through her. Dry-mouthed, she watched him strip.

'I like it when you can't take your eyes off me,' Gianni confessed huskily.

Her whole body tingled with the need to touch him. He was awesomely aroused. He strolled fluidly back to the bed and she felt as if her bones were about to melt beneath her skin. He stood her up with gentle hands and went down on his knees to tug her panties down over her hips.

'I have three years of erotic daydreams to live out.' Gianni's deep, dark drawl fractured as he pressed his mouth in a surprisingly tender salute against her stomach. She quivered like a sapling in a storm.

Curving strong hands to her slender hips, he lifted her back on the bed. She was weak with hunger. His first touch was like a match hitting a bale of hay. She was so ready she already ached for him, but Gianni was intent on reacquainting himself with every responsive inch of her wildly sensitised flesh. With silken finesse, he explored the hot, moist centre of her. She writhed out of control. Then he rearranged her, like a gourmet at a feast, and used his wickedly expert mouth and tongue to drive her crazy with an intimacy that drove her from ecstatic moans to choked and frantic pleas for satisfaction.

'*Dio*...I love torturing you with pleasure...I've had nothing else on my mind since the day I saw you at the airport, *cara mia*. I can't work; I can't sleep,' Gianni ground out, startling her.

Rising over her, he settled her beneath him. He entered her with an evocative groan of shuddering satisfaction. She met his shimmering dark eyes, feeling the sheer burning intensity of his pleasure for a split second before he plunged her back into sole awareness of her own.

'You feel like hot satin!' Gianni rasped.

And then, as he moved on her and in her, the hot, electrifying excitement took over and she wrapped herself round him, moaning her pleasure beneath his every thrust. Heart and body exulting as one, she gave herself without inhibition and reached a shattering climax that left her floating in shell-shocked contentment.

Releasing her from his weight, Gianni hauled her back into the circle of his arms. The almost forgotten reassurance of that continuing desire for physical closeness even after satiation filled her with brimming warmth.

He ran a slow fingertip down over one tear-wet cheek. 'Special,' he breathed almost harshly, gazing intently into her drowningly blue eyes, dark colour slowly rising to accentuate his sculpted cheekbones. 'And yet you have driven me crazy more times than any woman I've ever known...'

'Really?' Milly gave him a dreamy, unapologetic smile.

'Really, *cara mia*,' Gianni confirmed, hungrily kissing her again.

Gianni woke up and rolled over. Milly wasn't there. He sat up with a jerk to hit the lights and check his watch. It was midnight. Springing out of bed stark naked, he strode out of the bedroom.

He found Milly downstairs in the dimly lit state-of-the art kitchen. Her slender back turned to him, she was barefoot and wearing an oversized T-shirt that he recognised as having once been his. Humming softly to herself, she was checking something in the stainless steel oven. The almost forgotten aroma of baking apples and pastry assailed Gianni. He turned pale.

Breathing in shallow, quiet spurts to refill his straining lungs, Gianni slowly unclenched his coiled fists. He was in a cold sweat! Swinging soundlessly out of the doorway, he flung himself back against the wall in the dark corridor beyond. Where *did* you think she'd gone? His even white teeth gritted. He was outraged by the recognition of his own fear, alienated by the dark, deep stirrings of childhood memories he always kept locked away.

When he'd been barely more than a toddler, Gianni had learnt the hard way that he couldn't depend on anybody. Not his mother, who had thrown him out of the house for hours on end while she entertained her clients, not his supposed father, who had drunk himself into violent rages and seized on any excuse to lash out with his fists and his belt. Not his stepmother, who had loathed him on sight and humiliated him at every opportunity.

Not even his deeply religious uncle and aunt, who had removed him from the orphanage at the age of thirteen and flown him over to their London home to take the place of their own dead son. For a little while he had believed he was really wanted, until they'd started constantly reminding him of the debt he owed them. They had never formally adopted him, and had washed their hands of him entirely the instant they were forced to accept that he had no vocation to become a priest.

Yet Milly's warmth and affection had drawn Gianni even as he'd marvelled at her naivety in being so foolishly, dangerously open. Didn't she know he was going to hurt her? Didn't she know he had nothing to give back? That deep down inside, where she was all giving and feeling, he was just one big, empty hollow? But fate had had the last and cruellest laugh on him. The day Gianni had found Milly with his brother had been the day he'd finally realised how much he loved her.

Levering himself off the cold wall with sudden force, Gianni went back upstairs and headed straight for the shower, wrenching on the controls with angry hands. Love had been a breeze for Milly. But love had been a killer-chiller for him. So she needn't think that sneaking out of bed in the middle of the night to make some childish offering of his once favourite snack was likely to change the status quo!

*   *   *

Milly carried the tray upstairs. She was so happy. She was just so incredibly happy. Gianni had been so tender, so teasing, so warm. It had honestly been as if the Stefano episode had never happened.

How Gianni could shut it all out, *how* he could be like that with her while still believing what he did, she could not begin to comprehend. But suddenly it didn't seem to matter. If that worked for him right now, that was all right with her. Only once they were safely married Gianni was in for a rather unpleasant surprise, she conceded ruefully. If it took her fifty years, if it took chaining him to a wall in a locked room, she would make him listen to her about Stefano!

Fully awake, Gianni was lounging in bed, intent on his notebook computer. His black hair was still damp from the shower he had evidently taken. His sleek, powerful bronzed body was dark and exotic against the pale bed linen. Milly studied him with wholly possessive eyes. Externally he was absolutely gorgeous, internally he was a little bit complicated, but they finally had a future and she intended to make the most of the opportunity.

'I thought you might be hungry…' She slid the tray down beside him, suddenly feeling self-conscious. Possibly it had been slightly over the top to rush down to the kitchen and turn out a *tarte tatin*.

'I'm not, but don't let me inhibit you,' Gianni murmured, without taking his eyes from the screen.

'It's something you like,' she told him.

Gianni glanced at the laden tray. Then he glanced up at her, brilliant dark eyes cool, questioning, filling her with instant discomfiture. 'I may not employ a chef here, but whatever I want I *can* afford to send out for,' he reminded her with sardonic softness. 'So why the hell did you feel the need to get out of bed at this hour to bake?'

Hot, mortified pink flooded Milly's cheeks. She snatched the tray back off the bed, but she wanted to pitch it at him.

'I don't require cute little domesticated gestures from you now,' Gianni added in measured addition.

The tray rattled in her tensing grasp. But for the two cups of hot coffee, she would definitely have dumped the lot on his lap. Shaken and angered by his volatile change of mood, Milly returned the tray to the kitchen. Why was Gianni behaving like this all of a sudden?

In bed, he had been so different. Dear heaven, why was she always so stupid around Gianni? *In bed.* Within those two simple words dwelt the explanation. The minute Gianni had satisfied that high-voltage sex drive of his, he just went right back to despising her again. Well, she refused to put up with that sort of treatment. She hadn't sunk that low yet. Or *had* she?

Hadn't she let Gianni fly her over for the night like a call-girl? A sure thing? She had definitely been a sure thing. Anguish infiltrated Milly at that acknowledgement. And hadn't she played a full and uninhibited part in her own downfall? Tonight she had been his puppet on a string...his totally abandoned puppet on a string. She squirmed, fingers curling on the stack of plates she had left lying out on the counter.

'Are you coming back to bed?' Gianni enquired with studied casualness from the doorway.

As Milly turned, her eyes lit on him like burning blue stars. She grabbed up a plate and hurled it with all her might. Looking genuinely startled, Gianni ducked. The plate smashed bare inches from him. She sent a second plate flying with similar accuracy. 'If I wanted to hit you, I *could*,' she told him furiously. 'So get out of here before I forget that violence is not an answer!'

Gianni straightened with admirable cool. 'OK...if it's that important, I'll eat it,' he breathed grittily.

Milly studied him with huge blue eyes and slowly shook her golden head. 'Why are you so stupid?' she whispered helplessly.

'Why are you?' Gianni responded, ice-cold.

Milly spun away, denying the cruel message in his diamond-hard eyes. He could make passionate love to her over and over again but he wouldn't allow her to harbour the smallest illusion about the precise nature of their relationship *out* of bed. Sentimental touches of the 'cute' and 'domesticated' variety were out of line. When he had said he wanted everything the way it had once been between them, he had really been lying in his beautiful white teeth. All he really wanted was all the sex he could handle.

'If I hurt your feelings, I'm sorry, but we need to start out straight,' Gianni murmured flatly.

He'd done it deliberately. She knew he had rejected her stupid edible offering deliberately. But she also knew she didn't want to force a major confrontation *before* they got married. Was that proof of her intelligence or proof of her cowardice?

Feeling wretched, she cleaned up the broken plates and then went back upstairs to the bedroom. A small jeweller's box with a very impressive logo awaited her on her pillow. She lifted the tiny box and set it unopened on the cabinet.

Sliding into bed, she was careful not to even glance at Gianni, and she turned her back on him. She had let him see how much he had hurt her and that stung her pride.

'It's a ring,' Gianni advanced, without any expression at all.

Grudging curiosity stirred Milly, because he had never given her a ring before. Reclaiming the box, she flipped it open on a spectacular ruby surrounded by diamonds.

She threaded the ring onto her right hand and said, with all the enthusiasm of a woman confronting a huge pile of dirty washing, 'Fantastic. Thanks.'

'You're wearing it on the wrong finger,' Gianni informed her drily.

Milly frowned. 'Sorry?'

'It's an engagement ring,' Gianni extended in a charged undertone.

Milly flipped right over to look at him, blue eyes rounded with incredulity. 'An *engagement* ring?'

'Why not? We're getting married.' His bold profile rigid, Gianni doused the lights.

End of discussion. In the darkness, Milly fingered her engagement ring with rather more interest than she had been prepared to show a minute earlier. A romantic gesture? She reddened. Hardly. A conventional one? Gianni had yet to mention *when* they would marry. Milly tensed at that belated realisation. Was it possible that this was going to be a *very* long engagement? The sort of engagement that went on year after endless year until it became a positive joke to all onlookers?

'Hi...' Her expressive face pale and stiff, Milly slid behind the table in the dining room. An unfamiliar maid had wakened her.

'I'd have let you sleep, but I know you want to be back for Connor.' With a slow-burning smile that reminded Milly of how very lacking in restraint she had been around dawn, Gianni poured her a cup of coffee. 'You still look pretty tired.'

Milly reddened like an awkward teenager. While she had still been deliciously drowsy and defenceless Gianni had invaded her side of the bed, ruthlessly set on conquest. And even with all her experience of Gianni's incredible expertise she had been quite unprepared either for that level of slow, exquisite seduction or the intensity of his determination to give her the ultimate in pleasure. The intimate ache of her body had powered that smile he now felt able to bestow upon her.

She looked so miserable, Gianni reflected in frustration. He focused on her hand, where it rested on the table only about nine inches from his own. But Gianni was still challenged. Breathing in deep, he reached out suddenly to cover her tense fingers with his hand.

Milly froze in complete disconcertion. Gianni was not given to demonstrative gestures beyond the bedroom door.

She stared at him. His ridiculously lush black lashes semi-veiled his eyes, but his tension was pronounced.

'Last night, nothing went according to plan,' Gianni advanced, with the taut stiffness of a male who never normally allowed himself to explain anything he did. 'We had a reservation at Castel's. We were supposed to dine out. But coming back here, seeing you here again…'

As his hesitation threatened to stretch into a stark silence, Milly instinctively closed her other hand round his as well, literally holding him prisoner. 'Yes?' she encouraged in a breathless whisper.

'It was like we'd never been apart,' Gianni completed flatly.

'I thought that was what you wanted,' Milly muttered unevenly.

Gianni's strong jawline clenched. 'I did…I *do*…but for a while last night I didn't…'

Milly waited with bated breath, but the silence lingered. She was stunned by the extraordinary fact that Gianni had made the effort to explain that his passion had been entirely spontaneous and that he had originally planned a very different evening. Dinner and dancing at the most exclusive nightclub in Paris put the presentation of an engagement ring into a new light.

But his second admission had shaken her most of all. That had been Gianni telling her in as few words as possible that last night their unresolved past had returned to haunt him and caused his change of mood. It was such a gigantic step forward in communication that Milly's eyes glowed as if he had lit a neon light inside her. 'Gianni, I'm so pleased you told me this. I know how difficult—'

'And now that we've got that out of the way, *cara mia*,' Gianni interposed at speed, his lean, dark features lightening with barely concealed relief, 'We should talk about the wedding arrangements. I've applied for a special licence. We can get married this week.'

As a distraction, that change of subject worked. Having

been on the very brink of an emotional speech, Milly was stopped dead in her tracks. *'This week?'*

'Why not?' Gianni elevated a winged ebony brow. 'We have no good reason to wait.'

'I guess not...' Her attention welded to his spectacular dark eyes, Milly's response was rather weak. She had been so totally wrong in her suspicions. Gianni hadn't been using an engagement ring as a delaying tactic. If anything, he was prepared to *rush* her to the altar.

'Connor needs me around,' Gianni pointed out.

Her dreamy smile faded. 'Yes, of course he does.'

Louise Barclay watched Milly twirl in her wedding dress. Reminiscent of a romantic Edwardian tea gown, it was an incredibly elegant confection of silk adorned with exquisite handmade lace which enhanced her slender figure.

'You really, *really* love this guy, don't you?' Louise breathed with a slightly dazed expression on her freckled face.

Milly fell still in apparent dismay at that charge. 'How do you know that?'

Louise assumed a mock air of deep concentration. 'Oh, it might be the way Gianni's name enters just about every sentence. Then again, it might be the totally off-this-planet look you have when you say his name—'

'Louise!' Milly groaned.

'Or it could even be the fact that you've phoned him four times in the last two hours. I've heard of bridal nerves, but the last two times you called he was downstairs under this very same roof,' Louise pointed out gently.

Milly went pink. 'Phone calls are like a jokey thing between us.'

'Hey, I'm not criticising. Obviously he's crazy about you too.'

Eyes clouding, Milly turned away. She hadn't actually seen Gianni for four days. Business had kept him abroad. But, since her return from Paris, Gianni had made regular calls, and on the phone he was Gianni as she remembered him. Tender, teasing and warm. That was why the phone had become her lifeline.

Louise sighed. 'Why didn't Gianni just organise a media man-hunt when you went missing three years ago?'

Milly stiffened. 'Strictly speaking, I wasn't missing. I left Paris because we'd split up. We had some major problems.'

Her friend grinned. 'But nothing the two of you couldn't surmount within a week of finding each other again!'

But Milly knew better. The Stefano episode would never be forgotten. She was certain that her supposed betrayal had come back to haunt Gianni that night in Paris, and it would keep on coming back until she dealt with it. But how *was* she to clear her own name?

What, after all, had changed? It would still be her word against Stefano's. Stefano would never tell the truth; he had too much to lose. But for all that, Milly mused, Stefano would surely be very shocked to learn that she was back in Gianni's life in the infinitely more secure role of his wife.

Her portable phone buzzed. She snatched it up. 'Gianni…?'

'I'm now on my way to the church. We haven't yet met any roadblocks or fallen trees—'

'Don't be snide.'

'Of course, some gorgeous flame from my past could still throw herself across the church steps and prevent me from reaching the altar—'

'That's not funny!' Milly cut in hotly.

'Milly…proceed to the bedroom door. That's the large wooden oblong with the handle. Open the door, walk down the stairs and get into the transport waiting,' Gianni instructed with gentle satire. 'If you keep me hanging around at that church, I'll—'

'You'll what?' Milly whispered in breathless interruption as she moved towards the door.

'You'll find out tonight,' he promised, in a roughened

sexy undertone that made her heartbeat accelerate at the most astonishing rate.

'I'm going to be awfully late, Gianni…'

'I won't wait.'

'You will,' she muttered, smiling, and finished the call.

On her way down the stairs, she was amazed by the number of staff bustling in and out of the ballroom, and she was about to ask what was happening when Robin Jennings strolled out of the drawing room to extend his arm to her with a broad grin.

'Gianni wanted me to surprise you.'

Milly gave the older man a delighted smile and a welcoming hug. 'I'm so glad you're here to share this day with me.'

After that first surprise, the surprises simply got larger. The church car park and the road outside were packed with luxury cars. As Robin helped her out of the limo Gianni's security men surged forward to shield her from a pack of eager photographers and journalists shouting questions.

'What's going on?' Milly voiced her bewilderment in the church porch.

'Gianni did mention that he wanted to show you off to the whole world,' Robin Jennings confided then. 'Only I didn't realise he meant it so literally.'

There wasn't even standing room left in the church.

Gianni watched Milly walk down the aisle with glittering dark eyes of appreciation.

The simple ceremony filled her with emotion and optimism. Some day soon, she swore, she would be able to tell Gianni how much she loved him without him acting as if it was verbal abuse of the most offensive kind.

'Why didn't you tell me you were inviting all these people?' Milly squealed, the minute she got him on his own in the limo. 'We'll be in all the newspapers tomorrow, and you know how you hate that sort of stuff! Everything that's happened to me will come out as well.'

Gianni's dark, deep flashing eyes shimmered with amusement. 'In the words of one of my PR team...''just like a fairytale''. Less than cool, but romantic. You're a living cross between the Sleeping Beauty and Cinderella. I'm still working on being a prince.'

'Did you really say you wanted to show me off to the whole world?'

Slight colour burnished his stunning cheekbones. 'I don't remember.'

Plunged into a reception for five hundred guests back at Heywood House, Milly found her wedding day an increasingly breathless whirl.

Around three that afternoon she slid away to speak privately to Davina Jennings. After the older woman had listened to Connor's excited chatter and cuddled him, she explained that Edward had now become a junior partner in Jennings Engineering.

'He's bearing up very well to having lost you, I have to admit,' Davina confided ruefully. 'With hindsight, I can see that Edward *was* rather more interested in the partnership than he was in you. You made the right decision.'

Davina pressed a very familiar item of jewellery into Milly's hand. 'The bracelet. You left it behind in your room.'

'But I can't keep it. It belonged to your grandmother,' Milly protested.

'You're always going to be part of our family, Milly,' the older woman told her gently. 'But now that you've got your memory back, I'd love to know how you acquired the bracelet in the first place.'

'A couple of days before the accident, I bought it off a market stall.' Milly had turned the silver bracelet over and noticed the word 'Faith' inscribed on the back. It hadn't occurred to her that it might be a name. She had seen it in the light of a message to have faith, keep faith no matter how difficult things might seem. She had clasped it round her wrist like a talisman the same day she'd boarded the train to Cornwall.

'The bracelet belongs with you now. At least you liked it
enough to buy it,' Davina remarked wryly. 'Enough of that.
Have the police been in touch with you about the accident?'

'Gianni suggested that I get in touch with them, so I made
a fresh statement the day before yesterday,' Milly admitted
with a rueful twist of her lips. 'I'm afraid that even with my
memory back I still didn't have any useful facts to offer
them.'

'That can't be helped. By the way, Gianni mentioned the
enquiries he's having made on our behalf. If our long-lost
daughter *can* be traced, I've no doubt he's the man to do it.
Yet that awful day he made us tell you the truth I didn't
trust him an inch.' The older woman grimaced. 'I should've
recognised that, having found you, he was simply *terrified*
of losing you again!'

Milly laughed at that idea. 'Gianni has nerves of steel!'

'Not where you're concerned,' the older woman replied
with quiet conviction.

After a light supper was served at seven, Connor fell
asleep on Milly's lap. Gianni lifted his slumbering son
gently from her. 'It's time he went to bed.'

Barbara Withers was dancing, and very much preoccupied
with her partner. Gianni was ready to intervene, but Milly
scolded him with reproachful eyes and gave him a little lecture on the need to consider the feelings and the needs of
his employees.

'How many employees have you had?' Gianni enquired
as he carried Connor upstairs.

'None...but I know what's right,' Milly retorted, not one
whit deflated. 'And sometimes you're just a bit too bossy
and demanding.'

Gianni met her look of fearless challenge and threw back
his head to laugh. '*Dio mio*...how I have missed you in my
life!'

At that admission, her breath caught in her throat. ''Sometimes I wonder if I lost my memory because I couldn't handle remembering the pain,' she confided shakily.

The sudden silence that fell seemed to hang on a knife-edge. Aware that she had breached forbidden barriers, Milly scooped Connor out of Gianni's arms and got on with putting him to bed. By the time she had finished their exhausted toddler was no longer fast asleep.

'Play cars?' he mumbled drowsily to Gianni.

Hoping to distract their son until he went off again, Milly picked up a toy car and ran it along the top of his duvet. 'I can give you ten minutes.'

'Boys play cars,' Connor muttered dismissively.

'I wonder where he picks up these sexist ideas,' Gianni remarked, with sudden vibrant amusement.

'It's the Sicilian blood, Gianni. It's in his genes,' Milly teased, highly relieved that the awkward moment had been successfully bridged.

But it wasn't to be the last awkward moment. A pretty brunette teenager hurried up to speak to Gianni when they returned to the ballroom. 'Why's Stefano not here?' she asked baldly.

Gianni's long fingers tensed on Milly's spine. 'He's not well.'

'Gosh, is it serious?'

'I shouldn't think so,' Gianni countered.

'Poor Stefano,' the girl groaned sympathetically. 'He never seems to have much luck these days, and yet he used to be so much fun.'

'Maybe he just grew up,' Gianni suggested flatly.

He whirled Milly fluidly away onto the dance floor. It was some minutes before she could breath normally again, and even longer before she felt the worst of the tension ease in Gianni's big powerful frame. *Had* he invited Stefano to their wedding? Or had she just heard a social excuse to cover the absence of his one and only brother?

'I wanted this to be a wonderful day,' Gianni breathed harshly.

'It *has* been,' Milly argued. 'Don't you ever dare think otherwise! I've met hundreds of people, who have all been incredibly nice to me. I've got to be the centre of attention without anybody thinking I was a show-off! And for the first time in our entire relationship you have switched off your mobile phone!'

His dark, deep flashing eyes roamed over her animated face with an intensity that made her heart sing. Easing her closer, he complained about the frustrating difference in their heights and then, with a growl of very male impatience, he just lifted her high off her startled feet. He kissed her with such desperately hungry need she was trembling when he finally lowered her back to solid earth again.

'I need to be alone with you. I want you all to myself, *cara mia*,' Gianni growled in the circle of her arms.

'Well, you're just going to have to wait.'

'If we'd been able to take a honeymoon, we could have been out of here hours ago!' Gianni ground out in frustration.

'Why weren't we able?'

'Because we couldn't have taken Connor abroad with us. He has no documentation right now—'

Milly frowned. 'What do you mean?'

Gianni sighed. 'Milly, you slipped right back into your true identity because it was already established. Our son, however, was registered at birth as the child of Faith Jennings. That has to be legally sorted out before he can be issued with a new birth certificate.'

'My goodness, I never even thought about that!'

'It's in hand. Don't worry about it. But as soon as Christmas is over I have every intention of finding a hot, deserted beach and bringing in the New Year—'

'With Connor and a bucket and spade?'

'I'm not listening. Fantasy is all I've got right now,' Gianni muttered raggedly, whisking her deftly behind one of the marble pillars that edged the dance floor and hauling her up to his level again to repossess her soft mouth with hot, driven urgency.

Milly caught fire. 'Gianni—'

'You're like too much champagne in my blood.' He bowed his arrogant dark head over hers and snatched in a fracturing breath. 'You push me to the edge. Sometimes I need you so much it *hurts*.'

Already dizzy with desire, Milly experienced a joyous flare of sheer happiness. Had he noticed what he had said? Not want but *need*. Gianni, who prided himself on never needing anybody or anything, whose belief in self-sufficiency was legendary, had admitted that he needed her.

And yet a few hours later, when they were finally in the privacy of their own bedroom, surprisingly Gianni was patience personified. He removed her wedding dress with gentle, almost regretful hands. He told her how gorgeous she had looked all day. He made sweet, tender love to every sensitised, shivering inch of her he uncovered. He took his time—oh, yes, he took his time—until she was twisting and begging, lost in incoherent urgency. And when he at last sealed his lean, bronzed body to hers, and possessed her with aching sensuality, it was the most sensational experience they had ever shared.

Two weeks later, Gianni watched Milly turn on the lights on the big Christmas tree she had sited in the drawing room of Heywood House.

She smiled like a happy child when the lights worked first time. But then she'd had plenty of practice, Gianni conceded. This was the third tree she had dressed within as many days. Several shopping trips to Harrods and other well-known retail outlets had yielded a huge collection of ornaments and other necessities. It was a very big house, she had pointed out, in an apparent attempt to convince him that she was just doing what had to be done. But the truth was that Milly adored the festive season, gloried in every single tradition, no matter how naff, and still left out refreshment for Santa Claus as an adult.

'What do you think?' she prompted expectantly.

'Spectacular.' Gianni looked past the glimmering lights to

Milly, her fantastic hair tumbling round her shoulders, eyes bright as sapphires in her beautiful smiling face. 'Christmas just wasn't the same without you, *cara mia*.'

Milly stilled, veiling her eyes, not wanting to seem too conscious of that easy reference to the past. 'Wasn't it?'

'Like Scrooge, I stopped celebrating it,' Gianni admitted.

'Oh, Gianni!' Milly groaned, troubled by the imagery summoned up by that confession and heading towards him like a homing pigeon.

'And, like grumpy old Ebenezer, I took particular pleasure in doing it.'

Milly linked her arms tightly round his narrow waist. 'We're about to have the most wonderful Christmas ever!'

And it would be, Milly thought with warm confidence. They had spent every hour of the past two weeks together, loving and laughing. She had never been as happy as she was now. She had never known Gianni so relaxed or so content. She loved watching him with Connor, revelling in the rough-housing that little boys enjoy, but she loved him most of all for his acceptance of their son's occasional tantrums.

In fact, from that morning in Paris Gianni had been fantastic in every possible way. He had changed over their three years apart, she now acknowledged. He was more tolerant, more kind, less volatile, less driven. For Milly, it was deeply ironic that Gianni should be capable of showing her more caring tenderness now than he had shown her *before* he'd seen her wrestling on a bed with Stefano! And, unfortunately, that presented Milly with a major problem.

Every hour, on the hour, Gianni was proving that he could successfully put that sordid little scene behind him. As long as the subject was never broached, as long as it was left buried. She still couldn't really understand how he could contrive to achieve that miracle. Could it be because he knew that sexually nothing had really happened that night? Gianni had accepted his brother's lying explanation in its entirety. That *she* had been lonely and *he* had been drunk, that just for a few foolish minutes desire had overwhelmed decent boundaries.

Certainly Gianni had never doubted her guilt. She had been condemned for playing the temptress and punished much more heavily than Stefano. She was still very angry and bitter about that fact. But now she feared the risk she would be taking in challenging Gianni again. She might destroy everything they had recently regained; she might wreck their marriage.

And she still couldn't *prove* that she was innocent. To believe her, Gianni would have to accept that Stefano was an out-and-out liar, capable of behaviour that might well have landed him in court in any other circumstances. That was a very tall order. But, even as Milly confronted that truth, she knew that it wasn't possible for her to remain silent. She would just have to deal with the fall-out when it happened.

That same afternoon, Milly was coiled in Gianni's arms in front of the log fire in the library, telling him between kisses about the new rose garden she was planning, when a knock on the door interrupted them.

With a groan of annoyance, Gianni settled her into an armchair. Milly closed her eyes sleepily.

'Wake up, *cara mia*. We have a visitor.'

Something in Gianni's flat delivery spooked her. Her drowsy eyes opened very wide in dismay when she focused on the young man hovering in the centre of the magnificent rug. It was Stefano.

CHAPTER TEN

STEFANO had so much strain etched on his taut face he looked a lot older then he was. His hair was shorter now. He was a little too thin. His extrovert ebullience appeared to have deserted him. His dark eyes evaded both Milly's gaze and Gianni's.

Milly glanced at Gianni and just winced. The Sicilian side of Gianni's brooding temperament was in the ascendant. He looked grim as hell, but kind of satisfied too, content that his kid brother should be nervous as a cat in his radius. Milly began to revise her assumption that she had been punished more than Stefano. The two brothers had once been pretty close. Stefano, for all his brash talk and swagger, had been heavily dependent on Gianni's approval. And Gianni, she now recognised, had cut him loose from that support system.

Milly stood up. 'Anybody want a drink?' she gushed, to break the awful silence.

'No, thanks...I need to talk,' Stefano announced tautly.

'We'll talk elsewhere,' Gianni drawled, smooth as glass, but he shot Milly a grim, assessing glance, evidently having expected her to be more discomfited by Stefano's presence.

'I don't keep a hair shirt in my wardrobe,' Milly told Gianni defiantly.

'Milly has to be here,' Stefano stated stiffly. 'And you have to promise to hear me out, Gianni. I don't care what you do afterwards, but you've got to give me the chance to explain things.'

'Is there some point to that curious proviso?' Gianni enquired very drily.

Stefano lowered his head. 'You're my brother and I've wronged you,' he breathed tightly. 'I've lied to you, de-

167

ceived you, and I stood by and did nothing when I could have helped you. I followed the tabloid coverage after you got married. I found out what had happened to Milly…the hit-and-run and everything since…and I guess I just couldn't live with myself any more.'

Milly sank back down into her chair because her knees were wobbling. As far as the two men were concerned she might as well not have been there, and if the knowledge of their marriage had scared Stefano into confession mode, she had no desire to distract him.

Gianni was very still. '*How* have you lied?'

'About that night with Milly in New York,' his brother said gruffly.

'But you had no reason to lie. I saw the worst with my own eyes!' Gianni shot back at him.

'There's no way you'd ever have forgiven me for what I did!' Stefano burst out with sudden rawness. 'You'd have thought I was some sort of pervert. I *had* to lie! It was me or her, surely you can see that?'

Gianni was now the colour of ash beneath his bronzed skin, his hard facial bones fiercely prominent. 'Milly said you assaulted her…'

The silence hung like a giant sheet of glass, ready to crash.

Milly cleared her throat and spoke up. 'Stefano told me he loved me. He was drunk. I was feeling sick and I told him to go home,' she explained. 'I heard the front door slam while I was in the bathroom. I thought he'd left…'

'I opened the door and then I changed my mind,' the younger man mumbled.

'So I got into bed and went to sleep.'

Gianni scrutinised her taut face and then focused with mounting incredulity on his brother.

'I saw her sleeping. I just wanted to kiss her. That's all. I *swear*!' Stefano protested, weak as water now beneath the appalled look of menace and disgust flaring in Gianni's diamond-hard eyes.

'I think maybe you thought that if you kissed me, you'd be able to prove that I could respond to you,' Milly countered with contempt. 'You were angry with me. I'd dented your ego, and just for that you frightened the life out of me!'

'I was drunk as a skunk...I hardly knew what I was doing!'

Gianni's hands coiled into powerful punitive fists, and as he absorbed his kid brother's mute terror a look of very masculine revulsion crossed his lean, strong face. '*Accidenti*...I wonder how many sex offenders say that.'

Milly sprang upright again, her fine features flushed with turbulent emotion, and suddenly she was erupting like a volcano. '*You* needn't sound so blasted pious!' she fired bitterly at Gianni. 'If Stefano *had* been a rapist, you'd have given him open house. You just walked out and *left* me with him!'

Beneath the bite of that derisive attack Gianni froze, to stare back at Milly with stricken eyes.

Stefano's shoulders slumped as he too looked at Milly. 'I didn't mean to terrify you, but when you woke up you went crazy, like you were being attacked—'

'She *was* being attacked,' Gianni slotted in from between clenched teeth, his Sicilian accent thick as molasses as he visibly struggled to control his own rising fury. 'When you touch a woman without her consent, it's an assault.'

'I panicked! When you saw us, I was only trying to hold her still until she calmed down—'

'How the bloody hell do you expect me to believe that?' Gianni roared at the younger man in savage interruption. 'You are one sick bastard! *Per meraviglia*, you came to me that night in tears, sobbing out your penitence, telling me how you couldn't resist her, insinuating that she had led you on. It wasn't *enough* that you had assaulted a pregnant woman; you then chose to destroy our relationship to save your own useless hide!'

Stefano stumbled back against the desk for support. 'I didn't know she was pregnant then, Gianni. I'd never, ever have touched her if I'd known that! *Dio mio*...I pulled a crazy stunt and I frightened her, but I honestly didn't mean to!'

Milly studied the younger man with unconcealed scorn. 'I might be impressed by that defence if you'd thought better of your lies once you'd had time to appreciate what you'd done. But even weeks after that night in New York, you were still determined to keep on lying!'

Gianni's winged brows pleated. 'Are you saying that you saw Stefano *after* that night?' Gianni looked dazed.

'Gianni, once you asked me what I was doing in Cornwall three years ago. I'll tell you now. I went there to confront Stefano,' Milly stated crisply. 'I took a lot of trouble to find him. In the end I had to contact his girlfriend's mother and pretend to be a friend of hers to find out where they were staying.'

Stefano was now staring fixedly at the rug.

'You went to Cornwall to see him? *Why?*' Gianni's open bewilderment told her that shock had deprived him of his usual ability to add two and two.

'Milly wanted me to tell you the truth.' Stefano spoke up again in a sudden rush. 'She tried to shame me into it by telling me that she was pregnant, but I already knew that by then because you'd told me. I was furious she had tracked me down. I didn't want anything to do with her in case you found out. You might've started doubting my story, maybe thinking that we'd been having an affair...'

'Per amor di Dio...' Gianni gazed with incredulous dark eyes at his trembling kid brother, and then he simply turned his back.

'When I arrived at the cottage, Stefano had been drowning his sorrows again,' Milly revealed ruefully. 'He'd had a row with his girlfriend and she'd taken their hire car and driven back to London to fly home, leaving him stranded.'

'It was too *late* to tell the truth! I was in too deep by then. There was nothing else to do but face it out!' Stefano protested weakly.

Gianni's dark, haunted eyes were fixed to Milly. 'Tell me

that the night you're referring to was *not* the same night that you were hit by that car!' he urged, almost pleadingly.

'It *was* that night.' Milly shrugged fatalistically. 'I'd gone to the cottage in a taxi and then let it go.'

As Gianni rounded on Stefano, the younger man backed away, looking sick as a dog. 'Until I read about the hit-and-run in the papers last week, I didn't *know* what had happened to Milly that night! How *could* I have known? She just walked out on me. For all I knew she had a car parked further up the road—'

'You didn't give a damn either way,' Milly condemned helplessly. 'In a twisted way, you had started to blame *me* for the mess you were in with Gianni!'

'I called a cab the next morning and flew back to New York,' Stefano continued woodenly, as if she hadn't spoken. 'I had no idea that Milly had been injured after leaving the cottage.'

'But within days you were well aware that I was frantically trying to find her.' Gianni's tone was one of savage disbelief. 'Yet not one word did you breathe! You could have told me you'd seen her in Cornwall but you didn't. I spent months searching France for her. By then she had been wrongly identified as another woman.'

'I knew nothing about any of that,' Stefano reiterated, perspiration beading his strained face. 'And if I'm here now, it's because I couldn't stand all this on my conscience any more.'

'No, you're here now because Milly's my wife,' Gianni delivered with chillingly soft exactitude. 'Because you assumed I might already know all this, and the idea of confessing all and throwing yourself on my mercy seemed like the only option you had left.'

'That's not how it was, Gianni.' Stefano had turned a ghastly colour.

'Your conscience got to you too late. You hurt Milly not once, but twice. You also cost me the first years of my son's life,' Gianni condemned with lethal menace. 'But what I can never, ever forgive is my *own* mistake, Stefano. I put family loyalty first. And here you are, our father all over again. Weak, dishonest, unscrupulous. It's a just reward for my stupidity, isn't it?'

Looking at Gianni, Stefano seemed to crumple entirely. 'I'm not like that. I'm not. I've changed a whole lot since then. I *had* to lie… I was so scared—'

Gianni said something cold in Italian.

Stefano was openly begging now. 'How was I supposed to admit the truth, knowing that you'd kill me? Do you think I didn't realise that *she* came first with you when I saw how you reacted at the apartment? It was her or me…you've *got* to see that!'

Milly did not feel sorry for Stefano, but she was squirming for him. His best quality had always been the depth of his attachment to Gianni. He had always been measuring himself up against Gianni. He had probably developed a crush on her for the same reason. But alcohol, arrogance and sheer stupidity had combined to tear Stefano's privileged little world apart. He *had* been terrified that night in New York after Gianni had walked out on them both, terrified that Gianni, who had been more father than brother to him, would disown him.

'Go home, Stefano,' Milly suggested wearily.

Gianni said nothing. It was as if Stefano had become invisible. His brother slung him one last pleading glance and then hurried out of the room.

A hollow laugh that startled Milly was wrenched from Gianni then. '*Porca miseria!* To think I was jealous of that pathetic little punk!'

'Jealous?' Milly parroted in astonishment. 'Of *Stefano*?'

Gianni half spread expressive brown hands and then clenched them tight into defensive fists, his strong profile rigid as steel. He swallowed hard. 'Yes. Long before that night I saw you together at the apartment, I was *very* jealous,' he bit out raggedly.

Milly was stunned by that revelation. 'I can't believe that… I mean, why on earth—?'

'You had a bond with him. You talked about things I was totally out of touch with…*house* music, clubs. You used the same street dialect, shared the same *in* jokes,' Gianni enumerated with harsh emphasis. 'You were the same generation. I introduced you to dinner dates, antiques and art galleries, and occasionally you were bored out of your skull and I knew it.'

Milly was savaged by that shattering outpouring of feelings she would never have dreamt Gianni could experience. Insecurity, vulnerability concerning the age-gap between them. 'You couldn't expect us to share every taste, every interest…'

'I didn't feel that way until Stefano came into the picture.'

'I thought you were pleased we got on so well.'

'Sure I was pleased.' Gianni's agreement was raw with self-contempt. 'I'd ring you from the other side of the world and in the background my kid brother would be cracking jokes and making you laugh. I was *eaten* with jealousy and there was nothing I could do about it.' He moved restively about the room like a trapped animal, forced to pace round a too small cage. 'But until that night I saw you with him I *knew* it was all in my own mind; I *knew* I was being unreasonable!'

Suddenly Milly was grasping why Gianni had been so quick to believe her capable of betraying him. Jealousy rigidly suppressed—a fertile and dangerous breeding ground for distrust and suspicion. Yet she had never suspected that Gianni was jealous. Once he had even told her that he was grateful she had Stefano for company. His ferocious pride had ensured he went to great lengths to conceal his own weakness.

'I was planning to surprise you that night. I was in a really good mood. But I went haywire when I saw you on our bed with Stefano. That was my every worst fear come true. If I had stayed one second longer I would've torn him apart with my bare hands!' Gianni asserted in a smouldering undertone, ashen pale. 'I couldn't stand to even look at you. So I didn't.'

So I didn't. He always protected himself from what he didn't want to deal with emotionally.

'As usual, you took the easy out,' Milly sighed with immense regret.

The sudden silence seemed to swell.

'It wasn't the easy way out, *cara mia*,' Gianni contradicted from between bloodlessly compressed lips, feverish colour scoring his stunning cheekbones.

Milly hardened herself to the distinct shock spreading in the dark, deep flashing eyes pinned to hers. Now that the truth had come out, she wasn't prepared to allow him to duck that issue. 'Gianni, most men would've confronted us there and then. It's all right saying that you might have ripped Stefano apart. Frankly, I couldn't have cared less what you did to him that night! No, it was what you did *afterwards* that destroyed us.'

Gianni's breathing pattern fractured audibly. 'His *lies* destroyed us.'

'No. Your refusal to see me again did that,' Milly countered painfully, her blue eyes saddened. 'And I'm not interested in what you *thought* I'd done. I'd been with you for two years and I was carrying your child. I had the right to expect a meeting with you. But what did you do? You wouldn't even take a call from me and then you took off to the Caribbean with another woman!'

Gianni latched on to that last condemnation with something very much like relief. '*Accidenti*, you don't need to worry about that!' he assured her. 'We never actually made it between the same sheets. When it came down to it, I wasn't interested.'

'That's not the point,' Milly groaned, refused to be sidetracked into betraying the pleasure she'd received from that information. 'The point is that you let me down by refusing to face up to the situation between us.'

'Let me get this straight, *cara mia*,' Gianni breathed raggedly, as if she had suddenly discharged a shotgun into his back, brilliant eyes burning in stark golden disbelief. 'You're accusing me...Gianni D'Angelo...of running away like a spineless little jerk!'

Milly winced.

'Only you were trying to wrap it up a bit!' Gianni grated, outraged by her silence.

'Why did you take so long to tell Stefano that I was pregnant?'

Disconcerted, Gianni frowned. 'It was private, no business of his.'

'He's your brother.'

'When I hadn't yet decided how I intended to resolve the situation, I wasn't prepared to discuss it with anybody but you,' Gianni framed impressively.

'And not even with me if you could help it,' Milly tacked on helplessly. 'You spent that time trying to decide whether to keep me or dump me, didn't you?'

Gianni glowered at her. '*Dio*...it wasn't like that at all!'

'The speed with which you grabbed the first excuse you had to ditch me isn't in your favour,' Milly informed him.

'At the time, I was thinking of marrying you!'

'*Thinking?*' Milly repeated, unimpressed. 'Only it never got further than that. I trusted you. I relied on you. I loved you for two years and yet it still wasn't enough to convince you that we had something that it might have been worth trying to save.' Feeling her eyes smarting with oversensitive tears, Milly started to twist away.

Gianni reached out for her and pulled her into his arms, refusing to be held at bay by her resistance. 'Don't tear us apart with this,' he said unevenly. 'I made some mistakes. OK, I made a bloody *huge* mistake, but the minute I found out that you'd left Paris, I began looking for you.'

Milly was mutinous, unreachable. 'Because you had your child as an excuse. If it hadn't been for Connor, I'd still be out there, *lost*!'

'You're getting very worked up about this. You don't know what you're saying,' Gianni told her with stubborn conviction. 'OK, I didn't behave the way I should have after that business with Stefano, but once I came to terms with that—'

'Can't you even admit that you were *hurt*, like anybody else would?' Milly demanded emotionally, watching his devastatingly handsome features freeze and aching at the knowledge that he still wouldn't lower his barriers and let her in. 'Or did you stick me in a little compartment and just close the lid? Did you even manage to deal with it at all?'

Gianni's lean hands slid from her with a pronounced jerk. 'I'm going out for a while.'

'No, you are *not*! You walk out of this house now and you'll find barricades up when you try to walk back!' Milly warned him furiously.

'You are really angry with me right now. I have got nothing to say in my own defence,' Gianni spelt out thickly, rigid as a block of wood facing a very hungry bonfire. 'You haven't even given me the chance to apologise for misjudging you!'

'I don't want an apology. I accept that it looked bad for me that night. I accept that you were already jealous and so that much more likely to misinterpret what you saw. I even accept that Stefano is a convincing liar, and that you trusted him more than you could trust me.'

Gianni elevated an ebony brow with the kind of attitude that made her want to strangle him, stunning dark eyes coolly enquiring. 'So what *can't* you accept?'

'An emotional vacuum when we could have so much more!' she responded tautly.

'Enough is never enough for you, is it?'

'I'm not playing our marriage by your rules any more. Once I took all the risks, once I was the one who always went out on a limb...now it's your turn. I think I might enjoy seeing how good you are at expressing anything without sex.'

'Probably pretty hopeless,' Gianni admitted, disconcerting her. 'You want to humiliate me to pay me back for not believing in you three years ago.'

'Gianni...do you really think I'd do that to you?'

Gianni swung on his heel and strode out of the room. Milly emitted a strangled sob, suddenly wondering where all those crazy demands had come from and whether there was a certain unlovely grain of truth in his contention that she was trying to extract revenge.

She rubbed her eyes, knew she was smearing mascara everywhere, and finally she went off in search of Connor to console herself. But Gianni had got there first. He was in the playroom, sitting on the carpet in front of their son.

'Does she ask you how you're feeling all the time?' Gianni was asking broodingly while he set out Connor's toy train set. 'Does she want to know your every thought too?'

Connor gave him a winsome smile. 'Biscuit?' he said hopefully.

'Yes, I suspect that when you share your thoughts with Mamma it works very much to your advantage. Instant wish-fulfilment,' Gianni breathed reflectively. 'Do you think it could work that way for me?'

Milly reeled back against the wall outside the room and struggled to contain her laughter. But they looked so sweet together. Gianni chatting away, Connor giving up on the biscuit idea and getting down to play trains with all the accompanying choo-choo noises.

An hour later, Gianni walked into their bedroom. Fresh out of the shower, wrapped only in a towel, Milly fell still. Gianni sent her a disturbingly wolfish grin, exuding confidence in megawaves. 'Right, what do you want me to start talking about?'

'Us?' she practically whispered.

Gianni breathed in deep.

The silence was thunderous.

Milly couldn't bear it any longer. 'Why did you keep the house in Paris?'

'If you had ever decided to come back, you had to have somewhere to come back to,' Gianni pointed out levelly.

'But in all this time you hadn't changed anything at all!'

Gianni shrugged. 'Yes, I kept it like a shrine.'

Milly was poleaxed.

'When I wanted to feel close to you, I went there and sat for a while. I never stayed over. I used a hotel. Next question,' Gianni encouraged, as if he was competing in a fast and furious game.

'If you weren't able to talk to me like this before, how are you managing it now?' Milly whispered, wide-eyed.

'I've got to trust you. You're my wife.' Gianni breathed rather jerkily, as if that question had gone a little too deep.

Milly sighed. 'I've been so stupid. You wouldn't share things before because you thought I'd succumbed to Stefano.'

'I was protecting myself. I've probably protected myself more with you than any other woman,' Gianni admitted tautly, his strong facial bones now taut beneath his bronzed skin. 'Right from the start, I was vulnerable with you. Every time I walked away, I seemed to double back. I didn't like that. I didn't like the fact that I wasn't in full control.'

'But you were when you kept quiet?'

'It wasn't deliberate.' Gianni grimaced, his wide, sensual mouth tightening. 'You're always analysing emotions. I had learned to tune mine out and I was basically quite content like that. And when I met you you made it easy for me to go on that way. You knew what I wanted or what I didn't want before I had to say it. I didn't have to make an effort until you told me you were pregnant, and then you suddenly went silent and we were in trouble. One voice became no voice, *cara mia*.'

Milly was shaken by a truth she had never faced before.

'I'd always tried to *show* you that I cared, but all of a sudden that didn't seem to be enough. I really felt the change in you. I kept stalling on asking you to marry me,' he confessed ruefully. 'I didn't want you to say yes just because of the baby. I could see you weren't happy. That's why I became so jealous of Stefano. The cracks had appeared before he came along.'

'Yes,' Milly acknowledged, shaken yet again by his ability to put matters in their proper context. She *had* been different those last few months. 'I felt very insecure.'

'So you stopped telling me you loved me.' Gianni released a rather hollow laugh. 'You got me hooked on you saying it all the time and then you stopped. Considering that I never returned the favour, you had remarkable staying power, but I did wonder what was going on with you. I thought possibly you blamed me for getting you pregnant—'

'Oh, no!' Milly was pained by that misconception.

'So I tried not to mention the baby too much. I felt guilty. Of course I did,' Gianni shared heavily. 'I think I took those risks with you because on a subconscious level I was trying to push myself into making a real commitment to you.'

'But you were so upset when I told you I was pregnant.'

'I was scared I wouldn't live up to the challenge of being a parent,' Gianni admitted grimly.

'Gianni, you're a wonderful father,' Milly told him hotly.

'I'm learning.' Gianni shrugged, as if she had embarrassed him, brilliant beautiful dark eyes glimmering. 'You were right downstairs. I did let you down three years ago. I'm not proud of my behaviour. I'm ashamed that I listened to my brother instead of you. But I knew I could cope with him and I wasn't at all sure I could cope with you. And that word "hurt" doesn't cover what I was going through at the time.'

'I know.' Milly closed the distance between them to slide her arms round his lean hard body and feel her own heart beating as fast as a war drum.

'No, for once I don't think you *do* know,' Gianni countered almost roughly, framing her cheekbones with possessive hands. 'When I saw you with Stefano it was like somebody had taken my entire life and just blown it away. You had become so much a part of me that being without you was like being torn violently in two. And the half of me that was left was barely functioning afterwards.'

Milly stared up at him with mesmerised blue eyes.

'It took me a long time to fall in love, and it took even longer for me to realise that I did love you.' Gianni studied her with a raw intensity of unashamed emotion that touched her to the heart. 'And by the time I got the message, you'd vanished.'

'You loved me...' A strangled sob escaped Milly. She was overwhelmed by the poignancy of that confession, three years too late. 'Oh, that's awful!'

Gianni stooped to lift her up into his arms and carry her over to the bed. 'I'm only expecting to talk,' he told her loftily. 'I only want to comfort you.'

He held her close and her towel slipped. He watched the full swell of her pale breasts rise and fall with the rapidity of her breathing and an earthy groan was suddenly wrenched from him.

'I haven't really got that much more to talk about,' Gianni added in roughened continuation. 'You already know just how determined I was to get you back once I found you again.'

'You wanted Connor.'

'Behind every terrified male lurks a big liar,' Gianni shared, splaying long fingers satisfyingly wide over her slim hips and easing her into the hard cradle of his long, powerful thighs. I told you it was Connor I was really after. I told myself it was only sex I was after. I kept on telling myself that I couldn't trust you and then kept on forgetting it. But what I really wanted was everything back the way it was.'

'Your proposal really offended and hurt me...' Milly planted a fleeting kiss to his stubborn jawline.

'So I was trying to be cool. I didn't want to serve myself up on a plate. I certainly didn't want you to know that I was desperate for you to agree because I still loved you. I was trying not to admit that even to myself at that stage.'

'Oh, Gianni...' Milly sighed ecstatically. 'That's *all* I ever wanted, you know.'

'You put me through more hoops than a circus trainer,' Gianni growled feelingly. 'You really were that basic. When I did what you wanted, I was rewarded. When I didn't, I got time out as punishment. The first six months I was with you was like living in an earthquake zone.'

Milly ran a hand with provocative intent along the extended length of one lean, muscular thigh and watched his wonderful eyes narrow to a sexy shimmer of wildly appreciative gold. 'But I always loved you,' she said winsomely in her own favour.

'I adore you,' Gianni groaned with a slight shudder. 'You're gorgeous and smart and sexy and demanding—'

'*Very,*' she asserted.

'I'll never let anything or anybody hurt you again.' The most soul-destroyingly beautiful smile curved Gianni's mouth as he looked down at her.

Her heart tilted on its axis, but she knew she still had something important to say. 'But you still have to look after your brother,' she told him gently.

'Are you out of your mind?' Gianni demanded, staggered by that assertion.

'He was acting like a guy on the edge of a breakdown today, and deep down inside you know he needs you to sort him out. I know the way he was behaving makes you cringe,' Milly continued, with lashings of soothing understanding in her steady gaze, 'but you're all he's got, so he's your responsibility.'

'You couldn't possibly forgive him for what he did!'

'Three years ago, for the space of a minute, he give me a really bad scare...but afterwards he was much more scared than I was. Really scared people are not naturally noble or strong or honest. Think it over.'

'How come you're so compassionate about him but so tough on me?'

'You're like a great big thriving jungle plant and he's

more of a stunted seedling that needs help and encouragement to grow.'

Gianni flung his well-shaped head back on the pillows, dark eyes glinting with appreciation and amusement. 'You really know how to massage a guy's ego, *cara mia*.'

'Yours...oh, yes.'

'Did you realise that I was incredibly hungry the night you dumped that apple thing in Paris?'

'No, but I'm glad to hear it.'

'You can make it again for me.'

'Maybe...' Milly parted her lips with a shiver of delicious expectancy as his sensual mouth drifted downward.

Gianni stilled. 'I don't think we're likely to have a problem in the communication department again,' he proclaimed with satisfaction.

Tempted to tell him that she'd listened to him rehearsing with their son, Milly reared up, pushed his powerful shoulders back to the pillows and moaned in near desperation. 'Please shut up and kiss me!'

Six days later, on Christmas Eve, Milly watched Gianni finish reading a story about Santa Claus and his reindeer to Connor. He was able to answer all Connor's questions. Not a bad performance for a male who had never known a real Christmas as a child, Milly reflected with shimmering eyes.

After tucking their drowsy son in, Gianni straightened with a wry grin. 'We'll never get him to bed this early next year. He'll understand much more than he does now.'

They went downstairs together. Milly thought over the past week. It had been very eventful. All the publicity generated by their marriage and her mistaken identification as Faith Jennings had had stunning results as far as the Jennings family were concerned. Their long-lost daughter had written her parents a tentative letter from her home in the north of Scotland.

Divorced, and with three young children, the real Faith had admitted that the longer time went on the more difficult she had found it to get back in touch. They had since talked on the phone and were planning to meet in the New Year. Robin and Davina were anxious about how that reunion might go, but determined to be accepting of their adult daughter's independence. Milly believed it would be a happy reunion, because Faith had sounded rather lonely in her letter.

Gianni had also gone to see Stefano. They had talked. Gianni had emerged from that discussion feeling rather guilty, never having quite appreciated just how much Stefano relied on his approval, or indeed how devastated Stefano had been when Gianni had stopped treating him like a brother and given him only financial support. It was early days yet, but Milly reckoned that the healing process had started.

Gianni surveyed the drawing room of Heywood House. All the formality and the cool elegance had been banished. In all the rooms Milly used seasonal throws, glittery embellishments, festive padded cushions, unsophisticated homemade log, autumn leaf and berry arrangements and streams of paper chains ruled. Gianni even had to suffer a large fluffy Santa Claus toy on his library desk.

And he just loved it all, he acknowledged with a rueful smile of appreciation. He just loved the rich colour and warmth she brought into her surroundings, her innate ability to transform a house into a real home. He set a small parcel wrapped in beautiful paper down in front of her. 'You get your real presents tomorrow, but this is just a trifle I picked up ages ago,' he admitted, half under his breath.

Milly ripped off the paper and found herself looking at a delicate golden angel inside a crystal snowstorm on an ornate base. 'Oh, Gianni…' she sighed extravagantly. 'This is exquisite! Where did you get it?'

'New York.'

'But you haven't been there since—'

'Last year,' Gianni admitted, bracing himself.

'But you hadn't even found me then!' Milly gasped, instantly leaping up to envelop him in frantic hugs and kisses.

As desire flashed between them to instantaneous heat, Milly jerked back a step. 'Sometimes I love you so much it just hurts, *but* we still have a sooty bootprint to make on the hearth, so that Connor can see which chimney Santa Claus used as an entrance,' she explained apologetically.

'Maybe with the number of chimneys we've got we should put a flag on the roof so that the old guy doesn't get confused,' Gianni suggested deadpan as he curved her smoothly back into the possessive circle of his arms, knowing that bootprints could be faked after midnight as well as before it.

'Magic, doesn't need flags, Gianni!'

Against the backdrop of the flickering firelight and the glittering tree, Gianni scanned her wide, loving smile with softened dark eyes and pulled her close. 'You're the magic in my life, *cara mia*. I love you.'

HER SECRET SANTA

BY
DAY LECLAIRE

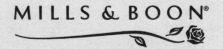
MILLS & BOON®

PROLOGUE

HE'D found her!

Mathias Blackstone allowed a small smile of satisfaction to touch his mouth. After all these months, he'd finally found Jacq Randell. The discovery brought him within one short step of his goal—to prove that the elusive Ms. Randell was the even more elusive Jack Rabbitt, author and illustrator of the most popular line of children's books currently on the market. His client would be pleased to hear the news.

Very pleased.

How interesting that he'd run her to ground in Seattle of all places, hiding right beneath his very nose. The fact that she'd turned out to be Turk Randell's daughter was even more ironic. Turk's public relations firm had been attempting to snag his attention for two solid years. It was a coincidence Mathias intended to use to his full advantage—once he came up with a client in need of a PR firm. Did Randell know his daughter was also Jack Rabbit? If not, it offered interesting possibilities.

After all the research he'd done, he was intensely curious to meet Jacq, which was why he'd accepted Turk Randell's invitation to this party. Mathias had hoped to meet her in an informal setting. The sketchy facts he'd gathered had captivated him, stirring an interest he hadn't felt in years. Studying her artwork—assuming it was hers—had only served to magnify that interest. She was twenty-eight, described by those who knew her as both strong and dainty, brilliant and vague, stubborn and

5

easygoing. The contrasting comments intrigued him. Only on one fact did all agree. Jacq Randell guarded her privacy with ruthless determination.

He folded his arms across his chest and waited patiently until the glittering array of guests cleared from his line of vision. He'd been forced to ask someone to point her out, but fortunately such a large party allowed him to maintain a certain level of anonymity. It gave him time to analyze the situation at his leisure, while searching for any vulnerabilities he could use. As the tide of humanity finally ebbed, he spotted Jacq by the buffet table and fought a sense of amazement.

He found it hard to believe that this bit of whimsy was Turk Randell's daughter. She looked nothing like her father. For that matter, she didn't look anything like her brother or sister, either. To a one they exuded a brittle sophistication—tall and handsome with sleek black hair, sleeker figures and brilliant jet-hued eyes.

But not Jacq.

She was as delicate as spun glass. Almost coltishly slender, she'd caught the weighty mass of streaked blond curls at the nape of her long fragile neck. As she bent to sample the hors d'oeuvres, her scoop-necked dress revealed the fine bones of her shoulders and offered a tantalizing glimpse of sweetly rounded breasts. His mouth tightened. Didn't they ever feed the woman? Apparently not, considering the way she devoured the bite-size appetizers, her greed as unconscious as that of a ravenous child. She peeked around just then, as though checking to see if any observed her voracity. Huge hazel eyes dominated her triangular face. They stared out at her surroundings with an avid curiosity so revealing, he longed to shield her from a world waiting to consume her.

And then it hit him.

He was the only one waiting to consume her. He was the one destined to hurt her.

Too bad, came the regretful thought. He hadn't felt this attracted to a woman in a long time. But as much as he might wish it otherwise, his client's need took precedence. There could be no doubt about how this chase would end. Like the rest of the Randells, this woodland sprite didn't stand a chance against him.

J.J. Randell caught her brother, Cord, by the arm. "You're not going to believe this!" she said in a gleeful undertone.

"What? What did I miss?"

"Mathias Blackstone is here." J.J. towed him toward their father. "No, no, you fool. Don't look. He'll see you."

"He came? Blackstone actually came?"

Turk Randell joined them, a broad grin spreading across his striking face. "Oh, he came, all right."

A sardonic expression gleamed deep in J.J.'s dark eyes. Her father was practically salivating over the unexpected coup. But then, why shouldn't he? He'd been striving to gain Blackstone's attention for two solid years. To have such a man connected with their public relations firm would be worth a fortune.

"The interesting question is...*why* did he come?" J.J. commented.

"What do you mean, why?" A frown marred Turk's chiseled features. "He must be interested in using Limelight International. What other explanation could there be?"

J.J. shook her head. "I don't think so. He's here for

a reason, all right. But not the one you'd hoped. Look who's snagged his attention.''

Like puppets on a string, her brother's and father's gaze swiveled from Blackstone to the source of his scrutiny....

Jacq.

"Damn."

"We're sunk."

"What the hell could he want with her?" Turk complained. "She doesn't even work for the company."

"Not anymore," J.J. couldn't resist needling. She studied Blackstone, adding sagely, "And I think his interest is obvious."

Her father's brows jerked together. "You can't mean he's— You don't seriously believe he'd want—" He gritted his teeth. "Don't be ridiculous!"

"Wait a second, Dad. I think J.J.'s right," Cord inserted. "I think Blackstone wants Jacq. It's a man/woman type deal. You know?"

"Only too well. I'm fifty, not dead," Turk snapped. "It just doesn't make sense. Why would a man of Blackstone's caliber want someone as artless as Jacq?"

J.J. smiled sadly. "How can you say that? She looks and acts exactly like Mom."

A momentary anguish flickered deep in Turk's black eyes. "She is like your mother," he whispered. "Isn't she?"

"And every bit as attractive in a pixieish sort of way."

Turk's mouth firmed. "You both think that's what he's after? You think he wants Jacq?"

"Without question," J.J. responded.

"Absolutely," Cord seconded.

Their father inclined his head. "In that case, let's make certain Mr. Blackstone gets what he wants."

Jacq examined the buffet table with unconcealed greed, popping something round and vaguely green in her mouth. Not bad. But then, considering she couldn't remember her last meal, she wasn't inclined to be choosy. In fact, if it hadn't been for severe hunger pangs, she'd never have ventured within a thousand miles of her father's public relation "do."

She risked a quick glance in Turk's direction and frowned, a shrimpy something-or-other halfway to her mouth. Uh-oh. No question about it. She'd chosen the worst possible party to crash. Her dear relatives—jungle cats to a one—were definitely on the prowl. They'd slunk to the far end of the room, amassing like black storm clouds, their joint gazes glued to... She craned to catch a peek and nearly choked on her shrimp.

Dear heavens! Had they completely lost their collective minds?

The source of their fascination had to be the most dangerously attractive man she'd ever seen in her entire life. Just a single glimpse made her itch to grab a sketch pad and set to work—from a safe distance, of course. Tall, beautifully proportioned and leanly muscled, his hair was a rich ebony. And his eyes... Even from across the room she could see that his eyes were an incredible shade of ice-green. They were cool—too cool for her taste—with a sharp intelligence that warned that he didn't miss a trick.

He turned that gaze in her direction just then and she froze, seeing the fire beneath the ice, sensed the power and determination that ruled his keen intellect. It was then that she realized how thoroughly she'd overestimated her relatives. They weren't jungle cats, but yapping scavengers, fighting over food scraps this lithe, dragonesque creature spurned. Whatever they wanted from him, they were way out of their league.

This was a man to be avoided at all costs.

The instant he turned his attention elsewhere, Jacq scooped a handful of hors d'oeuvres into a linen napkin and beat a hasty retreat. Limelight International hoped to get something from this man-dragon and the safest place for her was out of the line of fire. Besides, she couldn't wait to get to work. From the moment she'd glanced his way, a thousand images had leaped to mind, followed by a thousand story ideas—all inspired by this one man. She had to get to her studio.

Now.

"Mr. Blackstone." Turk greeted his guest with a meticulous blend of jovial friendliness and careful deference. "How kind of you to attend our little get-together."

Mathias inclined his head, his attention centered on Jacq's hurried exit. "Randell."

Turk noted Blackstone's interest. It would seem J.J. was right. Jacq had definitely captivated the man. Damn. Without question, that would complicate their situation. Knowing his eldest daughter, she'd make matters as difficult as possible. In fact, she had a singular talent for it.

"I hope your presence means you've decided at long last to utilize our firm," Turk said, determined to seize the opportunity at hand.

"Not quite. I've decided to give your firm a trial run."

Not as much of a concession as Turk had hoped, but still a definite coup. "I'm delighted to hear it. Might I suggest a meeting to discuss specifics?"

"Excellent suggestion." Mathias turned then and focused the full power of his pale green eyes on Turk. "Tomorrow evening at six would be convenient."

"Fine, fine. Shall we meet at your office or—"

"I'd prefer we meet here. I'd like to get acquainted with the rest of your family. Your *entire* family."

"Of...of course." *Damn*! It didn't take a genius to read the underlying message. Blackstone expected Jacq to be there. "You'll join us for dinner tomorrow?"

"I'm afraid that won't be possible. I have other plans."

"I see." For the first time in a dog's age, Turk found himself at a loss for words. Only thirty years' worth of experience dealing with difficult situations saved him now. "Tomorrow at six it is, then," he said, offering Blackstone his hand. "We look forward to meeting with you."

Mathias inclined his head. "And I look forward to meeting the rest of your family."

He departed without another word, leaving Turk cursing with equal virulence Blackstone's disconcerting personality and his daughter's contrary nature. Neither boded well for Limelight International's future.

CHAPTER ONE

"You have to come," J.J. wailed, pacing the library of the main house in long, frantic steps. "We promised Blackstone you would."

Jacq shrugged. "I guess you'll have to unpromise him. You know better than to make plans on my behalf." She selected the book she needed and turned, shooting her sister a cool look. "Especially without consulting me first."

"But, we couldn't ask," her sister argued. "Blackstone caught us by surprise with his request. He announced that the entire family had to be present at this meeting tonight and then walked off. Believe me, it didn't leave any room for discussion."

"I'm sure he meant the Limelight portion of the family," Jacq said, seizing on the probability with ill-concealed relief.

J.J. shook her head. "Not a chance. According to the information we've been able to gather, Mathias Blackstone is the most exacting man anyone has ever met. He made it clear that he expected all the Randells present tonight and that's what he meant."

Jacq frowned, wishing she knew enough about the man to argue the point. Unfortunately, she didn't. Besides, her sister might be only twenty-four, but she had the uncanny ability to assess a person's strong points and flaws with pinpoint accuracy. It was a skill Turk exploited with ruthless disregard. If J.J. said Mathias Blackstone expected all the Randells to show up, then chances were excellent that's what he meant. Jacq nibbled on her lower lip. The question she'd like answered was...*why*?

An image of rapacious green eyes leaped to mind—eyes that currently graced the fierce black dragon in her latest series of sketches. She'd planned on adding a dragon to her children's books for over a year now—she'd even written the story that would introduce him to her readers. But she'd never found the right model for such a dangerously elegant creature.

Until now.

She scowled at the plant book she held. The frustrating part was that she'd spent all of last night and half of this morning working on the project. But no matter how hard she'd tried, she'd been unable to get the dragon quite right. Even after dozens of sketches the essence of the beast continued to elude her.

"Jacq, please say you'll come. This is important."

"For you Limelighters, it's always important," Jacq retorted absently. Maybe it was the body. Mathias Blackstone had a lithe elegance about him. A grace to his movements that she'd had difficulty adapting to the larger, more cumbersome size of a dragon. Perhaps if she tried sketching him in flight it would work better.

"No, I mean this is *really* important. Dad's been working for two solid years to catch Blackstone's eye. He's...he's put a lot of money into the campaign."

That caught Jacq's attention. "How much money?" she questioned sharply.

"A *lot*. But don't you see? This time he's made the right decision. Blackstone's attendance last night proves that. He's interested. If we can obtain even a small portion of his business for our PR firm, it'll be worth every penny Dad spent. We'd be set for life."

Jacq's lashes flickered downward, concealing her expression. How many times had she heard that line before? "Why do you suppose Blackstone wants me there?"

J.J. shrugged. "Who knows. He's just like that."

"Like what?"

"I told you. Careful. Exacting. Thorough. Unbelievably precise. That's why it's taken so long to attract his interest. He likes to examine all the possible angles before he makes a decision."

"What's so tough about making a decision?" Jacq questioned in genuine confusion. "You just do it."

"Well, not Mathias Blackstone. Unlike normal people, once he reaches a decision, he never changes his mind."

"You're kidding. Never?"

"Never. I guess that's why he works so hard to get it right the first time."

"How very black-and-white of him." Jacq shot her sister an impish grin. "Personally, I need more elbow room. That's why I like all that colorful area in between. It offers so many intriguing possibilities."

"Not Blackstone," J.J. reiterated. "None of those colors exist for him. I don't even think they're in his vocabulary. He's the most ruthless, intimidating man I've ever met. And those eyes of his!" She shivered. "It's like looking into a sea of green ice. They freeze me solid."

No, they didn't freeze, Jacq silently corrected. They mesmerized, holding her while they searched. Searched for… Her brows drew together. Searched for… *What*? Why *had* he been looking at her so intently at the party? "I'd still like to know why I have to be there," she murmured. "I'm not a Limelighter."

"You were."

A wintry coldness settled into Jacq's tone. "Briefly. Since I'm not with the firm any longer, why insist I attend this meeting? I have no influence over how you three conduct business."

"Do you plan to hold that incident against Dad for ever?" J.J. questioned in distress. "It was horrible, I admit. But it worked out in the end, right? After all, you received Grandmother's inheritance. That went a long way toward compensating you for that fiasco, didn't it?"

Jacq fought for patience. "Grandmother Lacey gave me the cottage and exactly one thousand dollars."

"So you've said. But if that's true..." J.J. frowned. "Where does your money come from? You never leave the cottage to go to work, and yet—"

Jacq averted her gaze. Her secret identity was becoming more and more difficult to keep hidden from her family. Unfortunately if they ever found out, she'd lose the precious anonymity she'd enjoyed these past few years. "The rest of you received the main house. It was a fair division," Jacq finished with careful deliberation. Thankfully, the reminder succeeded in deflecting her sister's attention.

"We get to keep the main house only as long as we don't invade your privacy." A reluctant smile quivered at the edges of her mouth. "I can't even knock on your door without fear of violating the will."

"You can knock," Jacq replied mildly. "You just can't come in without an invitation."

"Look— Could we get back to the point of this conversation? Will you come tonight?"

"I'm thinking."

"Could you think a little faster? You're not

Blackstone. Give me a simple yes or no answer. We need time to invent an excuse if you refuse.''

Jacq sighed. Her choices were clear. Since her family wouldn't dare risk encroaching on her privacy, she could refuse their request and stay home without worrying about a herd of Randells descending on her door. Grandmother's will had seen to that. Or she could attend this little meeting her father had arranged and suffer through whatever unpleasant surprises he intended to spring. There was one distinct advantage to that plan of action.

If she went, she'd have another opportunity to study Mathias Blackstone. Only this time it would be up close and personal. She could analyze his various expressions, watch him move, pin down the exact shade of those odd green eyes. Getting better acquainted with Blackstone would breathe life into her still-sleeping dragon. The temptation proved too great to resist.

''Okay, I'll do it,'' she said. ''What time?''

''Si— Er, five-thirty. And for heaven's sake, don't be late!'' J.J. made a dismissive gesture. ''Although why I bother to tell you that, I don't know. It's like asking the sun not to shine.''

''It is rather pointless,'' Jacq conceded. ''But if it makes you feel any better, it isn't deliberate. Honest. I just lose track of time.''

''I don't know how that's possible,'' J.J. grumbled. ''It's not like you have anything else to occupy your thoughts. All you do is hide out in that cottage of yours and paint.'' A glint of curiosity shone in her dark eyes. ''At least, I assume you're painting. Not that you've ever bothered to show us the results.''

''Trust me. You wouldn't be interested,'' Jacq replied

with careful nonchalance. "Now if you'll excuse me, I'm going to hide out in my cottage some more."

"At least leave the phones plugged in so we can reach you," J.J. called. "Please?"

Jacq lifted a hand in acknowledgment as she left. Cutting through the sprawling garden at the back of the house, she headed toward the small cottage tucked at the far end of the property. Surrounded by a huge ivy-covered wall, it perched on the edge of Lake Washington. She adored her hideaway and thanked Grandmother Lacey every day for her unexpected benevolence.

After Jacq had left Limelight, she'd been adrift, not quite sure which direction her life should take. That question had been settled with one decisive conversation with her grandmother.

"You're finally going to fulfill your dream," Grandmother Lacey had announced two short months before her death. "You're going to paint. And you're going to paint full time, not just when Turk gives you the odd moment free. It's what you've always wanted and I'm going to see to it that you have a chance to succeed."

She'd been as good as her word. She'd set up a studio for Jacq in the cottage and insisted that the story ideas and sketches that had accumulated over the years be sent out to various publishing companies. Unfortunately, she hadn't lived long enough to witness Jacq's success. It had been a devastating loss. In fact, it wasn't until the will had been read that Jacq realized the full extent of her grandmother's love. She'd been left the cottage to use as a studio. And a stipulation had been included in the will ensuring privacy while she worked toward her goal. No one could enter the cottage without permission or they'd lose the main house to charity.

A sudden gust of wind tugged at her curls, whipping them into a frenzy. Wrapping her arms around her waist, Jacq ducked her head against the frigid air. The December morning felt raw, the steely gray clouds overhead heavy with the threat of rain. Next time she'd remember to grab her rain slicker. At least, she'd try to remember. Mundane matters such as that had a tendency to slip her mind. She'd lost count of the number of occasions she'd been caught in an unanticipated downpour. And in Seattle unanticipated downpours were always anticipated.

She arrived home the same instant as the skies opened. Darting inside, she slammed the heavy oak door against the elements and breathed a sigh of relief. Angelica meowed a greeting, leaping from a nearby table to rub with feline affection against her leg.

"Hello, sweetheart. I have messages, do I?"

The cat purred an acknowledgment and Jacq glanced at her answering machine. Sure enough, the light blinked with unmistakable urgency. The first six calls were from J.J., each more pressing than the last. Fortunately, Jacq had taken it into her head to go in search of a book on broad-leaved plants. She liked to make certain the background elements in her paintings were as accurate and detailed as possible. Her appearance up at the main house had spared J.J. the hassle of coming down and pounding at the front door. The last message on the tape was from her agent, raving about the sales figures on her latest children's book.

"Hello, Jack Rabbitt. Oops! Sorry, I just remembered. You don't want me leaving your pseudonym on your answering machine." Elena sighed. "I hate these stupid contraptions. I'll bet you have the phones turned off again, don't you? Anyway... I don't know what it is about elves and fairies and trolls, but your books are flying off the shelves. Those illustrations are pure magic. Hey, I have an idea. Have you ever given any thought to painting dinosaurs? They're still popular with the buying public. Or how about dragons? Can you do dragons by any chance? Just a thought.''

"Now there's a cosmic coincidence," Jacq murmured.

"Anyway, call me. Okay? *Ciao*, babe. Talk to you soon.''

Jacq grinned in satisfaction. "Pretty cool, Angel. Who'd have thought three years ago we'd make such a big splash? Bless Grandmother Lacey. If it hadn't been for her..." A momentary darkness settled on her piquant features. "She gave me back my life. Didn't she, sweetheart?''

Angelica's ears twitched and Jacq decided to take that as an agreement. Walking to the back half of the cottage with the cat at her heels, she carefully secured the door between the "public" section where she entertained the occasional visitor and the "private" area.

It was here that she became her alter ego—Jack Rabbitt—author and illustrator of some of the most popular children's books currently on the market. Three years ago the first Jack Rabbitt book had hit the stores and become an overnight sensation. Since then, her popularity had seen explosive growth. It had proved a mixed blessing. Although it provided her with the independence she so desperately craved, it also brought a notoriety she hated. So far, she'd managed to keep her identity a deep, dark secret. So far. With any luck at all, she could keep it that way for the next thirty to forty years.

Stepping into the studio, Jacq felt her tension drain away. This was the one and only place she felt truly at home. She studied her surroundings with a tiny smile. Pinned around the cavernous room were a series of sketches—every last one of them of an enormous black dragon with haunting green eyes.

"Hello, Nemesis," she whispered.

Angelica meowed plaintively, fixing the beast with a suspicious gaze.

"You're not sure about him yet, are you, sweetheart?" Jacq tilted her head to one side, contemplating her work. "Give it time. Soon, he'll be awake and breathing fire. Very soon now. And then you'll find him as attractive as I do."

At precisely six o'clock, Turk opened the massive front door to the Randell mansion. "Blackstone. I'm pleased you could make it." He offered his hand along with a hearty grin.

Mathias shook hands, lifting an eyebrow as he entered. "Did you doubt I'd come? I did arrange this meeting."

"Quite right. I just meant—" Turk cleared his throat and gestured down a long hallway. "I think you'll find the library a convenient place to discuss business. Plenty of room. We can get comfortable and answer any questions you might have about Limelight International." Taking the lead, he thrust open the first door they came to.

Mathias entered the room and glanced around. As Turk had indicated, the library had been designed for comfort while offering absolute business efficiency. An impressive array of books lined the walls while an imposing oak desk dominated one end of the room. Randell utilized the other half as a sitting area. Discreet lighting illuminated plush chairs, a couch, an extra-wide coffee table and a wet bar. The liquor cabinet stood open, glasses and bottles at the ready.

The hard sell would be accomplished there, Mathias realized with a touch of cynicism. As though to acknowledge that fact, Turk's son and youngest daughter hovered on either side of a couch, waiting for him to join them. Once seated, he'd be neatly hemmed in by Randells. His eyes narrowed in displeasure. Only one component was missing. A very small, very vital component.

Mathias turned to confront Turk. "Your entire family isn't here."

"Er, no. I expect Jacqueline will show up any moment now." Turk edged closer to the sitting area. "In the meantime, why don't we—"

"We'll wait."

With that, Mathias strolled to the bookcase and began an intent study of the contents. A whispered, distinctly agitated conversation ensued from the general direction of the sitting area. No doubt they were arguing over who would go and fetch Jacq. Before they reached their decision, a sudden flurry of activity sounded behind him. He turned in time to see Jacq breeze into the room and her family start en masse toward her. They stopped in their tracks the instant they realized how their actions might be interpreted—or misinterpreted.

"Sorry I'm late," Jacq announced casually, oblivious to the undercurrents swirling around her.

Her gaze fastened on Mathias and remained there. She studied him with the same direct intensity that he often

gave his own pursuits. It filled him with an absolute
certainty, an instinctive knowledge that the others in the
room no longer existed for her. For this brief moment
in time, he had become the center of her universe. His
eyes narrowed as he assessed his reaction. As someone
who worked hard to avoid attracting unnecessary attention, he'd never been the center of anyone's universe.
To his utter amazement, he discovered that he relished
the feeling—relished it far more than wisdom dictated.

"We haven't been introduced," he stated.

A delicious smile tilted her mouth. "No, we haven't."
She'd piled her wealth of curls on top of her head instead
of confining them at the nape of her neck. As she approached, a multitude of escaped ringlets bounced in
joyous abandonment about her slender neck and angled
cheekbones. She held out her hand, saying simply, "I'm
Jacq."

He captured her hand in his. "Mathias Blackstone."

She had strange eyes, the color quite unusual. One
moment the irises appeared sharply brown and gold before exploding with brilliant green and gray highlights.
It was as though her every thought had its own unique
color combination. Fascinating. Quite fascinating.

"Okay. I'm here," she announced. "Just out of curiosity… Would you care to tell me *why* you asked me
to come?"

He stilled, wondering if his expression revealed his
surprise at the directness of her question. Damn. He
hoped not. "I wanted to meet you," he answered just
as directly.

"Why?"

"Jacq, for crying out loud," Turk interrupted with a
groan. "Could we at least sit down and have a drink
before you start in on the man."

"But—"

"You'll have to excuse my daughter, Blackstone." He dropped a restraining hand on Jacq's shoulder. For all their slender elegance, his fingers threatened to crush the fragile bones trapped within his grasp. "She's not renowned for her tact."

For the first time in more years than he cared to remember, Mathias acted without thinking. He snatched Jacq from her father's hold and into his own sphere of influence. "Excuse us for just a minute. I'd like to speak with your daughter," he said, his voice taking on an unmistakable edge. When Turk continued to stand there, Mathias added pointedly, "Alone, if you don't mind."

"I didn't realize— I didn't mean—" With a muttered excuse, Turk crossed to the sitting area, exchanging confused glances with Cord and J.J.

"Are you all right?" Mathias asked in an undertone, brushing a gentle hand across her shoulder.

"Dad didn't mean anything by it," Jacq replied just as quietly, fixing him with a speculative look.

He understood that look. It asked why he'd interfered, why he'd reacted like a protective lover, instead of the stranger he happened to be. And the only response he could come up with was…damned if he knew. "Your father doesn't know his own strength."

She shook her head. "He'd never deliberately harm me. But he's under pressure tonight. And when that happens he sometimes forgets that I'm not built along the same proportions as Cord or J.J."

"It's time he remembered."

Inquisitiveness gave her eyes a misty gray tint. "Is that why you're here? To remind him?"

"No." He relaxed his guard enough to smile. "Would you believe I came to meet you?"

"Me?" She shook her head, laughing softly. It was a husky, full-bodied laugh, and as with everything else about her, it held irresistible appeal. "I find that hard to believe. Although as a line, it has definite potential."

"I'll work on it." He had himself back under control—a very tenuous control, true. But it should be enough to get him through this meeting. "Shall we join the others?"

She peeked around him toward the sitting area. "They are looking rather frayed around the edges," she murmured. "I hope you're planning to put them out of their misery."

"I'll be quick. I promise."

He walked with her to the couch, blocking access to the chair the Randells had left vacant for Jacq. "Shall we get started?" Mathias said. "I have a dinner engagement at seven."

"Have a seat, Blackstone," Turk said with forced heartiness. "What can I get you to drink?"

"Nothing, thanks. I won't be staying."

J.J. stirred. "Mr. Blackstone, perhaps you'd tell us why you arranged this meeting. Are you interested in utilizing Limelight's services?"

Mathias hesitated for a fraction of a second. Until this morning, he'd have been lying if he said he had someone in need of a PR firm. Fortunately, he'd been approached just today by a man who fit the bill. He'd most likely have turned the request down, too, if it hadn't provided him with the perfect excuse to approach Limelight. "I'm interested in giving Limelight a trial run," he announced.

"We're listening," Turk said, all business.

"I have a client who's starting up an investment company and needs the sort of creative publicity only a top-notch PR firm can provide. Fair warning, he's a rather particular client.''

"Particular as in difficult?" Cord asked with his father's frankness.

"Let's just say he requires special attention," Mathias replied, not in the least offended by Cord's candor. "If you're successful, I'll know your firm has the skill to handle my other business requirements." He lifted an eyebrow. "Are you interested?"

"We're interested," Turk responded. "When do we get started?"

"I'll fax you the details first thing in the morning." He spared a quick glance at his watch. "And now if you'll excuse me, I have to go. Jacq, I'd appreciate it if you'd see me out."

He could see the protest dawning in Turk's expression. Before it could find voice, Mathias snagged Jacq's elbow and walked to the door.

"We're leaving?" she asked, amused.

"We're leaving."

She didn't say anything until they reached the front door. He found that intriguing. Most women would have demanded an explanation. But not this one. Instead, she walked beside him, her gait light and easy, her expression curious yet patient. She glanced up at him and smiled. It was an open, appealing smile, filled with an electrifying vitality.

How the hell had Turk Randell fathered such a changeling? he couldn't help but wonder.

At the front door, she hesitated. "Considering what I know of your personality—which I confess isn't all that much—I have to assume you had a reason for asking me to show you out."

"Yes."

She tilted her head to one side. "Care to clue me in?"

"Would you have dinner with me?"

She blinked in astonishment. "Dinner."

"That's the meal you consume at the end of the day," he explained gravely. "Sometimes two people will share the meal. Are you familiar with the custom?"

Humor flickered within her gaze. "Somewhat. When did you have in mind?"

"Now."

"But you told my father—" Comprehension dawned and she laughed. "Sorry to be so slow. You caught me off guard."

It would be easy to get used to the sound of that laugh, he decided. All too easy. "You haven't answered my question. Will you join me for dinner?"

She took a moment to consider, studying him with a disconcerting intensity. "Is this a business dinner or personal?"

"I imagine it could go either way," he answered honestly. "Which would you prefer?"

"I'm not sure." A new array of colors sparkled within her eyes, shades Mathias had begun to associate with the more mischievous aspects of her personality. As though to confirm his suspicion, she pulled open the door and caught his arm in hers. "Why don't we find out?"

"Well I'll be a son of a—" Turk allowed the heavy drape to fall closed. "Seems you were right, J.J."

She smiled dispassionately. "Of course I was right."

"Walked off with the girl like he owned her." Turk's brows drew together as he analyzed the possible ramifications. "So now we know what *he* wants. But what about her? Never could figure out Jacq's thinking on anything."

"She went with him, didn't she?" Cord inserted. "She wouldn't do that unless she wanted to."

"Unfortunately, we can't count on that lasting," J.J. said. "You know Jacq."

The three fell into an unhappy silence, recognizing J.J.'s remark as an indisputable fact.

"So what now?" Cord asked.

"Now we treat Jacq the same way we would an un-cooperative business associate," Turk replied grimly.

J.J.'s expression cooled. She didn't like the sound of this one little bit. "You can't be suggesting blackmail."

Her father winced. "You always were far too blunt, J.J. I prefer to think of it as...persuasion. Gentle persuasion, if possible. We find a way to convince her to go along with our plans. Explain the advantages to her."

Cord snorted. "Yeah, right. Knowing Jacq, I'm sure that'll work."

Turk acknowledged his son's sarcasm with a chilly smile. "Oh, it'll work."

"How?" J.J. demanded. "If we tell her to turn left, she'll choose every direction except left. She's totally unpredictable. She doesn't even do the opposite of what we ask. She just does something different."

"There's no point in trying to second guess her," Turk agreed. "There's only one way to deal with Jacq."

"Which is?" J.J. asked apprehensively.

"We find the right angle."

"What do you mean, 'the right angle'?"

Annoyance flashed in Turk's dark eyes. "Don't be obtuse. You know what I mean. Everyone has a weakness. We just need to find Jacq's."

"Then you are talking about blackmail."

"Fine," Turk snapped, slamming his fist on the liquor cabinet. The bottles and glasses clattered discordantly.

"I'm talking about blackmail. I'm talking about finding out what she's been up to for the past three and a half years. Cord, you do the background check."

"No problem."

"J.J., I want to know her strengths and weaknesses, particularly her weaknesses. Her vulnerabilities. I want anything we can use to make her see the advantages of continuing a relationship with Blackstone."

"Dad—"

"I don't want to hear it," Turk interrupted coldly. "I don't like forcing her hand any better than you. But we don't have a choice. Do I have to remind you how much is at stake?"

"No, but—"

Turk cut her off again. "You're worrying about nothing. Jacq wouldn't have gone with Blackstone if she wasn't interested. All I'm asking is she stay interested long enough for us to strike a deal with the man." His tone turned aggrieved. "Is that so much to ask?"

"For some." J.J. turned away, wrapping her arms around her waist. "For some, it's asking the impossible."

CHAPTER TWO

"SO, WHERE are we going?" Jacq asked as they walked out the front door.

"To the home of an acquaintance." Mathias hesitated on the doorstep. "It's not far from here, but you might want to bring a coat."

She shook her head, not in the least concerned. It wasn't her coat she'd miss, but her satchel of paints. She rarely went anywhere without them, though it looked like tonight she'd be forced to make an exception. "I'd have to go back to my place to get my coat and I don't feel like taking the time," she said. Nor did she feel like running the risk of being bushwhacked by Limelighters.

"Your place? You don't live…?" He indicated the house behind them with a jerk of his head.

"No. I live in a little cottage at the far end of the property right on the lake. It used to be a garage. Then it was the caretaker's quarters." Satisfaction edged her voice. "Now it's mine."

"No purse. No coat." A hint of a frown touched his brow. "I didn't mean to rush you. I can wait while you get them."

"My sweater is wool, so I should be warm enough. I'll ask if I need anything else." She dismissed the mundane subject with an easy shrug and turned to one of far greater importance. "So, don't keep me in suspense. Who are these friends? Where do they live?"

He slanted her an amused glance as they followed a

sidewalk that wove an erratic path to the driveway. "You mean, what are they serving for dinner?"

She grinned, unabashed. "Did you hear my stomach growling? I'm starving! I can't remember when I last ate." She tilted her head to one side, considering. "Not only don't I remember when, I can't even remember what the meal consisted of."

"The when, I suspect, was Turk's reception last night. As to the what... You had half a dozen shrimp, crab dip and crackers, cheese and a handful of those little round green things. I won't mention the relish tray you nabbed on your way out."

She stared in astonishment. "How in the world do you know all that?"

"I'm observant."

"Now there's an understatement," she muttered. *He'd been watching her*! While she'd been watching her relatives watch him, he'd been... Her sense of the ridiculous caught up with her and she gave a light laugh. "I guess it would have been more socially acceptable to nibble." Her voice turned wistful. "But I was awfully hungry."

"Don't they feed you?"

"I'm supposed to be able to feed myself."

"But you get preoccupied and forget." It wasn't a question.

"How did you—" She held up her hands. "Never mind. I don't want to know. Some questions are best left unanswered and I suspect this is one of them."

"It's no great mystery. I put together a few facts based on observation and came up with—"

"An inspired guess?"

"An educated supposition," he corrected gently. "I don't guess."

"That's what J.J. said," Jacq admitted. "But I thought maybe she was exaggerating."

"Not in this case."

"Oh. Well. Never mind. I won't hold it against you." She smiled brightly. "About tonight…"

He took both her comment and the change in subject in stride. "I never did answer your questions, did I? You wanted to know about my friends. I've been invited to a small dinner party and hoped you'd accompany me."

"I see." Understanding dawned, taking the edge off her enthusiasm. "You need a date."

He stopped in the middle of the walkway and removed his coat. "I don't *need* a date," he informed her, draping the heavy black wool about her shoulders. He gathered the edges of the collar beneath her chin and waited until her gaze flickered reluctantly upward to meet his. "I invited you because I wanted to."

She was instantly captivated by his translucent green eyes. They were like flaming ice, came the bewildered realization, possessing the uncanny ability to freeze and scorch at the same time. She'd never seen anything like it before. "Why?" she couldn't help asking, snuggling into the folds of his jacket. It was deliciously soft, enfolding her in unrelenting masculine warmth. "Why did you invite me?"

"Because you're different from the rest of your family. And that difference intrigues me." He released her with notable reluctance and gestured toward the black Jaguar parked at the top of the circular driveway. It crouched beneath the protective embrace of an immense oak, looking sleek and fast and decidedly lethal. "Will you come with me?"

The words were innocuous enough. And yet she felt the dragon in him stirring, awakening before her very eyes. The change captivated her, her curiosity becoming an irresistible impetus. She could either enter the predator's domain or run for the safety of her snug little cottage. The choice was hers.

There was no point in pretending which she'd select. "Okay." He smiled at her response—a smile of genuine pleasure—and Jacq had the inexplicable impression that it had been a long time since he'd allowed himself that particular luxury. "I'll come."

"I'm glad," he replied.

His Jag gave a little chirp of welcome as he deactivated the alarm system and she halted beside the car, shaking her head. "I should have known. I really should have."

He lifted an eyebrow. "Excuse me?"

"I just realized. Your car. Your clothes. Everything's black."

He opened the passenger door. "It's a comfortable color for me."

Interesting. It would appear that this particular dragon preferred life in the shadows rather than basking in the sunshine. For some reason the knowledge saddened her. "I'll have to see what I can do about that," she informed him as she lowered herself into the low-slung seat.

"Don't bother. I'm satisfied with my life as it is."

Shutting the door to punctuate his comment, he circled the car and climbed in. With a quick flick of his wrist, he turned the key in the ignition. The Jag awoke with a throaty roar, before relaxing into a steady purr. Jacq studied Mathias in silence as they zipped down the driveway. He maneuvered the car with exquisite precision, every movement graceful and specific and economical. As usual, J.J.'s assessment of the man had been right on target. He was a creature whose world consisted of only black and white, who saw life in uncompromising terms of absolutes.

Up or down. Right or left. Yes or no. No exception to the rules.

"What are you thinking?" he asked unexpectedly.

Jacq decided to give him an honest, if blunt, response. "I'm thinking that I'm glad I'm me. I like my world to have colors in it."

She'd caught him off guard. "You think because I prefer black that my world lacks color?" he asked after a moment's consideration.

"Yes." She touched his arm, surprised when the muscles bunched beneath her fingers. "Oh, it's not just the fact that you like black. Black is an excellent color. I'm quite fond of it, myself." Especially for unruly dragons, she added the silent addendum.

"I'm relieved to hear it."

"But I'm afraid it suggests a certain rigidness of character."

"Rigid." His eyes narrowed and she began to wonder if she'd been a little too blunt. "And you prefer someone who's more... What?"

"Someone who's more spontaneous," she readily admitted.

"Inviting you out to dinner wasn't spontaneous enough for you?" he asked dryly.

"Ah, but was it? A spur-of-the-moment decision, I mean."

His frown deepened. "It was last night when I thought of it."

She regarded him in surprise. "You decided to invite me out then?"

"Yes."

Another possibility occurred to her. "Is that why you

arranged the meeting tonight with Turk? Why you insisted that the entire family be there?''

''Yes,'' he said again.

She couldn't quite believe it. ''You did all that just so you could ask me out?'' she demanded in astonishment.

''Sorry,'' he offered in a suspiciously humble voice. ''Considering my limited imagination, it was the best I could come up with on such short notice.''

She decided to take his comments seriously. ''That's okay. It was a sweet gesture. But now there's a problem.''

''Somehow, that doesn't surprise me. What sort of problem?''

''My father expects to do business with you. You can't very well tell him that the whole point of tonight's meeting was so you could ask me out.''

His gaze flickered briefly in her direction before returning to the winding road ahead. ''Will it offend you if I admit that the meeting this evening gave me an opportunity to address two separate issues? One business and the other personal. This investment company I mentioned needs a PR firm to help launch them in the community. If I put your father's firm together with King Investments, it will give Limelight a chance to prove themselves to my satisfaction while affording King the publicity they need to get off the ground.''

She sighed, vaguely disappointed. ''I see. You were killing two birds with one stone.''

He hit third gear with less than his normal precision. ''That's not quite how I'd have phrased it, but yes. The arrangements I made with Turk last night allowed me to have a preliminary meeting with Limelight. At the same time I could invite you out.''

"An economy of effort," she said in perfect under-standing. "Quite like you." She thought she heard him curse beneath his breath, but when she glanced in his direction, his expression remained blandly polite. "I don't suppose you've ever heard of a telephone?"

"Of course I have." His gaze flashed in her direction once again and she caught a fleeting glimpse of irony reflected there. "But in order to conduct a conversation, the other party has to have their phone plugged in."

Her mouth literally fell open. "How did you know that I keep it unplugged?"

"It's amazing what you can learn with a little re-search."

She fought off a feeling of unease. "That must be one heck of a research department you have," she muttered. Which brought up another question. "I never thought to ask J.J. what you did or why you need Limelight's help. She only mentioned that Turk's been trying to attract your attention for the last couple of years."

He lifted an eyebrow in response to that nugget of information, but didn't pursue it. "You don't know what I do for a living?" he asked instead.

"No." Jacq shrugged, feeling obligated to add, "Since I don't work for the company, I'm not up on all the pertinent details."

"But you used to work for them, didn't you?"

Her mouth compressed. "Briefly." She heard the clipped quality enter her voice, but couldn't help it. "Very briefly."

"What was your specialty?"

She shook her head, refusing to answer. "My turn. You still haven't said what you do for a living."

He turned into a narrow driveway that opened onto a sprawling estate. A dozen or so expensive foreign cars were parked close to the pillared front porch. Mathias found an open spot beneath a huge apple tree and pulled in, shutting off the engine.

"Well?" Jacq prompted impatiently. "Are you going to tell me or is it a deep, dark secret?"

"No secret. I'm a... I guess you could call me a procurer."

Releasing her seat belt, she swiveled to face him, staring in disbelief. "A *procurer*? Like a... A... You're kidding, right?"

"Nope. I'm dead serious."

She regarded him suspiciously. It couldn't be what she was thinking. Not her dragon. He wouldn't do anything so unethical. "Okay... Would you care to tell me what, precisely, you procure? Or is that a question you'd prefer I not ask?"

He relaxed into the leather seat, clearly at home in the darkness. "You have the most revealing eyes of anyone I've ever met," he commented reflectively. "You think I'm a white slaver or an international jewel thief, don't you?"

She squirmed beneath his unblinking gaze. "If it makes you feel any better, I almost immediately realized that you wouldn't do anything so awful," she confessed.

"You realized that, did you? After less than an hour's acquaintance you know me so well? Mind if I ask how you came to that conclusion?"

"It's because you're—"

He held up a hand, cutting her off. "Forget it. I suspect it has to do with colors again, doesn't it?"

"Well, yes. As a matter of fact, it does. I suspect your ethics are as well-defined as everything else in your life." She hoped he'd find the word "well-defined" a tactful alternative to "rigid." "But you did have me going for a minute there. The term 'procurer' does have a suggestive ring to it.''

"It's a fanciful word for a mundane job," he admitted with a smile. "I suppose I like it because it evokes a much more interesting response than when I say I'm a middleman.''

"A middleman, huh? And what is it you're in the middle of, exactly?''

"I don't have a specialty. People come to me because they're having difficulty obtaining something they want or need. I get it for them. It's as simple as that.''

"Somehow I doubt it is.''

"It can be a challenge at times," was all he'd concede.

"But you've never failed to meet that challenge, have you?'' she guessed shrewdly. "You've always succeeded in your various procurements.''

He hesitated before responding. "Since I started the business, I've never failed.''

Something in the way he phrased his response gave her pause. But she was too interested in learning more to dwell on it. "What sort of things do you procure?''

"Anything a person desires, so long as it's legal and ethical.''

"And who determines whether or not it's ethical?''

"I do.''

"Ah. That black-and-white quality of yours.'' A sudden thought occurred to her and she frowned. "And Limelight International? I can't quite see you pursuing the sort of media attention Turk specializes in. How do they fit into the picture?''

"Sometimes there's no alternative.''

"In which case Limelight is a necessary evil?'' she

inquired delicately. "If there's no other way to get what you want, you'd use Turk's services?"

His smile flashed in the darkness. "I have the occasional need for a public relations firm, either for a client or for my own personal use. Since I have a large client base, it could mean a lot of business for your family."

"You have regular customers?" She found that surprising. "I wouldn't have thought yours a profession that would get repeat business."

"There are quite a few corporations I assist on a regular business. Either they're looking for a specific type of person to employ, or they're after a product or service that's not readily available."

She thought about it for a moment. Thought about all the possibilities for a man with Mathias's abilities. She'd been woefully shortsighted. There had to be a thousand different people with a thousand different requests who would pay a fortune to obtain that one item they lacked. She gazed at him with new understanding. "You have to turn away business, don't you?"

"Yes," he said simply.

"And tonight? Let me guess… You're here to make a procurement, right?"

He stiffened and she realized she'd made a lucky hit based on wild speculation. "Very clever, Jacq."

She lowered her gaze in the hopes of concealing her disillusionment. "So who or what are you procuring?"

He leaned closer, snagging one of the curls brushing her temple. It wrapped around his finger with all the determination of a fast-growing vine. "Let's set the record straight, shall we? First, I invited you out tonight because I wanted to. It had nothing to do with Limelight. Nor did it have anything to do with this evening's procurement. And second, I'm obligated to attend this party.

I brought you along because it would make the occasion more enjoyable. Selfish, but true."

"Still… You're killing two birds with one stone again."

He sighed. "I can see that's a practice you don't appreciate. I'll make sure it doesn't happen again."

"Don't worry about it."

"Polite reply, though painfully stilted." He waited a beat, then asked, "What's wrong, Jacq?"

She took a deep breath. "I don't like mixing work and pleasure." She shot him a cool, direct look. "In particular, I dislike mixing Limelight business with a personal relationship. If you're using me to get information about my family, I'd rather you be frank about it. I'll tell you what you want to know, since they have nothing to hide. But don't lie to me about what you're after."

"Fair enough." He shifted closer, his eyes like flaming chips of green ice. "The truth is this… I don't give a damn about Limelight International. Any PR firm can handle the sort of business I plan to send their way, so long as they're ethical. Approaching Turk was the easiest way to get at you. Is that frank enough?"

It took a full minute to realize she was holding her breath. She released it on a ragged sigh. "Yes. That's frank enough for me."

"I could have had Turk come to my office. But since you don't work for him, I would have lost the opportunity to obtain an introduction."

"There were other ways to arrange a meeting," she reminded him.

"Such as phoning. We've already discussed why that wouldn't have worked." His thumb brushed the arch of her cheek, eliciting a helpless shiver. "This was the way that occurred to me, so it's the one I chose. Still frank enough?''

"Absolutely." If anything, he'd become too frank. As much as she wanted to pull away and end the conversation, the curl he'd snagged held her anchored to within inches of him.

"And finally, I didn't invite you tonight because I needed a date. Nor did I invite you because you'd provide a convenient 'cover' to hide my activities. If anything you're going to be one hell of a distraction. I invited you because I was too damned impatient to wait for a more convenient time. I wanted to get to know you right away.''

"J.J. says you never act without examining all the angles," she protested helplessly.

His gaze took fire. "I *have* examined all the angles. Every last one of them. And now I'm acting.''

"*Why*?" Bewilderment clouded her eyes. "Why me?''

"It's real simple, sweetheart. From the minute I saw you I wanted you. I've never experienced such an immediate attraction before. So instead of taking it slow, finding a more traditional means of approach, I came after you as hard and fast as I could.''

It was too much, too soon. She scrambled for a way to change the subject. "Tell me what you're hoping to procure tonight. Maybe I can help.''

"Now you want to help?" He released her curl with great care and eased back against his seat. "A minute ago you refused to mix business with pleasure.''

"Oh. Well, that was my business we couldn't mix. Your business is fine with me." His confused expression almost made her laugh. Confusion looked good on him, she decided. It devastated his self-control and allowed her a tantalizing peek at the man behind the mask. ''I mean... I don't mind helping if it doesn't have anything to do with me. So what are you after?''

He recovered his composure with amazing speed. ''I'm here to procure information about our hostess, Lynn Davenport.''

Instantly intrigued, Jacq asked, ''What sort of information do you hope to obtain?''

He hesitated. ''I'd like to get a fix on her personality. What type of woman is she? Is she content? What are her hopes, her dreams and aspirations?''

''That's expecting a lot from a simple meeting over the dinner table,'' Jacq advised him dryly. ''How do you plan to get all that out of her in one short evening of conversation?''

''That's easy. I'll talk to her until I have the facts I need.''

''You're going to sit down and grill her? That's your plan?'' She shook her head in disgust. ''How long did you say you've been doing this?''

His smile glimmered in the darkness and it gave her a surge of satisfaction. She had the distinct impression that there weren't many individuals who managed to win a smile from him. And she'd captured several already. It showed definite promise.

''You have a better idea?'' he questioned idly.

''Maybe. Just how spontaneous are you, Mathias Blackstone?''

''Ah... A challenge. I never could resist a challenge.''

''That's good to know. But you still haven't answered my question.''

''Why don't you try me and see how spontaneous I am.''

"I was hoping you'd say that." She offered a mischievous grin. "Do the Davenports know you well?"

He shook his head. "I helped her husband with a minor transaction last month. I suppose this invitation is his way of saying thank-you."

"Interesting coincidence that his wife is now the object of a procurement."

"It isn't a coincidence."

She blinked. "You... You helped Mr. Davenport in order to get at his wife?"

"Not to get at her," he corrected calmly. "It was so I could get to know her. And yes, I helped Mel obtain something he's wanted for a long time. A fair exchange, in my opinion. Now, if everything goes well, I'll do the same for my client, and possibly for Lynn Davenport, as well."

"This information you need... It won't hurt her, will it?" Jacq asked uneasily. "I mean, this *is* for a good cause, right?"

"It's for a very good cause."

She took a split second to decide. There was a gentle reassurance in his tone and a steadiness in his gaze that helped persuade her. Whatever this procurement involved, he'd make sure it didn't harm anyone. She gave a determined nod. "In that case, let's go have some fun." She opened the car door, calling over her shoulder, "Follow my lead. Okay?"

He almost laughed aloud and it was in that precise moment that Mathias realized he didn't want Jacq Randell for his client. He wanted her for himself. He wanted her with an intensity he'd never experienced with another woman, not even his former wife.

She paused in the middle of the walkway. "Are you coming?"

Curious to see what she intended, Mathias climbed from the car and followed. She still wore his jacket. In fact, it swamped her slender figure. Her brightly patterned skirt billowing out from underneath, flicking at him like a beckoning hand. She walked toward the front door with a purposeful step. He liked that, liked even more the way her brown and gold streaked curls bounced in rhythm with her stride.

One of these days he'd free those curls so they could spill across her creamy shoulders to the tender slopes of her breasts as nature intended. Then he'd lower her onto his bed and watch her hair tumble in glorious abandonment across the sheets. And finally he'd sink his fingers deep into those soft, vibrant curls at the same moment he sank himself deep into her soft, vibrant feminine warmth.

There was only one stumbling block. He suspected Jacq would prove a difficult woman to woo to bed. Her eyes reflected an intense wariness. She'd been burned at some point. Badly. And of course, there was that other matter to resolve. Once he'd proven to his satisfaction that Jacq Randell and Jack Rabbitt were one and the same, he'd have to deal with the problems that would create. But he'd find a way. Until then, he'd have to exercise both patience and delicacy.

Without a doubt, it would take a full measure of both to procure this particular woman.

CHAPTER THREE

THE minute Jacq stepped foot inside the Davenports', she knew she'd found a friend. Walking into Lynn Davenport's home was like viewing the woman's heart and soul. Jacq's first impression of the house was of elegance and warmth accented with a subtle blend of delicate colors. Next she noticed the natural-fibered rugs and furniture. Christmas decorations had made their appearance already, overrunning the place and proclaiming to the world that the Davenports thoroughly enjoyed the season. And even though it was December, fresh cut flowers filled a nearby vase.

Lynn had done the arrangement herself, Jacq would have bet on it. The blossoms hadn't been chosen to fit the decor, but rather because they were favored flowers. There was an artless grace to the display, an eclectic blending of colors and scents.

No question. Mathias had found himself a winner with this couple.

Mel Davenport, a large, gruff man at least ten years older than his late-thirties wife, introduced himself. "Mathias said he might bring a guest. Glad to have you join us."

Jacq held out her hand. "I'm Jacq Randell. You really don't mind that I tagged along? You see..." She beamed. "We just got engaged today."

Beside her, Mathias choked.

"Congratulations, you old son of a gun," Mel said, thudding Mathias on the back. "You sure are a deep one. Never gave a hint you were on the verge of marriage.''

''It was very sudden,'' Mathias replied in a masterpiece of understatement.

''Well, it's a lovely surprise,'' Lynn responded with a warm smile.

Jacq peeked up at Mathias. ''But a pleasant surprise, right, sweetheart?''

He wrapped an arm around her and growled into her ear, ''I'll show you how pleasant later tonight, darling.''

Lynn laughed at the byplay. ''Mathias Blackstone, you're every bit as wicked as Mel. He's a tease, too.''

Jacq snuggled against Mathias, amazed that she felt secure enough to do so. This man had the oddest effect on her. ''Just look at how they've decorated,'' she said, changing the subject to one of far greater importance. ''They have colors.''

Mathias sighed.

''You've done a wonderful job,'' Jacq chattered on to their hostess. ''I'm serious. It's quite beautiful.''

''Thank—''

''You didn't use a professional decorator, did you?''

''Jacq—'' Mathias muttered in warning.

She slanted him a puzzled look. ''Was I being rude? I meant it as a compliment. The colors, the furnishings, the flowers. Even the balance and flow of the room. It isn't just a setting. Haven't you realized?'' She gave him a sharp elbow to the ribs so he'd pay attention. Men could be so obtuse at times. The full spectrum of Lynn Davenport's personality was on display and he hadn't even noticed! ''Mathias, this house is an extension of a real, live person. To put it simply, it's Lynn.''

Mel Davenport spoke up. ''You're quite right. Lynn decorated the place without a lick of outside advice.''

He wrapped a loving arm around his wife. "Even when I'm alone in the house, her presence is all around me. It's a wonderful feeling."

Lynn positively glowed at the praise, the glance she shared with her husband sizzling the air. "I had no idea you thought that."

"Well, now you do. So don't you dare change a thing."

"I wouldn't dream of it. Not after such an effusive compliment."

Davenport turned his attention to Mathias. "I like your fiancée, Blackstone," he said. "She's a sharp cookie."

"Very sharp," Mathias agreed dryly, rubbing his bruised ribs. "She certainly keeps me jumping."

Davenport chuckled. "Now that I believe. Come on in and let me introduce you two around."

Jacq soon discovered that the Davenports' friends were an eclectic bunch and she found the next several hours a sheer delight. The major disadvantage with her current profession was how little time it afforded her to interact with others. She'd turned into a hermit, she realized in disgust. She'd allowed the unfortunate events of four years ago to change her view of the world and the people in it.

Well, tonight she'd escape her self-imposed prison and enjoy herself. By helping Mathias, perhaps she could help herself.

Perhaps she could learn to trust again.

"I'm starving!" Jacq announced with such undisguised enthusiasm that everyone at the table laughed in appreciation.

Mathias leaned back in his chair, content to simply

observe his "fiancée" in action. The Davenports and their guests had been kept amused all night—either by Jacq or by her outrageous stories or in response to one of her rapid-fire comebacks. Tonight had certainly been a revelation.

He wasn't quite sure what he'd expected—perhaps a more feminine version of Turk's bulldog nature. Instead he'd discovered an open, vibrant, exciting woman who took exquisite delight in the ridiculous. What she didn't realize was where her sense of the ridiculous would land her.

So they were engaged now, were they? He lifted his wineglass and studied her over the rim. Her impetuous announcement had not only sealed her fate, but would bring about an interesting—if inevitable—conclusion to her little game. Only one aspect of the entire situation surprised him—the conclusion he had in mind would occur far sooner than he'd envisioned.

He'd first become attracted to Jacq during his weeks of research. All the bits and pieces of information he'd gathered had added up to a very intriguing whole. The more he'd learned, the more he'd anticipated their eventual meeting. And then he'd attended the Limelight reception. From the moment he'd set eyes on Jacq, he'd known their paths were destined to merge. They'd just hit that juncture months ahead of schedule.

So much for meticulous planning.

He'd always thought he'd take his time weighing the pros and cons before taking another wife. After all, it was his nature to carefully analyze each move before acting. But with Jacq... He buried his smile in his wineglass. He'd simply known. Even with all the darkness shadowing his heart and soul, he'd still known. He'd taken one look at her and realized she was the only woman in the world capable of returning color to his bleak world.

"My goodness," Lynn said unexpectedly. "You're not wearing an engagement ring, Jacq. You didn't lose it, did you?"

Mathias glanced at his adorable bride-to-be, curious to see how she'd handle this one. Not that he need have worried.

"Oh, it didn't fit," she said blithely. "Mathias has to have it sized so it doesn't fall off in my soup."

"What a shame," Lynn sympathized. "I'd love to have seen it. Is it a diamond?"

Jacq peeked over at Mathias, her eyes bright with mischief. "It's not a traditional sort of ring at all. It's very unusual."

"For you, my dear, it would have to be," Mel said, lifting his glass in a salute.

"Don't keep us in suspense," another guest exclaimed. "Tell us what it looks like."

"It's a gold band fashioned into a dragon," Jacq said with an odd little smile. "And the tail wraps around my finger all the way to the knuckle."

"A dragon? That is unusual," Lynn commented. "I assume you collect them?"

"Oh, yes." Jacq's gaze fastened on Mathias. "It's a recent obsession. And this one is a particularly stunning piece of artwork. You see, he's clutching a heart-shaped ruby in his claws. And the eyes! They're the finest pair of emeralds I've ever seen."

"It sounds gorgeous." Lynn turned impulsively to Mathias. "You'll have to get it sized as soon as possible so Jacq can show it off the next time you come."

"I'll do my best," he replied. "But I rather the jew-

eler not rush. I wouldn't want him to botch the job because he's in too much of a hurry.''

"Oh, dear,'' Jacq piped up. "In that case, maybe you
shouldn't bother having it sized. I wouldn't want it
ruined. I could just wear the ring the way it is.'' She
waggled the fingers of her left hand at him, laughter
rippling through her voice. "Why don't I go ahead and
try?''

"That's what you said when I first gave you the
ring,'' he retorted blandly. "You didn't allow me a minute's peace until I gave in. Do I need to remind you
what happened then?''

Jacq cupped her chin in her hand. "Oh, yes, please!
Tell me what happened.''

Mel burst out laughing. "You act like you don't
know.''

She gave an abashed smile. "I just want Mathias to
have the opportunity to rub it in.''

Mathias inclined his head. "Very kind of you, my
love.''

"Well? Go ahead and say it.'' she prompted.

"Say what? I told you so?''

"It's only fair that I let him give me a hard time about
it,'' she supplied for the benefit of their audience, "because the ring fell off, just like he'd warned.''

"I have no intention of rubbing it in,'' he protested.
"That would be far too cruel…and far too easy.''

She chuckled. "True enough. You're very good to
me, I'm the first to admit. That's why I'll let you tell
everyone what happened after that.'' She looked at him,
her gaze full of anticipation, eagerly waiting to see
where he'd take the story next.

"We then spent a full hour searching my apartment

because I allowed sentiment to overrule common sense," he responded promptly.

She wrinkled her nose at him. "I'll bet *that* doesn't happen often."

"Only around you," he assured with complete sincerity. "If I hadn't thought to move the headboard away from the wall, I doubt we'd ever have found the damned thing."

She smiled sweetly. "That's what you get for trying to be creative. Next time don't tie me to the headboard and maybe I won't lose my ring behind the bed."

"Mmm. We could have used the ceiling hook and handcuffs, but they pinch. My wrists are still sore from our last go-round."

Jacq dismissed his comment with a wave of her hand. "That's just because you left them on too long. If you hadn't misplaced the key—"

"*I* didn't misplace it!"

"—it wouldn't have been nearly so painful." She heaved an exaggerated sigh. "Not that I'd want to go through all that again. I don't know why you couldn't have called a locksmith instead of bothering the police with our little predicament."

Mathias struggled to look suitably contrite. "Sorry, darling. My big toe couldn't manage more than 9-1-1."

Lynn stared from one to the other, openmouthed. Then she began to giggle. "Oh, you two! You're pulling our legs, aren't you?"

"Well... Maybe a little," Mathias conceded. "To be honest, we don't use handcuffs."

"Not anymore. They really do pinch," Jacq added irrepressibly.

"Have you set a date, yet?" Mel demanded once the laughter had died.

"Mathias insists on next Thursday," Jacq said, helping herself to another roll.

Mathias smiled in appreciation. Damn, she was quick. With one crazy conversation, she'd painted a fantasy life he craved to turn into reality. "*You* said Thursday, darling," he corrected. "If you'll recall, *I* said Christmas."

Her brows drew together and she paused in the middle of buttering her roll. "Not next Thursday? I could have sworn you said Thursday."

"Christmas *is* a Thursday. That's why we decided it would be more romantic if we waited until then. That way we could have the first baby by Halloween."

To his utter satisfaction, she choked on her roll.

He gave her a look of exaggerated concern. "You did say you wanted to start a family right away, didn't you?" To the table at large, he announced, "She'd like an even half dozen."

"Two," she hastened to correct.

"We'll compromise. Four."

Jacq's mouth curved upward and her hazel eyes gathered in the light, reflecting bits of sunny gold and rich brown and misty gray. "I give up. Four it is. But at least two of them have to be girls."

"Never fear. We'll just keep at it until you have your two girls." He offered a slow, teasing smile. "Even if it takes a dozen boys to get them."

Her laughter rang out, irresistible and thoroughly charming. "All right, all right. I give up. I'll take the first four I'm given. Just so long as they're happy and healthy, I don't care."

A fierce sense of possessiveness took hold, one Mathias couldn't control—one he had no desire to control. He saw an image of Jacq, large with his child, saw little girls with mops of blond-streaked curls and boys with bright hazel eyes. And though he waited, knowing the bitter consequences of chasing such an impossible dream, the darkness didn't come. With that one simple laugh, she banished the shadows, holding the terrible nightmares temporarily at bay.

There was no longer any question.

She was meant to be his.

Mathias caught hold of Jacq's hand and pulled her down beside him on the couch. To his private amusement, she nestled into his embrace as though they really were an engaged couple. Matters were progressing nicely on all fronts, he decided. But then, he'd found that careful planning usually guaranteed excellent results.

"What are you looking so smug about?" she asked suspiciously.

"I'm being thoughtful, not smug," he replied, deciding to avoid the truth at all costs and thus prevent a temporary setback to his master plan. He doubted "Miss Spontaneity" would appreciate the effort he'd expended in order to carry off this little dinner engagement. "How do you think the evening's going?"

She glanced toward the Davenports and their guests, all of whom were grouped around the painting Mathias had "procured" for Mel last month. "I like them," she replied, carefully sidestepping a direct answer. Not that he let her get away with it.

"So do I. But that isn't what I meant. What's your impression of Lynn?"

"She's wonderful. Gracious, charming, genuine."

"And…" he prompted.

"And shy. She's been hurt at some point in the past."

Mathias lifted an eyebrow. "What gives you that impression?"

"Two things. There's a certain wariness about the eyes. A bit of hesitation in the way she answers questions. And then there's Mel."

"What about him?"

"Haven't you noticed?" She shifted closer and Mathias obligingly lowered his head so she could whisper in his ear. He took full advantage of the opportunity to align her more firmly against him. Soft feminine curves calibrated precisely with hard masculine angles. The fit was sheer perfection. "See how protective he is?" she said.

"Of course he's protective. She's his woman."

"Oh, for—"

Her curls quivered in response to her exasperation, brushing the side of his face and branding him with silken fire. He gritted his teeth against the sensuous abrasion. What the hell had happened to his self-control? One touch from a pint-size sprite and it evaporated like desert dew. More than anything, he wanted to palm that stubborn little chin and kiss her senseless. It took every ounce of inner resolve to resist the temptation. This was neither the time nor the place. Although he'd better find that time and place—and soon.

"Isn't that what you meant?" he asked with remarkable calm for a man in his condition. "He's not being protective because she's his woman?"

"Yes. No!" She let out an aggrieved sigh. "For your information, I'm talking about something a little more refined than caveman etiquette."

His eyebrows winged upward. "Caveman etiquette?"

"You know what I mean." Her index finger thumped against his chest. "You, Tarzan. Me, Jane. Jane belong to Tarzan. Whack Jane on the head with a club and drag her off to the cave. Get it? Caveman etiquette."

"Um... Didn't Tarzan live in a tree?"

Her warm breath exploded against his ear, nearly taking the top of his head off. It was all he could do not to grab his enchanting fiancée by her curly topknot and make a beeline for the nearest cave. Or tree. Or bed.

"Will you be serious?" she demanded irritably.

"I am always serious," he said, perfectly serious.

"Oh, very funny." Before he could give her a personal demonstration of the level of his seriousness, she inclined her head toward the far side of the room. "Now pay attention and look at Mel. See how he's standing? And did you catch that look? It's more than a natural protectiveness. It's like she's a delicate piece of crystal that might shatter if touched."

Mathias frowned, becoming instantly focused. Damned if she wasn't right. "Was he like that earlier?"

Jacq's brows drew together. "You know..." she said slowly. "I don't think he was. I mean, he was. But not quite to this extent."

"Wonder what set him off?"

"Mathias?" She gazed up at him uneasily. "This procurement of yours. You're positive it's nothing that will harm Lynn? I like her."

"So do I, honey."

"No, I mean, I *really* like her. She's sweet and kind and nice. I haven't known a lot of people like that."

"Haven't you?" His eyes narrowed and he felt a renewed surge of caveman etiquette. Only this time, it had little to do with lust. Unless it was blood lust. "I'm real sorry to hear that. You'll have to tell me about it sometime."

"Too long and boring a story," she retorted crisply. And far too private, her expression clearly said. "Let's concentrate on Lynn. I'd feel just awful if we did something to hurt her.''

We. Damn, that sounded good. Did she even realize that she'd subconsciously paired them, that she openly referred to them as a team? ''We won't hurt her. That's why we're taking this approach. So we can get a feel for the situation.''

''Well, you'd better be right about that. Because I'm not the only one who'll kill you if you cause her any harm.'' Her gaze switched to their host. ''Mel will rend you limb from limb.''

''Then I'll have to be careful, won't I?'' he replied calmly.

Jacq bit down on her lip. ''*We'll* have to be careful.''

At that, Mathias allowed himself another brief smile of satisfaction.

Jacq nabbed Mathias's coat and stepped through the French doors onto the Davenports's deck. The chilly night air warned of a coming frost and she pulled the heavy wool more tightly about her. The evening was going well, she decided. Since her conversation with Mathias, she'd learned all sorts of fascinating details about both Davenports. With luck, it would help.

A small noise warned Jacq that she wasn't alone. Catching sight of a splash of pale peach at the far end of the deck, she called out, ''Lynn? Is that you?''

Lynn swiveled to face her, offering a smile that seemed a bit too bright and cheery. ''It was such a beautiful evening, I thought I'd look at the stars.''

''If it weren't for the clouds, they'd be beautiful,'' Jacq concurred.

''Oh.'' Lynn's smile faltered. ''I guess you caught me.''

"Is there something wrong?" Jacq questioned gently. "Perhaps it would help to talk."

"I…I don't want to burden you."

"It wouldn't be a burden." Jacq perched on the edge of the railing. "What's up?"

Lynn gazed out at the night, a sad smile playing about her mouth. "I guess it was all the talk about family and children at dinner. It can be…painful. Especially around Christmastime."

Jacq schooled her tone to reflect only a hint of the compassion that gripped her. "You don't have any children?"

"No. We wanted them. Desperately. But Mel…" She gave a helpless shrug. "It wasn't possible. Most of the time we don't mind. We're so happy together. It's just every once in a while, it catches up with me."

"I'm sorry I added to it," Jacq said sincerely.

Lynn's head jerked up. "Please! Don't be sorry. You weren't to know."

"Is there anything I can do?"

"Would you mind talking to me for a few minutes? Just until I get myself under control. These crying jags don't happen often. But when they do, I prefer to keep them from Mel."

"And he pretends not to notice."

"He tries." Lynn wrapped her arms around her waist. "It distresses him terribly when I get upset."

Jacq thought of Mathias and nodded. "Men have this uncontrollable urge to protect their women," she said in total understanding. "I imagine Mel feels helpless when it comes to something like this. He wants to make it right and he can't. For a powerful man, that can be a frustrating position."

"My husband was right. You are astute." Lynn forced

a brave smile to her lips. "Thank you for talking to me. You've helped immensely. Could I ask for one more favor?"

"Sure."

"Would you mind keeping this conversation between the two of us? It's so personal..." She trailed off awkwardly.

Jacq hopped off the railing. "My lips are sealed. Is there another way inside? We'll need to freshen up if we don't want to look like windblown disasters."

"Smart and tactful. Two rare qualities these days. I'm glad Mathias brought you along this evening so we could meet," Lynn said impulsively.

"So am I."

This time, Lynn's smile appeared more genuine. "He's a lucky man to have you."

"I'll be sure to tell him that."

"Tell me what?"

Jacq sent a startled look toward the far side of the porch. Mathias stepped from beneath the shadowed overhang of the house and approached. She planted her hands on her hips. "All this time we've been going together and I never realized how sneaky you were," she scolded.

"It's not my fault," he responded mildly. "It's the shoes. Have I interrupted something?"

"Not at all." Jacq crossed the deck to join him. "Miss me?"

He wrapped an arm around her. "More than you know. So what were you supposed to tell me?"

"How lucky you are to have me. At least according to our hostess." She caught the assessing glance he shot Lynn and hastened to distract him. "I was just on my way to find you."

"Looks like I've saved you the effort."

"So you did." She slipped from his grasp and tugged him back the way he'd come. "We'll catch up with you later, Lynn. Okay?"

"I'll meet you indoors," their hostess agreed.

As soon as she'd moved out of earshot, Mathias asked, "What was all that about?"

Jacq gazed at him, wide-eyed. "What was all what about?"

"Don't give me the innocent routine. I'm talking about your discussion with Lynn."

"Oh, that."

"Yeah, that."

"It was just girl talk."

"Oh, really?" He threw a glance over his shoulder, watching as the topic of their conversation disappeared inside. "If that's all, then why did you hustle me away from her like I'm some sort of plague-carrier? Tell me what you talked about."

"Actually, I can't," she informed him regretfully.

His gaze shifted to clash with hers and his eyes narrowed. "Can't? Or won't?"

"Can't. Won't." She shrugged. "Same difference. The point is, I promised Lynn. She asked that I keep our conversation confidential and I told her I would. You don't really expect me to betray her trust, now do you?"

"Yes, I damned well do. You seem to forget why we're here tonight."

"I haven't forgotten a thing. And just to set the record straight, obtaining information is the reason *you're* here tonight," she corrected carefully. "I came because you invited me out to dinner."

For some reason her comment annoyed him. His jaw

tensed and it took a minute before he responded. "Jacq, this is important."

"I know it's important." She turned, her expression serious. "But what you don't realize is that what Lynn said to me is something she'd never have said to you. If you'd come alone to do your procuring, you wouldn't have gotten this information, anyway. So my not giving it to you isn't going to change a thing."

"That has to be the most convoluted piece of logic I've ever heard!" he snapped.

"Give me time!" she snapped right back. "I can get much more convoluted than that."

"I don't doubt it for a minute."

They glared at each other for an endless minute. Then Jacq sighed. "You're not going to budge on this, are you?"

"Not an inch."

"Me, neither." A tiny frown puckered her brow. "It's been such a fun evening. I'd rather not spoil it with a fight. Do you suppose we could table this discussion for another time?"

He stilled and she wondered what she'd said to cause such an interesting reaction. And then she realized. "Another time" meant another time. It suggested they'd see each other again.

Before she could backtrack, he reached out and snagged her around the waist, tucking her securely against him. "An excellent suggestion. Now why don't we go wish everyone a pleasant evening. I'm sure they'll understand if we cut out early. After all, we are newly-weds."

"Newly engaged," she corrected, then sighed. "What am I saying?"

"You're saying that we've had an interesting first date. And you're looking forward to our next one."

She pulled back slightly to look up at him. "Is there going to be a next one?"

"There's no question about it. Shall I prove it to you?"

She stared at him, intrigued. "How?"

A hot glow lit his eyes, the green growing positively incandescent. "Like this...."

CHAPTER FOUR

MATHIAS cupped the back of Jacq's head and captured her mouth in a brief, intense kiss. Clearly a single sampling wasn't sufficient, for he came back for another. This one was slower and deeper, more passionate. Jacq wrapped her arms around his neck and gave herself over to sheer sensation. How had her sister described him?

Precise. Yes, that was it. Precise. If by that J.J. meant Mathias knew exactly what to do, Jacq couldn't argue with fact. He'd figured out how to stoke a woman's desire, to submerge her ever so gently into the flames. The decisive melding of lips, that delicious tangle of tongues, the sweet tasting of new, distinctive flavors. Pure precision.

Careful. That had been another of J.J.'s descriptions, Jacq recalled hazily. And Mathias was careful, all right. No question about that. He took care in the way he held her. Tight. Protective. Careful to lock hips and thighs. Close. Suggestive. Careful to ensure that he anticipated her every desire. Swift. Exacting. But most of all he was...

Thorough. Oh, yes. He was very thorough. Thorough, knowledgeable, delicious. Rocking her closer, he caught her lower lip in his teeth and ever so slowly tugged. An unexpected tingle started at her toes and flashed upward. She jumped, utterly shocked.

"What caused that?" she asked in wonder.

His surprise matched hers. "Electricity, if I'm not

mistaken. Or maybe lightning. We were definitely hit by something.''

''You…ah…'' She cleared her throat. ''You ever have that happen before?''

''Never.''

''Thank heavens. I thought maybe I'd been missing something all these years.'' She grinned, lifting her mouth to his. ''So we were zapped by electricity or lightning or something? That's good. Right?''

''Yeah. Real good.'' He lowered his head, his mouth brushing hers. ''Maybe we should try again, just to make a positive identification.''

Instantly, the tingle surged through her and she made an astounding discovery. Lightning did strike twice in the same place.

Jacq worked obsessively throughout the night, painting dragon after dragon. Still, she couldn't breathe life into her creation. It was the eyes, she finally decided, throwing down her brush in disgust. Those damned eyes of his. For the life of her she couldn't get the expression right—that intriguing mix of fire and ice. Nor had she found the perfect color. She'd blended every combination of green in her inventory and still hadn't hit on the right shade.

Finally, she gave up and crawled into bed.

An hour later, a pounding at the door woke her from a sound sleep. ''Go away!'' she said with a moan, dragging a pillow over her head.

''I know you're in there, Jacq!'' J.J.'s muffled shout came from the far side of the front door. ''We need to talk!''

Wearily, Jacq dragged herself from the bed and flung

open the door, squinting against the weak sunshine filtering through the clouds. "Who died?" she demanded.

"At a guess, I'd say it was you," J.J. informed her after a pointed scrutiny. "You look like something Angelica dragged in."

"Gee, thanks. I love you, too."

J.J. tapped an impeccably shod foot against the stone doorstep. "Well? Am I allowed in or not?"

Jacq propped herself against the doorjamb and swept a hand through the air in a halfhearted welcome. "What's up?" she asked as J.J. entered the cottage.

"You tell me. What's going on between you and Blackstone?"

"That's what you woke me to ask?" Jacq closed the front door and padded to the sofa. Collapsing onto the cushions, she flung an arm across her eyes. "There's nothing going on. May I go back to bed now?"

"You went out with him last night, didn't you? How long have you known him? Why didn't you tell us you two were… Were…"

Jacq peeked out from beneath her elbow. "Yes? Were…what?"

"You know!"

"We had dinner, that's all. We aren't…you know. We've never…you know. I doubt we ever will…you know. There. Feel better now?"

J.J. perched on the edge of the closest chair and shook her head. "Actually, I don't. Dad is desperate. He needs Blackstone's business. Correction. *We* need Blackstone's business. I think he was hoping that you and Blackstone were…"

"You knowing?" Jacq offered dryly. "Well, we're not."

"There isn't any chance that you will in the near future?" J.J. questioned delicately.

Jacq's eyes narrowed. "I thought Mathias was the only one in the procurement business. Or have you Limelighters found a new profession?"

Bright color leaped to J.J.'s cheeks. "I didn't mean that." She jumped to her feet and paced the small room. "All right, maybe I did, which just proves how bad the situation is." She turned to face Jacq. "Did Blackstone give you any idea whether or not we're in?"

"If you mean, whether or not Limelight is his PR firm of choice, no. He hasn't said a word. Isn't it dependent on how well you deal with this client of his?"

"Yes." J.J.'s ice-calm composure showed severe cracks. "But Dad's hoping you'll have some influence over the man. He wants you to make nice-nice, help him see the advantages of using our firm."

"I'm not a Limelighter anymore," Jacq said as gently as she could. "Remember?"

"You could still help. Drop a hint in his ear at an opportune moment."

Jacq sat up. "Please don't put me in the middle of this."

"You're already in the middle. Jacq…" J.J. moistened her lips. "It would be simpler if you'd cooperate. Dad will do *anything*, sacrifice *anything* to get at Blackstone."

"You mean any*one*, don't you?"

Slowly J.J. nodded. "He's not thinking straight. Whatever path leads to Blackstone is the path he'll take. Don't be on that path, Jacq. You'll either get swept along or run over."

Jacq set her chin at a stubborn angle. "I've played that game once before. I won't do it again."

"You may not have any choice. At least think about it. Limelight is in a precarious position right now and it's going to get worse if Blackstone doesn't come through. We need his business."

"And I'm supposed to get it?"

"I'm sorry, Jacq." A bleak darkness settled in J.J.'s gaze. "There may be no other option. The way our financial situation is right now, we either succeed with Blackstone or we go under."

The name on the smoked-glass door was very discreet. In clean, simple lettering, "Blackstone" had been etched in black. Pushing open the door, Jacq realized that she'd entered Mathias's personal lair. She couldn't help smiling. It reflected his personality exactly.

The reception area had been decorated in black, white and gray—clean white walls, plush dove gray carpeting, couches and chairs flecked with all three colors and a flashy black desk for the receptionist/secretary. Charcoal etchings framed in black lacquer decorated the walls and two huge shiny black urns filled with white and gray silk flowers flanked the couch.

"Oh, Mathias," Jacq muttered beneath her breath. "If I do nothing else, I swear I'm going to bring some color into your life."

"May I help you?" the black-gray-and-white-garbed receptionist asked in a I-know-you-don't-have-an-appointment tone of voice.

Jacq dutifully curtailed her perusal, almost choking when she read the woman's nameplate. "Just out of curiosity, Mrs. White," she couldn't resist asking, "was the name a prerequisite for the job?"

"I beg your pardon?"

Oops. Starchy, with no sense of humor. How unfortunate. Jacq offered a conciliatory smile. "Never mind. Is Mathias available? And no, I don't have an appointment." She might as well get that out of the way straight off. "If he can't see me, I'll just leave his coat with you."

Mrs. White picked up the phone. "And your name?"

Jacq couldn't resist. She should try, but apparently she didn't have the required strength of character. Dropping her satchel of paints to the rug, she perched on the edge of the desk and said, "Oh, just tell him it's his fiancée."

"His...?" The receiver crashed against the cradle and Mrs. White shoved back her chair. "One moment please." With a surprising lack of decorum, she bustled to a large set of black double doors, thrust them open and scurried inside. The doors slammed behind her.

Settling herself more comfortably on the desk, Jacq swung her foot and counted slowly to ten. When she reached six she glanced toward the double doors. Mathias stood in the threshold, leaning against the jamb. Mrs. White hovered not far behind, looking thoroughly flustered.

"Oh, hi, sweetheart," she said with a wide, sunny smile.

His mouth twitched in response. "Hello, darling." He approached, the elegance and grace of his walk enough to put even her cat, Angelica, to shame. Holding out his hand, he helped her off the desk. "Don't you like our chairs?" he asked.

"Not really." She nabbed her satchel from off the floor. "I'm allergic to the color."

"Then try the couch next time. You've thrown poor Mrs. White quite off stride sitting on her desk like that."

She wrinkled her nose at him. "And I'll bet you thought it couldn't be done."

"It just goes to show that you're a much better trou-blemaker than I gave you credit for. I'll file that away for future reference."

"Don't bother," she said, breezing past him toward his inner sanctum. "You'd be smart to keep that file right where you can get your hands on it."

He chuckled and Mrs. White's mouth dropped open in sheer astonishment. "I suspect you're right. Something tells me I'm going to need it very soon." Following her into the office, he said, "Hold my calls, Ebbie."

"Certainly, Mr. Blackstone." She scurried past them, shooting Jacq a look that contained equal parts fascina-tion and disapproval. "I'll buzz you when your two o'clock appointment arrives."

"Put her in the conference room, if you would. I'll meet with her there."

"Yes, sir."

Mathias closed the double doors and leaned against them. "This is a pleasant surprise."

Jacq crossed to the middle of the room and slowly turned around. "Good grief, Mathias! I don't think I've ever seen such thorough use of black lacquer before."

"I assume that's not a compliment."

She gave an apologetic shrug, then suddenly remem-bered that she still wore his coat. Slipping it off, she held it out to him. "This is my excuse for being here."

"You didn't need an excuse." He left his stance by the door and took the coat from her, tossing it across a nearby chair. "I appreciate your returning it, but I have to admit I'm puzzled."

She tilted her head to one side. "Really? About what?"

"What did you bring to wear home?"

She stared blankly at him for a long minute, then gave a reluctant laugh. "Good question. But, don't worry about it." She gave a careless shrug. "I'll make do."

"Let me guess. Your sweater is wool and will keep you warm enough."

"Something like that."

"I'd feel better if you'd take my coat when you leave." He held up a hand as she started to argue. "I insist."

She gave in with good grace. "Thanks. I appreciate it." Prowling restlessly toward his desk, she studied the surface. It was made of smoked glass, not so much as a fingerprint marring the surface. He'd centered the blotter directly in front of his chair. Files formed tidy, symmetrical stacks around the blotter. She bent over and examined the glass.

"What are you doing?"

"Just trying to see if the desktop is marked off in grids."

He gave her that bewildered look she so enjoyed. "You've lost me," he stated. "But then, I suspect that's going to be a commonplace occurrence with you."

There it was again. That hint that their relationship had a future. "Everything on your desk is so neatly organized, I just figured you must have rows and columns etched into the glass to help you keep it that way."

"No, it's a natural talent."

"Hmm. Somehow I'm not surprised. I suspected from the start that you were grid-oriented. This just proves it."

"Grid-oriented," he repeated. "An interesting concept. But I suspect that isn't what you came here to discuss. Do you want to get to it? Or would you prefer to continue dancing around the subject?"

She gave up on the desk and crossed to the black lacquer entertainment center. "I assume you're talking about Lynn," she said, glancing over her shoulder.

"Yes. I'm talking about Lynn. She gave you some personal information about herself last night, didn't she?"

"Yes, she did," Jacq admitted, seeing no point in lying. "What is this?" She picked up a heavy, vaguely octagonal object made out of some sort of coarse stone.

"I haven't a clue. It came with the decorator."

She lifted her eyebrows. "Is there anything in this office that you bought for yourself?"

"The desk, the stereo system and Mrs. White. Oh. And the cat."

That caught her attention. "A cat?" she asked in delight, returning the chunk of stone to its original position. "Where?"

He inclined his head to the corner of the room. There on a lamb's wool blanket sat a mangled marmalade tomcat. He watched warily as she approached, his raggedy ears twitching. She stooped in front of him and held out her hand. He sniffed her fingers suspiciously, then left the security of his nest and twined about her legs. A noisy rumble emitted from his throat.

"That's a first," Mathias observed. "Nemesis doesn't usually like people."

Nemesis! Jacq fought to hide her amusement. She found it an interesting coincidence. It would seem her sleeping dragon-to-be had been aptly named, after all. "So you don't like people," she murmured to the cat, giving his chin a gentle tickle. "Have they been mean to you?"

"He was one of my first procurements," Mathias ex-

plained. "My… A boy noticed the owner's abusive be-
havior and asked me to intervene."

"And you did," she said without question.

"I did." He folded his arms across his chest and
leaned against the edge of the desk. "As fascinating as
this discussion is, I don't think you came here to discuss
my cat any more than you came to discuss my being
grid-oriented."

"You're right," Jacq admitted, returning to the entertainment center. She wanted to look at the stereo since
it was the only other item in the room—besides the desk
and the cat—that Mathias had chosen. Nemesis followed, sitting attentively at her heels.

She examined the complex system. It contained a CD
player with a one hundred-piece changer, a cassette
deck, and a turntable—which came as a surprise. She'd
assumed turntables were obsolete. There was also one
piece of machinery that left her completely clueless, and
what she presumed was the actual stereo. Buttons and
digital readouts covered the front of each piece of equipment. Three remote controls were positioned in a neat
row on top of the unit. She picked up the first.

"Uh, Jacq?"

She stared at the array of buttons on the slim black
wand. Temptation beckoned. "Yes?"

"I wouldn't suggest—"

Her thumb clipped the largest and Wagner boomed
from the two huge sub-woofers and four smaller speak-
ers positioned equidistant around the room. She jumped,
the remote tumbling from her hand. Nemesis streaked
under the desk, his hair standing up in yellow and white
tufts. With an expression of calm resignation, Mathias
crossed to her side. Bending down, he picked up the
remote and keyed another button.

The silence was deafening.

Jacq sighed. "Sorry, Nemesis." To Mathias, she said, "Don't touch, right?"

Amusement glimmered in his eyes like sunlight bouncing off a clear mountain pool. "See if you can resist. If you can't, feel free to play with either of the others. They're not quite as lethal."

"Gee, thanks." She'd procrastinated as long as she could. Time to see how their relationship would handle this first little hiccup. "Tell me something, Mathias. What does your client want with Lynn?"

"Sorry. That's confidential information."

"I see. In other words, it's fine for me to betray a confidence, but not for you."

She could tell he hadn't considered it from that angle before. He frowned, adjusting one of the files on his desk. Apparently it had been a half millimeter off center. "You're right, of course. I don't know why that didn't occur to me before."

She shrugged. "You're too focused on your particular problem. Lots of people do that. It's sort of like looking at a painting."

His gaze flashed to hers, sharp as a laser. "A painting?"

"Sometimes people spend so much time studying the individual details of a piece of art, they forget to step back and look at the big picture."

"That's an interesting comparison." He hesitated, then asked, "Are you interested in art?"

"Sure. Isn't everyone?"

He started to say more, but then apparently changed his mind. "About Lynn…"

"Don't get sidetracked, right?"

He inclined his head. "We can discuss art another time."

There it was again—that reference to the future. "Okay. Let's stick with Lynn. Mathias…" She glanced at him unhappily. "I can't tell you what she said. If that causes problems between us, then I'm sorry. But I'm not going to change my mind."

"In that case, why don't we do what you suggested, and look at the big picture?"

"All right." She approached, perching beside him on his desk. "You have a client that wants something from Lynn. Is that about right?"

"Close enough."

"And you need to know whether or not Lynn is agreeable to giving your client whatever it is he or she wants."

"Exactly."

"But you can't tell me what it is and I can't tell you what Lynn said. Is that about the size of it?"

"'Fraid so."

"Why can't your client approach Lynn directly?"

Again Mathias hesitated, choosing his words with care. "She's afraid."

Jacq blinked in astonishment. "Of Lynn?"

He offered a crooked smile. "Crazy, isn't it?"

"Is there any chance I could meet this client of yours?"

"None."

She didn't take offense. "Well, then there's only one option. We need Lynn to tell you what she told me."

"Is that likely?"

"Not really," Jacq confessed. "But I'll do what I can."

"I'd appreciate that."

A soft knock sounded at the door and Mrs. White poked her head in. "I'm so sorry to interrupt, Mr. Blackstone. Mrs. Car—" She flashed Jacq a harried look. "I mean, your two o'clock is here early. She's terribly upset. I took her into the conference room as you requested, but I'm afraid she's going to run off if you don't come right away."

"I'll be along in a minute." Mathias glanced at Jacq. "I'm sorry about this. We'll have to postpone our conversation."

"No problem. I'll see myself out."

"You don't mind?"

"Not at all."

Mathias slipped his hand around the back of her head and gave her a swift kiss. He started to release her, then hesitated, his gaze consuming hers. His mouth returned and he deepened the kiss. She clung to him for several long minutes until reluctantly, he released her. For an instant neither of them moved, a look of perfect understanding passing between them. "I'll call you," he said. And then he left the room.

Jack picked up her satchel with a sigh and jiggled it. The glass jars inside bumped against each other, emitting a melodic clatter, a sound that never failed to soothe her. She'd transferred the paints from tubes into glass jars, an admitted eccentricity. But she found them easier to mix that way when she was away from home and less of a mess to clean up afterward. She frowned, bouncing the bag against her thigh as she considered her next move.

They really hadn't resolved anything, and they wouldn't unless she figured out how to get Lynn talking. Mathias was still as black-and-white as ever and unlikely to change anytime soon. The jars continued to tinkle merrily, giving her an idea. Well, there was one thing she could do for him before she left.

She could bring a little color into his world.

It didn't take long. Having sketched so many dragons over the past couple days helped the job go much faster. Hardly any time at all passed before she finished. Gazing at his desk in satisfaction, she put away her paints and carefully uncapped the long glass jar she used to store her wet brushes until she could get them home for a proper cleaning.

How long would it take Mathias to notice? she couldn't help but wonder. And how would he react when he did? A tiny smile crept across her mouth. Too bad she wouldn't be able to witness it.

Mrs. White's muffled shriek brought Mathias's head up with a jerk.

"Oh, my heavens," she said with a gasp. "Oh, Mr. Blackstone, I don't know what to say. Really I don't."

Mathias shifted his papers aside and fixed his secretary with a cool gaze. "Calm down, Ebbie. You don't know what to say about what?"

"About… About *that*!" She pointed toward one end of his desk. "This is all my fault. I never should have left her alone in your office."

Mathias shoved back his chair and stood. Circling the desk, he paused at the far corner and stared in amazement. How could he have overlooked this? He'd been sitting not four feet away from it for the past hour. Of course, it could only be the work of one person. And it didn't take much guesswork to figure out who that person might be. The style was too distinctive to mistake.

Jack Rabbitt had painted a baby dragon on his desk.

"I'll get it cleaned off this instant," Mrs. White promised.

Mathias sighed. "If you do, I'm afraid I'll be forced to fire you, Ebbie."

"You want me to leave it there?" she questioned in disbelief. "But...why?"

"It's an original piece of artwork."

A stunning piece of original artwork. Damn, but she was talented. She'd painted the baby dragon a rich, ruby red, the delicate scales tipped in gold. It appeared to be climbing onto the corner of his desk, it's gold claws skittering across the glass, leaving tiny scratch marks in their wake. Through the glass, he could see the creature's underbelly, one foot plastered to the bottom of the desk, the other stretched out and clinging to the far edge. A snakelike tail curled up onto the desk at right angles to the body, the spadelike tip anchored deep into the glass. She'd even painted tiny cracks and gouges around the embedded tail. They looked so real, he ran his finger over them just to prove to himself they weren't.

But the best part of all was the expression on the dragon's face. Mischievous. Daring. Brash. The emerald eyes mocked him, glittering with laughter, and a forked tongue lolling out of the side of its mouth. He knew that expression. He'd seen it on children's faces the world over as they attempted a new and difficult skill.

For a brief time, he'd seen it on his son's face.

"Ebbie?" he whispered.

"Yes, sir?"

"I'd like you to take the rest of the afternoon off."

"Mr. Blackstone?"

"And catch the lights as you go."

"Yes, sir. Right away." Without another word, she

turned and slipped from the room, flicking light switches as she went.

Mathias closed his eyes. Damnation. He'd worked so long and hard to bury the memories where they couldn't touch him anymore, just as he'd fought to close off that part of himself. It was either that or go insane. And with one simple painting, Jacq had brought the memories bursting to the surface, forcing him to face those dark, impossibly bleak days.

Christopher!

His hands clenched. How he missed him. Missed that bright, silly grin. Missed those huge mischievous eyes and tumble of black curls. Missed the impulsive hugs and wet, sticky kisses. One painting. One nonsensical painting and it all came back as if it were yesterday. As though sensing his anguish, Nemesis leaped onto his lap and gave a plaintive meow.

Mathias took a deep cleansing breath, fighting for control. Then he took another. And another. He focused on the rhythm of his breathing, struggling to get past the images trapped in his mind. But there was only one way he could do that.

He gave up the battle for control and allowed the images to come, allowed the pain to consume him. After he'd gone through each precious memory, he envisioned a strongbox and put the pictures inside. Then he locked the box and reburied it in the far reaches of his mind. Buried it deep where it couldn't touch him.

When he was done, he opened his eyes again and looked once more at Jacq's painting. This time he was able to study it objectively. Mathias sighed, realizing there couldn't be any further doubt.

Here before his eyes was confirmation of Jacq's identity.

"So what do I do now, Nemesis?" he murmured, stroking the short yellow fur.

Forty-eight hours ago he'd have known the answer. He'd have moved on to the second stage in the process, the same as always. His procedures were very carefully defined, steps he'd honed and perfected over the years. The first step was to confirm the authenticity of the object or person in question. Once he'd accomplished that, he proceeded to step two—find the best way to approach the subject. The final step often proved the most difficult—to get his hands on what he'd been hired to procure.

He doubted Jacq would make that last step easy for him.

"We'll have to find out why she keeps her identity a secret and how we can get her to give it up," he said at last.

Nemesis flexed his claws.

Mathias shook his head. "No, my friend. Force won't work."

His preferred method in situations such as this—the direct approach—wouldn't succeed, either. He'd tried that already when he'd contacted her agent and made the original request. He'd been turned down flat. No exceptions and no explanations. So, until he determined a workable alternative, he'd have to proceed very, very carefully. This was too vital a procurement to blow.

He drummed his fingers on his desk. What he needed to uncover was Jacq's weak spot, to find her greatest need. Once he knew that, he'd be in a position to bargain—he could make a procurement in exchange for what she'd be giving up. Of course, finding that weak spot would take careful and meticulous planning.

He tossed a legal pad on his desk, careful to keep it

clear of the baby dragon's claws. He knew of only one way to hold Jacq's full attention while he completed his analysis. So, she thought he lacked spontaneity, did she? No problem. He could ''plan'' enough spontaneity to satisfy even her exacting requirements.

Uncapping his pen, he wrote across the top, ''Spontaneous Activities Guaranteed To Capture Jack Rabbitt.''

CHAPTER FIVE

FOR the first time in months, Jacq left the phone plugged in. She didn't bother rationalizing the decision. She knew why she'd made it. She hoped Mathias would call.

And he did—waking her at the crack of dawn the next morning.

"I just got into the office," he announced without preliminary.

She fluffed her pillows behind her and cradled the receiver against her ear. "Am I your first call? I'm flattered," Jacq said, her sleepiness vanishing the instant she heard his distinctive voice. Angelica lifted her head from the nest of covers, her ears twitching.

"You should be. I haven't even had my coffee yet."

She released a low whistle. "The situation with Lynn must be more urgent than I realized."

"This isn't about Lynn," came his terse reply.

"Then what is it about?"

There was a curious silence before he said, "I'm not quite certain. But I think we should find out. Don't you?"

Without question. "What do you suggest?"

"That we get together again. I have several projects I'm working on. Since you enjoyed our evening with the Davenports so much, I thought you'd be interested in trying your hand at another procurement or two."

Interested? She found the idea incredibly appealing. The Davenports's party had been fun. A lot of fun. Still... Mathias never did anything without a reason.

"There isn't an ulterior motive behind your offer, is there?" she teased.

Again came that odd silence, as though he were analyzing her words for any hidden meaning. "What sort of ulterior motive?" he asked, his tone composed and nonchalant. Too nonchalant.

She sighed. "You're hoping that once I have an opportunity to watch you work, I'll change my mind about Lynn, right?"

He swore beneath his breath. "Jacq—"

It took all her self-control not to laugh. "You're doing it again, aren't you?" she cut in.

"Killing two birds with one stone? Sorry. It's second nature."

"Then let me warn you, I won't change my mind about Lynn. Now that we've cleared up that little misunderstanding, do you still want my help?"

"You're forgetting. My procurement problem is only one of the reasons I invited you today."

"And the other reason?"

This time there was no caution. No hesitation. Nothing but a rough, aggressive voice that stated, "I wanted to."

Her reply came just as swiftly. "In that case, I accept. I'd love to help with your next project."

"When can you come by?"

"I'll have to fit in a visit around my work schedule." Not that that would be any problem. With the preliminary manuscript on her "dragon" story finished, that just left the rough sketches for the "dummy" book to complete. She wouldn't start on the actual paintings until she'd received final approval from her editor and art director. And her agent would contact her when that happened. "I'll come by after lunch if that's okay?"

"Come by for lunch," he ordered. "We'll eat together and then you can sit in on my one o'clock appointment."

"Your client won't mind?"

"It's not a confidential matter."

"Oh." That was a relief. "I'll aim for noon."

"Good. I'll see you at twelve. And Jacq?"

"Yes?"

"Thanks for coming."

"My pleasure," she replied with a silly little grin.

Returning the receiver to the cradle, she hopped out
of bed. He hadn't mentioned the baby dragon she'd
painted on his desk, she suddenly realized. It would be
interesting to see if the ever-efficient Mrs. White had
cleaned it off or if Mathias had allowed it to stay.

"Well, what do you think, Angel?" Jacq asked as she
headed for the shower.

Angelica slinked into the bathroom voicing her opinion in no uncertain terms.

"If my baby dragon's still there, it means he's ready
to allow a little color into his life." She yanked her
nightgown over her head and tossed it on the floor.
"Right?"

Angelica meowed in agreement, assuming her
"throne" on top of the toilet seat lid. Only a cat could
look so intelligent while sitting on such a perch, Jacq
decided with a smile.

"But if it's been washed off," she continued, turning
the water on full blast, "I should bring a fast end to a
short relationship. Is that about the size of it?"

The cat's tail twitched aggressively.

"Hmm. I was afraid you'd agree. Considering my reaction to his kiss, I suspect *that* will be easier said than
done." Jacq stepped into the shower, then poked her

head around the curtain as a thought occurred to her. "Which reminds me! You've completely forgotten about Mathias. Knowing him, he'll have a word or two to say about ending our relationship. And I doubt any of them will be pleasant."

At that, Angelica blinked in wise acknowledgment of such an indisputable fact.

Jacq did her best to get to Mathias's office on time. She came close—she was only thirty-five minutes late. But those thirty-five minutes seemed to cause Mrs. White a great deal of concern.

"He's been waiting," she said with a severe frown.

"I would have gotten here sooner, but I saw these in a store window and had to stop." Jacq upended one of the huge plastic bags she held. Vivid rose and jade pillows tumbled onto the dove gray carpet. "Aren't they great?"

"I really don't think—"

"Don't think. Just look." She tossed them onto the couch and stepped back to assess her handiwork. The room was instantly transformed from coldly formal, to brightly welcoming.

Mrs. White sank into her seat. "My goodness," she said faintly.

"And if I just add this…"

From her second bag, Jacq pulled an assortment of silk flowers traversing the full spectrum of colors. She tucked them at random among the white and gray blooms already residing in the huge black floor vases. Stepping back, she admired the results. The vivid array lent a sunny ambience to the room that had been missing before, she decided. It made the reception area down-right homey.

"I don't know what Mr. Blackstone will say," Mrs. White fussed. "I really don't. He doesn't take well to colors."

"Mr. Blackstone will learn to take to them," Jacq replied firmly. "And I'll help."

"Now that I don't doubt," Mathias commented in a resigned voice. He stood in the doorway of his office scrutinizing the pillows and flowers. Emotion rippled beneath the surface of his calm green gaze, but whether he felt annoyance or amusement she wasn't quite certain. "You couldn't resist, could you?" he asked.

"'Fraid not." She swept the empty bags off the floor and approached. "Shall I return it all to the store?"

He looked again at the vibrant additions, then slowly shook his head. "Leave them there."

She knew then—without a single, solitary doubt—that the baby dragon still struggled to pull himself onto Mathias's slippery glass-topped desk.

Her smile was positively blinding. He responded with a smile of his own, one full of warmth and possession. One that started that odd tingle in the tips of her toes. It flashed upward, just as it did when he kissed her, shocking her so badly that she jumped.

"It shouldn't happen like that," she told him in an astonished undertone. "You're not even touching me."

"You shouldn't have been late," he responded gravely. "You built up quite a charge."

"Hmm. You could be right. Imagine if I'd been this late and we'd..." Her gaze strayed to his mouth and a warning tingle started in her toes again. "Have I kept you waiting very long?" she hastened to ask.

"Longer than you'll ever know."

There was no mistaking the expression in his eyes this time. The ice had temporarily melted, leaving behind a sizzling heat more potent than a live electrical wire. She stared, unable to look away. Why couldn't she get the color of his eyes right? she wondered helplessly. Perhaps because they changed with his moods—shifting from stormy arctic seas one minute, to a calm mountain pool the next, before burning with hot incandescent green sparks. She liked the sparks best of all.

He glanced past her to his secretary. "Warn me when my one o'clock arrives."

"Yes, sir. I'll put them in the conference room. They just called to say they're running late."

"That's convenient," Jacq said as she stepped into Mathias's office.

"Very convenient," he concurred. "Because it gives me the opportunity to do this...."

The minute the doors closed between the reception area and his office, his mouth captured hers. Then his arms locked around her and he leaned into her as though he couldn't tolerate so much as a breath of air between them. Her satchel of paints hit the floor with a melodic clatter and the plastic bags swirled around their ankles.

"Oh, Mathias," she whispered against his mouth. "You may have cured me."

He pulled back slightly. "Cured you? Of what?"

"I may never be late again." Her eyes fluttered closed. "Not if it means missing something like that."

"Good." Pure masculine frustration punctuated his words. "Because I don't think I could have lasted much longer without kissing you."

He cupped her face and kissed her over and over, his lips hard and heavy on hers. It wasn't enough. Not nearly enough. Her lips parted beneath the avid onslaught and she issued a soft sigh of welcome. He didn't wait for a second invitation. His tongue followed the velvety path inward in the sweetest of invasions.

It had never been like this with a man, she decided hazily. Not ever. She no longer felt a tingle when he touched her. It now felt like she'd caught the raw end of a live wire. It burned, arcing from lips to breast to belly before exploding outward in ever-intensifying waves.

His hands slipped from her face, bunching in the back of her sweater. He wanted her, she was certain, wanted her in the most basic way possible. But she knew he wouldn't act on that desire, no matter how hard-ridden he became. Not until the time was right. Not until she was ready to meet him on equal ground. His kind wasn't interested in submission. His kind respected strength and integrity.

His kind… Her dragon.

With a small murmur, she buried her face in the crook of his shoulder, fighting for breath. He was such a study in contrasts. Precise, yet intense. Fiercely determined, yet considerate. Always in command and yet living at the edge of chaos. Instinctive and urbane, he had a dragon's passion governed by a cool, exacting intellect. Right now, she held the dragon in her arms. But that wouldn't last much longer. Already she sensed his fight for control, felt him gathering his inner reserves to restore order to his universe.

"You're not going to get any lunch if we don't stop," he muttered.

Reluctantly she opened her eyes. "If you're asking which I prefer…" She touched her swollen mouth with the tip of her tongue.

He gave his full attention to the enticing movement. "I know which *I* prefer. Unfortunately, we have too little time to indulge that particular preference and too much time to take this any further without Mrs. White walking in at an inopportune moment.''

"Then I guess we'd better settle for lunch," she reluctantly agreed.

He found her mouth once more in a brief, hard caress. "Just for future reference, are you always late for appointments?"

"Always." She reached up to straighten his tie. "It's one of my more endearing qualities."

He offered a wry smile. "That's what I was afraid of. This might be a good time to set a few ground rules."

"Rules." Uh-oh. This didn't sound good.

"Right. Rules. You know, parameters that help define our relationship."

Definitely bad news. "Perhaps I should warn you that I'm not much of a rules and regulations sort of person." She shot him a worried glance. "I guess you hadn't noticed that about me."

"Believe it or not, I had noticed," he said gently. "But I'll try and keep the rules nice and simple and easy to follow."

"What happens if I break one?"

"Don't panic. You won't break any."

Her expression turned grim. "That's what they all say."

He didn't seem terribly concerned by her confession. "I'm sure. I'm also sure you've been quick to correct that misconception."

"Oh, I excel at it," she informed him darkly.

Laughter flickered in his gaze. "In that case, all I ask is that you do your best with these rules. Fair enough?"

"I suppose," she said without much enthusiasm.

"First. Call if you're going to miss a date altogether. Otherwise I'll expect you when I see you."

She blinked in surprise. "Really? No time limits like—if you're not here in ten minutes I go without you?"

He lifted an eyebrow. "Would a time limit work?"

"No," she admitted with brutal honesty.

"Somehow I didn't think so."

"When I'm working I tend to lose track of everything but what I'm doing," she felt obligated to explain. "But that doesn't stop some people from trying to turn me into a clock-watcher."

His mouth tightened ever so slightly. "I'm not 'some people'."

As if she could possibly mistake that not-so-minor detail. "What's rule number two?"

"Rule number two. I'll be where I say, when I say. If we miss each other, I'll give you my pager number. You can call me and we'll make new arrangements." He tucked an escaped curl behind her ear. "Now, are you ready to eat?"

"That's it?" she asked cautiously. "No other ground rules? No other parameters to worry about?"

"That's it. Unless you have a rule or two you'd like to add?"

"Not a one," she said in relief. "What's for lunch? I'm starved."

"Somehow I thought you might be."

He steered her toward where their meal awaited. Catching sight of the small table he indicated, she stumbled to a halt and stared. She'd never seen such an exquisite setting. The sight filled her with helpless confusion.

She smoothed a corner of the snowy damask table-cloth. "You did all this for me?" she managed to ask.

"I did it for us."

"For us." She hugged the words close, enchanted by the implication. "Is—is any of this food in season?"

"Champagne is always in season."

She laughed, waving a hand to indicate several of the dishes. "I meant the lobster and strawberries."

"I was afraid it might be the only meal you ate today. So I went a little overboard." He'd sidestepped a direct response, but she couldn't bring herself to call him on it. "I ordered the meal catered by House Milano. Are you familiar with them? As far as I'm concerned they're the best restaurant in Seattle."

"They provided everything? Even the Limoges?" She cautiously fingered the fine gold banding that edged the eggshell-thin plate. "It's almost museum quality."

"I suspect it's from Joe Milano's private collection."

Her gaze drifted to the crystal and cutlery. "And are the Lalique champagne flutes and Gorham silver from his private collection, too?" Mathias gave a careless shrug and her brows drew together. "This can't be part of their standard service."

"I told him I wanted the best."

"And he gave it to you."

"He owes me a favor or two."

His comment gave her an odd pang. "So you used up one of those favors on me?" His silence was all the confirmation she needed. "No one's ever done anything like this for me before," she murmured.

"Then it's time they did."

She bowed her head, totally overwhelmed. He must have sensed her confusion, for he bent and gave her a kiss of such warmth and gentleness it brought tears to

her eyes. Their lips clung and she knew in that instant
that their relationship had undergone an unmistakable
change. From the beginning they'd connected. But this
was something else, something that touched deep within,
that reached to that inner self she protected with such
zeal. In that timeless moment, the barriers she'd spent
so long erecting, tumbled. His name slipped out, filled
with vibrant longing.

His mouth caressed hers a final time. "I want you.
You know that, don't you?"

She didn't back away from the question, but fixed him
with a candid gaze. "Yes, I know. Because it's how I
feel, too."

For a brief instant the darkness consuming him eased,
revealing a man of indomitable strength and integrity, of
depth and determination. "Then I can wait until a more
appropriate time to continue this." A hard smile broke
across his face as he released her. "But it won't be
easy."

"Would lunch help?" she dared to tease.

"Possibly." He held out a chair. "Why don't we start
with champagne? I don't know about you, but I could
use a drink."

"Yes, please." Perhaps it would help calm the turmoil
he'd stirred. She eyed the striking planes of his face. On
the other hand, it could make it worse.

He filled her flute, then turned his attention to serving
a selection from the various covered dishes. "I think
you'll like my next client," he said, the change of subject giving her time to regain her composure. "I look
forward to introducing you."

Her gaze feasted on the chilled lobster he piled on her
plate. "Now I'm really sorry I'm late. I can eat fast."

"I don't want you to eat fast. I want you to enjoy

your lunch. If my clients arrive before you're through, you can join us later.''

''Do they know I'll be sitting in on the meeting?''

''Of course.'' A quick grin flashed across his mouth. ''I told them my fiancée would be helping me with their problem.''

She could hardly believe it. ''You told them I'm your fiancée?''

''If I didn't, I'm sure you would have,'' he retorted. ''Try the spinach and artichoke dip. It's a specialty of House Milano. Have you ever eaten there?''

''I had a date to go, but we never quite made it.''

''We?''

''My former fiancé and I.'' She managed a careless smile. ''The one before you.''

Fire and ice flared to life in his eyes once again. ''I gather he's no longer a concern?'' Mathias questioned mildly.

''No, he's not.'' She pushed the unpleasant memory aside and sampled the dip. ''Oh, this is wonderful!''

''I'm glad you like it.'' He gave her a moment to enjoy her lunch before asking, ''Was your former fiancé also the one who set the time limits?''

''Time limits, schedules, a whole list of require-ments.'' She stabbed her fork into a succulent piece of lobster. ''He had far more rules than you. And it an-noyed him no end when I'd break them.''

''Did you break them deliberately?''

Amusement had filtered into his voice and she sent him a look of indignation. ''No. I really tried to follow his silly rules. But it didn't work.''

''I gather it wasn't an amicable parting.''

''It was awful,'' she said flatly. ''Perhaps if my

mother had been alive, it wouldn't have been so bad. I suspect she'd have seen through him from the start.''

"Did the rest of your family like him?"

She grimaced. "They adored him. Everyone thought he'd be the perfect husband for me."

"I wonder why they thought that?" His idle tone was at direct odds with the grim look darkening his expression.

She gave the safest possible answer. "I don't know."

Mathias reached out and caught her hand, "Yes, you do," he said, refusing to let her evade the truth. "They thought he'd be perfect because he'd accomplish what they'd failed to. He'd bring you into line."

She attempted a careless shrug. "If it makes you feel any better, they paid a steeper price than me for trusting him. After he left I realized I couldn't change my nature and shouldn't try. So you might say my dear ex-fiancé did me a favor by dumping me."

She could tell he had a thousand questions he wanted answered. To her surprise, he didn't ask them, choosing instead to turn the conversation in a new direction. "Since you're not like your father, I have to assume you take after your mother."

Jacq nodded. "I look like her and our personalities are similar."

"You were thirteen when she died?"

"A week shy of my thirteenth birthday." She didn't bother asking how he knew. According to J.J. he knew everything about everyone. She slanted a surreptitious glance toward his desk. A telltale splash of red glistened in the corner. Well... He knew almost everything. "J.J. had just turned ten and Cord was only eight."

"And you did your best to try and fill your mother's role in the family." It wasn't a question.

"I tried…and failed miserably. Within a few weeks of her death I'd turned all of our clothing an interesting shade of either pink or blue because I kept putting colored clothes in with the whites."

"I suspect you were the only one who didn't mind."

She gave him a crooked smile. "Good guess. And then there were the meals. They were the worst part. Either I'd forget to take something out of the freezer or I'd forget to take it out of the oven. As soon as Dad realized I couldn't handle the responsibility, he hired a housekeeper."

"He should have done that right from the start instead of making you feel like a failure," Mathias bit out.

She realized then that she'd been far too frank. He was absolutely, down-to-the bone furious. She'd never realized anger could look so cold. The ice burned in his gaze and hardened his expression. For the first time she understood why her family considered Mathias so intimidating. She shivered, hoping he never had cause to direct that controlled fury her way.

"Dad wouldn't do anything to hurt me," she insisted, hoping to deflect his anger. Having Mathias upset with her father wouldn't be in Limelight's best interest, she belatedly realized. "Not on purpose."

"Nevertheless, he put a huge burden on a young child."

"You have to understand that it wasn't a good time for any of us. No one was thinking very straight." She struggled to explain what those dark days had been like. "It took everything we had just to get through each day without Mom. Dad grew more and more focused on business. Without her tempering influence, he became totally rules-and-regulations-oriented. J.J. and Cord had no problem following in his footsteps. But I..." She shrugged, trailing off.

"No grids for you."

A quick smile came and went. "No grids."

"And you'd lost the one person who understood you." To her relief, his anger had eased.

"I had my grandmother. She understood. But she didn't want to interfere in my relationship with my father. She felt we should work things out between us." Until the end. Until Jacq had nowhere else to turn.

"I'm beginning to regret having made even two rules for you to follow," he said.

"Really?" His confession delighted her. "If it makes you feel any better, I think there's a real possibility that I'll be able to handle them. At least you're not trying to change me."

"No," he said gently. "I like you just the way you are."

A soft burr sounded from the direction of his desk. Excusing himself, Mathias went to answer the phone. "Thank you, Ebbie. Offer them soft drinks. I'll be there in a few minutes."

"Your clients have arrived?" Jacq frowned, torn between two temptations—lunch and this latest procurement.

"There's no rush. Finish eating," Mathias insisted. "Oh, and one more thing." He reached into his pocket and pulled out a small box. Crossing to where she sat, he flipped open the lid and removed a ring. "For you."

She couldn't believe it. "I—I don't understand."

He lifted her left hand and slipped the heavy band onto her ring finger. "I can't have you running around telling everyone you're my fiancée without the proof to go along with it." Then he bent and kissed her.

Before she could react, he was gone.

She stared in shock at her finger. It couldn't be! A magnificent golden dragon clung there, its tail wrapping in circles all the way to her knuckle. Two fiery emeralds formed the eyes and it held a ruby heart clutched fast in its claws. She'd never seen anything so beautifully crafted, with such attention to detail. There was only one difference between this ring and the one she'd described at the Davenports's.

This one fit.

Jacq didn't know how long she sat there, lost in thought. When she finally awoke to her surroundings it was because the urge to find Mathias surpassed every other need. Only the knowledge that she wouldn't find him alone kept her from dashing from the room. She glanced again at the ring. Of course, she couldn't keep it. But perhaps she could find another way of expressing her appreciation.

Her gaze shifted to his desk and she walked slowly toward it. She thought she'd caught a glimpse of red earlier. Sure enough, the baby dragon still clung to the edge of the glass. Mathias had repositioned his files and papers so they didn't encroach on the dragon's territory and it gave her an idea.

She glanced toward the door, aware that she didn't have long. She was expected in the conference room soon and she had to admit—she was quite excited at the idea of helping with another procurement. Perhaps this time there wouldn't be a confidentiality problem. Pulling out tiny jars of paint, she frowned, considering the Davenport situation. There had to be a way she could obtain the information Mathias needed without betraying Lynn's confidence. It would just take some thought.

A short time later, Jacq finished her latest additions to

the desk. Packing away her paints and brushes, she studied her handiwork, wondering whether he'd say anything this time. If he didn't, she'd just keep adding to it. Considering how well he understood her personality, perhaps he'd also understand that this was her way of sharing herself with him.

CHAPTER SIX

MATHIAS spent the next half an hour going over his clients's request. As he discussed the situation with them, he waited for a familiar footstep, waited to hear an impetuous knock, followed by that husky, full-bodied laugh. What was it about Jacq that stirred such anticipation—that made him long to see a mop of gold-streaked curls poke around the open door and her mischievous, angled face fill up with a smile?

"Well, can you do it?" Patsie demanded in her typically forthright manner.

Mathias willed himself to concentrate on the task at hand. "You need to narrow the focus of your request some more," he replied. Although this particular procurement wasn't in the least complicated, he took his time so Jacq would have an opportunity to join them. He knew she'd be disappointed if she missed out. "Make a list of what you want and put it in the order of most important to least."

"I'll write everything down," Dana offered, tucking a lock of seal-brown hair behind her ear.

Just then Jacq breezed into the room. "Sorry I'm late," she said, offering the smile he'd spent the past half hour envisioning. "What have I missed?"

She still wore his ring, Mathias noted, and a fierce satisfaction seized hold. "This is my fiancée, Jacq Randell." He made the introductions. "She'll be working with me on your request. Jacq, this is Dana Ramsey and Patsie Tolson. They're both fourteen and best friends. They're also about to become sisters.''

Jacq held out her hand to each in turn, never revealing by so much as a flicker of an eyelash that she found the two a surprise. "It's a pleasure to meet you. What can I do to help?" she asked, taking the chair next to his.

"We want to give our parents a honeymoon," Patsie said. "And we're making a list of possibilities. We'd love to send them to Hawaii or Alaska, but we've only saved two hundred and twelve dollars. So we'll have to settle for whatever we can buy with that.''

Dana finished making a notation on her pad and glanced up with a frown. "We would have saved more, but we didn't find out in time.''

Catching Jacq's look of confusion, Mathias explained, "Dana's mother and Patsie's father are getting married. The girls were told that a honeymoon was out of the question because of work complications.''

"What a crock that turned out to be!" Patsie snorted, her bright red hair falling forward to graze a freckled cheek.

"Hey, you believed it, same as me," Dana said. "If we hadn't overheard them talking last week, we'd never have learned the truth.''

"What truth is that?" Jacq asked, glancing from one to the other.

"Instead of having a honeymoon, they're putting the money toward our college tuition." Patsie jumped to her feet and began pacing. "The minute we discovered that, we both took after-school jobs so we could give them a honeymoon as a joint Christmas and wedding present.''

"I just wish we'd known sooner so we could have saved more," said Dana. She peeked at Mathias from beneath her lashes. "When we read about your granting

Christmas wishes, we decided to call and see if this was something you'd be willing to help us with.''

Jacq shot Mathias a startled look. ''Christmas wishes?''

Damn. He hadn't intended for her to find out about that. At least, not yet. ''I'll explain later,'' he said easily, then returned his attention to the two girls. ''I assume you have some ideas for this honeymoon.''

''It has to be romantic,'' Dana said thoughtfully. ''Like a mountain hideaway or a fancy hotel or something.''

''We'd like it to have a fireplace and a Jacuzzi or whirlpool, if possible,'' Patsie added, peering over Dana's shoulder at the official list. ''Someplace where they can be private.''

''And flowers, if we can afford it.''

''And champagne. Definitely champagne.''

''When are they getting married?'' Jacq asked.

''Christmas night.'' Dana sighed. ''Isn't that romantic?''

Jacq locked gazes with Mathias, amusement stirring in her eyes. ''I have it on excellent authority that Christmas is the most romantic time of all to be married.''

''That's what we think, too. Which is why Patsie and I want them to have a honeymoon. It just wouldn't be right, otherwise.''

''I tried to make a reservation myself,'' Patsie claimed with a touch of indignation. ''But no one would let me. They all said I was too young and needed to have an adult handle it.''

Jacq didn't hesitate. ''We'll be happy to take care of the arrangements. Won't we, Mathias?''

He suppressed a smile. His fiancée's quixotic nature

didn't surprise him in the least, though he doubted she'd appreciate having the more predictable aspects of her personality pointed out. Not when she prided herself on spontaneity.

"Mathias?" she prompted, nudging him with a sharp little elbow.

He winced. He'd definitely have to break her of that habit before she fractured a damned rib. "Of course we'll help," he hastened to say.

"Mathias is excellent at research," she confided to the girls. "He'll find the perfect honeymoon location, I promise."

"We're still trying to earn more money," Dana said earnestly. "But considering how little we've managed to save, I'm afraid we'll have to settle for someplace wonderful instead of someplace spectacular."

Jacq waved her hand, dismissing Dana's concern. "You let us worry about the financial end of things. Just leave us your list and we'll get right to work on it. Won't we, Mathias?"

He didn't wait for the elbow this time. "Oh, absolutely."

The two girls grinned in delight. "This is great!" Patsie exclaimed. "Thank you so much."

Mathias stood. "Give us a couple days to check into your request." He shook hands with each of the girls. "I'll be in touch before the end of the week and we'll go from there."

Chattering excitedly, the girls left. Mathias glanced at Jacq, waiting for her comments. She sat at the table, studying the list Dana had concocted with single-minded intensity. After a few minutes she looked up, enthusiasm tinting her eyes the rich golden amber of autumn leaves.

"Giving their parents a honeymoon is such a sweet idea," she said. "Won't this be fun helping?"

"I thought you might enjoy it."

"Let's get to work right away. Where should we start?" She snapped her fingers. "I know. I'll contact a travel agency. Or maybe I could check the ads in the newspaper. They always run lots of holiday packages."

Mathias shook his head. "Not so fast, sweetheart. You're forgetting a step or two."

Her brows drew together. "What steps?" she asked warily.

"First we confirm their identities and the facts they've given us."

"You're kidding."

"'Fraid not. It's vital that we make sure they've told us the truth. We also need to ascertain whether or not this is a wish their parents would like to have granted."

"How can you doubt it?" she questioned in astonishment.

"If there's one certainty about people, it's that they're unpredictable." He rested a hip on the table next to her and picked up the list she'd been studying, flicking it with his finger. "By fulfilling this wish, I'm taking a level of control away from Dana and Patsie's parents. I'm making decisions for them that are personal. How would you feel in their position?"

"I think it would depend on the request being made," Jacq replied slowly. "It would also depend on why the person made the request in the first place and what effect the decision would have on me."

"I agree." He returned the list to the table. "Now suppose there's another reason why Mrs. Ramsey or Mr. Tolson have decided against a honeymoon. Dana and Patsie think they've discovered that reason—that it's a financial problem. But what if going on a honeymoon resurrects terrible memories. Or what if one of them really does have work obligations.''

"I never thought about those possibilities," Jacq admitted.

"It would be irresponsible to interfere in other people's lives without giving it due consideration.''

"So I'm beginning to realize." She sighed. "Tell me something. How are you going to find out whether or not Patsie and Dana's parents want to go on a honeymoon?''

"First, I'll do a background check on all of them and confirm their identities. I'll also confirm that the parents are getting married. Next I'll investigate their financial status and—''

"You can do all that?" Jacq interrupted in astonishment.

He lifted an eyebrow. "Of course.''

"What if everything the girls said is accurate? What then?''

"Then I'll make some discreet inquiries at their parents' places of employment. Once I'm satisfied that the wish is doable, we'll focus on providing the soon-to-be Mr. and Mrs. Tolsons with the perfect Christmas honeymoon.''

Enthusiasm reanimated Jacq's expression. "And that's where I come in.''

"Yes," he said, the corner of his mouth tilting upward. "That's where you come in.''

"Which reminds me. Dana said something about your granting Christmas wishes. What did she mean by that?''

He hesitated, considering how much to tell her. He didn't like exposing his December activities to public scrutiny. Although it might work to his advantage once he found the right angle for approaching "Jack Rabbitt," he'd rather not use these particular requests as emotional leverage. At least, not if he could help it.

"Certain procurements have to be completed before the end of the year. Dana's is one of them. I guess that's what she meant."

"Oh." A hint of disappointment colored her voice. "I thought maybe you were running around playing Santa or something."

If she only knew. "I don't think he'd appreciate my horning in on his business, do you?"

"That's all right, Mathias," she consoled. "I'm sure you do your best."

"Gee, thanks," he retorted dryly. "It gives 'damned with faint praise' a whole new meaning."

"Only when you're being compared to Santa Claus." Tilting her head to one side, she teased, "You would look fantastic in a red suit, however. No competition there."

He offered a lazy smile. "Most people who know me would agree. Though I suspect the red suit they have in mind comes with a tail, horns and a pitchfork."

Her laughter broke free. "You can't fool me with that one anymore. Others might find you tough and intimidating, but I happen to know it's all an act."

His smile faded. "You're mistaken, sweetheart. It's no act."

"How can you say that?" she scolded. "You work every day helping others. What could be more altruistic?"

As much as he appreciated her faith in him, it would be wrong to allow her to operate under such a delusion. Determination filled him—a determination that she see him for the man he was, instead of the man she'd like him to be.

"You think I'm altruistic?" He shook his head. "Let me set the record straight. My work isn't all fun and games. There are instances when my procurements have caused harm. A lot of harm."

"But you didn't do it deliberately," she protested.

"Yes. On occasion it has been deliberate." The time had come for brutal honesty. "I've turned people away, people who've needed my help."

"Why?"

"Various reasons. With some I chose not to help because their requests were unrealistic or impossible—"

"Or unethical?"

"That, too. Others I couldn't help."

"There's nothing wrong with that."

"Jacq…" He caught hold of her shoulders and pulled her free of the chair and into his arms. "I want you to know the truth. I've ferreted out secrets that individuals have worked hard to keep private—secrets I've then exposed to public scrutiny. I've hidden people whom others want found. And I've used every means at my disposal to tempt men and women into giving up their dearest treasures."

"Why?" she demanded again.

"Because I was paid to." He closed his eyes, stroking the fragile bones beneath his palms. She felt incredible, soft and supple and brimming with a warm vitality. It brought home how much he wanted her—and how likely he was to lose her. "I'm good at what I do, sweetheart. Very good. That's why people come to me, because they know I can get the job done."

"There has to be more to it than that." Desperation

edged her voice. "You wouldn't have made those procurements unless it was the right thing to do."

He didn't answer.

"I mean..." Her gaze swept to his face, fastening there with heartrending conviction. "The secrets you revealed, they belonged to individuals who'd done something wrong, didn't they?"

"No, Jacq. They were simply secrets that someone paid me to uncover. You of all people should know that secrets aren't always good or bad, right or wrong. And the reasons for exposing those secrets are as numerous as the reasons for keeping them." He spoke urgently, willing her to understand. "That's why I have to be so careful. I have to weigh the potential harm against the potential benefit."

"But the reasons— You said you make procurements only if they're legal and ethical."

"And I do my best. Unfortunately it doesn't always work out that way. Is it unethical to offer a person a huge sum of money to give up a possession that means the world to them? Is it unethical to reveal a secret if it's the truth? I walk a fine line. I do my best. But occasionally people are hurt as a result of my interference."

Alarm filled her gaze and he knew why. He wished he could level with her, wished he could warn her. But that would only defeat his own purpose. If there'd been a more forthright, more honorable solution, he'd have taken it long ago.

"I have to go," she murmured, pulling free of his grasp. "Will you contact me when you're through researching Patsie and Dana? In the meantime I'll make a few inquiries with local travel agents."

"Don't put too much work into it until I let you know the results of my investigation."

She lifted her gaze to his. The colors were muted, misted a turbid gray. "I don't need to wait," she insisted.

"Jacq—"

"I'm sure they'll check out just fine." She reached for her satchel. For the first time the glass jars within emitted a harsh rather than melodious jangle. "I know! I'll go ahead and jot down some of the more romantic hideaways I come across."

"Jacq—"

She refused to look at him. "Which reminds me…" She gave her full attention to sorting through the papers scattered across the table. "What did I do with Dana's list? I want to make certain the places I choose have all the necessary requirements—"

He caught hold of her, tugging her back into his arms. "I'm sorry I upset you," he murmured against the top of her head. "I didn't mean to."

The breath left her lungs in a gusty sigh and she burrowed into the crook of his shoulder. "Then why did you?" she asked in a muffled voice.

"You want the truth?"

Her head bobbed up and down, the riot of gold-streaked curls a silken caress along his jaw.

"I guess—" He pushed his response through gritted teeth. "I guess because I was afraid."

She stilled. "Afraid?" She peeked up, studying him with a nerve-racking intensity. "Afraid of what?"

"Afraid that you'd turn me into someone I'm not," he confessed. "Afraid you'd paint a fantasy image of me in your mind. An image I wouldn't have a prayer of living up to."

A tiny smile quivered at the corners of her mouth. "You're afraid I'll paint you all one color?"

"Yeah. I suppose I am."

"So you're determined to convince me that you're not a nice guy, is that it?" The steely gray had faded from her eyes. Now they gleamed with all the clarity of a bright autumn morning, filled with crisp golds and browns and greens. "You don't just procure for the good guys, you also procure for the bad?"

"Something like that."

"Okay. So you've convinced me you're a total louse." Her smile turned to a grin. "Now what?"

He released a gusty sigh. "I'm not a total louse."

"Just half a louse?" she teased.

"Yeah. I guess that about sums it up. Jacq... I need you to understand," he said softly, insistently. "I don't want you to blind yourself to the truth. And in some cases, the truth isn't pretty."

She remained silent for a long moment. Finally she asked, "Have you any regrets, Mathias? I mean... Have you ever taken on a procurement that afterward you were sorry you'd made?"

He thought about it, then shook his head. "No. Some have been tough decisions. A few have been close calls. But I can honestly say that there isn't a single one I regret."

"That's all I needed to know." The last of the clouds cleared from her expression. "By the way, I want to thank you for the ring. It was fun having the opportunity to wear it."

He stopped her before she could remove it. "Leave it on."

"I can't do that. People will think we're really engaged."

"Leave it on."

"Mathias, we're not engaged," she argued. "It wouldn't be right to wear a ring."

"Leave it."

To his relief she gave up, apparently conceding she wasn't going to win this particular argument. At least not at the moment. "I have to admit, I'd love to know how you were able to find a band that matched the one I described."

"It's my job to procure the unusual, remember?"

"But I invented that description." She studied the ring, a tiny frown puckering her brow. "I can't believe you were able to find it."

"I told you. I'm good at my job."

"Maybe I should write that down."

"Maybe this will help you remember." Gathering her into his arms, he bent to kiss her.

She met him halfway, impatience causing her mouth to collide with his. "I know we can do better than that," she said, chuckling at the momentary awkwardness.

"Prove it."

She didn't need any further prompting. Capturing his jaw within her palms, she stroked her thumbs across his lower lip. A groan of pleasure rumbled deep in his chest and she swayed closer. Whispering his name, she kissed him, her lips parting beneath his in sweet eagerness. There was an honest passion about her that stirred him, a sincerity he couldn't mistake. He cupped the nape of her neck, his fingers forking beneath the silken curls.

Her hands slipped from his jaw and she wrapped her arms around his waist, hugging him against her slender curves. The temptation to explore those curves drove him beyond endurance. He wanted to put his mark on her, to make her his. He wanted to carry her off to his penthouse apartment and stay there for as long as it took to turn the fantasy of the ring she wore into reality. But this was one procurement he didn't intend to rush.

Not when it was the most important he'd ever made.

As though sensing his thoughts, she pulled away, fixing him with a serious gaze. "I'd better leave."

"It's not what either of us wants."

"No, it's not. But we'll do it just the same. Won't we?"

"Apparently so." He snatched a final kiss and set her from him. "I'll call you tomorrow. And thanks for your help."

"I enjoyed it. It was fun."

"Be sure you take my coat and umbrella. It looks like rain."

"I was hoping you'd say that." She peeked at him from beneath her lashes, laughter gleaming in her eyes. "In fact... I was counting on it." Planting a final kiss on his jaw, she grabbed her satchel and dashed from the room.

Mathias walked into his office and started toward his desk when he suddenly realized the dragon painted in the corner of the glass top had companions. He detoured to that side and examined the changes, shaking his head in amusement. Jacq had added significantly to the painting. Three naked fairies now frolicked along the edge of the smoked glass just beneath the dragon. A forest had also sprung up, leaves, branches and vines positioned to preserve the winged sprites' modesty. He studied the newly-enlarged painting and grinned. He liked her sense of humor.

The first of the fairies clung to the baby dragon, attempting to help him onto the slippery glass. The second

fairy gripped the first around the waist. The third fairy—
heels threatening to slip out from under her—held fast
to the second fairy's wings, pulling with all her strength.
All three were on the verge of falling flat on their bare
bottoms.

His eyes narrowed as he examined her artwork. There
was something familiar about one of the fairies. Then it
hit him and he chuckled aloud. The last of the three was
the spitting image of Jacq's sister, J.J. The tiny creature
had the same thick cloud of ebony hair, the same fierce
black eyes and the same determined expression. It raised
a very interesting question. Were all of Jacq's books
peopled with familiar faces? And if so, did J.J. know
that she frolicked half-naked through them in the guise
of a fairy? Somehow he doubted that she did. He made
a mental note to check his collection of Jack Rabbitt
books when he returned to his apartment.

"Mr. Blackstone?" Ebbie White slipped into his office, carrying a stack of folders. "These are the last of
the Christmas requests. Oh! My goodness. Your fiancée's been busy, I see."

"Very busy," he concurred.

Ebbie peeked over his shoulder, examining the latest
additions. "She certainly is a talented young lady."

"That she is," he murmured. He took the folders from
his secretary and stacked them on the opposite end of
the desk from the paintings.

"I notice you're reluctant to put anything on top of
them, as well," Ebbie commented. "If Ms. Randell
keeps this up, you'll soon run out of desk space."

A quick grin slashed across his mouth. "I believe
that's the idea."

Amusement dawned in Ebbie's gaze. "It would appear I'm not the only one who thinks you work too hard.''

"I'm not sure that's the point of this particular exercise. Unless I'm mistaken, Jacq's trying to force some color into my life.''

"Thus the pillows and silk flowers and desk-painting.''

"You got it. I believe it's also supposed to make me less grid-oriented.''

"Grid-oriented?''

"I think that's her way of saying less neat and precise.''

Ebbie laughed. "Will it work?''

"I think,'' Mathias admitted with a sigh, "it just might.''

Jacq walked into her cottage and hung Mathias's coat in the hall closet. Angelica trotted over to greet her. Curling her tail around Jacq's ankle, she announced there were messages on the answering machine with a plaintive meow.

There was only one, but it was terse and to the point. "Come up to the house when you get in. We need your help.''

Only Turk could manage to make a request for help sound like an order. Returning to the closet, she grabbed Mathias's coat again. She could have worn one of the several she owned. But she liked wearing his. Even though the sleeves were ridiculously long and she had enough room inside its warm folds for at least two more people, she preferred the simple black wool over any of her more flamboyant garments. And it was for one simple reason—it belonged to Mathias.

Wrapping herself in the protective folds, she inhaled

the woodsy scent of his cologne. The faintest trace still lingered. For some reason, it gave her the fortitude she needed to face her relatives.

She ran the three to ground in the library. "Reporting as ordered," she joked as she entered the room.

As usual, her father ignored her attempt at humor. "Ah, Jacqueline. Thanks for dropping by."

"What's up?" she asked.

"Just a small matter we wanted to run by you," her father replied, getting right down to business. "We hoped to get your take on the situation."

"Is this Limelight business?" she asked, knowing full well it couldn't be anything else.

Her father and J.J. exchanged a quick look. Cord grimaced. It was answer enough.

"You know the agreement we made," she reminded gently.

"And we've kept that agreement," Turk retorted. "But this is serious. We wouldn't have called you otherwise. You know we wouldn't."

"Jacq... I've phoned Blackstone's client a dozen times in an attempt to set up an appointment," J.J. explained. "I can't get past the secretary. We're not asking you to help with the account. We wouldn't do that. All we want is for you to work some of that magic charm of yours and get to the owner."

Jacq frowned. "This doesn't make any sense. This client needs a PR firm, right?"

Turk shrugged. "As far as we know."

"Then why won't he take a meeting?"

No one had an answer.

"All right," Jacq said with a sigh. She slipped off Mathias's coat and tossed it over the arm of a nearby chair. "Give me a name and number. I'll see what I can do."

Cord shoved a piece of paper in her direction. "This is all the information we have."

The paper had a business name, King Investments, and a phone number. J.J. had scrawled the secretary's name at the bottom—Jewel Bright. "That's a joke, right?" Jacq demanded.

Turk shrugged. "Apparently not."

"Well, what's the client's name? Who owns this King Investments?"

"We haven't a clue," her father snapped. "I assume this is Mathias's idea of a test. He wants to see how well we handle the situation. If we pull it off, we're his PR firm of choice. Screw up and we're out. Right now, the chances of our succeeding are fading fast."

"Well, I'll give it a try and see what happens." She crossed to her father's desk, plucked the phone receiver from the cradle and punched in the number.

"King Investments," a sultry voice answered.

"Good afternoon," Jacq said pleasantly. "This is Jacq Randell with Limelight International."

"Yes?"

"I'd like to set up an appointment with your CEO."

"One moment, please." A short time later she returned to the line. "Did you say this was *Jacq Randell* with Limelight International?"

"That's correct."

"I have a few minutes available for you on Friday at three."

"That would be fine," Jacq said evenly. "One more thing... I need your CEO's name."

"I'm so sorry," the secretary replied. "I'm not at liberty to divulge that information."

"Why not?"

"I'm sure my employer will be only too happy to explain on Friday." And with that, the line went dead.

Jacq frowned as she hung up. "I don't like the feel of this," she said, turning to face her father.

"What did the woman say?"

"Very little," she admitted. "All I did was give my name. For some unknown reason, it worked like a charm. You now have an appointment at three on Friday."

"That's great," Cord enthused. But J.J. remained silent, her brow furrowed.

"No, it's not great," Jacq corrected, exchanging a quick look with her sister. "There's something funny about this setup. None of it makes sense. So, if you don't mind my making a suggestion... Be careful. Don't commit to anything. Research the company and the owner before you take this job."

"We've already taken the job, remember?" Turk retorted. "Blackstone warned us that his client requires special attention. He also made it clear that in order to handle any future business, we had to succeed with this account. So no matter what the setup is, we have to take it on. That's all there is to it."

"That isn't all there is," Jacq argued forcefully. "You're forgetting one very important fact. You don't have to take the job. If the owner of King Investments isn't on the up and up, you have every right to refuse to work with him. Sometimes the only right answer is a flat-out no."

"I'm sure once we meet, it will all work out. Thanks for your help, Jacq."

It was clearly a dismissal and she gave in, aware that nothing she said would make a difference. It was up to the Limelighters to deal with the situation. She could only hope her concerns had made an impact on Cord and J.J. "No problem, Dad," she said, pulling on Mathias's coat. "Good luck on Friday."

And with that, she left them to discuss their strategy for handling the mysterious owner of King Investments.

CHAPTER SEVEN

"YOUR cat doesn't like me."

"You're imagining it," Jacq protested. "Angelica loves everyone."

"I'm not imagining it." Mathias pulled onto the car ferry and nosed in close to the car ahead of him. "Angelica took an instant dislike to me. Which brings up another matter. That beast's name is a contradiction in terms."

A tiny frown appeared between Jacq's brows. "What are you talking about? How is it a contradiction in terms?"

He shut off the engine and swiveled in the seat to face her. "You have a black cat named Angelica who did nothing but hiss at me from the moment we were introduced. Any name but the one you chose would have been more suitable. How does Beelzebub grab you?"

She lifted an eyebrow. "What is it with you and names? First Nemesis and now Beelzebub."

"At least Nemesis is a hell of a lot more accurate than what you named your cat."

"Angel is an angel," she protested indignantly. "She wasn't serious when she hissed at you. She was just sizing you up."

"For her next meal, I don't doubt," he muttered, grabbing her overnight bag from the back seat.

Jacq slid from the car and waited while Mathias secured her suitcase in the trunk before explaining, "Angelica's intimidated by dragons. That's all."

"Dragons." He slammed the trunk closed and faced her. "I didn't realize you were having a problem with them," he commented dryly. "Have you thought about calling in an exterminator?"

"Don't be ridiculous! I'm not talking about real dragons. I meant you. Once Angelica realizes you aren't going to hurt her, she'll settle right down."

"She thinks *I'm* a dragon? Should I even bother having you explain that?"

"It's my fault," Jacq admitted with a sigh. "I made the mistake of comparing you to a dragon and she hasn't quite come to terms with it yet. Give her time."

He released a silent groan. "I get it. You're one of those pet people."

"Pet people?" Her eyes narrowed. "What's *that* supposed to mean?"

"You know full well what I mean. You're one of those types who act like their pet is a real person, aren't you? You anthropomorphize them."

"I most certainly do not. I'm well aware that my cat is a cat." She folded her arms across her chest. "But she can still have her feelings hurt like the rest of us. And speaking of anthropomorphizing animals... What about Nemesis?"

"What about him?"

"Don't tell me you treat him like a cat."

"Not only do I treat him like a cat, he *is* a cat!" Mathias snagged her elbow and headed for the steps leading to the passenger lounge. "He's an intelligent, affectionate animal who happens to share my taste in women. He's also a hell of a lot better behaved than your beast."

"Angelica has impeccable manners!"

His eyebrow winged upward. "I loved the way she displayed those impeccable manners."

"It was a hair ball," Jacq muttered. "It could have happened to anyone."

"Yeah, right. To anyone wearing Italian leather shoes."

Without question, a change of subject would benefit them both. "I'm so glad Patsie and Dana checked out. This research trip will be a lot of fun."

Aside from slanting her an amused glance, he took the abrupt switch in topic with good grace. "I'm looking forward to it, too. What made you decide on the Olympic peninsula?"

"I thought about finding a mountain hideaway in the Cascades, but this way the Tolsons will have the advantage of both the mountains and the ocean. I even found a listing for an island retreat. I wouldn't mind escaping to an island, would you?"

"It depends on whether or not they have indoor plumbing."

A broad grin spread across her mouth. "You don't like roughing it?"

"Not in December, thank you. And not if I were on my honeymoon. For some strange reason the words honeymoon and room service seem to go together a hell of a lot better than honeymoon, outhouses and cooking dinner on a wood-burning stove."

Her grin faded. "I hadn't thought about that."

"You would have eventually," he reassured. "Does this island getaway come equipped with electricity and central heating?"

"I don't know." She released a sigh of discouragement. "I was really hoping it would work out, though. But maybe we'd better call the rental agent and ask about the amenities. I doubt the Tolsons will want to stay there if it's too primitive."

"Good idea." He opened the door leading to the lounge and gestured for her to proceed. "The imagination often creates a much more attractive picture than reality. That's why I'd like to get a look at these places before we choose."

"You're right. I'd hate to disappoint Patsie and Dana, that's for sure." She played with the leather strap on her satchel, relaxing minimally when she heard the comforting rattle of her paint jars. "I'm trying hard to get this right. Did I tell you that I made a list and everything?"

He stilled. "*You* made a list?"

"Boggles the mind, doesn't it?"

"It certainly does." He wrapped an arm around her shoulder and dropped a quick kiss among the curls at her temple. "And just so you know… You're not going to disappoint them."

She bowed her head. "I never dreamed procuring could be so difficult. But it's a huge responsibility."

"It can be." He captured her chin in his hand, lifting her face. "Hey, cheer up. This is a fun procurement, remember? We've got two whole days to spend together researching the perfect honeymoon. What could be more enjoyable than that?"

She gave it serious consideration. "Nothing that I can think of," she finally admitted, her good humor returning.

"Come on. Let's go outside and see how long we can last before the cold drives us in."

"At least I brought a coat this time."

"I can't begin to tell you how relieved I am to hear that."

"Why?" she teased. "So I won't freeze or because I finally returned yours?"

"As far as I'm concerned, you can keep my damned coat. The only thing I care about is you."

His comment kept her warm for a long time.

Facing the frigid December wind as the ferry rumbled across Puget Sound gave Jacq the perfect excuse to snuggle in Mathias's arms. This past week had been a wonderful experience. She'd spent every single day with Mathias and enjoyed procuring almost as much as painting. Of course, she hadn't given up on her book. She'd worked on both the rough sketches for that as well as adding to Mathias's desk.

It intrigued her that he still hadn't said a word about her artwork. She also found it intriguing that the stacks of files and papers kept shifting so they wouldn't encroach on the fantasy world slowly unfolding across the smoked glass. A tiny smile flirted at the edges of her mouth. What would he do when she finished? Replace the desk?

"I see that smile. What's so funny?" he asked, tucking her more firmly against him.

Deciding to avoid the precise truth, she chose one of the procurements they'd worked on together to blame for her amusement. "I was thinking about Adele Gravis, her house and the Fearsome Foursome," Jacq responded promptly. Mathias had approached Adele for a client interested in purchasing her house—a beautiful Queen Anne mansion that she'd lived in since her newlywed days.

He chuckled. "Ah, yes. The Fearsome Foursome. Adele and her friends were certainly serious about their bridge game, weren't they?"

"Serious? Try ruthless. When I saw the tea service

and lace tablecloth and sponge cake, I figured, 'Oh, how sweet. A friendly little game of bridge.' Then Gladys cut the cards and started spitting them across the table. I never realized anyone could move that fast!''

"She could have taught a Vegas dealer a thing or two," Mathias concurred.

"Still… They were all so friendly and they enjoy playing so much. It's a shame they can't get together more often."

"Oh, really?" He glanced down at her. "I hadn't heard that. Why can't they?"

"Adele said the other ladies often have trouble finding a ride to her place. I suspect the other three aren't in the same financial position as Adele and can't always afford the cabfare over."

"That's too bad."

"Two of the women live in the same retirement home. I suppose Adele could move in with them if there was an opening. It seems a shame, though, to give up a huge, beautiful house in exchange for a tiny little room." Jacq caught her lip between her teeth, saying hesitantly, "I can understand why she's reluctant to sell. Can't you?"

He rested his chin on top of her head. "Yes, I can. Unfortunately, that's what my client has hired me to convince her to do."

She swiveled in his arms, grabbing at the lapels of his coat. "But what if that isn't what Adele wants?" she protested. "Oh, Mathias, you can't steal the house out from under her!"

His expression darkened. "Who the hell said anything about stealing it?"

"I didn't mean…" She shot him a swift, guilty look. "Well, yes. I guess I did. It's just that she's lived there for fifty-five years. I'd hate to hurt her."

She hadn't helped the situation any. His frown grew positively thunderous. "Who the hell said anything about hurting her?"

"I didn't—"

"Yes, you did. You said and meant precisely that. Haven't you learned a damned thing working with me this past week? I don't steal and I don't go out of my way to hurt people, especially not little old ladies with beagle puppies named Arthur and Guinevere."

Jacq seized the topic with relief. "They were cute, weren't they? And don't you think those big floppy bows were a perfect match for those big floppy ears—"

He cut her off. "I attempt to make reasonable procurements. If there's a way to satisfy the needs of both parties, that's what I do."

"I know," Jacq apologized. "I just can't see how you're going to satisfy both parties in this case."

"I haven't figured that out, either. But give me time." He fixed her with a steady gaze. "Now do you trust me to find a way or not?"

"Of course I trust you," she said without a moment's hesitation.

Warmth lit his eyes. "Then trust this, Ms. Randell. I won't force Adele Gravis to sell until she's ready."

"I believe you."

Satisfied, he cupped the back of her head and pulled her close for a quick kiss. "That's all I needed to hear."

Snuggling into his arms again, she moistened her lips, savoring the flavor that lingered there. She couldn't believe she'd been so lucky as to find someone like Mathias—not after Elliott. She gazed at him with adoring eyes. Her black-and-white man. Her sleeping dragon. She did believe in him. Why, she could even trust him with her heart.

*　　*　　*

As the daylight faded, so did Jacq's optimism. With the exception of the island cabin—which they'd crossed off her list due to the lack of amenities—all the resorts the travel agency had recommended were lovely. At least, she hadn't found anything wrong with them. She just hadn't found anything right, either. After a full day of driving, not one of the places they'd inspected had been "it."

"Don't give up," Mathias said, sensing her mood. "We'll find the one."

"What if we don't? I'd feel awful if we let Patsie and Dana down. They're counting on us."

"We won't let them down. I promise."

She examined the list for the umpteenth time, nibbling on the end of her pen. "Coldwater Resort wasn't so bad. It overlooked that bay, remember?"

"The lumber company had just cut a swath of trees not ten feet from the cabin. It was depressing. Besides, 'not so bad' isn't good enough. We're looking for a place where we'd want to spend our honeymoon."

That stopped her. "Our honeymoon?"

"Yeah. *Our* honeymoon."

The set of his jaw worried her, signifying an unmistakable masculine aggressiveness. She'd noticed the trait before, but until now she'd been successful at overlooking it. "I didn't realize we were planning one," she offered lightly.

The jaw inched further out. "You're still wearing my ring, aren't you? You're still telling people we're engaged."

"That's just a game we're playing," she protested.

He turned a fierce green gaze on her, trapping her for a heated instant. "I don't play games."

She swallowed. "Our engagement was just a way to put Lynn at her ease," she tried again.

"What about Patsie and Dana? And Adele Gravis?" he demanded. "What about all the other procurements we've worked on? Or Ebbie? Were you trying to make them feel more comfortable, too?"

"No," she admitted. But his questions provoked an uncomfortable question… Why *had* she kept up the fantasy?

A smaller road branched off to the right with a large wooden sign that read, "Heaven on Earth." Mathias pulled up the gravel road and parked in front of the resort office. Shutting off the engine, he turned to look at her. "Then why continue the pretense?" he asked, echoing her own thoughts.

She couldn't tell him the truth. She wasn't even sure what that truth might be—except that wearing his ring and being with him each day had become as vital to her as breathing. "It's too soon to have this conversation," she said, switching tactics. "We've only known each other a little over a week."

"I've known you a lifetime," he said roughly. "I just didn't find you until a week ago."

With that, he climbed from the car and slammed the door behind him. Jacq sat for several stunned seconds before finding the ability to move. He'd already started toward the office, a pretty white cabin with bluish-gray shutters and two huge Christmas wreaths hooked on the walls flanking the entrance. She chased after him, breathless by the time she'd joined him on the porch.

"Do you mean that?" she demanded as he opened the front door.

His mouth tightened. "What the hell do you think?

Does it sound like a line I hand out to every woman I meet?''

"No, but—"

He spun around and grabbed her shoulders. Hauling her close, he kissed her, kissed her long and hard. She could feel his anger, his impatience. She could also feel his intense hunger and longing.

Releasing her, he said, "I am not your ex-fiancé. When I say something, I damn well mean it. You got that?"

All she could do was nod.

"Well, Merry Christmas, folks," an amused voice greeted them from the vicinity of the front desk.

Jacq peeked around Mathias and smiled weakly at the elderly man beaming at them from behind the counter. "Oh, hello."

"Bobby Jacobs," he introduced himself. "Welcome to Heaven on Earth. Now, don't laugh at the name. My wife's something of a romantic and you'll hurt her feelings if you make fun of it."

Jacq bit down on her lip and shook her head.

"You two want accommodations for the evening?" he continued. "This time of year we don't keep many of our cabins open."

"Actually—" Jacq began.

"That would be great," Mathias interrupted. "We've spent the entire day on the road and we're both exhausted."

"We're looking for honeymoon accommodations for friends of ours," Jacq added. "It's our wedding gift to them. Would any of your cabins be appropriate for that?"

"I've got the perfect one," Bobby claimed. "We had it all stocked for a couple that was due in today. But she's come down with the flu and had to cancel at the last minute. How 'bout if I let you stay there for the night? Try it out and see if you don't agree that it's the perfect spot for a honeymoon. I'll even give you a break on the price.''

"Oh, that's fantastic," she enthused. "Isn't that great, Mathias?''

He gave her a curious look, then shrugged. "If it doesn't bother you, it doesn't bother me.''

"My wife decorated the interior herself," Bobby continued to chat as Mathias filled out the registration card. "You've got a spectacular view of the water and trees all around. Nice and private. If you feel like cooking your own meals, there's even a kitchen. Or you can go into Port Donovan. It's walkable when the weather's nice." He winked. "'Course, the restaurants will deliver if you're feelin' too lazy to make your way into town.''

Thanking him for the information, Jacq and Mathias collected the key and returned to the car, following the directions they'd been given to the cabin. "What do you think?" he asked, parking in front of the two-story A-frame.

"It's beautiful," she whispered, staring in awe.

The entire front was glass and offered a spectacular view of both water and woods. Walking inside, they discovered that it had been built with a reverse floor plan, the first level a giant master bedroom. In the small loft at the peak of the "A" they found a thoroughly modern kitchen as well as a dining area.

Mathias stood in front of the plate-glass windows upstairs. "It's like cooking in the treetops. I can't picture a better spot to have morning coffee.''

"This could be the one." Jacq hugged his arm enthusiastically. "Come on! Let's explore downstairs. Did you notice whether or not there was a fireplace?"

"You'll find it right next to the Jacuzzi and across from the king bed."

Her mouth dropped open. "You're kidding."

"Go look."

Sure enough, a raised tile dais held a Jacuzzi large enough to swim in. It was flanked on one side by the fireplace and on the other by a bank of windows. Lush ferns overflowed the sill and surrounded most of the tub.

"It must be like bathing in the middle of the forest." She could actually picture fingers of steam rising from the tub and stealing through the ferns while a fire crackled alongside.

"You'll have to give it a try."

It was tempting. Very tempting. If she were alone, she wouldn't hesitate. "I just might," she temporized.

"So are we agreed? Is this the place we want to send the Tolsons?"

Jacq nodded decisively. "This is definitely *it*. There's no point in looking any further."

"Excellent. I'll go unload the car."

As he started for the door, her gaze shifted to the king-size bed and clung there. How could she have overlooked *that*? It was then she realized precisely what she'd agreed to. Why in the world hadn't she thought of this sooner? She shot after him. "Mathias, wait!"

He turned unexpectedly, catching her as she tumbled into his arms. "Slow down, sweetheart. Where's the fire?"

"I just noticed. There's only one bed," she told the front of his shirt.

A chuckle rumbled through his chest. "How many beds did you expect the honeymoon cabin to have?"

No wonder he'd given her such a funny look when she'd suggested they spend the night here! She groaned. "I'm an idiot. I admit it, okay? But I can't... We can't..." She ground to a miserable halt.

"It's all right," he murmured, his arms tightening around her. "Everything will work out. I promise."

He knew, came the hazy realization. He knew what she'd been thinking, understood what she feared. She risked a quick look upward. "Mathias?"

"I'm not going anywhere, honey." He took a deep breath and spoke through gritted teeth. "And I won't try and seduce you tonight, if that's what's worrying you."

"Promise?"

"I promise."

He forked his hands through her hair and he kissed her just as he had in the resort office. At the first touch of his mouth, she relaxed. He wasn't like Elliott. She didn't have to worry about Mathias taking from her, deceiving her and then stealing off into the night. She trusted him. Trusted him more than she'd trusted anyone in her entire life.

Reluctantly, he released her. "Let's unpack and go explore Port Donovan. We can have dinner there and come back and relax in front of the tube."

"There's no TV," she noted.

"Oh, right." He frowned. "In that case, we'll buy a book. Several books. You brought your paints, didn't you?"

It was the first time he'd ever referred to her artwork. "Of course."

"Perfect. We'll both have something to keep us occupied."

She murmured an agreement, but thought privately that it would be interesting to see how long *that* lasted.

It lasted precisely half an hour from the moment they returned to the cabin.

Mathias jumped to his feet for the fourth time in five minutes and paced the length of the sitting room. He'd been a fool. A total idiot. How could he have imagined for one tiny second that he could spend an entire night alone with Jacq—and in a bedroom, no less—and keep his hands to himself? It was impossible. He'd been temporarily insane when he'd made that promise. A man couldn't be held responsible for his actions when he was insane, could he?

"Don't you like your book?" Jacq questioned absently as she made a small change to her sketch.

"It's fine." He glared at her downbent head. How did she do it? How did she manage to sit there looking so damned innocent while at the same time looking so damned sexy? "I'm going out for a walk," he announced abruptly.

That caught her attention. "But it's dark," she protested. "And cold."

He snagged his coat. "Cold. Good." Maybe cold would help cool him off. He opened the door and stopped dead, icy flakes slapping him in the face. Aw, hell. Cold, he welcomed. But he wasn't a total fool. Freezing cold wasn't an option. "Jacq, come look at this."

Tossing her sketch pad aside, she joined him in the doorway, staring out at the snow pelting earthward. "It's beautiful," she exclaimed, thrilled. "Do you think it'll stick? Do you think we'll get snowed in?"

He closed his eyes and groaned. Fate had a cruel sense of humor. "If we are, I'm going to need more books. A lot more books."

She linked arms with him. "Come back inside. You

can't walk in this. Why don't you start a fire and I'll check the cupboards. They must have some cocoa or coffee stashed around here somewhere.''

Reluctantly he shut the door, fighting for control. He'd be fine if she'd just stop touching him. ''Okay. But make it decaf.'' Tonight would be long enough without caffeine keeping him up half the night and adding to his edginess.

With a disgustingly cheerful smile, she headed upstairs and Mathias turned his attention to the fireplace. Not that there was much to do. It was already laid, only needing the touch of a match to start the blaze. Above him he heard Jacq opening and closing cupboard doors.

''Bobby wasn't kidding,'' she called. ''They're fully stocked. Oh! I have something you're going to appreciate.'' He heard the unmistakable tinkle of glasses just before she appeared on the circular staircase carrying two flutes and a bottle of champagne. She offered the magnum along with a smile that would have done Eve proud. ''You look like a man who could use a drink.''

Slowly he shook his head. ''There's only one thing I need. And it's not a drink.''

''Then what is it?''

She had a lot of nerve asking. His response was short and to the point. ''You.''

The stopper left the bottle with a muted pop and she jumped. But whether it was the sound that had caught her off guard or his comment, he couldn't determine. Without taking his eyes from her, he poured the champagne into the flutes. Heaven help him, she was beautiful. Firelight caressed her face, flickering across the sharp cheekbones and igniting the gold in her unique hazel-colored eyes. If he didn't find a way to break the

tension, he was going to do something he'd regret—
something they'd both regret.

"Sit down," he said, aware that the request sounded
more like an order. "Let's talk."

"About what?" she asked warily.

He racked his brains for an innocuous subject. "Why
don't we start with why you left Limelight. You never
told me that particular story."

She inclined her head, kneeling on the thick wool rug
in front of the fire. "Fair enough," she said, accepting
the glass he handed her. "But there's not that much to
tell."

"Humor me."

"Okay," she said with a shrug. "Let's see... I went
to college and took business classes as Dad requested.
Naturally, after graduation, I joined Limelight. Business
was booming, which was great, right? Only one small
problem. Much to everyone's dismay, we discovered
that I was a better idea person than administrator. J.J.
and Cord hadn't joined the company yet, and we needed
help. So, Dad hired Elliott Drescoll."

"The fiancé?"

"Ex-fiancé," she corrected carefully. She took a sip
of wine as though to rinse the sour taste of his name
from her mouth. "Shortly after we hired him, he began
working my accounts—with Dad's full approval, of
course."

"What happened?"

"Elliott threw a huge benefit for my one remaining
client—a cancer research organization. Only he deliberately made a hash of it. The organization actually lost
money as a result, at a very public and embarrassing
benefit. Everyone was furious and pointing fingers. In
the end, we all agreed that I'd take the blame and leave

the agency in an attempt to salvage what little remained
of Limelight's reputation.''

"*We* decided?''

"Dad and I.''

His mouth tightened, but he didn't comment. "And
Drescoll?''

"He scooped up the bulk of Limelight's clientele and
handed them over to our main competitor. He'd been
free-lancing for them all along. His job had been to join
our firm and turn as many clients as he could. Once he'd
done that, he was paid a hefty sum by our rival and
disappeared into the woodwork.''

"Where'd he go?''

"I don't know and could care less.'' She took another
sip of champagne. "He doesn't work for the competition. I do know that much. From what I gather, it was
just a clever, one-shot deal.''

"He did you a favor, you realize that?''

"Yes, I do. If it hadn't been for Elliott, I'd still be a
Limelighter and I'd be miserable.'' Cold anger filled her
eyes. "But that doesn't change the fact that he almost
ruined my father's company and caused irreparable damage to the cancer organization we were trying to help.
There's no calculating how much funding they lost or
how many needy people were harmed as a result.''

"Point taken.''

She drained her glass and gestured toward him. "Your
turn. How did you decide on such an unusual occupation? I've been wondering about that ever since we
met.''

"Pure chance. It started with one simple request and
grew from there.''

"Someone asked you to find an item for them and it

was such a snap, you decided to turn procuring into a full-time career?''

He swirled the wine in his glass. ''I failed at that first request.''

It took her a moment to absorb what he'd said. Surprise chased across her expressive features. ''You failed?''

''Crashed and burned.''

''But I thought you told me you'd never failed to make a procurement.''

''Since I started my business, no. At the time I tried to fulfill this request I was a stockbroker.''

''I...I don't understand. Just because you blew it, you turned your whole life upside down? Changed occupations and...'' She tilted her head to one side and he watched as slowly, ever so slowly, she crept closer to the bleak center of his soul. ''And your world lost its colors.'' she whispered.

''Yeah. Something like that.'' He refilled their glasses, the hiss of bursting champagne bubbles competing with the snapping of burning logs.

''What happened? What caused the colors to fade?''

It took him a full minute to push the words past clenched teeth. He wasn't even certain he'd ever said them aloud before. ''My son died.'' He closed his eyes. ''Christopher died and so did all the colors.''

CHAPTER EIGHT

ONE minute Mathias was alone with his pain and the next strong arms were wrapped around him, easing the agony. "Christopher made the request?" Jacq questioned.

"Yes."

"And you weren't able to fulfill it?"

"No. Not that first one."

It took her a moment to catch his meaning. "But there was another? One you were able to fulfill." She didn't wait for him to respond. "Nemesis," she said, her intuitive skills amazing him.

"Yeah, Nemesis. Chris was sick a long time and we kept his bed close to the window so he could look outside. He saw a neighbor mistreating the cat and begged me to save him."

"And you did."

"It wasn't hard. A few dollars along with a few threats and the man was happy to oblige." His mouth twisted. "Of course, after failing with that first request, I'd have done anything to get my hands on that cat."

"But instead you found a way to satisfy both parties," Jacq replied evenly.

He inclined his head in acknowledgment. "Christopher and Nemesis became the best of friends. They played together, slept and ate together, were inseparable. Until..." It took him a moment to continue. "Afterward, I quit my job to try my hand at procuring. But it was too much for Lisa."

"Your wife?"

"Yes. Without Chris, nothing was the same. The marriage fell apart and we went our separate ways."

"Which left you with Nemesis, a driving determination never to fail again…" Her voice grew softer. "And a world without colors."

He lifted his head and looked at her. "That changed recently."

A tender smile touched her mouth and she smoothed her hand along the taut line of his jaw. Firelight flared within her ring. Before his eyes, awareness stirred in the emerald eyes of the dragon and the ruby heart burned with new life. For the first time in a very long time, he felt the rekindling of hope.

And it was all due to one woman.

"Mathias… Do you remember the promise you made me?" she asked.

"I've made a number of them," he observed wryly. "Which are you referring to?"

"The one not to seduce me. That one."

He grimaced. "I remember it. All too well."

"Well, to be honest…" She moistened her lips, then said in a rush, "I'd appreciate it if you'd break that promise."

Jacq watched the refusal form in Mathias's eyes, the green turning as dark and turbulent as a winter sea.

"I don't want your pity," he snapped. "When we make love—"

"—it's going to be what we both want," she finished for him. "And it is."

"Prove it."

She traced the crevices bracketing his mouth. "Did you know that when you look at me, these lines disappear?"

He started to pull from her touch, then hesitated. "So?"

"So... They disappear and in their place little bitty crow's-feet form at the corners of your eyes. Care to guess why?"

He shook his head, tension lending his jaw a rock-hard set. "I haven't the faintest idea."

"It's because when I'm with you, you laugh," she said softly. "I've noticed other things, too."

"What?" The word seemed dragged from him.

"Your eyes turn color when I walk into the room."

That snagged his interest. "So do yours."

She caught her breath in delight. "Do they really? What color do they turn?"

"It's not one color, but a bunch of them. The gold gets brighter and there's this misty gray that shows up."

"Yours go a deep, dark green." Her brow furrowed. "I haven't quite got the exact shade worked out. But I will. It's sort of a hungry green."

A laugh broke from him. "Hungry?"

"Yeah. Hungry and determined and lustful."

His amusement faded. "I think we can both agree that I want you. Badly. I have from the first moment I saw you."

"Really?" She shivered, wishing he'd stop being so darned stubborn and kiss her.

"There's never been any question of that. But you still haven't proven the reverse is true."

"That's only because you haven't been looking." She captured his hand and cupped it to her breast. The nipple surged against his palm. "Do you feel it?" she whispered. "Is that proof enough for you? I want you so bad it actually hurts."

For a long minute the only sound in the room was the

ragged give and take of his breath. "Don't do this, Jacq," he demanded hoarsely. "Because I won't be able to stop if you keep pushing. It's been too long and I need you too much to be honorable."

"Honorable won't get me in your bed. And that's precisely where I'd like to be. This isn't pity, Mathias. Can't you tell the difference?"

"Not at this particular moment." He closed his eyes. "I have to think. I need to consider—"

"You don't have to consider anything but this."

She crept more fully into his arms, wrapping herself around him. He felt taut and powerful against her, a sharp contrast to her softer, more pliant curves. Their scents mingled, his as intensely masculine as hers was delicately feminine. He seemed to drink in the sweetness. His hands moved on her, shaping the swell of her breast before catching the swollen peak between his fingers. She rocked her hips against his.

He groaned harshly in response. "Honey, don't do that. You're killing me."

"I can't stop. I don't want to stop. You asked for proof? Well, here it is. This is desire." She caught the lobe of his ear between her teeth and tugged. "Real. Honest. Passionate. Desire."

He surged to his feet, bringing her with him. "I hope to hell you know what you're doing."

Oh, she knew, all right. She was finally giving herself to the man she loved with all her heart and soul.

He carried her to the king-size bed, releasing her only long enough to sweep back the covers. She sensed the desperate urgency he could barely contain, the battle he waged to be gentle.

"Clothes," he muttered. "We're still wearing clothes."

"They come off," she soothed.

She helped him work the buttons and zips, aware that if she didn't, he'd resort to ripping them from their bodies. A wildfire burned in his gaze, his face a mask of desperation. Her clothing disappeared first and he couldn't stop touching her—the sensitive nipples crowning her breasts, then the silken skin of her abdomen, and finally the nest of curls at the juncture of her thighs. He was intent on charting it all. All too soon an unmistakable urgency overrode his desire to explore. His shirt hit the floor, followed by his pants and shorts.

Jacq gazed in wonder. She'd always considered Mathias the most impressive man she'd ever met. But that was before she'd seen him nude. He truly was a dragon—fierce and untamed and powerful.

"You're beautiful. So incredibly beautiful," she told him. Her hands collided with the abrasive black hair of his chest and she traced the tough sinewy lines beneath, delighted by the well-formed muscles.

"Lower," he demanded.

She did as he ordered, following the arrow of hair to its source. He groaned at the first tentative touch, shuddering, every muscle drawn taut. He tried to say something, but only a guttural groan escaped his throat. Finally, he shook his head and palmed the sides of her face. He kissed her, again and again and again—her eyes, her cheeks, her chin and throat and then, at long last, her mouth. His tongue drove inward, hot and urgent and demanding. She couldn't get enough of him, her hunger spiraling to match his.

The bed rose up to meet them and she clasped her hands around his neck, reveling in the delicious press of his weight. She wanted him. Now. "Please, Mathias. Don't make me wait any longer."

For a brief instant he hesitated. "Tell me this isn't for Chris. I have to know before we take this any further."

It wasn't. But it did give her pause. "Mathias, listen—"

"I'm not sure I can." He buried his face in the curve of her shoulder, his breath hot against her throat. "Don't tell me it's pity. Anything but that."

"It's not pity. I promise." She held him close, fighting the urge to say to hell with everything but attaining the gratification Mathias offered. "Just listen to me for a minute. I'm not ready to start on the first of those four children," she said frankly. "And I don't think you are, either."

He lifted his head to look at her, his eyes black with unfulfilled passion. "An hour ago, I would have agreed with you. Now I'm not so sure." Meeting her serious gaze, he smoothed the curls from her face. "Don't worry, sweetheart. I'll take care of it. I have no intention of bringing a child into this world until it's what we both want."

It was all she needed to hear.

Tenderly, he found her mouth again and their passion became a dance, a fluid ballet of movement. He made love to her with every word and touch and kiss. And when he finally parted her legs and fit himself against her warmth, it felt as natural and undeniable as life itself.

What came next was ancient and timeless and perfect. It was the meeting and joining of souls, the most profound of all unions. It left an indelible impression Jacq would carry forever after. And in her heart, she knew Mathias would, too.

For in that timeless moment, they became one.

Mathias awoke to a familiar blackness. It was early. Or late. He couldn't be certain which. Only one thing mattered. Jacq lay secure within the haven of his arms. Her curls caressed his face and he closed his eyes, savoring the sensation. He didn't know how it happened, or why he'd been so gifted.

But at some point during the night this woman had returned color to his world.

Just as dawn crept through the windows, Jacq flipped her sketchbook closed and returned to bed. She snuggling into Mathias's waiting arms and smiled in drowsy satisfaction. Finally. Finally it had happened.

At some point during the night, her sleeping dragon had awoken.

Much to Bobby Jacobs's delight, Jacq and Mathias stayed at the resort for two more nights. If the proprietor found their excuse about not wanting to chance the snow-slick streets a trifle thin, he hid it well. But the unvarnished truth was, they couldn't bear to leave Heaven on Earth.

Early Monday morning Jacq reluctantly returned to her cottage. She listened patiently while Angel scolded her for being gone so long. Apparently it didn't matter that Jacq had arranged for a friend to stop by for a twice-daily feed-and-play session. After taking the time to soothe Angelica's hurt feelings, Jacq played back the single message on her recorder. It was from her father.

"Where are you?" he demanded. "We need you. It's serious."

With a sigh she retrieved her coat. Opening the front door she found her sister standing on the porch, her fist poised to knock. Jacq blinked in surprise. "Oh! Hello."

"I'm glad I found you before Dad," J.J. said in greet-

ing. And for the first time in over three years, she walked
in without requesting permission.

"What's happened?" Jacq asked in alarm. "You look
terrible."

"Gee, thanks." J.J. stopped in the middle of the living
room and eyed the overnight bag sitting there. She gestured toward it with the magazine she held rolled in her
hand. "Where did you go? We've been trying to reach
you for three whole days."

"I was with Mathias. That should make you happy.
Right?"

J.J. turned, her expression tight with anger. "It doesn't
make me happy in the least. Not after what he's done."

"Uh-oh. I assume that means the meeting with King
Investments didn't go well," Jacq guessed.

"Now there's the understatement of the century."

Jacq held up her hands. "I warned you I couldn't help
with this. You're on your own," she stated firmly. And
then she ruined it by asking, "Is the client really that
bad?"

"Maybe you'd better ask who the client is," J.J. suggested.

Despite the central heating, Jacq felt cold. Ice cold.
She sank into the nearest chair, clutching her coat more
tightly and wishing with all her heart that it was
Mathias's instead of her own. "It's Elliott, isn't it?" she
whispered.

"Yes," her sister confirmed with a ragged sigh. "It's
Elliott. He goes by the name Eddie Drysart now. But
it's still him."

Jacq shook her head. "I can't help you. I just can't."

"You may not have any choice."

"*Why*?"

J.J. unrolled the business magazine she held and offered it to Jacq. "Page forty, under the entertainment section."

Jacq flipped to the page and froze. There she found a photo of one of her paintings. "Jack Rabbitt—the author and illustrator whose identity remains shrouded in secrecy—now ranks number one with children worldwide," the article stated.

But it was the painting they'd chosen to run alongside the article that proved the most damning. It was one of her favorite, portraying a fairy riding a butterfly. The wings of the butterfly swept upward, concealing the fairy from the shoulders down. But sunlight turned the wings to gossamer, revealing the fairy's silhouette through a swirl of soft color.

Of course, the identity of the fairy was unmistakable.

"It's me," J.J. said. "Which means that you're the mysterious Jack Rabbitt."

Denials were pointless. "Has Dad seen this?"

"He's the one who showed me. We… We went out and bought all of your books. Good grief, Jacq!" she blurted. "They're beautiful. Why didn't you tell us what you were doing?"

"Do you really need to ask? After that fiasco with Elliott, I needed my privacy. I was desperate for anonymity. And Limelighters aren't exactly renowned for their discretion."

J.J. nodded. "That's true enough." She slanted her sister a humor-filled glance. "I can't believe you turned Cord into a troll, though."

Jacq grinned. "Don't knock it. He's one of my most popular characters."

"And you made Dad a king?"

"Fitting, don't you think?"

"He's so proud, I think he might pop." J.J.'s expression turned self-conscious. "And the fairy? Why did you choose that for me?"

"Symbolic. I keep hoping one day you'll break free and fly on your own."

"She's lovely."

"And naked," Jacq teased.

J.J. blushed. "Well... Fortunately, it *is* a children's book. You've been very clever at concealing her, ah—"

"Assets?" They broke into laughter and Jacq realized it had been a long time since she'd enjoyed such a light-hearted moment with her sister. "So I assume Dad's looking for a way to use my identity to Limelight's advantage. Or to force my hand so I'll help with Elliott."

Pain robbed the amusement from J.J.'s eyes. "I guess we deserve that," she said softly. "But you're wrong."

"He doesn't want Jack Rabbitt to save Limelight?" Jacq questioned in surprise.

"It isn't Dad who wants to use you."

"I don't understand. Who—" Jacq caught her breath in horror. "*Elliott*?"

J.J. nodded. "You should have seen Dad. As soon as he found out who owned King Investments, he gave Elliott hell and started to walk out. But then Elliott gave Dad the magazine and threatened to reveal your identity to the press."

"It doesn't matter! Limelight can't work with that—"

"It gets worse, Jacq. Elliott threatened to dredge up all those lies that were spread about you after the cancer benefit fiasco. He was horrible! Arrogant. Hateful. So sure of himself. He said no one would ever buy your books again once they found out who you really were and what you'd done all those years ago."

"What did Dad do?" Jacq asked numbly.

"Oh, Jacq, you would have been so proud of him. He

repeated your words almost verbatim. He very calmly said that sometimes the only right answer is a flat-out no. Then he told Elliott to go to hell and walked out.''

Tears gathered in Jacq's eyes. "Good for him. I wish I'd been there to see it."

J.J. glanced hesitantly at her sister. "Dad went to see Blackstone first thing this morning to explain our decision."

Jacq stared in alarm. "But Mathias doesn't know who I am."

"Don't worry. Dad won't spill the beans about that. He just wants to set the record straight about Elliott and tell Blackstone that Limelight International doesn't work for scum like Drescoll no matter what the financial incentive."

"Mathias doesn't, either," Jacq instantly leaped to his defense. "I guarantee he didn't know about Elliott or he'd never have taken him on as a client."

"That still doesn't solve the basic problem, though, does it?"

Jacq caught her lower lip between her teeth and shook her head. No. It didn't. If she didn't come up with a solution—and fast—she'd have her life destroyed all over again by Elliott. And she refused to allow that to happen. She jumped to her feet and grabbed the phone with only one thought in mind.

She had to speak to Mathias. He'd know what to do.

Jacq arrived at Mathias's office on the dot of twelve for their lunch appointment. To her surprise, Ebbie wasn't around. Neither was Mathias. Amazing. She couldn't remember his ever being late before. With a shrug, she closeted herself inside his office. At least she'd have an opportunity to add to her painting while she waited for him.

She dropped her satchel on the chair by his desk, amused to discover only one file cluttering the glass surface; he was fast running out of room for even that. She started to move the folder when the label caught her eye. "Christmas procurements," it read. Curiosity got the better of her and after a guilty glance toward the door, she flipped it open and scanned the contents. Ebbie had stapled a newspaper article to the inside cover and after reading it, Jacq shook her head.

"Oh, no, he says. I'm not playing Santa Claus. Ha!"

The article described a "mystery man" who donated his expertise for the month of December in order to grant a few deserving individuals their Christmas wish. Various requests filled the folder. She found a profile on Dana and Patsie. And the Davenports. And a whole slew of other familiar names. She saw Operation Toys in there, as well. She'd been actively helping with that one—calling on neighborhood businesses for toy donations that were then distributed to local shelters for the homeless and abused.

She closed the file with a smile. If someone had told her that one day she'd fall in love with Santa Claus, she'd have laughed in their face. Well, it would seem the laugh was on her, because that was precisely what she'd done.

Setting the file carefully to one side, she opened her satchel and began removing paints and brushes. Knowing Mathias needed the information about Lynn in order to fulfill some sort of Christmas wish, put a whole new light on the matter. She'd definitely have to reconsider how to handle that situation.

Bending over the desk, she quickly became engrossed

in her work, losing all track of time until the office door slammed closed. She jumped, knocking over a tiny vial of paint. Metallic yellow bled across the glass. Prepared to scold the offender for being so careless, she looked up and froze.

"Elliott." His name left in a breathless rush.

"Well, well," he murmured, leaning against the black double doors. "How convenient. The cause of all my troubles sitting here waiting for me."

"I'm not waiting for you. Mathias—"

"Isn't around," he cut in, advancing toward her. "But you are. Which gives me the opportunity to thank you personally for lousing up my latest little scam."

"What are you talking about? What scam?"

"My investment company scam. I had it all figured out, you know."

She moistened her lips, desperate to keep him talking until she could think of a way to escape. "Why don't you tell me about it?"

A humorless smile swept across his well-shaped lips, letting her know he wasn't fooled in the least by her question. "You can't delay the inevitable. I will make you pay for what you've done."

"At least satisfy my curiosity first." She prayed an appeal to his vanity would work as well now as it always had in the past. "What clever scheme did you come up with this time?"

To her intense relief, he took the bait. "I had it all figured. Approach Mathias Blackstone, the man with the impeccable reputation. Make my request intriguing enough so he'd take me on. Have him 'procure' the perfect location, the perfect clientele and the perfect publicity for King Investments. And then fleece as many investors as possible before retiring to a tropical island."

Fury darkened his expression. "The only thing I hadn't anticipated was Blackstone turning the job over to Limelight."

"It must have come as a nasty shock," she couldn't resist taunting.

She instantly regretted the crack, realizing it only served to feed his anger. "Very," he agreed, taking another threatening step toward the desk. "I almost took off then."

"What stopped you?"

"I came across the article on Jack Rabbitt. You really shouldn't have used your sister for a model," he chided. "It was a dead giveaway. That's when I realized I could blackmail your father into keeping quiet. And it would have worked, too, if you hadn't interfered."

She leaped to her feet, relieved to have the full width of Mathias's desk between them. "I didn't interfere. I didn't even know who the owner of King Investments was until this morning."

"But you told Blackstone my real identity and that's all that matters. He made it clear we wouldn't be doing business together now or ever. And I have you to thank for that." He fixed her with cold blue eyes and she wondered how she could have ever thought him attractive. "Of course, you'll soon regret sticking your nose where it doesn't belong. Once the buying public discovers your identity, your career will be over."

She said the first thing that came into her head. "Mathias will stop you. If you do anything to hurt me, he'll make sure you pay."

Elliott lifted an eyebrow. "And why would he do that?"

She opened her mouth to respond. But as it turned out, she didn't have to say a word. He reached the desk,

glanced casually at what she'd been painting and swore
viciously. Before she realized what he intended, he
rounded the desk and grabbed her arm, shaking her.

"What are you to him? Answer me!"

"We're engaged! See?" She held up a trembling hand
and showed him the ring. Emerald dragon's eyes flashed
a grim warning. "Now let go of me."

It was clear he hadn't known of their involvement. It
was equally clear the news unsettled him. Before he had
a chance to consider his next move, the door crashed
open and Jacq fought to free herself as a fire-breathing
dragon shot across the room toward them. It was over
in the blink of an eye. Elliott lay on the floor, cupping
his nose and Mathias stood over him, still breathing fire.

"My nob!" Elliott moaned. "You bwoke it!"

"Is that all?" Mathias curled his hands into fists.
"Then I suggest you get out before I decide to break
something more vital."

Elliott scrambled backward across the floor. "You'll
pay!" he shouted. "I'll make you both pay."

Mathias reached down, grabbed Elliott by the tic and
yanked him to his feet. "Listen up Drysart or Drescoll
or whatever the hell you call yourself. I've made a few
phone calls about you. I've even had a conversation with
several very angry law enforcement officials. For some
reason, they're real keen to get their hands on you. Now
why is that, do you suppose?"

Elliott turned white and moaned pitifully.

"I see you understand the situation. You do or say
anything to cause harm to Jacq or her family—if so
much as a single whisper comes to my ears, you'll wish
you'd never been born. Are we clear?"

"Give me a head start," Elliott pleaded. "I swear I

won't do anything, just give me a day to get out of town.''

''You better have that rock you're gonna crawl under all picked out. Because you have exactly one hour before I make that phone call.'' Mathias tossed Elliott toward the door. ''Now get out of here.''

The instant he'd left, Jacq threw herself into a pair of waiting arms. ''Oh, Mathias!'' she exclaimed tearfully. ''How could you?''

He looked thunderstruck. ''You didn't want me to hit him?''

''Of course I did. I meant how could you have broken rule number two? You said you'd always be where you said, when you said. And you weren't.''

He groaned. ''I'm so sorry, sweetheart. Are you all right? Did he hurt you?''

She nodded against his chest, barely stifling a sob. ''Yes, he did.''

''Where? Where are you hurt?'' He pushed her back, his gaze sweeping over her with unmistakable urgency. ''What did he do?''

''He ruined my painting!'' she informed him in tragic tones. ''Just look.''

Together they studied his desk. A huge black dragon lay sprawled in the very center, luminescent green eyes glaring warily at the world. Beneath one paw he'd trapped a nasty little rat that bore an uncanny resemblance to Elliott. And curled up at his side was another dragon, a rather feminine golden-brown dragon with laughing hazel eyes.

''What did he do?'' Mathias asked in confusion. ''It seems fine to me. Although if he saw that rat, I can understand why he lost his temper.''

''He made me smear the yellow all over—'' She

blinked, doing a quick double take. Yellow paint arrowed down from one corner and ended just at the top of the male dragon. It gave her an idea. A wonderful, exciting, delicious idea. "Never mind. You're right. It's perfect."

"I'm glad you—"

"Oh! By the way... This belongs to you." She picked up the file of Christmas procurements and held it out. "And before you ask, yes I looked."

He took the file and tossed it to one side. "Did you?"

"Yes. You know something else?" She threw her arms around him again, planting a quick kiss at the corner of his mouth. "I adore you."

"How much of the file did you read?" he asked in an expressionless voice.

"Just the article in front. Then I saw a page for Dana and Patsie. I also recognized Lynn's name as well as a few others."

"That's it?"

"I think so." She pulled back. "Why?"

"Those files are private, Jacq. I didn't want you to know about the Christmas wishes because—"

She gazed up at him with shining eyes. "Because I might think you're wonderful?"

"Because they're confidential. Sometimes they don't work out."

"I'm sorry. I'll be more careful in the future." She tipped her head to one side. "Am I forgiven?"

He closed his eyes. "It's me who's sorry, Jacq. I didn't mean to snap. I just have one procurement I'm working on that's proving more difficult than I'd anticipated."

"Is it anything I can help with?" she asked solicitously.

"Not yet. Maybe later on." He glanced at his watch. "Look. I have a client arriving any minute now. Could we get together tonight instead of for lunch?"

"I'd love to." Her brows drew together. "Are you positive you're all right?"

"You want proof?" Not waiting for an answer, he drew her into his arms and kissed her. It was a kiss that stirred memories of the weekend. Of bubble baths in the Jacuzzi and making love by a roaring fire. Of sitting quietly drinking coffee and sharing confidences. Of dawn's first light glistening on snowflakes as they tumbled from a wintry sky. And of peaceful sunsets over the water. "Does that reassure you?" he murmured.

"Mmm. Perfect." Reluctantly she left the haven of his arms and returned her paints and brushes to her satchel. "Would you like to come to the cottage for dinner? I could burn something for you."

He laughed. "Now how can I refuse an offer like that?"

She wrinkled her nose at him. "Most people find it amazingly easy."

"Well, not me. I'll be there at six. And I promise not to break rule number two again."

"I'm holding you to that," she warned and, giving him one last kiss, she left the office.

As she waited for the elevator, Jacq considered the finishing touches she'd put on the desk. For the first time in her life, she had something to thank Elliott for. If it hadn't been for him... The elevator doors opened and a woman stepped out.

"Lynn!" Jacq exclaimed in delight. "How great to—"

The woman cast her a bewildered look, clinging

tightly to the man at her side. "I'm sorry," she said. "My name's Shawna Carter. Do I...do I know you?"

It took Jacq a full thirty seconds to gather her wits sufficiently to respond. "No, no. I'm sorry. I thought you were someone else. You look so much like her." She smiled weakly. Only younger. And pregnant.

Tears gathered in soft blue eyes identical to Lynn's. "Do I? Look like her, I mean."

"Yeah, you do."

The man at Shawna's side stirred. "Come on, love. We're going to be late for our appointment."

"Nice talking to you," Jacq murmured.

Shawna nodded and allowed her husband to draw her along the hallway to Mathias's door. Jacq watched them go.

So Lynn had a daughter. A sweet, beautiful daughter. No question, this had to be Mathias's Christmas procurement. Which gave Jacq an idea. Maybe, just maybe she could help him grant this particular wish.

CHAPTER NINE

"I KNOW you don't understand," Jacq said patiently. She glanced over her shoulder and lowered her voice. "Listen, I'm with Lynn now. Can you get Shawna over to Sunset Hill Park at one? It's up on the bluff overlooking Shilshole Bay. Do you know where I mean?"

"I'm familiar with the area," Mathias replied. "But what excuse am I supposed to use?"

"You're inventive. Come up with something. I've got a plan that just might work. All you have to do is be at Sunset Hill Park by one. Choose a bench and plant yourself there, okay?"

"Jacq—"

She winced at the warning tone. "Relax. I can handle this. All you have to do is bring Shawna."

"You're not even supposed to know about Shawna. Now you're going to procure a mother for her?"

"It isn't my fault that I ran into her outside of your office," she retorted, stung. "Or that I put two and two together. Since I did, you might as well let me do what I can to help. All I need from you is a little cooperation."

"If this goes wrong..."

"You can blame me. Look, no one else will be aware of what's happening. If it works, I'll wave and you bring Shawna over. Otherwise, I'll shake my head and you cut out."

"How will I know it's what Lynn wants?"

"You won't. But I will." She released an exasperated sigh. "You'll have to trust me, Mathias."

"Dammit, Jacq!"

"I know. Love's hell. Will you do it?"

"Trust you? Absolutely."

She felt oddly humbled by his response. "Thanks," she said. "That means a lot. But what I meant was, will you bring Shawna to the park?"

"We'll be there. And, Jacq?"

"What?"

"I…" He sighed. "Be careful."

Jacq stifled a laugh. For a man so crazy in love, he sure had a difficult time saying the words. "I love you, too. 'Bye."

She hung up before he had a chance to respond. He'd say it. Soon. Once he sat down and analyzed every aspect, explored every option and alternative, he'd tell her how she felt in no uncertain terms. Until then she refused to try and force a declaration from him.

"Is everything all right?" Lynn asked curiously, joining her by the bank of pay phones. "Mathias didn't mind you breaking your lunch date?"

"He takes my whims surprisingly well. In fact, he's broken the rules more often than I have." It gave her a great deal of satisfaction to say that.

Lynn's eyes widened. "Rules?"

"Didn't I tell you about them?" Jacq linked arms with her newfound friend. "This should give you a chuckle…."

The rest of the morning passed in a pleasant frenzy of last-minute Christmas shopping. Finally, exhausted, the two loaded packages into the trunk of Jacq's tiny compact.

"I don't know what Mel will say when he sees all the things I bought," Lynn fussed.

"Well, I do," Jacq replied. "He'll roll his eyes in pretended exasperation, mutter something only a man would say about women and shopping. And then he'll decide he should run out and get you just one more stocking stuffer."

Lynn laughed in delight. "You're right. That's precisely what he'll do."

"I'm starved," Jacq mentioned casually. "How about stopping for lunch?"

"I hoped you'd say that. I know this fantastic deli. Their sandwiches are out of this world."

"Sounds great. And I know an even more fantastic spot to eat them. If you don't mind braving the cold, we can enjoy the December sunshine while it lasts and at the same time watch some boats go by."

Lynn shrugged. "I'm game if you are."

Shortly after one, they were parked on a bench overlooking Shilshole Bay and Puget Sound and staring at the white-tipped Olympic Mountains. It was a view guaranteed to appease even the most tortured soul.

Jacq glanced over her shoulder and saw Mathias climb from an unfamiliar car. Shawna and her husband were with him. As the three walked to the wire fence to take in the view, Jacq fought to control an unexpected and severe case of butterflies. This was the right thing to do. She'd never been more certain of anything. Still, she crossed her fingers, praying she wasn't about to make the biggest mistake of her life.

"Lynn… Would you mind if I ask a personal question?"

Relaxed and intent on the view, Lynn shrugged. "Not at all. Ask away."

"I know this is going to sound odd—"

"Something you have to say is going to sound odd?" Lynn teased. "Don't be ridiculous."

Jacq flashed a quick grin. "I guess when you put it like that…"

"I'm kidding. Go ahead. Ask anything you'd like."

"The thing is…" Jacq took a deep breath and plunged in. "I recently discovered that I've been working for Santa Claus."

Lynn blinked in amazement. "Come again?"

"To be honest, it surprised the hell out of me, too." Jacq turned to face her friend, resting a bent elbow on the back of the bench and cupping her chin in her palm. "I always thought Santa was this jolly fat man with a white beard and a red suit. But he's not."

"He isn't?" Lynn asked in confusion.

"No. He's actually quite beautiful. And sexy. Very sexy."

"Jacq? Are you feeling okay? Do you want me to call someone?"

"I'm fine. Honest." She frowned. "To get back to Santa Claus… I just found out something rather wonderful. You see, he has the most amazing ability to grant wishes." She paused to consider. "I suppose he could be an angel. Although, even I'm forced to admit he has a few too many faults for that. So, I guess we'd better stick with the Santa Claus theory."

Lynn gave an incredulous laugh. "You can't be serious!"

"I'm very serious," Jacq replied calmly. "And I was thinking…. Since this guy's running around granting all these Christmas wishes, why don't I try and get him to grant one for you."

Lynn fought to keep a straight face. "Well, that's very nice of you, but I already have everything I need."

Jacq shook her head. "I'm not talking about something you *need*. I'm talking about something you want with all your heart." She gave Lynn a moment to absorb her comment, then said, "Just think. If you could have any wish fulfilled, no matter how impossible, what would it be?"

Lynn gave a bewildered shrug. "Okay. I'll play along. One wish, right?"

"Yep. Anything you want."

"I don't know. How about a million dollars?"

"They aren't those sorts of wishes," Jacq explained. "They're more personal."

"Oh. Then you already know the answer. I'd wish Mel and I could have had children." Lynn's smile turned bittersweet. "Somehow I don't think your Santa can grant that wish, can he?"

"No, I'm afraid not. And since that isn't possible?" Jacq prompted gently. "What else would you choose?"

"Then I'd wish…" Her brows drew together as she deliberated. "I'd wish for the next best thing."

"Which is?"

"I'd wish—" Lynn drew a shaky breath, tears unexpectedly filling her eyes. "Oh, Jacq. Why are you doing this?"

"Because you're my friend and I want to make you happy."

Lynn bowed her head, the words torn from her. "I'd wish I could have known my—" She covered her face with her hands, clearly unable to go on.

"You'd wish you could have known your daughter?" Jacq finished softly.

Slowly, Lynn lowered her hands, every scrap of color draining from her face. "What did you say?"

"If that's not your wish, I can tell Santa I was wrong," Jacq began in alarm.

"No, it's my wish!" Her voice broke. "It really is my wish! It is!"

"In that case..." Slowly, Jacq shifted on the bench so Lynn could see past her to where Mathias stood with Shawna. "Her name is Shawna Carter. And her one Christmas wish in all the world is to meet her mother. I hoped it would be your Christmas wish, as well."

Lynn lifted shaking hands to her mouth, tears rolling freely down her cheeks. "My daughter," she half moaned. "My daughter."

As though sensing something odd, Shawna's head jerked up. Slowly, she turned in their direction, locking gazes with her mother. Fear and hope were written in equal measures on her youthful face. Lynn stood, walking tentatively in Shawna's direction. And then they were both running, meeting halfway and throwing their arms around each other, talking in frantic gasps. At one point they pulled apart and Lynn touched Shawna's rounded stomach with a gentle hand. And then they were hugging again.

Jacq sat, unable to move, surprised to discover that her own face was wet with tears. Thank heaven it had worked out. Oh, thank heaven.

"You did good, sweetheart," Mathias murmured from behind.

She'd been so focused on Lynn and Shawna, Jacq hadn't even noticed his approach. She flew off the bench and into his arms. "I was so scared," she confessed tearfully. "I started to worry about what would happen if I was wrong. Maybe I should have taken more time,

talked to Lynn some more. Maybe I was being too impulsive.''

"You did fine,'' he soothed. "Turn around and look.''

She did as he directed. The two women had moved
to a nearby bench where they sat, their heads close together. Shawna's husband stood beside them, beaming
in relief.

"I never stopped to consider,'' Jacq murmured.
"Lynn couldn't have been more than just a baby when
she gave birth.''

"Sixteen. Five years younger than Shawna is now.''

"It must have been incredibly difficult to put her child
up for adoption.'' She turned a questioning gaze on
Mathias. "And Shawna? What made her come looking
for Lynn?''

"I think her pregnancy prompted the search.''

"Shawna's adoptive parents don't object?''

"Her mother died when she was eight. Her father
passed away just recently. But even if they'd lived, they
wouldn't have objected. Shawna had a wonderful relationship with them both.''

"And now Shawna has a grandmother for her baby,''
Jacq commented softly. "And if she'll allow it, a mother
for herself. Lucky girl. She's going to adore Lynn.''

"And Mel, too, I hope.'' Mathias glanced over his
shoulder. "Here he is now. Right on time.''

"You called him?'' Jacq asked in surprise.

"I figured no matter how this turned out, Lynn would
want him here.''

"How did he take the news?''

"Don't look so nervous,'' Mathias reassured. "He's
always known about the baby Lynn gave up.''

"Does he... Does he mind that Shawna's decided to
approach Lynn after all these years?''

"He's thrilled—for his wife's sake as well as his own. When we spoke he said he'd always wanted a daughter and with a grandchild on the way it would be a double blessing."

Mel lifted a hand in greeting, clearly torn between the urge to be polite and the overwhelming desire to get to his wife. Mathias waved him off and with a look of relief, Mel joined Lynn and Shawna.

Jacq heaved a sigh. "I want to stay and watch, but we shouldn't intrude. They need time alone." She caught Mathias by the hand. "Come on, Santa. Our work here is through. Let's climb into your sleigh and head back to the North Pole."

"I'd love to. There's only one problem."

She smiled. "Reindeers on strike?"

"Nope. My sleigh has a broken runner."

"Okay. We'll use my Ford." She cast him a teasing glance. "But you'd better get that runner fixed and quick. Otherwise you're going to look pretty silly landing on roofs in my compact."

He flicked the tip of her nose. "Not as silly as you'll look, pulling it, Rudolph."

"Is my nose red?" she asked self-consciously.

"A delightful shade of pink."

"That happens whenever I cry." She cast a wistful glance toward Lynn and Shawna. "I just can't help it. I'm sentimental."

"I'm glad you are." Mathias gave her a lingering kiss. "Very glad."

"You've *what*?"

"Now, Mathias," Jacq began nervously. "You told me to make the arrangements for Operation Toys and I did."

"Making the arrangements means delivering the toys to the various shelters and homes. It does not mean filling my office building with a hundred screaming kids. Nor does it mean putting up a twenty-foot tree. And it especially doesn't mean decorating this place so it looks like—" He glanced around, glaring.

"So it looks like Christmas?" she offered mildly.

"Yes! No. Dammit, Jacq! And what's this?" He indicated the huge box she'd put on his chair.

"A Santa suit. It's for when you hand out the presents."

He jerked back as though it might bite him. "Oh, no. I'm not wearing that Santa suit and I'm certainly not handing out any presents."

"Why not?" she demanded. "Do you have something better to do with your time?"

"Yes! No. Dammit, Jacq!"

She planted her hands on her hips. "It's easy to simply throw money at a problem and hope it goes away."

"I don't do that," he retorted, stung.

"Normally, that's true. But in this case, that seems to be precisely what you're doing. Come on, Mathias," she wheedled. "It's just one day out of your life. And it's for a good cause. Besides, they're—"

She stopped abruptly, realizing what she'd been about to say, realizing too why he was so desperate to wriggle out of the arrangements she'd made.

He sighed in defeat. "They're children."

"Oh, Mathias." She wrapped her arms around his waist. "I'm sorry. I didn't think."

He rested his chin on the top of her head, her curls tickling his chin and mouth. "No, you're right. It is only one day. I'll hand out the presents. But I'm *not* wearing the suit. And that's final."

"You don't have to," she soothed. "The kids can do without a Santa this year."

He winced. "All right. You win. I'll wear the damned suit. But those kids are absolutely, positively, not allowed to sit on my knee. I have to draw the line somewhere."

She snuggled deeper into his embrace. "Whatever you think best. I'm sure they'll understand about the knee thing. And if they don't, you can explain it to them."

He sighed. "I'm not going to win this fight, am I?"

She looked up in surprise. "Did you think you would?"

The smile he gave her came with astonishing ease. "I think I'd have been disappointed if I had."

The day of the Christmas party proved an unqualified success. Jacq tried to hide her nervousness from Mathias as the event initially got rolling. She couldn't help worrying about how he'd handle having an office building full of children. But her fears were swiftly alleviated. After an initial hesitation, he jumped right into the thick of things.

Soon she found him organizing the decorating of the Christmas tree, busily lifting one child after another so they could hang their ornaments. Not long after that he manned the food table, distributing punch and cookies. And later still she caught him playing a fierce game of freeze tag. Toward the end of the day, he donned the Santa suit and handed out toys. The instant everyone had a gift, he got down on the floor and played.

Silently she thanked her lucky stars that once again her impulsiveness hadn't caused any harm.

At dusk, the party began to break up and before long

the last sleepy child reluctantly departed. The resulting silence was deafening.

"It looks like we were hit by a tornado," Jacq said, and then groaned. "Oh, no! I just realized something."

Mathias leaned against the nearest wall and slowly sank to the floor. At some point he'd discarded his red velvet jacket, fake beard and padding. Only his Santa cap remained. But it had slipped to one side so it sat cocked low over one red-rimmed eye. "What did you just realize?" he asked with a huge yawn.

She slid to the floor beside him and drew her knees to her chest. "I didn't arrange for a cleanup crew to come and take care of this mess."

He grinned smugly. "Fortunately, I did."

That perked her up for an instant. "Really?"

"Santa never lies," he informed her gravely.

Jacq lowered her head to his lap. "Does Santa sleep?" she mumbled.

He tilted his head back against the wall. "Oh, yeah. Santa definitely does that."

Jacq had no idea what time she finally awoke. Late, past midnight, she guessed, and the building had taken on an eerie silence. Mathias continued to sleep but she was suddenly wide awake and possessed by a truly brilliant idea. One or two of the toys they'd collected from various neighborhood businesses had been confiscated because they were inappropriate for young children. Ebbie had hidden them away in a storage closet and Jacq intended to make use of them. Right now.

Sneaking into the closet she removed two huge plastic slingshots and the "balls" that went with them—each of which contained a different colored glow-in-the-dark powder. She crept back to where Mathias slept and gently placed one of the slingshots and a bag of ammunition in his lap. Then she tiptoed through the building, switching off most of the lights.

Rejoining Mathias, she hesitated. As much as she wanted to sneak up and pelt him with one of the powdered balls, she decided it would be too cruel to wake him in such a manner. So instead she aimed for the wall over his head. Powder splattered a foot above him and rained down in a bright yellow cloud. It was then she realized she'd made a serious tactical error.

Mathias wasn't asleep.

Before she could stop laughing long enough to reload, he fired off a series of shots. It turned out he had impeccable aim. Orange, indigo and pink powder smoked her arms and stomach. With a screech of dismay, she took off running. For half an hour, they stalked each other through the darkened building. If it hadn't been for the glow-in-the-dark powder, she doubted they'd have ever found each other. Finally, only two balls remained and she decided to make them count. She snuck toward Mathias's office, certain the ever-methodical Mr. Blackstone would soon track her down. Crouching behind the door just inside his office, she waited.

It didn't take long. Five minutes later, the door cautiously swung open and he eased into the room. She wouldn't get a better opportunity. Jumping up, she shot him square in the back. The powder bullet exploded on impact, leaving a beautiful ring of glow-in-the-dark green on his shirt.

He whirled and ducked just as she got off her final round. It whizzed over his head and landed with a splat on a stack of files. Papers scattered, forming a blizzard of white and glowing red powder.

"You're going to regret that," he growled, and

blasted her square in the chest with a brilliant circle of purple.

Jacq giggled. "I give up. Don't shoot." She flung down her slingshot and switched on the overhead lights. Looking around, she gasped, torn between amusement and dismay. "We'd better get this place cleaned up before Ebbie comes in."

Mathias collapsed in his chair, shaking yellow powder from his hair. "Don't bother. I'll take care of it if the cleaning crew doesn't."

"I don't mind helping. Besides, I'd feel awful if Ebbie walked in here and saw this. She'd probably faint dead away."

"She almost did the first time she saw what you'd done to my desk." He leaned back and closed his eyes, smiling at the memory. "I had to threaten her with unemployment to keep her from washing it off."

"You did? Really?"

He opened one eye. "I did. Really."

"That was sweet of you." Jacq knelt on the floor and began to gather up the loose paper. "It's almost done, you know. The desk, I mean. I just have one final addition to make and—"

Before she could finish her comment, Mathias catapulted out of his chair. "*Jacq!*"

She looked up, astonished by the harshness of his voice. "What is it? What's wrong?"

"Put the papers down," he ordered tautly. "Just leave them for the cleaning crew, all right?"

Afterward, she couldn't say what tipped her off. She vaguely remembered staring at him, absorbing the intensity of emotion reflected in his eyes. The green turned a shade she'd never seen before and in that moment time slowed, stretched. She recalled shaking her head and whispering, "Oh, no." And then she glanced down and really looked at the papers she held in her hands.

The one on top was yellow—a color she'd always considered sunny and cheerful and rather hopeful. It had been ripped from a legal pad. The heading leaped out at her, written in bold caps. She knew it was Mathias's handwriting. It matched the printing on the reservation card he'd filled out at the Heaven on Earth resort. It read, "Spontaneous Activities Guaranteed To Capture Jack Rabbitt." And there on the paper, carefully numbered, he'd detailed everything they'd done since they'd first met.

She could hear J.J.'s voice cataloguing Mathias's personality traits. *Careful. Exacting. Thorough. Unbelievably precise.*

"I think," she whispered. "I'm going to be sick."

Mathias knelt beside Jacq, easing the papers from her grasp. "Sweetheart, I can explain."

"Please don't touch me," she requested politely.

"Honey, listen."

"I'm a procurement, aren't I?"

"Yes, but—"

"How silly of me not to have realized sooner." A pained laugh escaped. "No wonder you never asked what I did for a living. You already knew, didn't you?"

"I suspected. After you painted the baby dragon on my desk, it confirmed your identity."

She closed her eyes, overwhelmed by the sheer irony of it all. "You want to know something funny?"

"At this point, I think we could really use a bit of levity."

"I painted that dragon out of gratitude for lunch. Remember? You'd had it catered from House Milano. After you left to meet with Patsie and Dana, it occurred to me how I might bring some color into your life.'' Her laugh took on a harsh edge. ''It was my way of thanking you. But instead it trapped me.''

''It's not a trap! I set out to procure you for a client. Instead I fell in love. I didn't plan it. It just happened. And it happened the moment I set eyes on you.''

''No! I don't believe you.''

''Why not? It's the truth.''

''The *truth*?'' She glared at him, knocking the papers from his grasp. They scattered like autumn leaves before a harsh north wind. ''What would you know about the truth? Our entire relationship is based on lies.''

''I'm not lying about this.''

''How can you expect me to believe anything you have to say? I've been there, remember? Done that.''

''I am not Elliott,'' he stated through gritted teeth.

She lifted an eyebrow. ''Oh, really? Tell me… What's the difference? You both had an ulterior motive for romancing me. You both professed to love me. And then you both used me to further your own career. There's only one tiny step left. The one where you take what you want and walk out the door.''

''That's not going to happen.''

''You're right. It's not. Because I'm walking through that door first.''

''Jacq, you've worked with me on a number of procurements. You must know by now that I don't operate like that.''

''Don't you?'' She picked up the yellow sheet of paper and shook it at him. ''It's all here in black and white, Mathias. It's obvious that our dates were a series of tests to determine the best way to approach Jack Rabbitt. Do you deny it?''

''No!'' Frustration burned in his gaze. ''I can't deny

planning ways to hold your interest. But I'd hoped to find something to offer in exchange for your help. And I figured that if there wasn't anything I could give you, maybe by working with me you'd see that my procurements were well-intentioned. That I try and help people. Do you think I would have used deception if the need wasn't great and the cause just?''

''I don't know what I think anymore.'' She stood, putting as much distance between them as possible. ''Just out of curiosity… What were you going to offer in exchange for my identity?''

His expression closed over. ''What I have to offer, you apparently don't want.''

''You're right. There's nothing you have that I want.'' Tears blurred her eyes and she fought to control them. She would not cry. At least not now. Carefully, she removed his ring from her finger and set it on the desk. ''I won't be needing this anymore. Maybe the person you procured it from would like it back.''

''I didn't procure it. I had a jeweler make it based on your description.''

She bit down on her lip, refusing to acknowledge how much his confession meant to her. ''Tell your client I'm sorry. It was never my intention to be your first failed procurement.''

She'd gotten all the way to the door before she heard his reply.

''Second.''

Fury shot through her and she spun in her tracks. ''How could you! Don't you dare throw Christopher in my face.''

''I wasn't.'' He rubbed a weary hand across his face. ''Go on, Jacq. Leave. I'll tell my client I wasn't able to procure Jack Rabbitt. You're off the hook.''

It took every ounce of self-possession to open the door and walk out when what she wanted more than anything was to race across the room and throw herself into his arms. Unfortunately, she'd been down that path before and barely survived the emotional battering. She wouldn't survive again. If she stayed, it would destroy her.

CHAPTER TEN

MATHIAS leaned back in his chair and studied his desk. Jacq's painting was stunning, he thought for the hundredth time. Brilliant, in fact. There was only one minor problem…. She hadn't finished it. Scratching Nemesis behind the ears, he deliberately closed his eyes to shut out the sight. It didn't do any good. The damned thing continued to haunt him.

A knock sounded on the office door and Ebbie walked in. "Good morning, Mr. Blackstone," she said in a disgustingly cheerful voice. "I have the file on the Gravis house. I assume you'll want to sign off on it."

"Put it on the desk, please."

"How did the party go?" she chattered on. "Well, I hope."

"Great."

She carefully placed the file in the tiny section of the desktop not yet painted. "Oh! Ms. Randell left her ring. She must have forgotten it after the party."

With a plaintive meow, Nemesis leaped from Mathias's lap and slipped under the desk. "She didn't forget it."

"She didn't…?" Ebbie cast him a stricken look. "I assume—I assume that means she found out the truth."

"Good assumption."

"And she wouldn't help?" Ebbie questioned, clearly shocked. "I don't believe it. She's worked with you on all those other Christmas procurements, why in the world wouldn't she help with this one?"

"She didn't say. The discussion centered around the fact that I'd deceived her and pretty much stayed there."

"But once you explained why—"

"We never quite got to the whys and wherefores."

Ebbie frowned. "Mathias, didn't you tell her about the Johnsons?"

"She knows about the Johnsons," he snapped, surging to his feet and taking up a stance by the windows. He tossed the words over his shoulder. "I wrote volumes about the Johnsons both to her agent as well as to her publishing company. Apparently none of them give a damn."

"I don't believe it," Ebbie repeated stubbornly. "Jacq isn't like that. I'm telling you, she doesn't know why you procured her or she wouldn't have returned your ring. You have to talk to her again."

"And say what?" He shook his head. "I did the one thing she couldn't forgive. I lied to her. What's left to discuss?"

Ebbie tilted her chin to a defiant angle. "I'll tell you what...."

"What do you mean, it's over?" J.J. stared in disbelief. "Have you lost your ever-loving mind? You're crazy about him. And Blackstone is crazy about you, too."

Jacq slouched further down on the couch, throwing an arm across her eyes. "Correction. He's crazy about Jack Rabbitt."

J.J. said something short, succinct and painfully rude. "Okay. So from what you've told me, he initially intended to go after Jack Rabbitt. When his client first approached him that was undoubtedly his plan. But those plans changed at the Limelight reception. From that mo-

ment on he wanted you. *You*. Jacq Randell. Not Billie
Bunny.''

"Jack Rabbitt. And it was all an act. He pretended to
be interested so he could figure out how to procure me
for this client of his."

"You're forgetting something. I was there. As was
Cord and Dad. The three of us stood there watching
Blackstone watch you. If you'd stuck around a little
longer, he'd probably have had you right then and
there."

Jacq glared. "Don't be crude."

"Actually, I didn't mean it like that. Interesting that
that's how you took it." She tilted her head to one side.
"I wonder what would have happened if he'd made his
move that night."

Jacq groaned. No question there. She'd have tumbled
into his arms just as readily as she had one week later.
She sat up and scowled at her sister. "What does it mat-
ter? The bottom linc is—he deceived me. Just like
Elliott. He had an ulterior motive for coming on to me.
Like Elliott. And he planned to use me. Like Elliott."

"What if he'd gone after you in a more direct manner? What if he'd knocked on the door of this safe little
hideaway of yours and said, 'Hi, there. I'm Mathias
Blackstone, procurer extraordinaire, and I want Holly
Hare for a client of mine.' How would you have responded?"

"I'd have slammed the door in his face." Well...
Maybe she'd have kissed him first and then slammed the
door.

"My point exactly," J.J. said triumphantly. "So how
can you blame him for coming after you in a more cir-
cuitous fashion?"

"He didn't have to romance me for his client. He

didn't have to pretend he was spontaneous.'' Tears pricked her eyes. And he certainly didn't have to make love to her.

''Now there's a contradiction for you—using the words Blackstone and spontaneous in the same sentence. That alone should have tipped you off.''

''He is spontaneous.'' Jacq instantly leaped to his defense. ''He just has to plan it a little.''

J.J. smothered a grin. ''Uh-huh. Whatever you say. By the way, who was this client Blackstone tried to procure you for?''

''I don't know,'' Jacq admitted.

Her sister lifted an eyebrow. ''Well, why did his client want to meet Connie Cottontail?''

''Jack Rabbitt. And Mathias never said.''

J.J. frowned. ''Didn't you ask?''

''We were a little busy shouting at each other,'' Jacq retorted defensively. ''It didn't occur to me to stop mid-scream and ask detailed questions.''

''I can understand that. But, what about his other procurements? Can't you get an idea from them?''

''Not really. They're all different.''

''Oh, really? Tell me about them. What kinds of things does he procure?''

Jacq shrugged. ''Like I said, it varies.'' She ticked off on her fingers. ''He found a painting for Mel. He brought about a meeting between a mother and the child she'd given up for adoption. There were two teenage girls who wanted to find the perfect honeymoon retreat for their parents. I helped him with those as well as the Operation Toys program—''

''You mean that Christmas party you threw?''

''Right.''

''The one where he dressed up as Santa Claus for a

bunch of kids even though he'd lost his own son not so long ago?''

Jacq had trouble meeting her sister's eyes. "Yes."

"In other words, his job is to fulfill wishes. Good wishes. Beneficial wishes."

"Not all of them are beneficial," Jacq insisted. "He has one client who wants to buy a house belonging to this sweet little old lady."

"And Mathias stole it from her? Threatened her? Turned her out into the street?''

"Not yet." Jacq glowered. "But there's plenty of time. He still has four days until Christmas."

"You're right." J.J. leaped to her feet and began to pace. "I'll just bet he's gonna go over there on Christmas Eve, drag the woman out by her graying bun and chuck poor granny and all her stuff into the gutter. The bastard."

Jacq gave a reluctant laugh. "Okay. Maybe he won't do that."

"Oh, no?" J.J. questioned gently. "Why not?"

"Because he's hoping to find a way to satisfy both parties." Jacq bowed her head. "It's sort of a thing with him."

"A thing. You mean, like a principle or something?"

"I guess you could say that."

"Uh-huh."

"You think I'm wrong, don't you?"

"I think maybe you'd better find out why Mathias wanted to find Jack Rabbitt so badly," J.J. suggested softly. "There must have been a very powerful reason to make him forego his principles enough to deceive you."

"He's not Elliott, is he?" Jacq whispered, stating what she already knew in her heart.

"No, Jacq. He's not."

Why, oh why, hadn't she realized that sooner? Jacq wondered in despair. And now that she had... Was it too late to make things right? There was only one way to find out. She leaped to her feet.

She had to talk to Mathias. Now.

Jacq opened the smoked-glass door marked "Blackstone," fighting to remain calm. Her grip tightened on her satchel of paints but for the first time ever, the familiar clatter of jars did nothing to reassure her. Ebbie sat behind her desk and looked up, surprise and relief written all over her expressive features.

"Oh, Ms. Randell. Thank heavens you're here."

"I'm sorry it's taken so long for me to come to my senses," Jacq said contritely. "Is Mathias in? I'd like to see him."

Ebbie shook her head. "He's visiting a client."

"Oh." Jacq nibbled on her lip and thought fast. "I wonder if I could ask a favor."

"Of course."

"Do you think he'd object if I finished the painting on his desk?"

"I think it would mean a lot to him." The secretary hesitated and then removed a folder from her drawer. "And would you mind leaving this for him? He'll want to see it when he returns."

"Sure." Jacq accepted the file and started toward the office.

Outside the set of black double doors she paused long enough to draw a deep breath. Then she shoved them open and strode into the darkened room. She switched on the light nearest his desk and started to put the folder on his chair when she noticed the name on the tab.

Jack Rabbitt.

There was no doubt that Ebbie had given her the file for a reason. Slowly Jacq flipped it open and began to read.

There was a lot of general information detailing his search—all very precise and thorough and methodical. Typical of Mathias, she thought with a reluctant smile. She turned the pages, delving deeper. Next came months' worth of correspondence between Mathias and her agent and editor. Mathias's letters were a long string of requests to meet with the author and illustrator known as Jack Rabbitt and the reason behind his request. The reason left her stunned. And in response were an equal number of letters in reply. Each was polite, though adamant, in refusing his request, explaining they were legally bound to maintain Jack Rabbitt's confidentiality. The author refused to even discuss the subject of a personal appearance.

Tears filled her eyes. Every word was true, just as every word condemned her. No wonder Mathias had chosen to approach her the way he had. She wiped the moisture from her cheeks and turned to the very last page in the file—the damning sheet of yellow legal paper.

She read it for a second time, giving it more attention than she had before. Why hadn't she noticed how much thought he'd put into the activities he'd chosen? It must have been very difficult to open himself, to allow an outsider such an intimate peek into his life. She drew a shaken breath. But he'd done it anyway, because his client's need outweighed his own. Something had been written on the back of the paper. She flipped it over and saw it was another list.

Only this one read, "Reasons Why Jacq Should Marry

Me.'' The column of ''cons'' ran the full length of the page and some of the itemized notations nearly broke her heart. He was too rigid, too black-and-white. Too grid-oriented. He'd hurt her by exposing her secret. He lacked spontaneity. He'd steal the color from her world and give nothing in return. On the opposite side were the ''pros.''

There was only one.

I love her, he'd scrawled in a heavy hand.

It took a long time before she'd composed herself enough to complete the painting. As she worked she wondered how Mathias would respond when he saw it—and how he'd answer the question she left there. Nemesis came by at one point to watch her work.

''You and Angelica had better get along, that's all I can say,'' she muttered. ''Would you like a companion?''

To her relief, Nemesis gave a reassuring purr.

Half an hour later all that remained was one final detail. Her signature. Then she picked up the phone and called home.

''Turk Randell,'' her father answered brusquely.

''It's me.''

''You sound odd, Jacq. Is everything all right?''

''Not really.'' She wound the telephone cord around her finger. ''Dad... I need your help.''

There was a long moment of silence. And then in a voice heavy with emotion, Turk said, ''I've waited three and half long years to hear you say that. Tell me what you need and it's yours.''

Mathias strode into his office, exhaustion riding him hard. He'd gone to visit the Johnsons personally and it had been a painful meeting. Nemesis sat in his chair behind the desk and meowed a greeting. Crossing to give the cat a scratch, Mathias glanced automatically at Jacq's painting.

"My, God," he muttered beneath his breath. "She finished it. She actually finished it."

The two dragons still held center stage—only the male's eyes were no longer wary. Instead it was the female's expression that held a question. Shafts of gold-flecked sunlight pierced the surrounding jungle and poured down toward the pair without quite reaching them. Something danced within the golden light and it took Mathias a few minutes to realize what it was. Dragons. Four infant dragons. And while the male dragon still held a decidedly wretched rat beneath one claw, he reached toward the light with the other. Reached toward the children with a beseeching look in his green eyes. And where the light touched the black of his scales, they glowed, glittering with all the colors in the rainbow.

He never knew how long he sat there or how long it took him to notice that one last detail. Even after he'd spotted it, he still didn't immediately understand the significance. But once it dawned on him, he shot to his feet and bolted for the door.

In the most revealing gesture of all, she'd signed the painting Jacq Randell instead of using her pseudonym.

Jacq poked her head around the doorway of the hospital room and smiled at the young girl she found there. "Hi," she said with a friendly grin.

Huge dark eyes stared curiously at her for a moment and then a hesitant smile slipped across the seven-year-old's pale face. "Hello."

"Are you Tosha Johnson?" Jacq asked, stepping into the room.

"Yes." Wariness crept into her gaze. "Are you a doctor?"

Jacq shook her head. "I write books and I understand you wanted to meet me. My name's Jacq. Jack Rabbitt."

Tosha's reaction was heart-breaking. A look of radiant joy spread over her delicate features and she grasped the sheet so tightly her fingers turned white. "I wished and wished for you to come and visit me. Everybody said no. They said you wouldn't come. But I knew you would. I just knew it."

"I—" Jacq swallowed hard, painfully aware of how close she'd come to destroying this little girl's dreams. She held out the gift she'd brought. "Merry Christmas."

"What's that?"

"Something I brought for you."

Slowly Tosha took the package, studying the cheery wrapping paper and huge floppy bow in stunned silence. Finally, she asked, "May I open it?"

"I wish you would. Do you mind if I sit down for a minute?"

"Sure. My mom will be back soon. Do you want to use her chair?"

"I'd like that. Thanks." While Tosha carefully unwrapped the present, Jacq took a seat and removed her sketch pad, paints and brushes from her satchel.

"Oh! It's one of your books." She hugged it to her chest. "Thank you."

"You're very welcome. Take a look inside."

Tosha opened the book and blinked in surprise. "You wrote my name and signed it and everything."

"You're the only one I've ever done that for."

"Wait until all my friends see." She looked uncertainly at Jacq. "Do you think they'll believe it was really you? Maybe they'll say I made it up."

"They'll believe you. I promise." Jacq rested her sketch pad on her knee. "Tell me something, Tosha. Who's your favorite character in my books?"

"The fairies," she replied promptly. "I like them best because they're so pretty and they can fly anywhere they want." She regarded Jacq curiously. "Are you going to make a painting?"

"I sure am. I'm going to make a painting just for you."

The gratitude that lit Tosha's eyes was humbling. Jacq swallowed against the knot in her throat and determinedly set to work. The next few hours were a delight with the two of them laughing and talking about everything from school to pets to favorite TV shows. At one point Tosha nodded off and her mother returned. Jacq introduced herself and Michelle Johnson promptly burst into tears.

"I didn't think Mathias would be able to pull it off. He said he'd tried everything and couldn't find you."

Jacq blinked hard. "It's Christmas," she responded lightly. "It's the time for miracles."

"Tosha's going to need more than one, I'm afraid."

"She has to have a bone marrow transplant, doesn't she?" At Michelle's nod, Jacq asked, "Have they found a donor, yet?"

"No. It's her genetic makeup that's making it so difficult. Mathias had the same problem with Christopher because Lisa had such an interesting heritage."

"Christopher had leukemia?" Jacq questioned in distress.

"Didn't Mathias tell you? You see, minorities are the most difficult of all to match and Tosha has a bit of everything. West Indian, African-American, even Native American Indian.''

''I wonder… Perhaps a public appeal will help,'' Jacq suggested diffidently.

''We've tried that.'' Michelle's shoulders slumped in defeat. ''There was an article or two in the local newspapers, a brief flurry of responses. And then nothing.''

''I'm thinking along the lines of a national appeal.''

Michelle stared blankly. ''National? Why would anyone give Tosha's situation national publicity? She's just one of thousands of similar cases.''

Jacq blushed. ''Well… They wouldn't if it were Tosha alone, more's the shame. But maybe Jack Rabbitt could pull a string or two. My father owns a PR firm and if you don't object, we'll use my name to draw attention to Tosha's plight. I have to warn you, it could mean a lot of media attention. That can be pretty overwhelming if you're not used to it.''

''It would also mean helping a lot of people just like Tosha,'' Michelle said slowly.

Jacq nodded. ''Yes, it would.''

''But…'' Michelle fought back a resurgence of tears. ''Are you sure you want to do that? You'd have to reveal your identity. Mathias said it was really important for you to keep it a secret.''

Jacq shrugged. ''Helping Tosha is more important.''

At the sound of her name, the little girl stirred. Her lashes fluttered and she opened her eyes, smiling when she saw Jacq. ''You're still here.''

''I sure am. And look what I have for you.'' She held up the painting she'd completed. ''It's still wet, but as soon as it dries, it's all yours.''

''Mommy! Mommy, look! I'm a fairy.''

Michelle smiled in wonder. ''I see that, sweetie.''

"How'd you like to be in my next book?" Jacq offered.

Tosha's eyes widened. "Can I? Will you let me?"

Jacq nodded. "I promise. All you have to do is work real hard at getting well."

Color blossomed across Tosha's cheekbones. "Will you make me a fairy again?"

"Absolutely. I'll even give you a dragon for a playmate."

"A baby dragon?" a voice asked from the doorway.

Jacq spun around with a silent gasp and met Mathias's impassive gaze with a hint of trepidation.

"Well?" he prompted, leaning against the door frame. "Will it be a baby dragon?"

Uncertainty filled her. Obviously he'd seen the changes she'd made to the desk. But how did he feel about it? "I think that's up to you. Baby dragons need a lot of sunlight in order to survive."

"And color?"

"That, too."

"Then that's what we'll have to give them. Won't we?"

It was all the answer she needed. With an inarticulate cry, she flew into his welcoming arms. They remained with Tosha for another hour before making reluctant farewells, promising to return again in the morning. And then they were in his car, speeding northward through Seattle. Jacq wasn't the least surprised when Mathias eventually stopped at the park above Shilshole Bay. It looked far different than the last time they'd visited, though. The Olympic Mountains were well hidden behind a bank of heavy gray clouds and the Sound boiled with choppy waves.

"You haven't asked me about Adele Gravis or her house," he commented as they left the car.

She sent him a quick sidelong glance. "You mean your first failed procurement?"

"Ebbie told you?" he asked wryly.

"No, she didn't. I worked it out for myself. I can even guess how you resolved the situation."

He lifted an eyebrow. "You can, huh?"

She leaned against the fence at the edge of the bluff and nodded. "If I were a betting woman, I'd lay odds Adele has three brand new boarders. And I'd also bet they all play a mean game of bridge."

He shook his head in admiration. "How'd you figure that out?"

She gave him a smug grin. "Simple. It's exactly what I would have done. How did your client take it?"

"He was disappointed, but not surprised. We're looking at other houses." Mathias hesitated a minute, then asked, "Why did you do it?"

"Go and visit Tosha?" He nodded and she admitted, "I realized you weren't the only one living in the shadows. I was, too. And I decided I'd been there long enough."

"Life's to be lived, is that it?"

"Something along those lines." Snow flurries filled the air, driven by a cold northwestern wind. Mathias opened the front of his coat and Jacq stepped into the warm haven of his arms. She sighed in delight as he closed the heavy wool around them. "I've asked Dad to arrange for an auction. I'm going to sell one of my paintings and donate the proceeds to the National Marrow Donor Program. I'm hoping the resulting publicity will help find a match for Tosha."

"Not bad for your first solo procurement. Which painting are you going to auction off?"

Jacq grinned. "The one with the fairy riding a butterfly."

A quiet laugh rumbled through his chest. "J.J.'s going to kill you when she finds out."

"It's her own fault. She's the one who convinced me to give you a second chance."

He glanced down at her. "Did you need much convincing?"

"Not much," she confessed, wrapping her arms more tightly about his waist. "I'm sorry, Mathias. I had no idea you were trying to get hold of Jack Rabbitt for such an important reason. Neither my editor nor my agent ever approached me about it. And that's my fault, too. I'd made it clear that I didn't want to know about any of the requests they might receive. It didn't occur to me that some of them might be for such vital causes."

"Ebbie suggested that might be the case." He rested his chin on top of her head and sighed. "I've spent a very long time looking for you, Ms. Rabbitt. You've proved to be one tough bunny to snare."

"A long time?" Three months wasn't long. Not long at all. And then it clicked and the pain hit so hard she had trouble catching her breath. "Oh, no. Oh, no," she whispered over and over before dissolving into tears. "*Christopher*! I was Christopher's first request, wasn't I? The one you couldn't fulfill."

He didn't bother with denials. He just held on to her, rocking her until she'd regained her composure enough to speak.

"You must hate me," she said in a tired voice.

"I could never hate you." He cupped her face, forcing her to meet his impassioned gaze. "I love you, Jacq. I' fell in love with you three years ago, when I held my son each night and read your first book to him. I fell in love with your joy for life and your spirit and the sweetness of your stories. And then the first time I saw you, I fell even harder.''

"You couldn't have known what I was like. Not enough to—"

"I knew. It was there for me to see. All I had to do was look. That night at the Davenports's I realized I'd found my other half. I knew I'd found the one woman who could make me whole again.'' He reached into his pocket and retrieved her ring. "Will you marry me, Jacq? A real engagement, this time?"

Tears glittered on the ends of her lashes. "Do you suppose there's still time for a Christmas wedding?"

"If not, we can hold it on New Year's Day. I can't think of a better time to start a new life together.''

A hint of mischief replaced her tears. "It would still give us time to have our first baby by Halloween.''

"Especially if we get started right away.''

And then he lowered his head and kissed her. It was a kiss of hope and determination, of sunshine and color. Of trust and faith and renewal. It was a promise for the future. But most of all it was a kiss of love.

LIMELIGHT INTERNATIONAL: PRESS RELEASE

Jack Rabbitt's fifteenth book, *Celebration*, is just that. A celebration. And with good cause. Devoted readers may remember young Tosha Johnson, the seven-year-old girl in desperate need of a bone marrow transplant to cure her leukemia. Her plight prompted Jack Rabbitt to come out of hiding and make a national appeal for donors—an appeal that resulted in a successful match for young Tosha!

Well, *Celebration* is dedicated to young Tosha—in honor of her thirteenth birthday! Happy Birthday, Tosha! With your leukemia cured, we're certain you'll celebrate many, many more.

EPILOGUE

JACQ'S first baby didn't arrive by Halloween as they'd hoped. Instead, their son was born on Thanksgiving Day. He was every bit as happy and healthy as they could have wished and had Mathias's dark hair and Jacq's bright hazel eyes.

As the years progressed, Mathias never forgot the tragedy of his first son's death. But he did find the love he'd thought forever lost to him. He found it in the faces of the children he ultimately raised and in the eyes of the woman he loved most in all the world. And he found it grew with each day, its intensity banishing the few remaining shadows.

He never did replace his dragon desk, instead he protected it with a glass cover. Over time, it became as well-known as Jacq's books and he displayed it proudly to visitors from all over the world. Only three final changes were made to the desk before it was deemed completed.

The questioning expression in the female dragon's eyes turned to contentment and joy.

The name "Blackstone" was added to Jacq's signature.

And infant dragons frolicking at their parents' feet.

There were four altogether. Two boys and two girls, just as Mathias had promised.

A FAMILY CHRISTMAS!

BY
JOSIE METCALFE

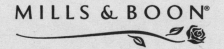

MILLS & BOON®

CHAPTER ONE

'CATCH him, whoever you are!'

The deep voice called from somewhere out of sight as a child came flying through the tinsel-adorned door Callie had just opened and cannoned into her legs.

Long years of practice had her swooping down to field the giggling youngster and she quickly settled him onto her hip—the one unhampered by the burden already cradled in her other arm. There was no time to worry about the fact that her skirt had probably been hiked up far enough to show that she'd had to resort to stockings when her last pair of tights disintegrated.

'And where are *you* off to in such a hurry, young man?' she demanded with an attempt at sternness, but she was unable to help the broad smile that overtook her in answer to her wriggling captive's wholehearted grin.

'Thank God your reactions were quick enough,' came the deep voice again, relief clearly mixed with exasperation as he joined her in the doorway to the children's ward. 'Come on, Mark-the-Shark, I know we should be on our way home by now, but you promised me there would be no more jailbreaks. If you're going to keep breaking your parole am I going to have to resort to handcuffs?'

The muscular arm that reached out to relieve her of her wriggling burden had a rumpled white shirtsleeve rolled up above the elbow and was attached to an impressively wide set of shoulders.

Her gaze was drawn inevitably upwards to meet blue eyes that almost seemed to glitter with silver shards as he grinned down at her.

'Snap!' he said when he finished his lightning glance over the white-swaddled figure she shifted from one arm to the other, still amazed at how heavy such a tiny baby could grow within the space of a few minutes. 'But mine's bigger than yours.'

'Is yours an absconding patient or just a visitor who's had enough?' she asked, the boy's robust little body making her doubt that there could be anything wrong with him.

'Neither,' he said, with a rueful shake of his head. 'This one's mine, for my sins. Aren't you, Mark-the-Shark?'

He lifted the youngster up in the air and made him giggle, the sound infectious in its spontaneity. Callie was surprised to find her spirits strangely subdued and had to push her unwarranted disappointment to the back of her mind. What business was it of hers if her unfairly attractive new colleague was a married man with a family?

She saw the moment when Mark's new vantage point gave him his first clear view of the bundle cradled in the crook of one arm.

'Is that a baby?' demanded the little tearaway, wriggling round and leaning precariously towards Callie, obviously without any fear that the man holding him would let him fall. 'Look! She got a baby!'

'So I see, Mark-the-Shark,' he murmured, with a wry twist to his mouth that emphasised that single wicked dimple. 'And she's looking just a little bit lost and flustered, too. Can I offer you directions, or is your expression just part and parcel of parenthood?'

'Both,' Callie admitted, and blew a stream of air at the strands of hair that were already beginning to escape from the hasty twist confining it. She'd been so determined to look competent and efficient when she arrived for her first shift at St Lawrence's, and look at the state of her. No one would think she'd had more than half a day to get ready.

Unfortunately, four-week-old Zoe could have no idea how important the impression she made today would be for their future.

An unexpected bout of colicky sickness after her morning feed followed by yet another dirty nappy had necessitated a quick change of clothes for both of them, and had ruined all Callie's good intentions. It had probably been her own fault for losing track of time and then trying to hurry.

Now, she was not only too late for a leisurely handing-over as she delivered Zoe to the hospital's staff crèche for the first time, but she probably hadn't even managed to arrive on the ward in time to meet her opposite number before he finished his own shift.

She couldn't help watching the interplay between adult and child with a pang. It seemed impossible that she would ever develop that sort of ease with Zoe.

Unlike her fumbling attempts, the confident way he was handling the youngster spoke well for their relationship, and the fact that he was obviously at home in the ward made Callie realise that he would probably know who she was looking for.

'You wouldn't happen to know if Dr Kendrick is

still on the ward, would you? I know he's supposed
to be off duty now, but I was hoping to—'

'*I'm* Ross Kendrick,' he supplied with an easy
smile in spite of the fact that his young charge was
now using him as a mobile climbing frame. 'You're
lucky to have caught me. I should have disappeared
about half an hour ago, as you can probably tell from
Mark-the-Shark's air of hyperactivity. And you are?'

'I hate to say it, but I think I'm the reason why
you're still here,' she said apologetically, freeing one
hand to offer it towards him with trepidation. 'I'm
Callie Bell.'

She knew the swift frown that drew his brows together wasn't a good sign, nor was the disappointed
expression that passed briefly over his suddenly aus-
tere features.

In spite of the fact that he didn't hesitate to envelop
her hand fleetingly in the lean strength of his, Callie's
stomach dropped towards her eminently sensible
shoes.

'I'd planned to be here far earlier,' she said ruefully, hurrying to explain in the hopes that she could
minimise the damage she'd done to her own reputation while her hand tingled strangely from the momentary contact with his. 'Unfortunately, Zoe's a little young to understand that there wasn't time for a
bout of colic today, and then she needed a change of
nappy…' Horribly conscious that she was babbling,
she finally gave up.

'Luckily, this end of the day's been fairly quiet, so
there's no harm done,' he said crisply, all trace of that
engaging grin gone. 'What will happen later on is
anyone's guess, of course, and tomorrow morning
there's a full list for Theatre. We'll probably be work-

ing to capacity over the next few weeks to clear as many as possible before we start trying to empty the department for Christmas.'

'Is that her? Can we go home now?' interrupted a belligerent young male voice, and Callie suddenly realised that there was someone watching them from a doorway just along the short corridor—two some-ones, in fact.

'Not long now, Andy,' Ross promised, with a quick glance over his shoulder before he led Callie in their direction.

Callie's attention was drawn towards the sulky-looking young man as he slouched his way across the room to sprawl crossways in an armchair, his trainers dangling luridly against the dull upholstery. He couldn't have been more than ten or eleven but she could tell that the expression on his face didn't bode well for a smooth transition through his teenage years.

'You've been saying that for hours,' he pointed out rudely, accusation clear in eyes just a shade or two darker than those of the man he resembled so clearly.

'Andrew…' Ross began firmly. Callie could hear a warning coming but before he could deliver it an-other voice broke in.

'Why are you being so mean all the time, Andy?' demanded the last member of the quartet, her little cheeks pink and her hands clenched into fists. 'It's not his fault—he's got to go to work. Anyway, it doesn't make much difference whether we waited here or watched television back at the flat—*you* still got to watch the programmes *you* wanted to.'

'All right, Fliss,' Ross said, and from the resigna-tion in his tone it sounded as if it wasn't the first time he'd had to step between the two of them.

Callie's guilt grew as she realised how much trouble her lateness had caused. The whole family seemed to be at each other's throats and it was all her fault.

'Please… I'm very sorry for holding you up. If you could just point me in the right direction for the crèche before you go, I should be back here before the rest of the staff know it.'

'I'm sure you could,' Ross agreed. 'But that's hardly the right way to ensure that our patients are properly taken care of. It won't hurt this mob to wait a little while longer before we embark on the excitement of a trip to the supermarket while battling the pre-Christmas hordes.'

Callie found her sympathies drawn towards the two children when she saw the glare Ross directed at them.

The little girl he'd called Fliss looked so like the older boy that they couldn't be anything other than brother and sister, but everything else about them couldn't have been more different.

At a guess, she was a couple of years younger but, where his posture shouted *attitude*, she was sitting as neatly and tidily as if expecting to take tea with a duchess. He was dressed as if he didn't care what he'd put on when he got up this morning, while the berry-red skirt of her winter wool dress was smoothed all the way down to the tops of coltish bony knees covered by dark green tights.

'The two of you can share the last of the orange juice while you're waiting. Don't make a mess,' Ross directed sternly as he turned towards the door with the youngest child once more safely in his grasp, and gestured for Callie to make her way out of the ward.

'I do apologise for making you—'

'I'm sorry about their lack of—'

Almost as soon as the child-proof lock on the main door into the department snapped closed behind them they both began to speak, then broke off in disarray.

Ross chuckled briefly as he pointed out the signs for the nearby crèche, his long legs forcing her to hurry just to keep up with him.

'You're sorry for being late and I'm sorry for their lack of manners,' he continued wryly. 'Shall we take it as read that we've kept the score even with apologies? My crew are good kids at heart but they're obviously having a few problems with the social niceties at the moment.'

Callie shifted Zoe from one shoulder to the other and was rewarded with a loud burp.

'As you can hear, my little monster is taking full advantage of the fact that no one expects her to have mastered *any* of the social niceties yet,' Callie pointed out, her instinctive embarrassment demolished by young Mark's chuckle of delight at the way the rude noise echoed along the corridor.

It didn't take her long to hand the sleepy baby over to the staff at the crèche, confident that the hospital would have made certain that they were all properly qualified. Even so, she could tell from the way everyone's eyes softened when they saw her that Zoe wasn't going to want for attention.

'Lots of babies,' Mark pronounced brightly. 'Can we take one home?'

'Mark…'

'*Please,*' he added quickly, and Callie couldn't help smiling when she realised that he obviously thought he was only being reminded of his manners. 'Just one?'

'Don't you think there are enough of us, young man?' Ross demanded in exaggeratedly horrified tones. 'If we try to move any more people into the flat, you'll end up sleeping in the wardrobe with a hanger in the back of your pyjamas.'

Callie scored Ross a silent point for successfully side-tracking the child from his wish to take a baby home, but she couldn't help laughing at the expression on the child's face. He was obviously intrigued by the idea of being hung away for the night.

'You might regret putting that idea in his head,' she pointed out softly. 'Still, if he goes missing tonight, at least you'll know where to look.'

Ross groaned. 'Me and my big mouth. The kids will all have left me by the time I get the hang of this parenting lark.'

In no time they'd retraced their steps and he was leading her back into the children's ward where he promised to make short work of the introductions.

'This is obviously good timing,' he said as he stuck his head round the door of the small staffroom and found a meeting in progress. 'Any of that coffee going spare, Sister? We'll need two.'

He beckoned Callie forward into a room that seemed to be full of chairs, each one home to someone whose eyes were now fixed firmly on her.

'Listen up, you horrible lot,' he began, his tone almost identical to the one he'd used on the children not long ago. Callie seemed to be the only one surprised at his form of address... The rest of them, from the lowliest member of staff upwards, were grinning at him as if they didn't expect anything else.

'This is Dr Callie Bell,' he announced, with a wave in her direction of the enormous steaming mug of coffee he'd just been passed. 'She's the one who will—single-handedly—keep me sane by taking you off my hands for hours at a time, so I want you all to be very, very nice to her.'

An elegantly slender woman in the dark blue uniform of ward sister rose to offer Callie her hand.

'Naomi Henzie,' she said, her wide smile only intensifying the impact of perfect cheekbones. 'What the good doctor has failed to mention is that if you can manage to keep *him* sane that will stop him from driving *us* insane too.'

Callie laughed as he mimed a fatal wound to his heart but her attention was divided. She had the strange feeling that she'd seen the woman somewhere before and had to drag her eyes away from the uncannily familiar face.

'Well, I'm not a miracle-worker, but I'll do my best,' she assured them, glad to find that everyone seemed so willing to accept a complete stranger so easily into their midst. 'I'll apologise in advance for getting lost as I learn my way round the hospital, and for forgetting everyone's names almost as soon as you tell me, as long as you promise to put me right.'

Her mind was going over and over the faces of the staff at the hospital where she'd trained, and those she'd worked with since then, trying to match a face with the one in front of her. Even when she went further back, to the many faces she'd known as she and her sister were passed from pillar to post through the fostering system after their parents died, she couldn't think where she'd seen the woman before. Then, suddenly...

'Naomi Campbell!' she exclaimed out loud as she recognised the clear resemblance to the internationally familiar model, then, when everyone in the room burst out laughing, she wished the ground would open up and swallow her.

'I wish!' the ward sister exclaimed ruefully, obviously not in the least upset. 'I don't think my earnings in a *year* match what she can pull in for a day!'

'I'm sorry,' Callie said hurriedly, aghast at her *faux pas* in the first moments of her new job. 'I didn't mean to be so rude, but...'

'Don't worry about it—it happens. In fact, you're quicker than most to make the connection,' Sister Henzie said dismissively. 'It was more of a problem when I worked up on the men's wards. Their fantasies about models are even more lurid than their ones about nurses. At least, down here, most of the kids are more into cartoon characters.'

Ross had been standing quietly by but his young burden had obviously decided he'd been still long enough and demanded to be released from captivity.

'Listen, I've left the other two watching television at the other end,' he began, with a quick glance at the plain steel watch strapped to his wrist.

'And you don't know how long it'll be before World War Three breaks out,' Callie finished for him, understanding his problem and knowing that part of it was her fault. There were an awful lot of questions she needed to ask him; an awful lot of things she needed to know before she would feel completely happy about being left in charge for the next shift.

But then, when would she ever feel as if she knew enough to be completely in control of every case? Most of her career so far had been one learning situation after another and she firmly believed that it was the only way to improve and progress.

There was no way she was going to admit, even to herself, the feeling that she didn't want Ross Kendrick to stick around *just* for the information he could give her. She wasn't even going to *think* about the effect his silver-shot blue eyes and wicked dimple had on her pulse rate—where was the point when he was obviously married? Even now, he was relinquishing the youngest of his three children into the temporary care of a willing junior with promises of a swift return home.

'You might as well escape while you can,' Callie forced herself to say with a breeziness she didn't really feel. 'I'm sure everyone here will be able to tell me where to go and what to do, and, if not, the infernal bleeper will.'

'Ah! Bleeper!' he said, and delved in each of his pockets in turn. 'Here we are!' He presented the little grey plastic box with all the panache of a conjuror producing it out of a hat. 'Your very own little piece of technological torment. May you be very happy together!'

Callie pulled a face at him, knowing that happy was probably the last thing she'd be feeling the first time the wretched thing woke her up.

She went to slip it into her pocket and felt the sharp edges of the letter she'd stuffed in there on her way out of the house this morning.

For just a second, the problems she was going to be facing at the end of her shift intruded, then she made herself force them away as she clipped the gadget to her belt instead.

It was another ten minutes before she stood watching Ross usher his little brood out of the ward—ten minutes in which he'd given her a thumbnail sketch of the current situation with each of the patients on the ward. He'd finished off with a crash course in the idiosyncrasies of the hospital call system and wished her luck on her first shift.

'Do you really mean that?' she'd challenged softly, and had seen a shadow of his former animation flicker in his eyes.

'Actually, I do,' he'd admitted candidly, his tired smile giving her just a glimpse of that elusive dimple again. 'It's a good hospital and I hope you're going to enjoy working here—for my sake, if nothing else.'

It was twelve long hours before Callie collapsed on her unmade bed, totally exhausted.

A slight snuffling sound had her holding her breath and crossing her fingers, but this time Zoe slept on.

'What a nightmare,' she breathed, shutting her eyes to avoid staring up at the naked light bulb hanging down from the centre of the room.

A small corner of her brain registered that the reason why her sister had never got around to putting the lampshade up was the small pile of paint tins and decorating equipment in one corner of the room, but the frivolous thought evaporated in the face of more desperate concerns.

With a soft groan she forced herself to roll over and slide quietly off the bed, her stockinged feet almost silent as she crept out of the room and back into the kitchen.

There, on the table, was the cause of her greatest problem—an innocent-looking piece of paper that had shot all her plans to pieces. How was she ever going to get herself out of this mess?

She skirted the table, eyeing the letter as if it were

a poisonous snake lying in wait, and reached for the kettle.

Her first shift at St Lawrence's had gone smoother than she could have hoped and, after numerous trips backwards and forwards between various departments, she had finally memorised her way around. Now, all she wanted to do was crash out and recharge her batteries for more of the same tomorrow, this time with the added stress of a ward full of post-operative cases on top.

Unfortunately, what she needed to do was sit down with her cheque-book and calculator and work out if she was going to be able to afford to buy the next container of milk for Zoe, let alone food for herself.

She sat at the table and forced herself to concentrate on the letter she'd been carrying about with her, as if she hadn't read it often enough to memorise the words. The logo of the mortgage company at the top seemed quite benign in comparison with the dire consequences threatened in the contents.

It wasn't the first time she'd wondered if she'd made a disastrous mistake in giving up her job and moving across country, but when she'd made the decision she'd thought she was going to be staying with her sister.

For months, ever since Steph had told her that her boyfriend had moved out, Callie had known that the last precious member of her family was becoming severely depressed. When she'd finally admitted that she was pregnant and begged for her big sister's help, what else could Callie do?

The last thing she had expected was that Zoe's birth, several weeks early, would end in such a disastrous way.

She still couldn't believe it. It was three weeks since she'd taken emergency leave and had arrived to find her sister dead from a totally unexpected pulmonary embolism with her tiny daughter still cradled in her arms.

Callie dragged shaky fingers through the bedraggled strands of blonde hair that had caused the two of them to be mistaken for twins on more than one occasion. It looked as if Zoe had inherited the same colouring, but the blue of her new-born eyes already looked as if it was changing to hazel and her similarity to Steph was clear enough to be heartbreaking.

Callie took a mouthful of the rapidly cooling coffee and grimaced. It was going to be hard enough to switch off at this time of day, and with these worries on her mind, without filling her system with caffeine. The thought that she and Zoe could end up out on the streets with an enormous debt around their necks and no way to pay it back was the last way to guarantee dreamless sleep.

If she was very lucky, she would be able to come to some arrangement with the mortgage company about paying it off in instalments. If not...

It would have been so different if she'd known what she was getting into.

Why hadn't Steph told her that, apart from being abandoned by her boyfriend, she was months behind with her payments? Thinking that the property was rented, Callie had spent the last couple of weeks concentrating on the possibilities of saving money by moving out into a smaller flat.

Well, there was nothing she could do about any of it until she'd had some sleep. She was so tired she was nearly falling over. If only Zoe would give her a full four hours before she demanded attention, her brain might start to lose its fuzzy edges.

Perhaps she could phone later to arrange meetings with the bank and the mortgage company. There must be something she could salvage out of the situation. If not, she could see herself looking for a full-time post just to earn enough to pay off her sister's debts, in spite of the fact that this would leave her with no time to take proper care of Zoe.

Then what would happen to the solemn promise she'd made to Steph?

During their years in the various types of institutional care, the two of them had talked and dreamed about the way they would raise their own children, once they arrived. Now it looked as if she was going to fail Zoe right from the outset; to break the vow she'd made at Steph's graveside.

As if she knew Callie was thinking about her, Zoe stirred and whimpered.

With a heavy sigh, Callie stood up and poured the rest of her cold coffee down the sink and started to prepare the bottles she would need for the next few hours. The last thing she wanted to do was scrabble about with her eyes closed while her feet turned to ice blocks and a four-week-old martinet screamed at full volume about the poor service.

At least if she was fed as soon as she wakened she didn't seem to get herself so worked up and the feeds stayed down better. The trouble was, it was turning Callie into a nervous wreck who couldn't sleep through the slightest sound, knowing that she was solely responsible for Zoe's health and welfare.

When she finally curled up under the bedclothes and began to relax she was disgruntled to find Ross

Kendrick's handsome face hovering in her mind's eye.

'I bet he never had to get out of bed to take care of a screaming baby,' she mumbled. 'Probably left that side of things to his wife.'

The mental image of his rapport with young Mark made her feel guilty for such uncharitable thoughts. He was obviously the sort of hands-on father she and Steph had dreamed about finding, and she could be excused a twinge of jealousy over the fact that he already belonged to someone else.

She relived the frisson of attraction she'd felt the first time that she'd been treated to the sight of that single wicked dimple. There was no room in her life for married men—no room for *any* men, with the mountain of responsibilities that had landed on her shoulders in the last few weeks.

Still, she thought muzzily as she began to drift off, a tired smile lifting the corners of her mouth, that didn't mean she couldn't look at him…and he was certainly worth looking at…

She was married!

Ross tried to slide his numb arm out from under Mark's head but the sleeping youngster just burrowed closer, pushing him right to the edge of a bed that had always seemed perfectly big enough before.

He sighed as the memory of the disastrous day tried to swamp him and concentrated on his new colleague, the only bright spark in the whole fiasco.

There'd been no ring on her finger—he'd caught himself looking for one—but that didn't mean much these days, and with that well-wrapped bundle in her arms it was obvious that she was a recent mother returning to her profession part-time.

He'd felt a strange sensation when she'd told him her name, as if his stomach was diving swiftly· towards his boots, and it had brought him to his senses.

What did it matter whether she was married or not? She might be the most appealing woman he'd met in a long time but, in spite of the fact that his hormones had reacted as instantaneously as if he were still a teenager, he had enough on his plate without getting tangled up in any sort of relationship. Even with someone who wore stockings…

As if he'd have time!

A less than subtle blow to his ribs with a sturdy knee activated his instincts for self-preservation just in time to avoid the foot aiming for a more tender portion of his anatomy as Mark wriggled again.

The youngster drew in a ragged breath, legacy of the tears he'd shed when he hadn't been able to find his beloved soft toy at bedtime. The fact that Andy had been responsible for hiding the wretched thing had been just one more frustration in an increasingly impossible situation.

The reminder from the young lady who had been keeping an eye on the children after school that she was going away skiing for Christmas had warned him that the school holidays were bearing down on him at a rapid rate of knots. So far, he had no idea how he was going to replace her.

If the tense confrontation with his neighbours was anything to go by, no one would be happy if they ended up cooped up in the flat for the duration. Three children undoubtedly made more noise than this essentially 'singles' set-up was used to.

A spreading dampness made Ross groan aloud as he rolled out of bed with the dripping culprit held at arm's length, hoping that he'd moved fast enough. If he'd soaked this mattress, too...

'Come on, Mark-the-Shark,' he muttered as he hurried the sleepy child towards the bathroom. 'Let's get you emptied out and changed so we can both get some sleep.'

Poor little chap, he thought fuzzily as sleep began to claim him. The last year hadn't been very easy on any of them. They were obviously missing their mother, each reacting in their own unique way.

Andy had retreated into surliness, relieved only by periods of bossiness towards his younger siblings, and Mark had retreated back towards babyhood, with frequent episodes of bed-wetting and a return to dependence on much loved toys.

It was Fliss who worried him most, though. At nine years of age she should still be playing like a little girl, largely oblivious to the cares of the world around her. The ultra-polite little wraith tucked away in a spare room hardly bigger than a large cupboard was nothing like the giggly chatterbox she used to be, and confrontations were often enough to reduce her to tears.

Still, with Callie Bell settling in at St Lawrence's, at least he might have some time to spend with the three of them.

A stray image of the long-legged sun-shot blonde loveliness of his new colleague was swiftly banished in favour of a fervent hope that she was going to fit well in the department. He'd been trying to keep everything going for nearly three months, now, and hoping for the best, but with the Christmas holidays looming he'd realised that it couldn't go on any longer. It just wasn't fair to his colleagues or their patients.

Thank goodness the powers-that-be had been understanding, albeit a little amused, when he'd asked to be treated like a married woman with children to accommodate around her schedule.

The job-sharing scheme sounded as if it would solve most of his problems, allowing him to continue working while taking care of Andy, Fliss and Mark. Other problems, like the sheer lack of space in his flat for three growing children, were another matter, and it looked as if it was something he was going to have to solve before the end of the school term arrived.

He shelved that problem for another day. Time enough for that when he was certain that the department wasn't going to suffer under the new regime, with his usual workload shared between himself and Callie.

She was very slender for her height, he found himself musing, his thoughts circling back to their original focus as he remembered how she'd looked in that first lightning glance. She was fine-boned...looked almost as if a stiff breeze would blow her away. She'd certainly regained her figure far faster than Megan had after Mark, or either of the others. You'd hardly know that she'd been pregnant at all...

He snorted silently when he realised how his mental eyes were traversing the length of her slender body, those stocking-encased legs and the stomach as taut and flat as...

'Enough!' he muttered in disgust at himself. 'She's

a married woman with a new baby. All you're interested in is whether she can do the job…and whether
she can get herself organised enough to turn up on
time for her shift.'

CHAPTER TWO

'AT LEAST I'm on time today,' Callie muttered to a fitfully sleeping Zoe as she hurried towards the crèche. Her restless charge was muffled up to her little button nose, tucked out of harm's way inside Callie's thoroughly dampened coat.

With bulging bags dangling from each elbow, she'd been glad of the electronic eye to open the doors into the unit. Who would have thought that such a tiny being would need so much *stuff*?

Unfortunately, her punctuality was about the *only* thing that had gone right since she'd woken up and found the letter pushed under her door.

Just when she'd thought things were as bad as they could be, something had come along to prove her wrong.

When she'd moved in, she'd known that Steph had been sharing the pretty little detached house with a young couple upstairs to help with her shaky finances. Callie had foreseen that her sister's impending motherhood would leave her in desperate financial straits and it had been one of the major reasons why she had wanted the position at St Lawrence's.

Unfortunately, according to their obviously hastily scribbled note, it looked as if her erstwhile housemates had been unofficially subletting the rooms from Steph and her boyfriend and were already several months behind with the rent.

They were very sorry, they'd written, but they just didn't have the money to pay.

'Neither have I,' Callie had fumed impotently, knowing that all the careful calculations she'd done to impress her bank meant nothing if they weren't there to pay their share of the expenses. They obviously had no intention of honouring their debts, either.

'At this rate, I might have to move into the crèche myself,' she murmured with a sigh as she let herself into the ward. 'The size of the beds would be a bit of a problem, but at least we'd have a roof over our... Oof!'

'I'm sorry. Are you all right?' Ross Kendrick's quick reactions were the only thing that prevented her landing on her bottom in the middle of the corridor. His grasp on her elbow was reassuringly firm as she regained her balance.

'I'm sorry, I didn't see you until it was too late,' she apologised, silently berating herself for yet another less than sedate entry into his life. When was she ever going to get her act together? Ever since they met, she seemed to have been a one-woman disaster area.

'Too busy muttering to yourself to hear me coming,' he teased, with a weary smile that told of the end of a long day. 'Perhaps I need to hang some of these reindeer bells around my neck to give you warning.' He held up the end of a tinkling string that stretched back round the corner into the main part of the ward.

She certainly needed warning about that smile, she thought as she watched him reach up to attach the string to the top of a notice-board, having to bat aside a brightly coloured bouquet of balloons to reach the top.

He might be tired and she was definitely discouraged but his smile, coupled with a close-up view of an impressive set of shoulders, was still enough to jump-start her heartbeat into double time.

'Well, at least I'm not late today,' she pointed out when he finished his task and turned suddenly to face her. She'd hurried into speech, half afraid he'd caught her admiring gaze, then realised how defensive she sounded and pulled herself together, aiming for calm professionalism. 'If you're ready to give me a rundown of what's been happening on your shift you might even be able to leave a few minutes early.

Ross was obviously quick on the uptake, matching his tone to hers.

'It was a full list this morning. Two hernia repairs, picked up at pre-school medicals. Ditto, one undescended testicle. Kidney stones removed from a twelve-year-old and a ureter implanted in the lcft kidney of a four-year-old. No complications and all doing well, so far.'

Ross briefly took her through each set of notes, concisely detailing what procedures had been used and confirming levels of pain relief. While he answered a couple of questions for her, Callie found herself distracted by the way he was rubbing the back of his neck with one hand. The poor man didn't look as if he'd had much more sleep than she'd had.

The side of her that was so strangely attracted to him wanted to do something to take care of him, but that was not her responsibility. The sooner he went home, the sooner he'd be able to get some rest.

'Well, it looks as if you're ready to go now,' she

said cheerfully, more than willing to make up for the time she'd kept him waiting yesterday.

'I can't tell you how grateful I am,' he rejoined fervently. 'With any luck we won't have to stand another evening of Andy reminding us that he was royally ticked off with the situation. You could have cut the atmosphere with a knife and poor Fliss got herself so wound up she didn't get to sleep for ages. As for Mark…' He shook his head and when she saw him shudder she decided not to ask what Mark had done.

'Teenage hell looming?' she asked, more drawn to him than ever, even though all he was doing was detailing the problems he was having with his children.

'God, I hope not,' he said fervently, then glanced at his watch. 'Got time for a coffee? This is my last chance for adult conversation until tomorrow morning.'

Callie didn't need much persuading and he led the way to the little staff kitchen and plugged the kettle in. 'The teenage years are still officially nearly two years away, but the way things are going I don't think I'd survive if I had to keep them that long.'

'Keep them?' Callie parroted, confused. 'You mean, they don't usually live with you?' Did his wife have custody? Were they separated…divorced?

There was a sudden unseemly lift to her spirits at the thought that this gorgeous man might not be married after all.

She squashed it firmly. With everything going on in her life—Zoe and now her disastrous finances—she didn't have time to breathe, let alone start a relationship.

'No, thank goodness.' He rubbed his hands over his face and the rasp of his emerging beard vied for her attention with his heavy sigh. 'God, that sounds terrible, doesn't it? Especially for someone specialising in paediatrics.'

'Everyone has those sorts of days,' she said, offering the words as an excuse.

'This has been months rather than days, and it might be continuing indefinitely,' he said grimly. 'It's not general knowledge but I would have thought someone might have told you what was going on yesterday.'

'I don't listen to gossip. People's private lives are their own business,' she said stiffly, stung that he thought she might have asked questions about him as soon as he was out of the door. The fact that she'd wanted to was another matter entirely.

'This is hardly gossip,' he said as he leant back against the waist-high work surface and wrapped both hands around a steaming mug of strong black coffee. 'It's the reason why your job was advertised in the first place.'

Callie had wondered about that. She'd been so delighted that she'd secured the part-time post she'd needed so badly that it hadn't occurred to her to ask why she was going to be sharing it with a man.

'Tim and Megan, my brother and sister-in-law, had been going through a bit of a rocky patch. He's an engineer dealing with big Government contracts and sometimes has to be away for days and even weeks at a time.'

'That can certainly put a strain on things,' she commented when he paused, wondering where the narrative was taking him.

'When his partner had a fall and broke his leg, Tim knew he was going to have to take off to supervise a major project on the other side of the world. Unfortunately, he'd promised faithfully that he wasn't doing the field work on this one and Megan went ballistic.'

Callie sipped her own drink and let him get to the point of the story in his own time. She still couldn't see what all this had to do with his own situation.

'I couldn't stand back and watch everything go to the wall without doing something to help, so I suggested that Megan went with him for a couple of weeks—a bit like a second honeymoon. There was no way I could commute to St Lawrence's from their house so I said their children could stay with me and the babysitter could ferry them to school.'

'Their children... You mean they're not *yours*?' That was one explanation that hadn't even crossed her mind, in spite of her own situation with Zoe.

'Mine? Good Lord, no!' Ross exclaimed, and burst out laughing, the deep, full-throated sound drawing an answering chuckle from Callie.

'I don't see why you're so surprised. They look just like you, and the way you handle them—especially Mark—you could easily be their father.'

'Thank you for the compliment. I only hope I don't have to find out whether I can sustain it over the long haul. The kidnapping means it's already been far longer than any of us anticipated.'

'Kidnapping?' Callie repeated, shocked. 'Who's been kidnapped?'

'Tim and Megan, just before she was due to fly back.'

'But... Why? Who?'

'It was several weeks before we found out that they were even alive,' he explained sombrely, all trace of humour gone. 'Apparently, some of the locals object to large areas of their most productive land being drowned under millions of gallons of water to provide power for cities they'll never even visit. The fact that they were never even consulted about the project didn't help.'

'So what's going to happen to them? Is anything being done to rescue them? God, those poor children. They must be worried out of their minds.' That went some way to explaining the tensions she'd seen simmering between the group. They were far too young to have to cope with such a situation.

'They don't know,' he said bluntly. 'They were upset enough by all the arguments between Tim and Megan, so I decided not to say anything about the kidnapping until we know they've been released.'

'But…' Callie shook her head. That didn't seem right to her, having been in the same position herself. Well-meaning social workers had told her that her parents had gone away and it had been years before she realised what they'd really meant and stopped waiting for them to return. 'How on earth did you explain the fact that their mother didn't come back?'

'I said she'd decided to stay with their dad a bit longer.'

'And if the worst happens to their parents? The children will know that you lied to them and you'll have lost their trust,' she accused heatedly, her heart going out to the three of them.

Mark was probably too young for it to have such a lasting effect on him, but Andy and Fliss were definitely not happy. She wouldn't be at all surprised if the two of them had already got wind of what was

going on. Either that, or they'd drawn their own, even
more disastrous scenario.

'Well, it's not a situation I've come across before,
so I'm just taking it one day at a time. Unfortunately,
the rest of the people in the flats around me are reaching the end of their tethers before I do.'

'What have they got to do with it?' She'd been
ready to argue her case for telling the children what
was going on but he'd completely side-tracked her.

'You mean, apart from the fact that there are now
four people crammed into a bachelor flat, three of
whom have never had to think about the fact that their
feet will sound like a herd of elephants to the people
below?' He pulled a wry face. 'And that's before they
break up for the Christmas holidays. Heaven only
knows what I'm going to do with them when they're
home all day, especially as I'm losing my baby-sitter,
too!'

No wonder he looked tired, she thought, suddenly
wanting to do nothing more than give him a hug. The
poor man *was* almost at the end of his tether.

'I know Andy and Fliss are probably too old, but
have you tried any of the agencies that provide nannies? They might have a suggestion.'

'I tried them and they did, but it involved moving
the lot of us, lock, stock and barrel, into a much larger
house.'

'And?' With no end to the situation in sight, it
seemed an eminently sensible suggestion to Callie,
but then, she was the person who only needed a tiny
flat and was swimming around in a house far too big
and too expensive for her needs.

'I know it would be a good idea for everyone's
sake, but…' He gave a gusty sigh and seemed very

intent on watching his thumb smoothing repeatedly over the curve of the mug handle. 'It just seems…almost as if I'm giving up on Tim and Megan ever coming back if I make such a permanent move, if you know what I mean?'

He looked up at her, his sombre blue-grey gaze meeting hers for a fleeting second.

The darkening tint across his lean cheeks told her that he was embarrassed to admit to such a superstitious feeling, but she felt no inclination to mock. She'd played too many similar games herself while she'd waited for her family to come and fetch Stephanie and herself.

As if keeping her room perfectly neat and tidy or avoiding walking on the cracks on the pavement would make any difference…

He glanced down at the plain steel watch strapped to his wrist then reached across to tip the dregs of his coffee into the sink.

'It's time I went to retrieve my little gang and tried to find something to do with them before they have to be cooped up inside for the night,' he said as he ran the tap to wash his empty mug out. 'It wouldn't be so bad if it didn't get dark so early; I could take them to a park, or something. As it is, the flat is far too small and cramped. At least in a house there would be room for them to get away from each other when they'd had a disagreement.'

Callie shivered when she remembered that, at the end of her shift, she was going to be going home to a completely empty house. It was the first time that the thought had struck her and she realised that she didn't much like the idea.

It wasn't so much the fact that she would be

lonely—she'd long been accustomed to her own company, ever since she'd reached eighteen and had to leave Steph and the home. It just worried her that she hadn't even met her neighbours and would have no one she could call on in case she needed help.

Ross had reached the doorway and was just wishing her a quiet shift when the solution to both of their problems struck her.

'You could come and live with me,' she blurted.

The arrested expression on his face made her realise what she'd said and she felt her face go up in flames.

'I mean, you and the children could move into the other half of the house,' she explained hastily.

'Oh, don't spoil it. That was the best offer I've had in years,' he complained, his dimple much in evidence again. 'But won't your husband have something to say about you inviting a horde of strangers to stay?'

'Oh, I'm not married. I live alone...well, with Zoe, and she doesn't pay rent, even though she takes up most of the space. I don't know what Steph was thinking about, moving into something so big.' Once again her tongue took over.

'Steph?' He'd patiently leant one shoulder against the doorframe as though waiting for her to ramble herself to a halt.

'My sister, Stephanie. Zoe's mother.'

'Zoe's mother?'

It was the startled expression on his face that told her he'd been making assumptions, too. He hadn't been able to stop his eyes dropping swiftly from her less than spectacular breasts towards her never-been-pregnant waistline and she couldn't help chuckling out loud.

Steph had told her, amid tearful laughter, that almost as soon as she'd become pregnant she'd developed a bustline big enough to launch a thousand ships. In comparison, her own probably wasn't enough for a very small dinghy.

'I'd have been doing very well to have got my figure back this quickly,' she pointed out with a dismissive gesture at herself. 'Zoe's only four weeks old.'

Callie glanced up at him in time to see the renewed flush of embarrassment darkening his cheeks at being seen looking at her body like that. She was seized with an unexpectedly wicked intention of teasing him about it but caught sight of someone moving into view in the corridor behind him just before Sister Henzie's distinctive voice broke in on their conversation.

'I'm sorry to interrupt, Doctors, but we've had a call from Casualty. Can somebody go down and have a look at a child who had an argument with a motorbike on a pedestrian crossing?'

'I'm on my way.'

'I'll go.'

They both spoke together and Naomi laughed.

'That's what I like to hear—people keen to work. I'll let you fight it out between you,' she added with a dismissive wave, and disappeared from sight.

'*I'll* take it,' Callie reiterated firmly. 'It's my shift now, remember? You're on your way home.'

He conceded with a silent wave of his hand for her to proceed, waiting until she was reaching for the child-proof lock before he spoke again.

'I'll think about your offer and come in a few minutes early tomorrow morning to talk about it,' he called, and set her heart thumping in a totally different rhythm.

'Drat the man,' she muttered as she hurried towards the brand-new accident and emergency wing and her waiting patient. 'What on earth made me open my big mouth? The last thing I need is *him* underfoot.' Especially now she knew that he wasn't married, a little voice added in the back of her head, but she pretended she hadn't heard.

'Sister, you rang up for someone to take a look at a child knocked down by a motorbike?' she said as soon as she reached the department. Thank goodness she could rely on her professionalism kicking in to exclude other extraneous considerations, such as the lick of fire that had seared over her skin from her breasts to her belly in the wake of a certain doctor's gaze.

'This way.' The older woman turned smartly to lead the way and, in spite of her much longer legs, Callie had to stride out to keep up with her. 'Brought in by a passer-by—a motorist who witnessed the accident. The child—Richard—is three years old and looks badly battered. Mother's too hysterical to be much use.'

Callie's first impression as she entered the room was that the sister had been very exact in her appraisal.

The child, a young lad roughly the same size and build as Mark, was lying on the bed whimpering into the mask covering the lower half of his face, his little neck completely hidden by the protective cervical collar.

The young woman perched on the edge of the chair beside the bed was shielding the rest of his body from Callie's sight, her arms wrapped around herself as she rocked herself backwards and forwards with tears streaming down her cheeks.

Callie stepped forward and took her first close look at him, dread tightening its fist inside her when she saw that one corner of his forehead already bore the spreading evidence of a heavy blow.

She didn't need to see the pile of tattered clothes that had been cut away from his body to know that he'd been dragged along the road; the evidence was there in the multitude of bloody scrapes right down one side of his body.

'Was the mother injured at all?' Callie demanded in a low-voiced aside, a swift look at the distressed woman failing to reveal any damage to her clothing.

'Not at all. She's just badly shocked—she says it's all her fault.'

'In that case, I think it would be a good idea if she's taken somewhere quiet and given a hot, sweet cup of tea while we get on with our job. It won't do her guilt any good if she has to watch us put this little chap through the mill.'

Callie spared a brief moment to introduce herself and promise that she would do what she could to take care of Richard, then turned back to her poor little charge.

Before the door had time to swing shut she was demanding status reports on his pulse, respiration and blood pressure.

No one was surprised that his pulse and respiration were higher than normal, but the clear evidence of a

steady downward trend in his blood pressure was far
more worrying.

It didn't take long before Callie had isolated not
one but two possible causes.

'Is the radiographer ready?' she rapped out sharply.
'His left femur's broken up close to the hip joint and
I don't know whether he might have damage to his
spleen. We'll also need to scan his head to rule out
brain damage.'

Callie was impressed by the speed with which
things were accomplished. It seemed no time at all
before the child was ready for his urgent journey up
to the top floor and an appointment with a waiting
orthopaedic surgeon.

'Have you got time to have a word with his
mother?' Sister asked as Callie fired her discarded
gloves into the bin. 'The man who brought them in
has been sitting talking to her and she's much calmer
now.'

Callie nodded. Now that she'd handed Richard over
into other hands she could concentrate on explaining
the situation to his mother. Doubtless she would be
seeing both of them fairly often over the next few
days, when the child arrived on her ward for post-
operative care.

'Is he all right?' demanded a fierce young man as
soon as Callie entered the little interview room. For
a moment she was taken aback. For some reason she
hadn't expected him to be the epitome of a yuppie
young executive, and she certainly hadn't expected to
find him holding the young woman's hand.

'He's broken the long bone in the top of his left
leg and he's had a bang on his head. He's covered in
scrapes and bruises but they're all relatively minor.'

Thank goodness her worry about his spleen had proved to be unfounded. 'He's losing quite a bit of blood into the tissues of his leg and needs an operation to fix the ends of the bone together so they can heal properly, then he'll be having a scan to make sure he hasn't done any damage to his skull.'

'When?' It was the first word Callie had heard the woman utter but she could hear the anguish in it.

'He's ready to go into Theatre now. Would you like to go up with him to give him a kiss before he goes to sleep? He's a bit groggy but he'll still know it's you.'

'Can I?' She glanced from Callie to her companion and back again. 'Can we both go, only…?' She drew in a shuddering breath. 'It's all *my* fault. It wouldn't have happened if I'd made him wear his safety lead thing. He hates wearing it, but at least he wouldn't have been able to run on ahead.'

'That's not true,' her companion butted in heatedly. 'It's *not* all your fault. The traffic had stopped and you were already on the pedestrian crossing but that idiot on the bike still thought he had time to roar across. He could have killed both of you.'

Callie wasn't going to get involved in the rights and wrongs of the situation. It was enough for her that, whoever he was, the young woman's white knight was giving her the support she needed so she could give Callie's little patient the support *he* needed.

'While you're here…' said a voice at her elbow as Callie watched the little group hurrying towards the bank of lifts.

Callie grinned wryly. 'Oh, dear. Should I have made my escape while the coast was clear?'

'Probably. We're always on the lookout for willing hands, but if they're unavailable we're not averse to press-ganging people into doing what we want,' the older woman said with a friendly smile. 'I was wondering if you'd be prepared to do a bit of embroidery on a budding hairdresser. It's going to take someone who's a dab hand with a needle to do a neat enough job on it, and if you've seen the size of the hands on the chap on duty...'

'You've caught my interest,' she admitted. 'What have you got?'

'A young lady who got hold of her mother's dressmaking scissors and decided to have a go at her own hair. Unfortunately, she missed her aim and tried to take her ear off as well.'

'Ouch!' Callie winced.

'And messy, too. Why do ears always seem to bleed so much?'

'Don't say any more or you'll put me off,' Callie warned as she followed her towards one of the curtained cubicles down the side of the department.

A quick examination of the mutilated ear revealed that it was, indeed, going to be a messy and time-consuming job.

Callie settled herself down on a stool and began to distract her tearful patient from the sharp discomfort of a series of anaesthetic injections by asking lots of questions about the Disney characters on her T-shirt.

It was amazing how scathing a five-year-old could be when you deliberately mistook the Little Mermaid for Beauty and the Beast, Callie thought with a smothered smile as she caught the mother's eye.

By the time the eleventh tiny stitch had been carefully placed, she even felt that she might have per-

suaded her little patient that she was going to grow
her hair as long as the Little Mermaid and leave the
chopping to a real hairdresser.

'The stitches should come out at the end of the
week,' she told a grateful mother. 'Sister will organise
a note for you to take to your doctor so you don't
need to come back to the hospital.'

'Wouldn't it be better to come back here?' she demanded with a worried frown.

'It might be more convenient for you, if we're
closer, but for something as minor as removing
stitches it certainly won't be better. Just think about
how many years your GP has been doing the job and
then think how many doctors in accident and emergency departments are newly qualified.'

'I never thought of it like that,' she said in amazement. 'And if I make an appointment for our doctor
to do it we'll get seen pretty close to the time of our
appointment.'

'Whereas here, as a non-urgent case, you could end
up waiting for hours until someone was free,' Callie
finished, doing her little bit for patient education.

Out of sight, Sister was giving her a thumbs-up and
Callie had to turn her grin of complicity into a smile
of farewell.

'Will you let me escape now?' she asked as another
set of disposable gloves landed in the bin.

'Until the next time. When does your shift end?'

Callie explained briefly about her job-sharing with
Ross and suddenly remembered that he was going to
be coming in before the end of her shift to talk to
her.

She could have done without the reminder. All the

while she was busy she could forget that she'd made such an outlandish suggestion.

What had she been thinking of? She'd always hated the lack of privacy that communal living entailed and now she'd suggested that he move in and bring three less than happy children with him.

Obviously she had no idea what he was going to decide, but if it weren't for the disastrous state of her finances she would begin their meeting by withdrawing her suggestion.

She'd got enough problems in her life already and sharing a house with Ross Kendrick was the last thing she needed.

CHAPTER THREE

'ABOUT your suggestion,' Ross began, coming straight to the point before Callie had time to draw breath. 'How big is your house, exactly? Would there be room for all four of us? And how far away is it from the hospital?'

As he had promised, he'd arrived in the department more than half an hour before she was due to clock off, but instead of looking well-rested after a good night's sleep he was looking rather frazzled. And if she wasn't very much mistaken he was still wearing the same shirt he'd worn yesterday. Either that or he had two with identical mismatched buttons sewn on the cuffs.

It was unlikely that he'd spent a night on the tiles, not with three children depending on him. That led her to the sneaking suspicion that all might not be well on the domestic front—particularly in the laundry department.

The thought that he might be having problems coping with the housework three children would entail dissipated most of her fears in one fell swoop.

She'd spent several hours carefully wording a little speech to tell him she'd changed her mind. It had been full of evasive disclaimers but she knew, deep down, that there was only one real reason—for the sake of her sanity she would have to avoid sharing her house with a man who did such strange things to her pulse.

But how could she be worried about that same man when he didn't seem to have the time to get his laundry done? He certainly wouldn't have time to pay her any attention—not with three little chaperons in residence…four if she counted Zoe.

'It's a little detached house about three-quarters of a mile from here,' she began, hurrying into speech when she saw the frown starting to pull his tawny brows together. 'There are three bedrooms upstairs, a bathroom and a tiny room being used as a kitchenette. There's even a small garden out the back.'

'How many of the rooms do you need? Does Zoe share your room?'

'Oh, no, I live downstairs,' she said, and hurried into an abbreviated version of the events that had led her to offer to share her accommodation.

'So,' he summarised, 'you got left holding the baby and with a mortgage on a four-bedroom house to pay on a junior doctor's salary.'

'Not forgetting a pile of debts,' she reminded him.

'I hope that's something you *can* forget about,' he said, to her surprise. 'I'll get a lawyer friend to check up on it, but I vaguely remember something about a person's debts dying with them. If I'm right, you might only be liable for the costs since you moved into the house.'

'That would be fantastic if it were true, but that still leaves me with a mortgage to pay.'

'And when I move in with my little crew your share would go down to a manageable one-third, if we divide it by the number of bodies.'

She'd been expecting to have to pay half but she wasn't foolish enough to argue. She was still slightly reeling at the fact that he seemed to be assuming that everything was settled.

'You haven't even seen the place yet,' she pointed out warily, not wanting to get her hopes up too high.

'That's the next step, then. When would be convenient? Not that I think it's going to make any difference. You wouldn't have made the suggestion if you didn't think it was a viable idea. When will we be off duty together?'

The two of them compared shift patterns but while Callie was holding a perfectly lucid conversation, arranging for Ross to come over that Thursday afternoon, she was very conscious of a warm glow settling around her heart.

It had been just a throwaway line to him...'You wouldn't have made the suggestion if you didn't think it was a viable idea'...but it was the first real evidence she'd had that he valued her opinion.

'Damn,' Callie muttered as she tottered on the top step of a set of decidedly rickety stepladders. The strident ring of the doorbell had startled her so much that she'd nearly fallen off.

'Coming!' she called as she stretched up one last time to try to twist the light bulb back into the socket, the newly installed shade swinging wildly as she fought with it.

The days had seemed to stretch endlessly into the distance as she waited for Thursday to arrive, and she'd thought she would have plenty of time to get things looking a little tidier. Now he was here, and the place still looked as if she was packing up to leave rather than settle in.

She'd even contemplated hiding the poor state of

the walls and paintwork by hanging Christmas decorations. She already had a small box of the ones she'd saved from last year's celebrations with Steph, but they were still packed somewhere in the boxes piled all along one wall.

Anyway, there just hadn't been time, not with Zoe waking her up every three hours, and by the time she'd been fed and…

'What are you doing?' demanded a deep voice from the doorway, and she nearly leapt out of her skin.

Without a thought for her precarious position she started to swing round to face her unexpected company and lost her balance.

Arms windmilling wildly, she tried to grab for the top of the ladder but the room was tilting alarmingly and she gave one startled shriek as gravity won the battle.

She just had time to catch one glimpse of the horrified expression on Ross Kendrick's face before she closed her eyes and prepared for the inevitable painful crash.

His reactions must have been superb because the next thing she felt was a strong arm tightening around her to jerk her descent to a halt.

'Stupid woman,' he hissed in her ear when his other arm had joined the first to support her weight as easily as though she weighed no more than Mark.

Her eyes snapped open in renewed shock, the illusion of safety destroyed by the anger heating his eyes to molten steel. 'You could have broken your neck on that thing,' he added harshly, giving her a shake for good measure.

That got her vocal cords working again in a hurry.

'Put me down,' she demanded, feeling at a definite disadvantage. 'I wouldn't have fallen at all if you hadn't startled me.' She certainly hadn't expected to have the wretched man walking in on her like that.

He lowered her feet to the floor but held onto her arms as if to steady her. When she would have stepped back from him to break the contact between them she found her back against the ladders and was reduced to glaring up at him.

'What are you doing in here anyway?' she demanded, knowing she would have felt much more in command of the situation if she'd been able to welcome him calmly at the door.

'You said to come in,' he retorted with annoying composure as he finally released her and tucked his fingers in the pockets of his well-worn jeans. 'And the door wasn't locked.'

'I said I was coming,' she countered, and heard for herself how he could have mistaken her words. Not that it mattered much. He was here now and she'd just have to gather her tattered dignity around herself and carry on.

She shrugged slightly and released her chagrin with a brief sigh as she looked up the half-dozen or so inches into his eyes.

They really were beautiful eyes, she thought distractedly, somehow unable to look away. Their colour almost seemed to change with his moods. Just moments ago, when he'd entered the room, they'd been stormy, more grey than blue. Now they'd softened, darkened, the pupils enlarging even as she watched, almost as if he were becoming aroused...

'What are you doing, Uncle Ross?' demanded a little voice, and the two of them jerked apart almost guiltily to face the three children standing watching them from the doorway.

'Ah, I was…ah…'

'We…he…just stopped me from falling off the ladder,' Callie explained, fumbling for an explanation that would take the suspicious glare off Andy's face.

She followed his gaze briefly up to the lampshade still swinging gently over their heads and when she saw him relax realised that her answer seemed to have satisfied him. What did surprise Callie was the realisation that the same evidence proved just how little time had passed since Ross had come into the room. She had been concentrating so intently on him that time had ceased to have any real meaning. The only thing that eased her mind was the fact that his own reaction to his nephew's question must mean that he'd been equally engrossed in her.

'The children came out of school early today for a staff meeting,' Ross explained briefly. 'I hope you don't mind them coming along, too?'

'Not at all,' Callie replied, her manners on automatic pilot as she tried to sort through the strange haziness in her brain.

What on earth was the matter with her? She'd invited the man to look at the house with a view to helping her to keep a roof over her head.

The other side of the equation was that Ross needed the extra space to give his niece and nephews somewhere more suitable to live. It was a two-sided coin, each of them needing the other to help solve a problem. There would be no time for either of them to indulge in any extra-curricular activities…even if they wanted to…

'Well, are we going to have a look at this house,

then?' Andy prompted impatiently, his measuring glance strangely adult as he scanned what once must have been the dining room.

'Of course we are,' Callie agreed briskly, and set off towards the door. All of a sudden, she felt an urgent need to get Ross out of the room she slept in. After that strangely electric interlude between them, it felt too intimate somehow to have him in there.

'Is baby coming too?' demanded Mark, and she suddenly noticed that while the rest of them had been concentrating on their slightly uncomfortable conversation he and Fliss had quietly approached Zoe's portable cot and were standing gazing at her with enthralled expressions on their little faces.

'Hey, you two, don't wake the baby up,' Ross admonished softly.

'We haven't, Uncle Ross. It's still asleep,' Fliss assured him earnestly in a stage whisper.

'She,' Callie corrected her with a smile. 'Her name's Zoe…it means life.' Steph hadn't been able to decide what to call her daughter and it had been left to Callie to think long and hard about it, even buying a book of names. First she'd thought of naming her Stephanie, after the mother she would never know, but that didn't seem to fit. She'd reached the very end of the alphabet before she'd found the perfect one.

'Why?' Fliss demanded. 'Why does it mean life?'

'Lots of names have meanings,' she explained, and when she saw the light of interest kindle guessed what was coming next.

'Everyone calls me Fliss but I'm really Felicity. What does that mean?' she asked eagerly.

'That's an easy one,' Callie said with a smile. 'It means happiness.'

'What about Andy and Mark? What do they mean?'

'I don't know those off hand, but I've got a book, so we could look them up.'

'Now?' she demanded, her eyes scanning the room, obviously in hopes of spotting the book herself.

'Not yet, Fliss,' her uncle said decisively, but Callie noticed that his hand was gentle as he reached out to smooth a wayward strand of hair from the child's face. 'We've come to look at Dr Bell's house, remember?'

'Why do we have to look at her house?' Andy demanded belligerently. 'We like living with you.'

'I explained all that,' Ross reminded him patiently. 'It's only a bachelor flat and there really isn't room for all of us there.'

'But it isn't worth us moving,' Andy insisted, and Callie could hear more than a hint of desperation in his voice. 'Mum will be back soon and we'll all be going home and then you'll only have to move back again.'

If his mother came back, Callie corrected silently, her heart going out to the unhappy child. She knew what it was like to live from minute to minute not knowing what was going to happen to you, and all the time knowing that the grown-ups around you were keeping secrets.

'In the meantime,' Callie said brightly as she led the way through to the inner hallway and up the stairs, 'you'll be able to have room for your toys and games and space to get away from each other when you want to.'

She stood aside at each doorway so that the four of them could examine the size of the three rooms.

It was the first time she'd taken the time to have a good look round up here, and as far as she could tell one had been used as a bedroom and the other as a living room. The third had obviously been used as storage for packing boxes and junk, most of which had been left behind in the hasty move.

'There's a kitchen in there and the bathroom is here.' She pointed at the door leading into the smallest of the rooms and pushed open the last door beside her.

'Hardly a kitchen without a sink,' Ross commented wryly. 'They must have done the washing-up in the bath.'

Callie's heart sank. It didn't sound as if he was very keen, and if he didn't want to move in her finances were shot. What on earth was she going to do about finding somewhere to move Zoe? If it were only herself, she could probably persuade someone to allow her to sleep on the floor for a few days. She doubted anyone would be very keen to offer an invitation that included a baby who didn't seem to be able to sleep longer than three hours, day or night.

As if on cue, there was the distinctive sound of her little nemesis letting the world know, at full volume, that it was time she had some attention.

'If you'll excuse me for a minute,' she said, and seized the chance to hurry down the stairs with the excuse that she needed to pick Zoe up before her little charge got herself really worked up.

In fact she was grateful for the opportunity to get away from Ross for a moment. The frowning expression pleating his brow was enough to tell her that he'd been trying to find a polite way of turning her proposition down. It would be less embarrassing for both of them if she gave him some time to find the words for a polite refusal.

She'd just finished changing Zoe's nappy when she heard the sound of assorted feet descending the stairs. For about fifteen minutes she'd been listening to the four of them wandering about over her head, her mouth lifting into a brief smile when she heard the sound of Mark's exuberant shout as he ran full-pelt from one end of the hallway to the other.

She sighed as she braced herself for a refusal. It would have been nice to have the four of them up there, she thought wistfully. Apart from being her financial salvation, the sounds of their footsteps and voices above her would have helped to drive the dreadful loneliness away.

'Come in,' she called in answer to the childish knocking on her door.

'We've had a family conference,' Ross announced when they'd all trooped into her room. Fliss and Mark had immediately hurried across to join her on the edge of her bed, one on either side of her to be as close to Zoe as possible. Andy was hovering close to the door, his expression telling Callie that whatever had been decided was without his approval.

Ross was the one who drew her gaze as he leant silently against the wall beside the fireplace and watched her as she settled Zoe against her shoulder.

'I know it's much bigger than the flat we're in at the moment,' he began, and Callie braced herself for disappointment. It was hardly the opening comment of someone who was thinking of moving in.

'But?' she prompted, wanting to get it over with.

'But we're interested, if we can come to some agreement on sharing of space?'

'Sharing of space?' she repeated blankly, trying to absorb the fact that he hadn't immediately turned it down.

'Yes,' Fliss jumped in eagerly, not waiting for her uncle to continue. 'We want to know if you will let us use your kitchen if we let you use our bathroom?'

'The kitchen?' she repeated, her brain obviously two steps behind. 'But—?'

'What we thought,' Ross interrupted, his hands thrust into his jeans pockets giving him an air of total relaxation as he settled himself into a slouch and crossed his feet at the ankle, 'was if we gutted that excuse for a kitchen we could turn it into a bedroom for Mark, and...'

'And then there would be a bedroom for each of us,' Fliss butted in excitedly. 'No one would have to share with anyone so none of our things would get mixed up.'

Ross grinned at her. 'Did you notice I managed to say all that without moving my lips?'

'Uncle Ross!' Fliss exclaimed, her cheeks growing pink. Callie suddenly realised just how pretty she was, and that it was the most animation she'd seen from her since she'd met her nearly a week ago.

'I have got my own bathroom downstairs,' she admitted honestly while her hopes rose like helium-filled balloons.

'It's only got a shower in it, which won't be very convenient when Zoe gets too big for her baby bath,' Ross pointed out quietly, proving that he'd had a quick peep at her rooms on the way through. 'Anyway, that kitchen upstairs would never be big enough for the four of us, while yours down here has enough space for a dining table and chairs in the corner by the door.'

Callie wasn't going to argue with the man. He could take over the whole house except for this one room if it would solve her problems.

'So, you're going to move in?' She crossed her fingers out of sight within the blanket wrapped around Zoe and held her breath while she waited for his answer.

'If you're happy with sharing the kitchen and bathroom,' he agreed. 'If I can hire a van of some sort, we could bring the first lot of things over tomorrow.'

So soon! Callie's head was whirling at the speed things had started moving.

'Morning or afternoon?' she asked with a false semblance of calm, as if it really made any difference.

She barely heard his reply, her brain filled by an annoying little voice prophesying that doom and catastrophe were surely going to follow such foolish decisions.

If the expression on Andy's face was anything to go by, he was even less pleased by the situation. He glared at her one last time as the four of them took their leave of her, the only one who wasn't saying 'see you tomorrow' with a smile. Just for a moment, Callie thought she saw the threat of tears in his eyes and, behind them, an ocean of fear and misery waiting to break their banks and overwhelm him.

By the time the rental van pulled up outside the front of the house, Callie was dressed ready to set off for St Lawrence's with a warmly bundled Zoe settled into a sling against her chest.

'I'll be glad to go to work to have a rest,' she whispered to her sleeping charge as she picked up the bulging bag of necessities and set off to open the front door.

Ever since Ross had left yesterday afternoon she'd been upstairs clearing up the mess left behind by her erstwhile tenants.

There hadn't been a lot she could do about the dingy colour scheme, but at least all the rubbish had gone now, bagged and dumped outside by the bin. Early this morning, courtesy of Zoe's inbuilt alarm system, she'd set to again with cleanser and disinfectant and had scrubbed everything to within an inch of its life.

At least she was leaving them to move their belongings in knowing that the place was clean enough not to pose a threat to the children and, now that she'd finally worked out how to regulate the boiler, warm enough for comfort.

'Here, you'd better have this,' she said as she opened the door to Ross and held out the key she'd left waiting for just that purpose.

'You're going?' His breath steamed in the chilly air and it almost seemed as if he was disappointed.

'On duty soon,' she pointed out.

He glanced down at his watch and did a double take. 'Is that really the time? I never realised how long it would take to pack things up and load them into a van.'

'Especially without three children "helping"?' she queried with a grin. 'Best of luck with the rest of the job. I've always found it takes longer to get straight when you unpack than when you pack.'

'Thanks very much for the encouragement,' he

groaned. 'At least I've got a couple of hours to get this lot shifted before I've got them underfoot again. One of the other children invited the three of them to a birthday party after school so I might get something done before I have to pick them up.'

The ward was busy that night, with three children brought in suffering from bad asthma attacks to add to the numbers.

Each time, Callie was called down to have a look at the youngster to confer over the severity of the attack, and each time she had erred on the side of caution.

'I'd rather they spent a few extra hours under observation than for you to get home and have to come all the way back in again,' she explained each time. 'In the long run, it's a lot less wearing on all of us, especially the patient.'

'We're well used to it by now,' said one parent, his other child sleeping in his arms as his wife concentrated on the little patient struggling for breath. 'At least, here, the staff are sympathetic to the idea of wait and see. The last place we lived they seemed to want to shove us out of the door as quickly as possible.'

Callie knew that often this was just the impression some hospitals could give in their attempt at efficiency. She had often noticed that as long as the staff made certain to seem easygoing about the length of time it was taking to stabilise the situation a lot of tension simply disappeared. This could only be good for the patient's state of mind.

'Doctor, about a year ago there was something on the television about a new way of controlling asthma.

Did you see it?' queried the grandmother of one little girl at about three o'clock in the morning.

It had taken a couple of hours for her breathing to ease but she was now settled on the ward and dozing peacefully after her exhausting struggle for breath.

'Was it some drug they were talking about?' Callie asked, glad for something to talk about to keep her mind from wondering how far Ross had got with his removals. He'd managed to wangle a shift swap so she wouldn't be seeing him at the hospital when she handed over at the end of her shift. She'd have to wait until he came over with the next load of furniture to find out how things were going.

'No, it wasn't drugs. It was some Russian doctor who was training some volunteers to be able to control an attack.'

'Control it, how?' Callie was intrigued, especially with the incidence of asthma on the increase.

'As far as I could tell, it looked as if he was teaching them how to control their breathing to stop an attack getting hold.' She pulled a wry face. 'It wasn't very clear, but then, if he's trying to make his living teaching it, I suppose he wouldn't want to give all the details away.'

'And was it successful?'

'It seemed to be…very.' She was obviously delving in her memory for details. 'There were only three guinea pigs but the cameras went back to visit them some time later. Apparently, one of them was managing to sleep right through the night for the first time in years, one had improved so much he'd been able to start learning to play golf and the third one was off drugs completely.'

'That sounds fantastic.' Callie was genuinely impressed. Asthma could completely take over a person's life and if there was some way of breaking its stranglehold...

'The programme said there was a doctor's surgery somewhere in the middle of England where the asthmatics were being trained in this breathing, and their drugs' bill was down to a third of what it was before.'

Callie was still thinking about the breathing technique for controlling asthma attacks when she let herself in the house later that morning and dumped two bags of shopping inside the door.

As she settled Zoe into her bassinet, she realised that she vaguely remembered watching the programme, now that her memory had been jogged, and she wondered whether Ross would know whether there was any such scheme being run locally. She would have to remember to ask him.

It didn't take long to carry the shopping into the kitchen but when she opened the door she stopped in her tracks.

'Wow, you've been busy,' she murmured in amazement when she looked around the room. There, in the corner, were the table and chairs he'd talked about, one end of the table piled high with unidentified boxes and gadgets. The short work surface running partway along one side of the large square room was laden, too, with boxes of tins and packages obviously waiting to find a home.

'We're going to need some more cupboards...or at least some shelves,' she murmured, silently admitting that what the kitchen really needed was a major refit. Chance would be a fine thing, she thought as she filled the kettle, and she kept herself busy stacking her purchases in the fridge while she waited for it to boil.

'Next stop, the bathroom,' she promised herself. She'd been looking forward to a real wallow ever since she'd realised that their agreement to share kitchen and bathroom gave her the rights to more than the cramped shower she'd been using.

It didn't take long to grab the last clean nightshirt out of the drawer. It was worn decidedly thin but it was so comfortable that she was loath to throw it away, yet. Unfortunately, each time she wore it became the signal that it was time to do another load of washing. If she set the machine going before she climbed into bed it could be waiting for her when Zoe next woke her up.

She'd been a little worried about leaving Zoe at the other end of the house while she had her bath but, not wanting to disturb her by carrying her upstairs, had compromised by leaving the bathroom door ajar so that the sound of her cries would carry.

'Ah-h!' she groaned blissfully as she leant back in the bath and retrieved her mug of tea. 'Luxury. Absolute luxury.'

She closed her eyes, determined to empty her mind of everything but the heat and warmth surrounding her like a cocoon. For as long as the bath lasted she wouldn't think once about the patients she'd left behind or the financial problems she still faced. She certainly wasn't going to think about all the possible pitfalls of sharing a house with Ross and his unhappy little crew...especially not Ross...especially when she was sprawled naked in the bath...

The water had begun to cool and, while she'd have loved to top it up and soak a little longer, she would be needing the hot water for the load of laundry begging for attention.

She'd just finished rinsing the last of the shampoo out of her hair when she thought she heard Zoe stirring.

'Already!' she moaned as she quickly wrapped a towel around the dripping mass, glad that at least she'd had a clear half an hour to pamper herself.

Faced with the choice of trying to drag her nightshirt on over wet skin or taking a few extra seconds to rub herself dry, Callie took the more comfortable option and grabbed a second towel.

She was just trying to manoeuvre her towel-wrapped head through the opening without tearing the flimsy fabric when, without warning, the bathroom door swung open and Ross stood framed in the opening.

CHAPTER FOUR

FOR several interminable seconds Callie was frozen in surprise, her hands raised up above her head so that her whole naked body was exposed to his gaze.

'Oh!' Suddenly she realised that she was standing there like some Greek caryatid and yanked her night-dress down over herself. There was an ominous tearing sound and she winced, but that was the least of her concerns now.

A fierce blush spread its way upwards from her breasts to her hairline and honesty compelled her to admit that it had little to do with her embarrassment at being caught naked. She closed her eyes and shivered as she recalled the heated expression she'd surprised in his eyes as they'd raked her from top to toe and back again.

For just a second she'd thought he was going to come closer, then, as if suddenly remembering where he was, he'd stepped swiftly back and pulled the door closed again.

The sharp click as the latch caught was an audible punctuation mark to the whole episode.

Her hands were shaking as she collected up her belongings and dread infused her. How was she going to be able to face the man?

She'd never dreamed that he would arrive so early. Surely, on a Saturday, the children wouldn't have been so amenable to getting up early. He could hardly have left them alone in his flat—Andy was too young to be landed with that much responsibility.

No matter how she tried to side-track her thoughts, they kept returning to the same subject—those few brief embarrassing seconds when she'd all but posed for him.

If only she'd stuck to her own shower. Would Ross think she'd left the door open on purpose? Surely not. With three children living with him for the foreseeable future, he had even more responsibilities than she had. Neither of them was in the position to start a relationship, even if they were attracted to each other.

Callie had just decided to make a run for her room when there was a sharp tap on the bathroom door.

'Ready for some breakfast, or have you already eaten?' Ross called cheerfully, seeming as unaffected by the embarrassment of the last few minutes as if they'd all been in her imagination.

She opened her mouth but not a sound emerged. What could she say without sounding as if she was swallowing her tongue?

'Callie?'

Damn him for his persistence. Why couldn't he just disappear and let her bolt for her room and bury her head under her pillow for the next twenty years? 'I'm going to do some toast and a pot of tea. Are you interested?'

If she were honest, she was interested in a lot more than a piece of toast and a cup of tea, but if that was all that was on offer…

'Y-yes, please,' she croaked, frantically trying to get her unruly thoughts under control. 'I-I'll be down in a minute.'

'Do you want scrambled eggs on that toast or would you prefer bacon?'

She sighed in resignation. If he could be so resolutely upbeat she must have imagined that heated look in his eyes when he'd seen her a few minutes ago. Was it a symptom of frustrated spinsterhood—imagining that every man a woman met was lusting after her?

'Am I allowed to have both?' she called back, then held her breath while she waited for his answer.

In a sudden flash of comprehension, she believed she knew what he was trying to do. The two of them had agreed, for their own reasons, to share the house. If they allowed an isolated incident to create a strained atmosphere between them...

'Bacon and scrambled eggs it is,' he agreed. 'But I hope you realise you're stretching my bachelor cooking skills to the limit.'

There was the sound of laughter in his voice and as she heard him going down the stairs she relaxed her death-grip on her clothes. Her stomach rumbled loudly and Callie allowed herself to smile.

There was a spring in her step and a little quiver of excitement somewhere deep inside her as she emerged from the bathroom.

It wasn't worth getting dressed again but there was no way she was going to sit down at the table with him in a nightdress torn from waist to hem. She would have to detour into her room to find her faithful old towelling dressing gown, but then...

Half an hour later she leant back in her chair and sighed.

'That was utterly delicious, but I think I've eaten so much that I won't be able to sleep.'

'Do you need to get your head down straight away?' he asked, his enormous coffee mug cradled in one long-fingered hand, refilled for at least the third time.

He was leaning back in his chair, his long legs stretched out under the table almost to the other side, and he looked thoroughly disreputable.

It wasn't just the fact that he was wearing well-worn denims and a sweatshirt long past its best; he'd been wearing something similar last time she'd seen him. This time he looked almost as if he'd only just climbed out of bed, his hair rumpled and at least a day's worth of tawny stubble lending his face a piratical air.

It was quite an effort for her to remember his question and she found she could only concentrate by looking away from him.

'Well, I've got a load of washing to put on before I go, but I try to get as much sleep as I can between feeding Zoe. There isn't a problem, is there?'

He was silent for a moment, and her gaze found its way back in time to see a thoughtful frown pleating his forehead.

'Yes and no,' he said at last, and the vague unease that had been hovering in the background of her mind suddenly mushroomed into a black cloud of dread. He wasn't going to tell her that he'd changed his mind, was he?

The silence began to stretch out again and this time it seemed as if he was avoiding her eyes.

Callie suddenly wondered if it was up to her to make the first move. After all, the whole thing would never have happened if she'd locked the door.

'I'm sorry I didn't—'

'I apologise for barging in—'

Once again, they began to speak simultaneously and broke off in confusion.

'This is getting to be a habit,' Ross said with a wry smile. 'Both trying to apologise at the same time.'

'At least we're still all square, if you're keeping score,' Callie pointed out. 'Anyway, I promise it won't happen again. I'd only left the door open so I could hear if Zoe woke up. I wasn't expecting you to arrive quite so early this morning, as it's a Saturday. What have you done with the children?'

'I'd only been out to deliver them to the lady who's been minding them for me when I'm at work,' he explained. 'As a final favour, she said she'd keep them for the day while I finish moving in. Unfortunately, things were so topsy-turvy this morning that I didn't have a chance to get to the bathroom before it was time to take them.'

He rubbed a rueful hand over the tawny stubble on his chin and when Callie heard the rasp of his emerging beard she found herself wondering if it was as bristly as it sounded.

'So, you think you'll finish moving in today?' she asked, dragging her thoughts back to the matter in hand. 'Are the children looking forward to living here?'

'None of them settled down very quickly last night—that's why everything was such a rush this morning. It didn't help matters when they realised I'd left the box of breakfast cereals back at the flat. It'll be better when they get used to it.'

'You mean, you slept *here* last night?' Callie was amazed. She hadn't bothered looking into any of the bedrooms on her way to the bathroom so she hadn't

realised. How had he managed to get everything organised so quickly?

Ross scowled. 'It was rather a case of having to,
in the end. It was either that or go stark raving mad
trying to keep track of the three of them.'

'Why? What were they doing? I would have
thought they were all old enough to be able to help
a bit.'

'They should be, but Fliss and Mark are so keen
to move in, they're flinging everything into the boxes
regardless of whether they're breakable or not, and
Andy's so much against it that he's being as obstructive as possible.'

'How much more have you got to transport? Is
there anything I can do to help?'

'I've got a small removals van arriving at the flat
in about an hour to take the rest of the furniture, and
there will probably be two more carloads of the small
stuff. Most of it's mine because the children only
brought enough with them for an extended visit. They
weren't supposed to be staying this long, so they've
been putting up with makeshift beds. It seemed...'
He paused for a moment as though he couldn't decide
whether to continue, then did. 'Somehow, it seemed
as if buying furniture for the children for an extended
stay...well, it made it seem as if I'd given up hope
that Tim and Megan were coming back.'

Callie caught a glimpse of the deep sorrow in his
eyes as he thought about his missing brother and sister-in-law. She glanced away at the clock on the wall
above the cooker to allow him a semblance of privacy
while she thought of some way to change the topic
of conversation.

'How long do you think it will take to load up and drive here? Till about midday?'

'Or thereabouts,' he agreed, with a shrug that drew her attention to enviably broad shoulders under the disreputable sweatshirt. 'Why?'

A squeak from Zoe's direction warned Callie that it was time to bring the conversation to a swift close. She was surprised how long she'd slept this time— long enough for a bath *and* a leisurely breakfast. Was she finally getting into some sort of routine?

'Well, if you promise not to wake me up before one o'clock, I'll help you straighten things out a bit before you have to fetch the children.'

She hurried over to the fridge to retrieve the bottle she'd prepared earlier and turned to set the power level and timer on the microwave.

'Offer accepted,' he said quickly. 'In fact, if you want to get your laundry organised, I'll start feeding Zoe for you. How's that for a fair exchange?'

Callie blinked. That was the last thing she'd expected him to say.

'Are you sure? She tends to be very colicky so I have to feed her slowly or the whole lot comes straight back up with the first bubble of wind.'

'It's hardly going to make a great deal of difference to what I'm wearing,' he pointed out, with a disparaging look at his clothing. 'If it had been Armani or Versace, I might not have been so keen to offer.'

'You mean they're *not* Armani?' she said with faked amazement, and had a tea-towel thrown at her for her pains.

It didn't take long to sort through the pile in the linen basket and set the first load going, all the while listening out in case Ross was having any problems with Zoe.

There hadn't been a sound from her little charge by the time she was ready to return to the bedroom, just a low rumbling sound that told her that Ross was talking.

She paused in the doorway, entranced at the sight that met her eyes.

Ross had settled himself on her bed, her pillow propped against the headboard to make himself comfortable. Zoe was cradled happily in the crook of his arm, apparently enthralled by the stream of nonsense he was speaking as he held the bottle to her mouth. Callie couldn't help smiling when she saw the way one tiny starfish hand was curled possessively round his much longer finger.

'There you are,' he was saying softly. 'I told you if you'd only calm down and take the time to enjoy it you'd feel so much better. There's no point in rushing it if you really want to appreciate it, but you're a typical woman—no patience at all. I'm sure it's something to do with that double X chromosome. I think it means you've all got a double helping of stubbornness. If you'd only listen to us men, everything would be so much easier and we'd all be much happier.'

Callie knew the host of double meanings couldn't be accidental, but there was no way she was going to mention them—not now, when all she could think about was the quote from a song about a lover with slow hands.

'As soon as she's old enough, I'll have to explain the concept of subversion,' she murmured as she fought a grin. 'I've heard of brainwashing but don't you think you're starting a little young?'

'Well, it's an important job, making sure the female half of the population is brought up right, so I thought I'd get a head start on one of the newer recruits,' he murmured in return, his wicked dimple confirming her suspicion that he'd known she was there all along.

'Has she nearly finished?' Callie leant against the doorframe to enjoy the peaceful scene in front of her. For a big man he looked totally at home dealing with such a tiny child.

The one thing she didn't want to think about was the fact that that big man was sprawled barefoot and dishevelled on top of *her* bed, looking far too tempting for her peace of mind. And she certainly wasn't going to acknowledge the fact that his low voice was a seduction all on its own, stirring to life things that would have been better left sleeping.

'She's almost asleep,' he murmured, his voice a velvety soft rumble in the quiet of the room. 'I've already changed her nappy, so if I hand her over to you you can bring the last of her wind up and put her down to sleep.'

'Wow. That was speed and efficiency.' Callie was impressed. For a bachelor he was very proficient, with far more hands-on experience than his qualifications in paediatrics would suggest.

'I did all my learning on my three horrors,' he explained with a grin that displayed that heart-stopping dimple again. 'My brother was only too willing to hand them over when it was his turn to change them. It was the only time I could get my hands on them without a fight!'

'I can imagine!' Callie smiled in return, still amazed that he would have volunteered for the job often enough to have become so proficient. What a pity neither of them was in line for a relationship. He would be ideal—a man willing to cook breakfast and take care of a baby was something of a rarity, by all accounts.

Not that she'd conducted any extensive surveys, herself. She'd been totally committed to gaining her qualifications and hadn't bothered to take the time to go out on dates, other than a few group outings.

There was a moment's awkwardness as Ross swung his legs over the side of the bed and Callie had to step forward between his spread thighs to get close enough to reach for Zoe. It wasn't until she had to bend forward to slide her hands under his fragile burden that she realised just how much the neckline of her nightdress gaped.

Callie's cheeks were still burning when she scooted under the covers and pulled them right up to her ears.

It wouldn't have been so bad if she hadn't looked up from her embarrassing discovery straight into his eyes and found that Ross had noticed too. What was worse, there had been no mistaking his sharp intake of breath nor the way his pupils had suddenly dilated.

She turned over again and punched her pillow into a more comfortable shape. It always took her a little time to get used to sleeping at the wrong time of day. It wouldn't be so bad if only Zoe would! She rarely needed to set her alarm these days, but just in case Ross turned up and found her still in bed she'd wound it up fully this time. Two embarrassing situations was the most she could cope with in a day.

No matter how hard she tried, she couldn't empty her head of the sight of his face when he'd stood in the open bathroom doorway. Even when she closed her eyes tightly and concentrated on relaxing each muscle in turn she couldn't stop the quiver of excitement that tightened deep inside her when she thought about seeing Ross again.

His jaw would be freshly shaven and his blue eyes gleaming with silver shards as he took those fateful steps that brought him towards her naked body...

'All right, Zoe, I can hear you,' Callie grumbled, dragged out of an unexpectedly vivid dream by the baby's strident cries. 'You could at least have let me get my hands on him before you woke me up.'

She stumbled her way out of bed, still more asleep than awake, and fumbled her way into her dressing gown.

'All right, sweetheart. Up you come and let's find you a bottle.'

As she staggered her way into the kitchen, the first thing she was aware of was the annoying beep of the washing machine telling her that the load she'd put on earlier was ready for her attention. The second thing was the sound of the front door closing, signalling that Ross had returned, and here she was standing in the middle of the room in a rumpled nightshirt torn right up to the waist even if it was covered by her dressing gown.

'Callie?' she heard him call softly, obviously keeping his voice down in case Zoe was still asleep.

The timing of the shriek let out by the tiny child in her arms sounded almost as if she were answering Ross. In any other circumstances it would have struck Callie as funny. In her present predicament, it didn't.

'Everything under control?' he asked in a more

normal tone of voice, the sound growing louder as he drew nearer.

'I'm not ready yet,' she said hurriedly, panic-struck that he was going to come in and catch her like that. 'If you make a start, I'll join you as soon as I've fed Zoe.'

'Anything I can do to help?' His head appeared around the edge of the door and she hastily turned herself and positioned Zoe to cover as much as possible of her less than elegant clothing.

'Hello? Anybody there?'

The sound of a stranger's voice accompanying a brisk tattoo on the front door was her salvation.

'You'd better go and let him in,' she suggested, trying to keep the relief out of her voice. It was difficult trying to stand there looking unconcerned when all she could feel was the heat of his eyes as they grazed over her once more. 'Then the two of you can get started on the heavy stuff.'

Half an hour later she was no closer to going to help out.

She'd heard a lot of thumps and bangs and even a smothered imprecation or two, but anything other than that had been drowned out by Zoe's strident cries.

Callie was close to tears.

She'd been patience itself as she'd tried to persuade the little mite to take her feed, but she'd refused to calm down long enough to take more than a mouthful or two.

'You're clean and dry and it's four hours since your last feed, so I know you must be hungry,' Callie crooned, fighting to keep her tone encouraging. 'If only you could tell me what's the matter.'

'Problems?' asked Ross as he paused by the partly open door. 'She doesn't sound very happy.'

'That's an understatement,' Callie retorted. 'My ears are ringing.'

'Shall I give you a break? We've finished carrying that lot in.' He ambled forward, apparently completely at home in spite of the fact that this was her part of the house, not his. 'Here, sweetheart. Come to Uncle Ross and tell him all about it.'

He plucked the squirming infant off her lap and swung her deftly up against his shoulder, her little body looking even smaller cradled in his broad hands as he began to rock her.

Almost instantly, the volume of her cries began to decrease and, within seconds, had dwindled to an occasional whimper.

'You must be a magician,' Callie whispered, not certain whether to feel delighted or slighted that he could achieve in seconds what she had failed to do in over half an hour. 'I could develop a severe inferiority complex around you.'

'Not if you saw the state of those rooms upstairs,' he said with a grimace. 'I'll do you a trade. I'll take care of this little problem down here if you'll make a start on organising me upstairs.'

'Oh, but…I can't sort your things out. How will I know where you want them to go?'

'Almost anywhere other than in piles and boxes on the floor,' he said glumly. 'I've really got no idea where to start.'

'Well, if you bring Zoe upstairs you could supervise while you try to get her to take her bottle. I'll need to know what belongs to whom or you'll be in a worse state than ever.'

'Done!' he exclaimed with pleasing alacrity, and reached for the bottle standing abandoned on top of the pile of cardboard boxes nearest to her own rumpled bed.

'You might be making a mistake,' she pointed out. 'My own decor isn't exactly a sterling example of *Homes and Gardens*.'

'No trying to wriggle out of it, now,' he warned, and led the way out into the hall. 'I might hold Zoe as hostage until you've fulfilled your part of the bargain.'

'Dangerous move,' she muttered, with the memories of too much broken sleep very clear in her mind. '*I* might just let you keep her.'

'You don't really mean that,' he chided indulgently, pausing for a moment at the top of the stairs to meet her gaze head-on. 'I've seen the way you look after her. You love her to pieces.'

Callie conceded with a sigh. 'In spite of everything, you're right,' she admitted. 'It was a shock when Steph told me she was pregnant and her boyfriend had abandoned her, but I was sure I'd be able to give her the support she needed to get her back on her feet. The last thing I'd expected was to end up taking care of Zoe all on my own.'

Ross must have heard how choked her voice had become at the memory of her sister's death but he was silent as he led the way through to the smallest room—the one that used to be the kitchen. He gestured towards the neatly folded pile of cartoon-covered bedlinen that had been dumped in the middle of the bed.

There was a less orderly pile of toys overflowing a chair and another of jumbled clothing interspersed between a matching chest of drawers and wardrobe, all the furniture very obviously new.

He perched himself on the end of the bed and arranged Zoe comfortably in the crook of his arm before offering her the bottle.

'What happened to her father?' he asked quietly when, with typical contrariness, she accepted her feed without a murmur.

'Apparently, he just took off when Steph told him she was pregnant,' Callie told him, tight-lipped, as she transferred another neatly folded pile of clothes into the chest of drawers. 'She tried to get in touch with him after the baby was born and when he didn't reply… I think that's what finally tipped her over the edge.'

'Have *you* tried to contact him?' he asked.

'Why should I? He obviously didn't want to know.' She moved several battered-looking toys to a temporary home on top of the chest of drawers and gestured for Ross to transfer from the end of the bed to the newly emptied chair so that she could make the bed.

'But he's the father,' he reminded her quietly.

'Biologically, yes, but not in any way that matters,' she snapped, taking her anger out on the sheets as she tugged them tight enough to bounce pennies off.

'Legally?' he added softly, and her hands froze.

She straightened up slowly, a heavy weight settling around her heart and beginning to squeeze.

'You mean…he could take Zoe away from me?' Her knees felt decidedly weak and she sank onto the edge of the bed.

'He could certainly try. He's got a closer blood relationship to her than you have.'

'But… But he was the one who didn't want to have anything to do with her. Why would he change his mind now?'

'I'm not saying he will. Just that it's a possibility.' He smiled down at Zoe, now feeding steadily while they talked, as if there'd been no screaming fit to contend with just a few minutes ago.

'Can I stop him?' she demanded, her hands shaking now as she forced herself to stand up again and smooth the duvet into position.

'I don't know, but I could find out the name of a solicitor who could help you to find out. For Zoe's sake, you really ought to get the legal position straightened out as soon as possible.'

Callie thought about the possibility of losing Steph's precious little daughter and shuddered. It would be bad enough now, when she'd only had her for a few weeks. What it would be like if it happened months or even years in the future didn't bear thinking about.

'If you could find out that name, I'd be very grateful,' she said quietly. 'I want to make absolutely certain that she can't be taken away from me. She's all I've got left of Steph, now.'

She straightened up and glanced around the room, putting a brisker tone into her voice.

'How's that, then? Will it pass inspection?'

Ross grinned when he saw the way she'd tucked a very battered-looking teddy bear under the covers as though he was just waiting for Mark to come and join him. The rest of his menagerie was propped casually against the wall as though they were having some sort of toys' convention.

'That's perfect,' he said, and she felt a warm glow

start to loosen the tight knots caused by their topic of conversation. 'It looks really welcoming.'

'I've put his hard toys—the cars and trucks—on top of the chest of drawers until I find something to use as a toy box.'

'I think when he arrived he brought them in a carrier bag, originally.' He straightened up out of the chair and propped Zoe up against his shoulder to stroke her back. He was shaking his head with a bemused expression on his face. 'You'd hardly know it was the same room.'

'It would be better with a different colour scheme, but that's something for another day. Which room next?'

She decided she was rather enjoying herself. Somehow, helping someone else to sort their unpacking and tidying was a very different job from doing her own. It certainly couldn't be the topic of conversation that made the task seem so satisfying. Was it just the fact that she had company, or was it the fact that she was able to bask a little in his approval?

'Felicity's room, please,' he said promptly. 'She's such a funny little thing that I'm sure she'd be as disapproving as my old great-aunt if she thought I'd been dealing with her underwear.'

Callie chuckled. 'How on earth do you cope with the laundry?'

'We've worked out a system. I let her know when the machine's ready to switch on and she puts her own things in and closes the door.'

'She's probably feeling very outnumbered in a house full of men,' she pointed out.

'Well, the numbers are even here. There are three

men and three women now we've moved in with you.'

Moved in with you...

She knew what he meant, but somehow the words sounded very different when he said them and they set off that strange quivering deep inside her again.

As he followed her through into the room that Fliss had claimed she tried to keep her mind on the task in hand but it kept straying to impossible scenarios...such as what it would be like if Ross really had moved in with her...

The only antidote for her rambling thoughts was hard work and conversation and by the time another couple of hours had passed there was only the master bedroom left to do.

'You can manage your own room, can't you?' she suggested, rather unnerved by the implied intimacy of helping him to straighten out his belongings.

'Hey! That's not fair!' he complained, with a mock pout. 'Everyone else will come home to a tidy room and mine will still be messy.'

'But...'

'Please?' He grinned at her, sensing that she was weakening, and she wondered just how many times he'd used that wicked dimple to get his own way. 'It won't take long with both of us working.'

'On one condition...no, two conditions,' she demanded, trying to sound stern.

'And they are...?'

'First, that you come down and help me with my mess in return.'

'And second?'

'That wc each sort out our own clothes.' The thought of Ross seeing her less than glamorous underwear was even more disturbing than the idea of dealing with his.

'Spoilsport,' he grumbled, with another flash of that demon dimple. 'That should have been one of the perks of the job.'

CHAPTER FIVE

THE ward was very busy that evening but Callie was finding it hard to concentrate.

It had been bad enough that she'd spent hours with Ross while they'd talked and laughed their way through the tedious job of tidying the house. Oh, she'd enjoyed it, every minute of it, but it wasn't doing much to help her follow her resolution to keep him at arm's length.

The whole situation had been made much worse by his suggestion that she should leave Zoe with him while she went to work. As her niece had been wide awake for several hours during the afternoon and had just gone to sleep, his suggestion had made sense. She certainly didn't want to wake the baby up when there was no need, but, once again, it meant that Ross featured prominently in every other thought.

It wasn't that she didn't trust him to look after Zoe and keep her safe. She'd already had ample proof that he seemed to be able to cope with her little niece better than she could.

Given that neither of them was free to pursue any sort of relationship with each other, it was an uncomfortable feeling that this could be the thin edge of a very insidious wedge.

Her thoughts were interrupted sharply by the familiar insistent bleep of her pager. Ross hadn't been joking when he'd said that she would soon grow to hate the sound.

'Dr Bell, here,' she said briskly when she dialled through on the nearest phone. She'd only just come back up to the ward after a trip down to the casualty department and crossed her fingers that this wouldn't be a return journey.

'Sorry, Doctor, but could you come back down to Casualty? We've got a little boy here who's been knocked down and dragged along by a car.'

Callie uncrossed her fingers and paused just long enough to let Naomi Henzie know where she was going, then she took off at a run.

'If I'd known I was going to be up and down between the ward and Casualty all evening, I would have done less housework today,' she puffed as she reached her destination and was met by the same staff nurse she'd been working with not ten minutes ago. 'What have you got for me this time?'

'Simon Prentiss. An eleven-year-old boy hit on a pedestrian crossing by a four-wheel drive with bull bars on the front. His jacket got caught up on the wretched thing and he was dragged about thirty yards before a young man stepped out into the road and forced the driver to stop,' the young staff nurse began, her anger evident in the amount of detail she was giving.

'What injuries?' Callie prompted, helping to focus her mind.

'He's badly shocked, rubbed completely raw along one side, one shoulder is dislocated and he might have some broken ribs. His lungs sound OK, so far. He's in a cervical collar, on oxygen and the paramedic got an IV of saline running.'

'Right, then, let's have a look.' Callie smiled at the young nurse and murmured in an aside, 'If it's any consolation, I favour running the owners of these stupid bull bars over with their own cars and dragging *them* along the road, too. Maybe *then* they'll realise how dangerous their fashion accessories are.'

She heard a startled chuckle behind her as she turned away to enter the cubicle.

'Hello, Simon. I'm Dr Bell. I hear you lost an argument with a set of bull bars.'

'And my new football strip!' he exclaimed in disgust, his voice muffled by the Entonox mask. 'That nurse cut it to pieces.'

'We bought it for him as an early Christmas present,' the woman seated beside the bed offered, her reddened eyes mute testimony to the tears that she'd shed over her young son. 'He'd only had it for a couple of days and now it's useless.'

'The nurse had to cut it off you in case you'd broken any bones. You wouldn't have liked her to do any more damage trying to peel it off,' Callie explained. 'As it is, you've got a very painful arm.'

The way he was cradling one arm protectively with the other and the strange appearance of that shoulder were very marked. 'Did the police come to the scene of the accident?'

'Yes,' his mother answered. 'And they made the driver take a Breathalyser test in case he'd been drinking.'

'In which case you should be able to find out from them about his insurance company and, apart from Simon's injuries, you should be able to put in a claim to have the clothing replaced.'

She turned to direct the rest of her words to the pale youngster lying quietly on the bed. 'You might not get the new kit in time for Christmas, but maybe in time for when you're ready to play football again.'

While she'd been talking to the two of them she'd begun her examination and found little to add to the initial findings.

'What you need now is to have some X-rays taken of your neck, your ribs and your shoulder, just to make sure you haven't broken anything, then we can make a start on sorting you out.'

She gently peeled away the large pad of gauze covering the deep graze along his hip and silently cursed the driver. If he'd stopped as soon as he'd hit Simon the poor boy wouldn't be looking at the painful possibility of months of skin grafts. Still, she wouldn't mention *that* until she'd got someone down from the plastic surgery department to take a look at it. All she could do was thank goodness that the stupid man hadn't run Simon over, as well.

'Staff Nurse will get everything organised and I'll probably see you again a bit later,' she said, mentally crossing her fingers that the X-rays wouldn't reveal too many additional problems.

She was passing one of the visitors' pay-phones when she was overcome by the urge to phone Ross.

'Hello?' His deep voice answered so swiftly and sounded so intimate in her ear that for a moment she was struck silent by her reaction to it.

'Er, Ross...it's Callie. I just wanted to make sure that everything's all right.'

'If you mean Zoe, she's fine. The children think she's wonderful. At least, Fliss and Mark do. They helped me to give her a bath.'

There was laughter in his voice and she felt an answering smile creep over her face.

'What happened?' she demanded, already having a good idea.

'Well, I'm not certain which one of us got the wet-test, but the bathroom floor won't need washing again for a month of Sundays.'

'That's one thing Zoe really enjoys—a splash in the bath,' Callie laughed, remembering the times she'd been caught by the overflow from a particularly vigorous kick.

'I think next time I do it I'll strip down to swim-ming trunks,' he suggested wryly, and Callie's imag-ination immediately went into overdrive.

'Any major problems at work?' he asked, his vel-vety voice breaking into her heated thoughts.

'Boy versus bull bars,' she said succinctly.

'Damn, not another one,' he muttered. 'How much damage this time?'

'So far, dislocated shoulder and bad bruising, but the blighter dragged him along the road and it's touch and go whether he's going to need skin grafts. I'll know more when the X-rays come back and Plastics have had a look.'

'I'll let you get back to it, then. And don't worry. As far as I can see, child-rearing is ten per cent skill and ninety per cent blatant bribery and I've got the ninety per cent off perfectly. Everything's under con-trol at the end. Don't forget, you get to look after them tomorrow.'

Callie put the phone down and grinned. His last comments had almost made it sound as if they were an old married couple.

She permitted herself just a couple of seconds to wallow in a few 'what ifs' before she firmly shelved them away with all the other things she wouldn't allow herself to pine after.

She had a swift mental image of his bedroom and the enormous double bed that dominated the space. His room had been just as chaotic as the rest, with furniture and clothing all dumped in heaps wherever she looked. But it was the bed that had inexorably drawn her eyes.

She knew what he looked like propped against her headboard with Zoe cradled in his arms. What would he look like sprawled across that expanse…naked?

Was that where he'd been when he'd answered the phone? Unlikely, this early in the evening. He was probably relaxing in his recliner chair which he and the removals man had positioned strategically in front of his wide-screen television in the sitting room.

'There will probably be another one coming to join us,' she told Naomi Henzie when she returned to the ward and gave her the pertinent details.

'So he'll be coming straight here as long as he hasn't broken anything?'

'As far as I know, yes, but it will depend on how long it takes for him to go through X-Ray whether we'll see him sooner or later. Apparently, there was already a queue forming because of the Saturday-night crazies.'

'Well, all I can say is I'm glad I work on the children's ward. At least we don't often have to deal with drunks.'

'Although it's definitely more common than it was, say, ten years ago,' Callie pointed out. 'That's just one of the reasons why so many hospitals, like St Lawrence's, are starting to open specialist adolescent units.'

Her first love would always be dealing with their younger patients, but she'd found during her training that she had an instinctive rapport with the older children and could understand why they felt isolated when their only choices were to be surrounded by babies or old people.

It was a sad fact of modern life that drink and drug abuse were ruining more and more young lives before they'd had a chance to realise their true potential.

'Have you heard—they've announced that the dedication of the new unit will take place on schedule just before Christmas? There was a circular came round some time in the last day or so.'

'If they're opening it just before Christmas, they're probably hoping they can get all the organisational wrinkles ironed out while the numbers are kept low for the holidays,' Callie guessed. 'I just hope they'll have it fully staffed by the New Year because if I have to run backwards and forwards between three destinations I can foresee problems.'

'Ross always complains that he needs to be schizophrenic to keep up with the ward *and* downstairs,' Naomi pointed out. 'It's all very well having staff on call to look at particular accident victims, but if they're already fully committed to a ward full of post-operative patients…'

She didn't finish the sentence but Callie knew what she was implying. She'd often wondered what she would do if she was dealing with a patient on the ward with an unexpected post-operative complication and was bleeped to go down to accident victims. If she was also overseeing the adolescent unit she was going to be stretched very thin.

Thank goodness for experienced staff such as Naomi Henzie.

The rest of her shift was relatively quiet and, while Callie was delighted for the rest after her strenuous afternoon, she wondered whether that boded well for the person she would hand over to.

Simon finally joined them on the ward just before midnight.

'He hasn't broken anything,' Mrs Prentiss told her, with another bout of tears, this time of relief. 'He's got a lot of bruises…one big one on his head…but they're only going to keep him in long enough to see how his skin heals on his hip.'

'He's been a very lucky boy,' Callie agreed, having read the reports attached to his file when he'd arrived on the ward. 'Things could have been very much worse.'

'It wouldn't be so bad if he hadn't been in the right,' she complained. 'I've always told him to cross at the crossing and he'll be safe, and what happens? Some idiot in a tarted-up Jeep decides to plough straight through him.'

'Well, the police will probably throw the book at him, so he won't be feeling quite so clever when they've finished,' Callie reminded her. 'You make sure you get onto them about Simon's clothes.'

She spent a few minutes with the youngster when he'd been settled into bed.

'My head hurts,' he whispered, mindful that the rest of the children on the ward were probably fast asleep.

'Where?' Callie knew he'd been scanned to check for damage but it never did to be complacent. The sudden onset of a headache could signal a bleed inside his skull.

'Here.' He put his hand up to the side, gingerly touching the area with his fingertips.

'May I?' Callie probed gently and found a soft swelling right where his notes had detailed a large bruise. 'Ah! I've found it. I think you're growing a doorknob on the side of your head.'

He gaped for a second in surprise then giggled softly.

'Is it bad? Would you like a painkiller?' she offered, reaching for his notes to check what level of analgesia he'd already received.

'Not if I have to have another needle in my bum,' he said quickly. 'It just hurts when it presses against the pillow.'

Callie showed his mother how to use a spare pillow to wedge him onto his side so he wouldn't roll over and left them to sort themselves out.

He was a nice lad with a supportive mother and was obviously resilient enough to cope with this setback. At least he should be well on the mend by Christmas.

She glanced around the ward as she got ready to end her shift and was surprised to see just how many decorations had appeared in the last couple of days. There were balloons and tinsel and, on top of every available surface, forests of cards, the Christmas greetings nearly rivalling the get-well ones.

The countdown to the big day was marked on the home-made calendar and she suddenly realised just how little time there was left.

Not that she had anyone to buy presents for, yet.

Zoe was too young to appreciate it this year, but in a year's time…

Her wandering thoughts came to a sudden halt when she realised that she *did* have someone to buy for this year…in fact, four someones. Unless Ross had other members of his family nearby to invite him and his surrogate family to share their celebrations, there would be six of them in the house, and so far they'd done absolutely nothing to mark the season.

'It's only been two days,' she muttered, trying to find an excuse for her complete lack of involvement in the growing excitement gripping her patients. 'And until this afternoon I didn't even know where to find the box of decorations.'

That excuse wouldn't hold water any more. At his insistence, Ross had repaid her favour by helping her to shift furniture and boxes in what had once been the dining room of the house.

She'd been surprised how big the room had looked once she'd unpacked the most obvious things and found homes for them in the elderly wardrobe and chest of drawers. She'd even found the patchwork quilt she'd bought in a charity shop and spread it over her bed so that it looked less like the place she slept and more like a spacious settee.

'Whoever lived here before certainly loved chintz and cabbage roses,' Ross had muttered, with a glare at the busy pink wallpaper still gracing one wall.

'What are you complaining about? You got the room with putty-coloured wood-chip. At least you don't have to go to sleep dreaming of triffids coming to get you.'

'Just creeping blandness,' he'd retorted. 'Still, at least it's actually intended to be easy to paint over.

All I have to do is find the energy and inclination and buy the paint.'

'I think if you're thinking of doing some decorating Andy's room should be first on the list,' she'd warned. 'I don't know many eleven-year-olds who would willingly put up with a pink and purple herbaceous border from floor to ceiling.'

Ross had conceded her point. 'It might even make him feel better about moving here...although I've no idea why he's being so negative about it. He was the one who did the most complaining about the cramped situation back at my flat.'

'Is he one of those kids who just doesn't like change?'

'Not usually. He was really keen to stay with me at first.'

'Then he's probably missing his parents,' Callie had suggested easily, but, now that she remembered Andy's attitude towards the world the first time she'd met him, she had a feeling that there was something far more serious at the root of it.

Perhaps he would cheer up when they began to get the house ready for Christmas. She would have to see if she could enlist his help to put some decorations up and remind Ross to take the three of them out to choose a tree.

'Callie. Ready to go home?'

She knew it was Ross as soon as she heard his voice, and whirled to find him leaning nonchalantly against the wall just outside the main door to the ward. In his arms was a well-wrapped pink and white bundle and he seemed totally oblivious to the speculative looks he was receiving from the people passing by.

'Ross. What's the matter with Zoe? Is she ill?'

'Stop panicking. She's perfectly all right,' he soothed. 'I could hardly leave her at home alone, or supervised by three children under twelve, so they all came along for the ride.'

'But...'

'The other three are waiting in the car just outside the main entrance. One of the ambulance crews is keeping them entertained while I hand little miss over to you. My car's got children's safety belts fitted so you'd better drive that. I can use yours to get home.'

Bemused, Callie obediently handed over her keys and held out her hands while Ross carefully transferred the sleeping baby. Where was the point of arguing when he'd worked everything out so logically?

'See you later, sweetheart,' he said, and Callie's pulse rate gave a crazy leap at the unexpected endearment until she saw him bend forward to stroke a careful finger over the curve of Zoe's cheek.

'Yes, well, I'd better get out to your gang,' she said as her heart slowly resumed its normal rhythm again.

'I've left messages with several agencies who provide nannies and au pairs, so hopefully they'll find me someone reliable soon. I'll be finishing a bit earlier today, so I should be back in time to cook them a meal. Thanks for keeping an eye on them for me in the meantime.'

'No problem,' she began easily, only to lose her train of thought when he stroked the tip of the same finger down *her* cheek to end up at the corner of her mouth.

Her eyes snapped up to meet his just in time to see his pupils dilate with sudden awareness. Without thinking, her tongue flicked out to moisten her lips and grazed his finger and he jerked his hand away as if he'd just been burned.

'I'll…we'll see you later, then,' she said when she managed to unscramble her brains. It was hard to concentrate on forming a coherent sentence when all she was conscious of was the tang of salt on her tongue where it had touched him.

She had the feeling that someone was watching her and glanced back over her shoulder just before she turned the corner by the lifts. What she saw was Ross standing in the middle of the corridor staring after her with his fists planted on his hips and a deep frown etched between his brows.

By the time Ross was due home, Callie couldn't wait to see him.

It wasn't that the children had been disobedient— they were fairly well behaved on the whole. It was more their attitude that she couldn't cope with.

Well, if she were strictly honest, it was Andy's attitude that had soured the day.

It didn't seem to matter what she suggested, he'd found some reason not to do it, and had persuaded Fliss and Mark that they didn't want to do it either.

The only time he'd shown any animation was when she'd mentioned the fact that she hated the wallpaper in the house.

'You mean you didn't put it up?' he demanded sceptically.

'Oh, please!' Callie exclaimed. 'It gives me nightmares!'

'So why don't you do something about it?'

Callie knew a challenge when she heard it.

'Like what?'

'Strip it off or paint over it, of course,' he said with an eleven-year-old's imitation of strained patience.

'I'm afraid I haven't had time yet, but I'm hoping to get it done soon. The paint's already waiting in the corner.' She pointed to the stack of decorating supplies Ross had helped her to tidy away.

'So what's stopping you? I could help.'

'And me,' Fliss joined in eagerly. Her little face had been screwed up with concern as she'd followed the various stalemates throughout the day. This time she seemed to think that they were all on the same side.

'Me too,' chimed in Mark, looking up from his private game with his cars, desperate not to be left out.

'So where do you think we should start?' Callie asked, far from certain that this was a good idea.

She didn't yet know whether the mortgage company was going to let her take the house on now that neither Steph nor her boyfriend lived here. She didn't even know if she could afford to take it on, and the last thing she would need if it had to be sold was for the whole place to look as if a bomb had dropped in the middle of it.

'This room has already had the paper taken off some walls,' he pointed out. 'If we took the rest off, you could paint it.'

'And then you could put up a Christmas tree and decorations,' Fliss added with a shy smile.

'Yeah. Father Christmas tree,' Mark cheered. 'And lots of toys.'

Callie looked from one face to the other and took a deep breath.

'All right, gang. Let's do it!'

There was pandemonium for a minute as Mark ran round in circles cheering while Andy and Fliss made a beeline for the nearest patch of wallpaper.

It took several minutes for her to get them back under control and organise their efforts into teamwork. Once they realised that everything needed to be cleared away from the sides of the room before work could begin they set to with a will.

In no time at all everything had been moved to the centre of the room and they had spread drop cloths around the perimeter. Then she was issuing them with sponges and demonstrating how to soak the paper to release the glue without soaking the floor.

Callie was so busy supervising and trying to manage damage control that she hardly noticed that Ross was at least an hour later than he'd said.

The first she knew that he'd arrived was the moment the door swung open just as the last long run of paper peeled away from the wall. As she watched from her perch on top of the ladder behind the door, it slithered down to drape itself over the top of the door and onto his head.

'What *have* you kids done?' he demanded as he gingerly peeled it away and dropped it on the floor, obviously horrified by the sight that met his eyes. 'This is Callie's house and you had no right to do such a thing.'

'But Uncle Ross—' Andy began, but got no further.

'I'm surprised at you, Andy. I thought you would have had more sense...'

'Ross! Stop!' Callie called as she leapt down from the ladder and emerged from behind the door. 'They're *helping* me. I asked them to do it.' Well, it wasn't strictly true. Andy had almost dared her to let them loose on it. But the atmosphere between herself and the three children, and even between the children themselves, had been so much better since they'd started their orgy of destruction.

'You *asked* them to?' he demanded, looking around the ugly bare walls and back at her as if she must be completely mad.

'Of course,' she replied, as if it were the obvious answer, and grinned at each of the apprehensive faces. 'Where else could I get an expert team that would agree to work this hard just on the promise of a pizza for tea?'

'Yeah! Pizza!' shouted Mark. 'Uncle Ross gets the pizza!'

Ross looked round again and shook his head.

'OK,' he conceded, 'I'll get the pizza, but by the time I get back with it you must all be clean enough to eat it.'

'Done!' Callie agreed with a broad grin. 'Right, gang, overalls off and in a pile by the door. We'll have to move fast or Uncle Ross might eat the whole pizza by himself.'

There was an instant stampede for the doorway with three bodies wriggling to shed an assortment of elderly shirts and T-shirts.

Out of their sight, Callie signalled to Ross to give them fifteen minutes before he returned. He shrugged and nodded before roaring that they were all cheating.

'You started before I did,' he complained as he fought his way towards the front door, Andy and Fliss laughing as they grabbed at him to slow him down.

As soon as the door closed behind him Callie chased the three of them upstairs to collect soap,

shampoo and towels and told them to grab their pyjamas.

'We can race him if we use my shower,' she suggested. 'How about it?'

As ever, Mark was willing and eager to try anything and she scooped him up and hurried back downstairs.

By the time Fliss and Andy joined them she'd
cleared her own toiletries out of the way and regulated
the water temperature so it was safe.

'First one in,' she ordered Mark as she stripped his
clothing off with an efficiency born of much practice
in the homes she and Steph had shared. 'Put this flannel over your eyes and shut them tight.'

It didn't take long to shampoo the last traces of
wallpaper paste out of his hair and a soapy flannel
took care of the rest of his wriggly little body.

'Here you are, Andy. Wrap him up in a big towel
and rub his hair with a small one. Now it's your turn,
Fliss.'

Without a trace of concern, Fliss had already begun
to fling her sticky clothes on top of Mark's. Within
seconds she was under the shower with a flannel over
her eyes and luxuriating in the thick froth of shampoo
cleaning the muck out of her hair. She didn't need
prompting to complete the rest of the de-glueing with
plenty of soap.

'It's so clean it squeaks,' she said with a broad grin
as she fingered the strands while Callie tried to wrap
it in a towel. 'It's not the same when I do it in the
bath.'

'Well, we'll have to tell Uncle Ross that I don't
mind you using the shower to wash your hair, as long

as you don't mind if I use your bath to have a lovely lazy soak.'

Eleven-year-old Andy was a totally different prospect and Callie already knew enough about him not to suggest that he might need her help.

'I've left the water running for you and the soap and shampoo are on that little shelf in the corner,' she told him as she came out of the way to take over drying Mark. 'You've got two minutes to get all the glue out of your hair and another two to wash yourself before your uncle will be on his way home.'

She turned her back to give him some privacy and gave Mark a last swipe with the enormous towel before grabbing his pyjamas.

'OK, Mark, here we go. One foot, please.'

As soon as he was dressed she scooped him up again and hurried through to her bedroom. She put her finger to his lips to remind him not to wake Zoe while she grabbed the hairdryer and retreated to the kitchen to use it.

His fine silky hair took no time at all to dry and she left him with a handful of cutlery to set out round the table as she went to check up on Andy and Fliss.

'Ready for the hairdryer?' she asked from the doorway, still trying to make sure she gave them a modicum of privacy.

'I'm ready,' Fliss announced as she scurried out into the hallway in her pretty pink pyjamas. Her towel was already starting to sag round her shoulders. 'Andy's just getting out of the shower. He turned it off when he finished.'

'Thank you, Andy,' Callie called softly. 'See you in the kitchen in a minute.'

It took a little longer to dry the little girl's hair but when it was done it gleamed.

'It's all soft and shiny, just like when Mummy does it,' Fliss whispered, holding the strands up to her face. 'Will you do it in one of those French things?'

'There isn't time at the moment if we want to be ready for the pizza, but I could lend you a spare scrunchy,' she suggested.

Andy was just coming into the kitchen as she was on her way out, his hair standing up in endearing spikes just like his uncle's after an obviously vigorous rubbing. She pointed to the dryer and actually received a smile as she hurried to fetch the promised hairband.

Ross had just arrived outside the front door as she reached the hallway and she hurried to open it.

'Shh!' she whispered, and beckoned him in. 'They need another minute and they'll be ready.'

'What on earth's been going on?' he demanded softly. 'You worked like a slave yesterday to get that room tidy and now...'

'I'll tell you about it later,' she promised. 'Give me a minute then announce your arrival.'

She hurried back to the kitchen as Andy finished with the dryer.

'Can you get some plates out of that cupboard?' she directed with her chin as she smoothed the long strands into a jaunty ponytail and wound the elasticated fabric round it. 'There you are, Fliss. All done. Let's pull the chairs out and—'

'Pizza delivery,' called a voice from the hallway as Ross shut the front door with a convincing clunk.

'He's here! He's here,' Fliss hissed. 'Sit down, everybody.'

'Where is everybody?' Ross demanded loudly. 'If your hands and faces aren't squeaky clean I shall have to eat this delicious pizza all by myself.'

'We're clean! We're clean!' chanted Mark as Ross appeared in the doorway.

'You certainly are,' Ross agreed, with a nod of approval. 'And you've all washed your hair, too. How did you manage that while I was out cooking your pizza?'

'You didn't cook it!' Andy exclaimed.

'We went in Callie's shower,' Fliss explained.

'Want pizza,' Mark demanded single-mindedly, his knife and fork already held tightly in each hand.

While Ross took charge of serving large wedges of the steaming savoury onto each plate everyone seemed to be talking at once but as soon as everyone took the first bit silence reigned for a moment of appreciation.

Fliss was the first to take up her topic of conversation. 'Callie said I could use her shower when I want to wash my hair,' she told Ross proudly.

'She said we could all use it,' Andy corrected her. 'Especially so she could use our bath for a long soak.'

Callie's eyes flew across the table, her thoughts full of the way things had ended the last time she'd taken a long soak in the bath. From the intensity in his eyes, she could tell that Ross was remembering it too.

CHAPTER SIX

'RIGHT, woman, it's time you sat down and told me what's been going on here,' Ross demanded when Callie finally returned to the kitchen. He handed her a large mug of tea and pulled one of the chairs out from the table for her.

In the time that she'd been reading Mark the first instalment of her own very battered copy of *The Velveteen Rabbit*, Ross had been busy restoring the kitchen to some sort of order. In the corner, the washing machine was churning its way through one load of clothes while a familiar pile of damp, sticky ones waited their turn nearby.

Callie sighed as she remembered the way the day had started. 'Well, it's like this,' she began, and told him the whole story. He scowled when he heard how obstructive Andy had been right up until she'd agreed to their paper-stripping stint.

'So you let them destroy a room just on a whim?'

'They didn't destroy it,' she contradicted fiercely. 'They did a jolly good job. It won't take much more work before it's ready to begin painting.'

'And had you intended painting it so soon?'

'Well, no. But...but I thought it would look so much better when it's been done that the mortgage company will probably be able to sell the house and get back the money they're owed.'

Ross blinked as if he hadn't expected her to come

up with such a ready answer and for just a moment he almost looked guilty.

'About the mortgage company,' he said, apparently concentrating on inspecting the design on his mug. 'I wasn't prying, but when I was sitting in the other room last night I couldn't help seeing the letter they sent—the one about the arrears.'

'Frightening, isn't it?' Callie murmured. 'If they say I *am* responsible for paying it back...'

'Actually, I hope you don't mind but I wrote them a letter today, telling them I'm making an offer for the house.'

'Making an offer?' she repeated. 'You mean, you want to buy the house? But you were only going to move in as a temporary measure, weren't you?'

'I also spoke to a friend of mine who gave me the name of that solicitor,' he continued, apparently unperturbed by the panicky tone in her voice.

'Solicitor?' she parroted, beginning to feel even more as if events were being whirled out of her grasp.

'He's going to make the relevant notifications so you can get started on making your guardianship of Zoe legal.'

'I don't just want to be her guardian,' Callie corrected him quickly. 'I want to adopt her properly and bring her up as my daughter. I don't think I could love her any more if she *were* my daughter, even when she keeps me awake, screams at me and spits her milk up all over me.'

'I also asked him how to trace her father,' he added quietly, and Callie's heart stopped.

'What?' she whispered, horrified. It took several seconds before the enormity of what he had done struck her, but then her anger soared. 'Why did you do that? How dare you interfere? If he knows I want to adopt her he might try to take her away from me.'

'He has rights,' Ross said quietly, his arms braced on the edge of the table as he cradled his mug between his hands.

'Rights! He didn't care about his rights when he abandoned my sister and ignored the birth of his daughter,' she said heatedly.

'Nevertheless, he has legal rights and I don't think you'd be allowed to adopt Zoe *unless* he's notified.'

He was so calm in the face of her rage that she had to believe him. As if he'd burst a balloon her anger deflated and she sagged dispiritedly in her chair.

'Oh, Ross, I can't lose her now,' she whispered sadly. 'But what chance have I got of keeping her when I won't even have a place to live? They're not going to approve of someone who—'

'Whoa, Callie. What are you talking about? Of course you'll have somewhere to live.'

'But…you've decided you want to buy the place. You're not going to want a lodger with a noisy baby.'

'If that lodger is the one who got my crew to work together in harmony for the first time in weeks, *and* got all three of them washed, dried and dressed in little more than fifteen minutes, I'll certainly want her to stay,' he said in a teasing voice.

'But…'

'Listen, Callie, I've been doing some thinking,' he interrupted, his tone so serious that she couldn't help but listen. 'There's no guarantee that Tim and Megan are going to be back any time in the next few days. It could be weeks or even months before they're released.'

The dark shadows in his eyes told her that he was

carefully avoiding talking about the possibility that they might *never* return.

'It was all very well having the three of them for a couple of weeks—we could all put up with the inconvenience of makeshift living conditions by pretending it was some sort of camping trip.'

'I'm in a similar position,' Callie admitted, fully understanding what he was telling her. 'It was one thing to arrange to spend some time with Steph while she got on her feet and into some sort of routine, but it's completely different now that all the responsibility has fallen on my shoulders.'

'That's my point exactly,' he said eagerly. 'We've both ended up taking on a bigger burden than we ever imagined, and with the best will in the world it's always going to be too much for one person to manage on their own.'

'So, what you're suggesting is that we...what? Pool our resources?'

'Something like that,' he agreed. 'We're already job-sharing, so it isn't going to be difficult to arrange our shifts so that one of us can be home with the children at all times. As I told you, I've put out feelers for an agency to find us some help, but I'm not terribly hopeful, not at this time of year.'

'So, how would we sort it all out? If you buy the house, would you be my landlord?'

'We can decide on the details when we find out what the mortgage company will agree to. In the meantime, it should take the pressure off both of us if we can share the load.'

Callie sat and thought for a moment. It would certainly be better for Zoe if she didn't have to travel backwards and forwards to the crèche each day. She seemed to have slept much better today in spite of all the extra noise in the house.

She had no qualms about leaving the baby with Ross, although she was slightly more worried about being in sole charge of his three for any length of time. The emotional stresses they were trying to cope with, first with their parents arguing all the time, then leaving the three of them with their uncle and not returning on the due date, were obviously an ongoing problem that she wasn't certain she was equipped to deal with.

It wouldn't be too bad while they were still at school, but the holidays were looming ever nearer on the horizon and she could remember with awful clarity just how hyper children could get as Christmas drew near.

'What do you think?' His quiet question was accompanied by a brief contact as he touched the back of her hand with his fingers to draw her attention.

Callie felt a tingle travel up her arm as every tiny hair stood to attention, and had to admit that *that* was one very good reason for turning his suggestion down.

In all her twenty-eight years she'd never before met a man who affected her so strongly, and she was actually contemplating living with him and sharing his chores and children. She must need her head examined.

'I've never lived with a man before,' she blurted out, then closed her eyes as a deep blush suffused her face when she realised that she'd spoken her thoughts aloud.

Ross chuckled briefly. 'I hadn't really thought of it like that, but I suppose, technically, we are,' he said thoughtfully. 'That'll give the hospital grapevine something to talk about.'

'Oh, God, don't!' Callie groaned as she imagined the gossips having a field day. She hadn't been working at St Lawrence's very long, but she'd realised that it was no different from any other place she'd worked when it came to embroidering rumours.

'In the end, it's *our* business what we do and how we organise our lives,' he said with a return to seriousness. 'Unless…have you got a serious relationship that might suffer for the notoriety?'

'No,' she replied honestly, glad that he couldn't know that there had never been anyone serious in her social life. Someone as good-looking as Ross would never have lacked for female companionship so he couldn't possibly understand. 'It's more likely that you've got some pretty nurse whose nose is going to be put out of joint when she finds out about the arrangement.'

'No. Nothing like that,' he admitted with half a smile. 'I've been waiting to meet someone special and I'm not prepared to put up with second best in the meantime.'

'That sounds very…serious.' She found she couldn't be light-hearted at the thought that he was waiting for perfection. She would be no one's idea of perfect and she was surprised to discover how much it mattered that Ross would never be likely to look in her direction.

'What I want is the sort of marriage that my parents had, so I suppose I'm looking for the same sort of woman as my mother was.'

*   *   *

'Hair styled with an egg-whisk,' Callie groaned when she got out of bed the next day.

It was all *his* fault. If Ross hadn't mentioned his parents she wouldn't have remembered the photos she'd seen in his room. Every one of them bore witness to the fact that he had come from a happy home and she couldn't help making comparisons with her own—which had been anything but happy.

Perhaps, she'd mused as she'd listened to the house growing still and quiet, perhaps that was why he always seemed to see the good in people and situations, while she...

It was no good thinking about it. She couldn't change the past and it didn't seem as if the future was going to be any different.

At least it looked as if her financial worries were going to disappear fairly shortly, although unfortunately she was going to have to deal with another set of problems. Ross might be perfectly happy to share the house with her and treat her as a glorified housekeeper, but she certainly couldn't see herself treating him as a male nanny.

Callie was grateful that the ward was busy that day.

She had a feeling she might not be firing on all cylinders because she hadn't been able to switch her brain off long enough to go to sleep. At least work helped to take her mind off the situation back at the house.

There had been an accident victim admitted to the ward since she was here last—the reason why Ross had been late home the previous evening.

Somehow the young lad had got hold of some fireworks left over from bonfire night. Unfortunately, the private display he had envisaged in the shed at the bottom of the garden had turned into a raging inferno with spectacular explosions as the rest of the fireworks caught light.

'He was very lucky to get away so lightly, by all accounts,' murmured a young staff nurse when Callie had returned from speaking to his parents. 'The whole shed burned down and he nearly got trapped in it.'

'I doubt he's feeling very lucky at the moment,' Callie pointed out. 'There's every possibility he'll still be in here for Christmas. One of the burns on his hand is full thickness and the back of his head and his shoulders are a mess.'

'Will he need to go to a specialist burns unit?'

'They're trying to find him a place now. St Lawrence's record for treating burns victims is good and it's not too far away for the family to be able to visit. Unfortunately, they're worried about the possibility of reconstruction work if he's to retain enough use of his hand and he's going to need extensive grafting on his head.'

'At least Simon Prentiss has avoided that,' the young woman pointed out. 'When the plastics consultant came round he said it looked as if he was going to be redundant. He was amazed how quickly Simon is healing.'

Mrs Prentiss had told Callie the same thing, her tears this time of relief.

'He said Simon might be able to come home in a week, but he promised that he would be home for Christmas.'

'Provided there aren't any complications,' Callie warned her, erring on the side of caution.

'He said that too, but I'm certain there won't be.

Simon's such a good boy he deserves to get better quickly, especially as the accident wasn't even his fault.'

If only life worked that way, Callie mused as she hurried down to the casualty department to look at one of the hospital regulars—a ten-year-old girl with yet another asthmatic attack.

It didn't take long to decide that Lissa would benefit from a short stay on the ward while they got her symptoms under control again and by the time that was organised there had been a flood of assorted injuries from a crashed school mini-bus.

None of the injuries was life-threatening but most of the children had succumbed to tears as they continually relived the shock. It seemed almost coincidental that several of them needed stitches and one ended up with a backslab cast on a cracked arm.

Callie was amazed to discover that, for the first time, she was putting herself in the parents' position, worrying about how she would cope if it were Fliss or Andy or little Mark who'd been injured.

By the time the last of them had been collected by their parents it was time for Callie to go home.

She was just on her way out of the staff cloakroom when she was accosted by a very elegant woman who wasted no time on polite introductions.

'Are you the one who's living with Ross Kendrick?' she demanded bluntly. Her pale china-blue eyes went over Callie from head to foot and left her in no doubt that she wasn't impressed by what she saw.

You're very much mistaken if you think you can intimidate me, Callie thought, her chin lifting to what

Steph had always called that 'just-you-dare-try-it' an-gle.

'Who wants to know?' she retorted calmly as she fished for her keys in the pocket of her thickly padded jacket.

'I'm Jacqueline de'Ath, and you can't be very close to him if he hasn't told you that,' she sniffed. 'Are you sleeping with him?'

Callie gasped silently at the effrontery of the woman. She might be dressed like a lady but she certainly didn't have the manners of one.

'Well, Jackie,' she began, her face a picture of in-nocence as she delighted in the other woman's wince at the common diminutive. 'When Ross and I are to-gether, we're far too busy to waste time talking about our various acquaintances. And we certainly don't *sleep* together.'

It wasn't until she heard the words emerge from her own mouth that she realised that they could be taken two ways.

A stifled sound behind her was the only warning she had that the two of them were no longer alone. She didn't need the look of fury on the woman's face as she glared at the person who had joined them to tell her who it was. Just the way the hairs on the back of her neck stood up told her that Ross was now standing right behind her.

'Hello, Jackie,' he said, and Callie could hear the thread of laughter in his tone that told her he had heard everything.

He'd stopped right beside her, his shoulder brush-ing hers, but still she was surprised when he slid one arm around her and pulled her close. The gesture was blatantly possessive and wasn't in the least diminished by the pink and white bundle he carried in the crook of his other arm.

His hair had been rumpled by the wind so that his resemblance to Andy and Mark was even more noticeable. The cold had reddened his cheeks and the tops of his ears and he'd surrounded her with the scent of fresh air and healthy man to combat the smell of disinfectant.

'Zoe and I have just come to collect Callie and tell her where the car is parked. Will you excuse us?'

Without giving the woman a chance to catch her breath he turned Callie and led her towards the lifts.

'Ross, I'm sorry if I've upset…' she began as soon as the doors slid closed to give them some privacy.

'Callie, you're wonderful!' he exclaimed with a delighted chuckle, completely ignoring her halting attempt at an apology as he tightened his arm around her. 'I've been trying to tell the wretched woman I'm not interested for months.'

'So you're not angry? She wasn't your…?'

'Good Lord, no,' he said hastily. 'As if I could ever want to get involved with a human icicle called Death.'

'That's *de'Ath*.' Callie mimicked the woman's pronunciation wickedly and joined in his laughter, wondering when he was going to realise that he still had his arm around her shoulders.

'What I don't understand is how she found out,' Callie mused as Ross fastened Zoe into her cot and checked the newly fitted restraints holding it in position. 'I certainly haven't mentioned it to anyone.'

'That might be my fault,' he admitted as he straightened up to lean back against the car. 'I had a word about our shifts—about making sure they don't

overlap either way. That's why I came in—to warn
you what might happen—but the grapevine obviously
moved faster than I did.'

'What can we do about it? Everyone's going to
think we're living together.' Even in the chill
December wind she could feel the surge of embarrassed heat in her cheeks.

'But we *are* living together,' he reminded her, with
another tantalising glimpse of that wicked dimple.

'You know what I mean,' she said, her hand curling up into a threatening fist.

'Look, they're all going to think whatever they
want to, no matter what we say,' he said gently as he
caught her small hand in his and stroked it until it
uncurled against his chest. 'The only thing that matters is that *we* know what's going on, right?'

Callie had almost forgotten that they were standing
in the hospital car park in full view of anyone looking
their way. Half mesmerised by the shards of light
gleaming in his eyes, and conscious only of the way
his heart was beating heavily under her hand, she nodded her agreement.

They were already halfway home by the time her
brain started working properly again and she replayed
his argument in her mind.

He was right that the only thing that mattered was
that the two of them knew what was going on. But
did they?

Even her brain and her heart seemed to be in conflict about it. Neither side of her wanted to get involved in a relationship; both recognised that it could
be an absolute disaster; but every time she saw the
man she realised more clearly that it seemed to be
happening anyway.

Ross seemed to be deep in thought too and he was parking the car in the drive before he spoke again.

'We've got a couple of hours before the children are due home so I thought we could move Zoe upstairs well away from any fumes and get the first coat on those walls.'

'You want to decorate? But...aren't you going to work?' Callie liked the idea of getting the room finished and tidy as soon as possible but she didn't know whether she was up to spending so much time with Ross. She had an awful lot to think about.

'I'll give you the choice,' he offered as he released the catches and lifted the cot out of the car. 'One of us needs to put the kettle on while the other deals with Zoe and settles her down. Then I must bring you up to date on the phone calls I've made.'

'Well, as you're more proficient with Zoe you can sort her out. I'll bring her bottle and your tea through together.'

They parted company in the hallway and Callie found herself breathing a small sigh of relief as she hurried through to the kitchen.

While she waited for the kettle to boil she braced her hands on the edge of the sink and stared out of the kitchen window. The garden that went with the house wasn't very big, but it would certainly be enough for the children to play in. At the moment it looked dead and dreary and very much in need of a complete make-over. The grassy area was so overgrown it couldn't honestly be called a lawn. By the time spring came, small children could be in danger of getting lost in it.

By the time spring came...

Was there any point in trying to plan that far

ahead? Ross had no idea whether he would still be
taking care of his little gang, so she had no idea
whether she was still going to be welcome as a lodger.

The kettle boiled and, on automatic pilot, she
turned to make the tea, her mind still travelling along
the same tracks.

It was difficult trying to predict events as far ahead
as Christmas, and that was just a couple of weeks
away. The thought of living here day after day, having to watch Ross taking care of the children and
doing the thousand and one little things that consti-
tuted normal life, was going to become harder and
harder.

If only her realisation that she was so strongly
drawn to him hadn't been so closely followed by his
assertion that he was searching for the perfect woman.
She'd had no time to indulge in rosy dreams before
they were taken away from her.

Unfortunately, that hadn't lessened her attraction
towards him. It was going to take commitment and
concentration to live beside him without letting him
guess at her growing feelings.

'One drink for each of us,' she said brightly as she
brought the small tray through with Zoe's bottle and
two mugs of tea on it.

'And chocolate biscuits,' he gloated with a grin. 'A
typically balanced doctor's diet—the three Cs: caffeine, calories and cholesterol.'

'Dreadful habits we get into when there's no time
for proper meals,' Callie agreed as she opened the
packet and took the first one off the top before offering it across.

'You'll have to feed me with it,' Ross said, with a
quick glance down at his fully occupied hands. Once

again Zoe was gripping his finger tightly, almost as if she was afraid that he was going to take the bottle away.

Callie smiled at the contented picture they made, the utterly masculine figure sprawled against her headboard while he took care of the fragile baby.

'Callie? Are you going to hog the whole packet?'

She glanced down at her hands and realised that she was already on her second biscuit.

'Sorry. Here…' She held one out towards him and smiled as he opened his mouth for it just like Zoe asking for her bottle.

The second bite brought his lips much closer to her fingers and with a sudden clenching of muscles deep inside her she realised that soon there would be no way of escaping the possibility that her fingers might touch his lips.

A small shower of crumbs landed on Zoe's pink and white blanket and gave her the perfect justification for stopping while she still had a voice.

'It's going all over the baby so I'd better leave these by your tea,' she suggested hurriedly.

She caught a glimpse of a very knowing expression in his eyes, as though he'd guessed that she'd been looking for an excuse, and hurried into speech before he could challenge her on it.

'You said you'd made some progress with telephone calls?' she prompted as she sat down on top of a pile of books and picked up her tea.

Briefly he outlined the steps his friend had made in putting Ross in touch with a solicitor in the right branch of law.

'He'll be able to advise you about the proper steps to take to adopt Zoe legally, and I also authorised him to employ a private investigator to track her father down.'

'Private investigator?' Callie repeated, somewhat bemused. 'I thought it was only people on American TV shows who used them; in fact I thought they only existed in America.'

'They certainly seem to use them a lot more over there, but he suggested it might be the quickest way to find out where her father's disappeared to.'

Somehow, talking to Ross about it made the whole process seem a lot less daunting. Perhaps it really was true that a problem shared was a problem halved.

'What about the mortgage company? Any word from them?'

'Probably not for several days. They're such vast enterprises these days that it will take them that long to find the file and make a decision.'

'In the meantime…'

'In the meantime, it's time you took over winding Zoe so I can drink my tea before it's cold…and grab another biscuit. Then it's time for a bit of real work.'

It took just over an hour to paint the first coat right around the walls of the sitting room. Fortunately the plaster was in such good condition the walls hadn't needed lining.

Callie was amazed how much bigger and brighter the room looked now that the dingy walls were the colour of rich cream.

'From here, it hardly looks as if it needs a second coat,' she said, glowing with a sense of achievement. 'Before it absorbed light and now it reflects it.'

'It'll still be worth doing the second coat, especially

as it's the first time it's been done in years. Have you thought what you're going to do with the floor?'

'By the time I'm ready for that, it won't be my house any more,' she pointed out. 'In fact, I'm not even sure if it is *now*.'

'But what would you suggest?' he persisted. 'Ideally, I'd like a fairly pale carpet to keep it light in here, but I suppose that's totally impractical with four kids.'

'You could always sand and polish the floor and seal it with one of those special Scandinavian varnishes,' she suggested.

'Is the floor good enough for that? You don't want to be permanently taking splinters out of the children.'

'From what I saw when we moved things out of the way for our wallpaper-stripping session, it looked nearly perfect. I'd guess that once it's sealed it will be a cross between honey and pale gold, almost like having sunshine in the room all the year round.'

While she'd been speaking Ross had gathered up the paintbrushes and rollers and had replaced the lids firmly on the tins.

'Time to clean up and get ready for the children,' he reminded her. 'I should just about have time to hear the gory details about their day before I have to get going to the hospital.'

He led the way into the kitchen and was just about to dump the paint-covered equipment in the sink when Callie stopped him.

'Wrap them individually in plastic or foil and put them in the fridge,' she suggested. 'That way you don't waste so much paint and they'll still be fresh to use the next day.'

She was just finding space in the bottom of the fridge while Ross started scrubbing his hands when he commented on a problem with the tap.

'Problem?' she repeated, her head buried behind the fridge door.

'Either it's stuck or it's just very stiff. Have you had a problem with it?'

'Is it just because your hands are slippery? Shall I have a go?' She leant round him to reach for it as he gave another twist and the whole thing came off in his hand, sending a fountain of water straight up in the air.

CHAPTER SEVEN

'OH, MY God, turn it off!' Callie shrieked as icy cold water landed on her in a drenching waterfall.

'I would if I could,' Ross retorted grimly. 'Where's the stopcock? Under the sink?'

'I've no idea. You'll have to look, but hurry!' She grabbed a handful of tea-towels and hand towels and held them firmly over the source of the gushing water.

For a moment the pressure managed to force its way out in a jet straight at her but then she worked out how to direct it into the sink and the devastation slowed down.

While Ross rummaged through the packets and tins crammed in the cupboard beside her she took a despairing look around the room. Everything was soaked...

'Nothing here,' Ross said as he backed out of the cupboard. 'Where's the stopcock for the cold water mains? In the front garden?'

'I haven't got a clue! I haven't needed to look for it before. Please hurry...my hands are freezing.'

Callie knew when he opened the front door because a stream of chilly December wind howled down the hallway to surround her. She would have loved to grab something to wrap around her sodden shoulders but there was no way she could take her hands away from the cloths diverting the flow into the sink.

With her first glance around the room it had seemed as if everything would be ruined but by the time the worst of the water had stopped dripping off the ceiling she realised with a lifting of her heart that there would probably be little permanent damage.

That didn't mean that she wouldn't have an awful lot of water to mop up off the floor.

Callie felt the pressure easing under her frozen hands and realised that Ross must have found the tap to turn the water supply off.

'Found it!' he announced in evident relief as he came back into the room.

Callie dumped the sodden towels in the sink. 'What do we do now?' she asked as she turned to face him, using both hands to drag soggy tendrils of hair off her face.

'I'll have to find the name of a plumber and persuade him to come out as an emergency,' Ross said as he straightened up. 'It'll probably cost an arm and a leg, because they can charge what they like for that sort of...'

He stopped talking when Callie had her first good look at him and saw what he looked like. She burst into helpless giggles.

'You look like a drowned rat,' she chortled, gesturing towards his dripping hair and the clothing plastered to his body.

'You're no better,' he retorted with a grin of his own. 'Your hair's hanging down like seaweed and your...'

His voice died and she suddenly realised that his eyes were riveted on her body.

She looked down at herself to discover that not only was her shirt soaking wet but it had turned completely transparent.

With her arms raised to pull her hair back off her

face the cloth was pulled tightly across her breasts to
show in clear detail the effect of the cold water on
her tightly beaded nipples.

'Oh, Lord,' she breathed, and brought her arms
down swiftly to wrap them around herself.

Ross groaned and the unexpected sound dragged
her gaze up to meet his again.

'Are you doing it deliberately?' he demanded, his
tone holding something more than exasperation.

'Doing what?' she said with a frown. '*I* didn't
break the tap.'

'*That's* not what I meant. How many times am I
supposed to resist temptation?'

'Temptation?' She followed the line of his gaze and
found that she was being less than successful at hiding her near-nakedness.

'Yes. Temptation.' He stepped forward the few
inches necessary to bring her within his reach and it
felt almost as if there was a force field humming between them.

They'd both been drenched in icy water and he'd
even spent several minutes outside in the chilly
December air but she was certain she could feel the
heat from his body radiating towards her.

Suddenly she didn't feel cold any more and there
didn't seem to be any point in wrapping her arms
around herself...not when she would far rather wrap
them around Ross...

'Callie,' he growled, his voice husky and deep in
his throat as he cradled her cheek in one hand and
slid the other around her to pull her towards him.

The shock of her body touching his was electric,
every nerve-ending overloaded with sensations of
heat and strength and size.

They were so close that she couldn't help but be aware that he was also fully aroused.

'I thought that cold water was supposed to have a certain effect on that sort of…problem,' she whispered uncertainly, totally out of her depth with the emotions he was arousing in her.

'Not with you around, it doesn't,' he said through his teeth. 'I've tried it before—several times.'

'But—'

'Woman, you've had me in this state almost from the first moment I met you—even when I thought you were a married woman returning to work after maternity leave.'

'But I'm not—' She was confused. No one had ever found her irresistible before, certainly not at first sight.

'Then I walk in on you posing naked like a Greek statue come to life—'

'I *wasn't* posing!' she denied hotly. 'I was trying to put my nightdress on and you walked into the bathroom.'

He drew in a harsh breath and pressed his forehead to hers as he slowly released it.

'I don't know how I made myself walk out of there,' he whispered. 'All I wanted to do was…'

He tilted his head that last little bit to bring their lips together.

They were warm and gentle and so beguiling as he brushed them fleetingly over hers then returned with a hotter contact as he parted them and slid the tip of his tongue out to meet hers.

'What are you doing?' demanded Andy.

'Why is the floor all wet?' enquired Fliss.

'Uncle Ross! We're home!' Mark announced, oblivious.

The three voices spoke simultaneously from the kitchen doorway and Callie sprang away from Ross as if she'd had a genuine electric shock.

'You're home,' she said, and blinked, unable to formulate another word in the face of Andy's accusing glare.

'What happened to the floor?' Fliss repeated as she approached gingerly. 'Where did all the water come from?'

'Wait by the door, Fliss, or you might slip over. The tap broke and sprayed water everywhere,' Ross explained. 'Callie was helping me to get it under control and we both got soaked with cold water.'

It hadn't felt cold when they'd been pressed tightly together, Callie thought. In fact, she wouldn't have been surprised if it had turned instantly to steam and they were now both dry.

'I'll phone for a plumber,' he continued, reaching for the water-spotted telephone directory. 'In the meantime, Callie, it might be an idea if you change into something dry.'

He turned his head to glance pointedly at her and she realised that not only was the heat in his gaze undiminished by the fact that the children had interrupted them but her body's response was even more evident.

'Meanwhile, I shall put the kettle on and make all of us a warm drink.'

Callie felt very uncomfortable, almost as if she was having to run the gauntlet, when she had to walk out past the children.

Mark looked amused by the whole business but

Fliss had picked up on the tensions in the room and looked vaguely perplexed. It was Andy's eyes that felt as if they seared her back with condemnation as she hurried away from them along the corridor.

'They're only children,' she muttered when she found herself pausing at her bedroom door to delay her return. 'And Ross and I weren't doing anything wrong.'

That was not to discount what they might have done if the children hadn't arrived when they did. Callie had never known such an overwhelming emotion—and he'd barely begun to kiss her.

'Do it by *self*!' she heard Mark insist as she approached the kitchen. '*My* drink!'

'But you might spill it,' Fliss said, obviously trying to mother him.

'If he spills it then he won't have anything to drink, will he, Fliss?' Ross said calmly. 'Let him choose.'

Callie watched quietly as Mark considered his options and realised anew how well Ross dealt with them.

In Mark's hands was a large insulated beaker of gently steaming blackcurrant drink with a brightly coloured twisty straw sticking up out of it.

At the table, Andy was already sitting down and Fliss was hovering between the two.

Mark made his move.

Silently he took the end of the straw in his mouth and swallowed several large gulps, lowering the level in the beaker far enough to lessen the risk of an accident.

'Do it by *self*,' he said with a big grin, and made his way carefully to the table.

'Well done, Mark-the-Shark,' Ross said with a smile.

'That boy will go far,' Callie murmured as she joined him by the pot of tea. 'He's already thinking laterally to get what he wants.'

'Not always a good thing. Too many teachers can only cope with pupils who conform,' he replied, and there was a slight edge to his voice that made Callie wonder if he had been one of those pupils who didn't.

'I contacted a plumber who said he should be here within the hour. I've written his number on the notepad by the phone.'

'So we should have water on again in time for the children's baths?'

'With any luck.' He pushed her mug along the surface towards her. 'I should just have time to drink this before I need to go.'

'Is there anything special I need to do with the children; any special routines or preferences?'

'Homework,' Ross said with a groan, adding under his breath, 'That alone is a good reason for contraception.'

Callie nearly choked on her tea trying to smother her surprised laughter, and had to turn away to concentrate on the task of mopping up the rest of the water.

Ross had cleared enough of the floor to make it safe for the children to come in but there was plenty more to do. Callie didn't mind the job and, anyway, she felt it was important that he spend a little time talking to the three of them before he left.

'We don't need you to help us,' Andy announced rudely when Callie reminded the two eldest that it was time to do their homework.

'That's all right, then,' Callie replied, trying not to show her disappointment at his reversal in attitude. She'd thought they'd gone beyond that during their paper-stripping session. 'I can get on with making the supper.'

'What are you cooking?' Fliss asked, with a quick glance towards Andy.

'Spaghetti carbonara,' Callie said.

Andy scowled. 'We don't like all that fancy stuff,' he said.

'I like pa-sketti,' Mark announced. ''Cept it always wiggles off my fork so Uncle Ross cuts it up and I use a spoon.'

'What's spaghetti carbonara?' Fliss wanted to know. 'Is it very fancy?'

'Only if you think bacon and scrambled eggs are fancy,' Callie teased, trying to find a way to steer between the hidden shoals in her relationships with the three of them. 'I think it's just a fancy name for something very simple.'

The homework session was interrupted by the arrival of the plumber, who made short work of completely replacing the cold water tap and turning the water back on, all the while chatting to the children about other plumbing disasters he'd had to attend.

She'd hoped that by the time the meal was served Andy might have unbent a little but the best he managed was to completely clear his plate of every morsel she put on it.

'Right, now will the three of you tiptoe your way upstairs and collect your night things while I draw your bath?' she said when she'd stacked the dirty

plates in a sink full of piping hot water. It wouldn't
be long now before the baby would need feeding
again, so the washing-up would have to wait. Would
she ever get the hang of this mothering bit? Was
everyone this disorganised?

'Why do we have to tiptoe? Because of Zoe?' Fliss
asked in a whisper.

'Yes. She's upstairs in your uncle's bedroom,'
Callie explained.

'Why?' demanded Andy, more belligerently than
ever. 'She's *your* baby, not his. He's got us.'

'He carried her up there so she wouldn't be too
close to the paint fumes,' Callie said calmly. 'He
didn't want her to get ill, especially as she's so tiny.'

'You did painting today? In the sitting room? What
does it look like?' Fliss was almost bouncing with
excitement, her voice growing louder with every
question.

'Shh! Yes. In the sitting room and we'll have a
peep inside the door as we go past.'

When they reached the door to the sitting room she
reached round to turn the light on and swung the door
wide.

'Doesn't it look clean?' Fliss breathed. 'When we
were pulling all the paper off it looked all yucky.'

'Well, by the time it's had a second coat and the
furniture's been straightened out, I think it will be a
good room to start putting up the Christmas decorations.'

'Yeah!' Mark cheered, and was promptly shushed
by the other two.

'Don't wake Zoe,' Fliss reminded him as they began to tiptoe up the stairs.

When they were finally ready to settle into their

respective beds Callie suggested that Andy and Fliss might like to keep their lights on to do some reading of their own while she read the next instalment of *The Velveteen Rabbit* to Mark.

'Can I come and listen with Mark?' Fliss begged. 'I could hear you reading last time so I know the story.'

Andy silently turned and took himself off to his room, pointedly pushing the door almost closed.

Callie gave a mental shrug and emptied her mind of everything but passing on her favourite story to a new generation.

She'd just turned the light out for Mark when Zoe demanded attention, and as Callie began to feed her she realised she could see a marked difference in the little child in just the few days since Ross had moved in.

The most noticeable change, apart from the fact that she was almost visibly growing, was that she seemed so much calmer about taking her bottle these days. Whether it was because Ross had a special knack or whether it was the calming effect of his voice as he murmured nonsense to her, Callie didn't know. If it allowed her to get a good night's sleep she was just very grateful.

It wasn't long before Zoe was fast asleep against her shoulder and it was still far too early to contemplate going to bed.

'I could do the second coat on the walls,' she mused aloud, knowing that her internal clock would take at least a day or two before it got accustomed to her new shift. Hopefully, she and Ross would be able to sort out a regimen that suited both their own needs and the hospital's requirements. Until then, she was

living from day to day and week to week thanking
her lucky stars that the two of them had found a way
to share the load.

Callie groaned when she turned over in the bed to
swat the alarm clock and couldn't find it until her
third attempt.

She'd thought at the time that it was a mistake to
paint a coat of brilliant white on the ceiling as well
and her muscles were confirming it.

The trouble was, she hadn't been sleepy and the
ceiling had looked so sad against the newly painted
walls that she hadn't been able to resist.

She forced her eyes open and looked at the clock
then catapulted upright when she realised that the
room was completely silent. Zoe wasn't making a
sound.

She staggered to her feet with the nightmare scenario of cot death screaming in her head before she
realised that the baby's bed wasn't even in the room
with her. In fact this wasn't even her room.

She stood there swaying for several seconds while
she tried to work out what was happening.

'I left her upstairs while I finished the painting,'
she whispered, going through it step by step.

She could remember showering to remove the spots
and splashes of paint from her hair and skin then rubbing her hair dry and donning her nightdress.

She'd gone upstairs to retrieve Zoe and carry her
bed back downstairs and could remember sitting on
the edge of the bed—the big burgundy and navy covered double bed that Ross should be sleeping in.

'I must have fallen asleep,' she wailed in disbelief,

dreading finding out what Ross had thought of the situation.

Where had he slept when he'd come in from work and where had he taken Zoe?

She grabbed a towel from the pile of clean ones to take into the shower, groaning when yet again it looked as if she was going to be facing him without being properly dressed. She was going to have to borrow his towelling robe to go downstairs as it was.

'It's partly his fault I was so tired,' she muttered as she fought to subdue her hair—it must still have been damp when she went to sleep because it had dried looking like an exploding hayrick.

She tightened the belt around her waist and wondered just how long the thing was on Ross. It reached almost to her ankles and the mixture of soap and musk that surrounded her made her recall what it had felt like when he'd pulled her against his body and kissed her.

'If he hadn't kissed me I wouldn't have been in such a state, and if I hadn't been in such a state I'd have been ready to go to sleep at a more civilised time and I wouldn't have fallen asleep when I came up to bring Zoe down.'

She finished her muttered tirade right outside the door to her room but before she could open the door the large message stuck to the door caught her eye.

'Good morning, Sleeping Beauty. Don't worry, Zoe and I are fine. Wake me before you go so I can take the kids to school.'

It was signed with the flowing letter R that she'd grown accustomed to seeing as part of his signature on their patients' charts.

She hesitated for a moment then took him at his word and turned her steps towards the kitchen.

With her immediate responsibility for Zoe taken out of her hands she indulged herself with a breakfast of cereal *and* toast, only the second leisurely one she could remember enjoying since she'd arrived here.

With five minutes left before she was due to go she poured a mug of coffee for Ross and set off towards her room again. She couldn't afford to wait any longer if she was going to grab her clothes and get dressed.

She had to tap twice before there was an answering sound inside the room and when she opened the door the first thing she saw was the stirring sight of Ross Kendrick struggling out from under her peaches-and-cream quilt like a sleepy bear emerging from hibernation.

'Ross?' She swallowed hard, trying to control the quiver in her voice as her pulse took off like a rocket. She'd certainly never imagined that she would ever watch him waking up in her bed. 'You asked me to wake you before I went to work?'

He scrubbed one hand over his face, his hair standing up in endearing spikes all over his head.

'I hope that's a mug of coffee and I hope it's for me,' he growled in a sleep-roughened voice that Callie could all too easily imagine waking her up in the morning after a night spent in his arms.

'Ah…yes. I thought it might help to wake you up and I needed to get some things out of the room.'

He beckoned her over as he scooted back against the headboard, seeming to remember just in time to make sure that he took the bedclothes with him.

Not that Callie would have minded finding out

what the rest of him looked like. His shoulders and chest were every bit as magnificent as they'd seemed under his wet clothing and she had no doubt that the rest of him would be every bit as...

'What time is it?'

His prosaic question brought her back to earth with a bump.

'Time I was gone,' she said, with a quick look at her watch. 'I just wanted to apologise for...for kicking you out of your bed. I went up to get Zoe and...I don't know how it happened but I must have fallen asleep.'

'I'm not surprised after your mammoth effort on the sitting room. You must be half dead this morning.'

'Let's just say I would far rather that today turned out to be a very quiet day,' she said wryly as she tried to circle first one shoulder then the other then had to grab for the gaping neckline of the robe as it started to slide off her shoulders.

Zoe made a funny sound as she stirred in her bed beside him and they both watched her stretch as she woke.

'Time I was up, too,' Ross said, and took a hefty swallow of his coffee. 'By the way, thanks for putting the children's clothes out ready for this morning. That's something I hadn't thought about.'

Callie had grabbed the clothes she needed but she was strangely loath to leave him, enjoying the unaccustomed intimacy of talking to a man lazing in bed without him being one of her patients.

'Well, I'll see you this afternoon,' she said lamely as she forced herself to turn and walk away. She still had a couple of frantic minutes to get into her clothes before she could leave the house.

'You forgot something,' Ross called softly as she reached the door.

'I forgot...what?' She paused to check the pile in her hands then looked back at him over her shoulder. When she saw that wicked dimple, she took it as a warning that he was now wide awake.

'You forgot to give me my kiss good morning,' he said with a sexy pout. 'Coffee's not sweet enough without it.'

Callie's heart leapt at the thought of walking back across the room and delivering a kiss, but she knew she couldn't afford to take his teasing seriously.

'I'll put more sugar in it tomorrow,' she said dryly, and pulled the door closed behind her.

It was almost a relief to immerse herself in the work of the children's ward.

All the way to the hospital she'd been replaying his teasing request for a kiss and had been horrified by how willing she'd been to comply. It had only been that little voice in the back of her head at the last second shouting, Danger! Danger! that had enabled her to laugh it off.

The trouble was, she didn't know whether it would work again if he were to make a similar request. How could she resist him when her feelings towards him were growing faster than she'd ever thought possible?

For the moment, she had a ward filled almost to capacity and, doubtless, numerous calls to Casualty to cope with, and in spite of the fact that every bone and muscle in her body was aching she was glad of the need to concentrate.

The most recent admission was a case in point—a young lad barely into his teens and, although slightly small for his age, definitely big on attitude.

He'd apparently had an accident on his bike on the way to school and was sporting some spectacular scrapes and bruises including a rather nasty one on his neck.

'The strap of my bag did that,' he told Callie belligerently. 'When I fell off my bike it went round my neck.'

'How's the bike? Did you do much damage to it?' Callie questioned lightly, a slight niggle at the back of her mind telling her that something wasn't quite right here.

'It's wrecked,' he said gruffly. 'Got all twisted and bent.' After that he turned onto his side and she knew that was the end of the conversation.

She sighed as she walked away, grateful that at least his injuries hadn't been too serious. He'd be kept under observation for a few hours in view of the fact that he'd obviously hit his head quite hard when he fell, but then he'd be well enough to go home.

'Hey, is it true?' Naomi Henzie quizzed her in a whisper halfway through the morning, having lured her into the office with the promise of a coffee.

'Is what true?' Callie countered, silently groaning that she wasn't going to escape Ross even when he was nowhere in sight.

'That you and Dr Ross are living together, of course,' she said impatiently. 'I must say, you're a quick worker. You've hardly been here more than a day or two and you walk off with the prize right from under everyone's noses.'

'That would be fast work if it were true,' Callie

agreed wearily, wondering how many times she was going to hear the same rumour. 'Ross was trying to cope with three children in a bachelor flat and I was about to get thrown out of a house that I was rattling around in with one tiny baby. It just made sense for him to move into the flat upstairs and solve both our problems.'

'Oh.' She sounded quite disappointed. 'No one told me it was two flats; they just said you were living together.'

'Same address, different rumour,' Callie said with a laugh, hiding her crossed fingers in the pocket of her white coat. What the hospital grapevine would make of it if they knew she'd woken up in his bed this morning, heaven only knew. It would probably completely ignore the fact that Ross hadn't been in it at the time.

'Still, it does give you a head start over the rest of the female population,' Naomi said as she rallied her spirits. 'You're the one on the spot and I'm sure, if you played your cards right...'

'I never have been much of a gambler, and with a tiny baby to look after...' She left the sentence unfinished, knowing Naomi would get her drift. 'Anyway, you know very well that the two of us are job-sharing so we never see each other. You probably have more chance with him than I do. You've known him much longer and you get on really well.'

'Uh-uh. Not interested.' Naomi shook her head. 'I've got my own man wriggling on a hook just trying to persuade me to marry him.'

Callie chuckled at the imagery. 'Tell me, tell me. Does he work at the hospital?'

'He's a visiting consultant.'

'In paediatrics?' Callie was trying to think who he could be but Naomi was being very coy.

'Other end of the spectrum. Geriatrics,' she said with a mischievous grin, knowing that Callie would never guess—she just hadn't been at the hospital long enough to know the staff in other specialities. 'He's tall and gorgeous—'

'You'll make a perfect pair, then,' she interrupted, already getting a clear mental image.

'Thank you kindly. He looks a bit like Dr Benton on that American hospital drama, but without the moodiness or the American accent.'

'And you're head over heels,' Callie finished, hoping her envy didn't show. 'Well, I hope you invite all of us to the wedding.'

It was great to hear of someone as lovely as Naomi preparing to embark on marriage, but afterwards Callie found that the conversation had left her feeling quite melancholic.

When her dedication to her training had left her with too little time to form the sort of relationships that might lead to marriage, she'd begun to resign herself to the fact that happily-ever-after probably wasn't going to happen for her.

Now, although she hadn't been looking, she'd found the perfect man, and was falling for him harder than a ton of bricks…and it was all a waste of time.

The trouble was, if things carried on the way they'd started, she was going to become every bit as attached to Andy, Fliss and Mark as she was to Zoe. If that happened, it was going to break her heart when they eventually had to part company.

By the time she arrived back at the house at the end of her shift she'd come to the decision that, in future, she was going to treat the children the same way as she treated the patients on the ward. She would help Ross to take care of them and make sure they were safe, but she wouldn't let herself get too close to them.

The same thing applied to Ross.

He was a good-looking man with a teasing, easy-going way about him that had fooled her heart into thinking she had a chance with him.

From now on, there were going to be no heated imaginings or wistful wishes. As she'd told Naomi, he was just another person who happened to be sharing the house with her.

The trouble was, as soon as she walked into the house and saw him standing barefoot in the doorway to the sitting room with only a pair of low-slung dusty denims on, all her resolutions evaporated and blew away.

CHAPTER EIGHT

'GOOD Lord! Is that the time already?' he exclaimed. 'Where does the time go?'

'They say it flies when you're enjoying yourself, so what have you been doing today?' Her heart was doing a silly tap-dance in her chest as he continued to stand there looking at her. The smile that had creased his sweaty, dusty face as soon as she'd come in the door had lifted her spirits like champagne bubbles, and the sight of all that naked flesh...

'Come and see,' he invited, and stepped into the sitting room again. 'I decided I wasn't going to be outdone by your efforts on the ceiling and walls.'

'Oh, my...' Callie breathed as she stood in the doorway and took in the scene in front of her. 'How ever did you do all that?'

The room was completely bare of any furniture and belongings apart from a strange-looking machine parked in the middle of the freshly sanded floor. It looked fantastic.

'I moved everything out while Zoe slept then she came with me to pick the machine up from the hire place.'

'But it must have taken hours. You can't have had any sleep at all.'

'Zoe and I have had to come to an arrangement about co-ordinating our sleeping so I could get this done, but the next stage is going to be a bit more tricky.'

'Next stage?'

'I managed to track down that special Scandinavian sealant but it's probably going to take three coats to do a good job and there's a warning on the container about fumes.'

'And you don't think it's going to be safe for Zoe?'

'I think she'd probably be better off in the crèche at the hospital for a couple of days until I get the floor finished. She's far too precious to risk for the sake of a bit of organisation.'

Callie toed off her shoes and walked gingerly into the middle of the room before she turned in a full circle.

'It's going to be so beautiful,' she breathed. She could feel the smile wreathing her face and knew that he would be able to tell how foolishly elated she was about their joint achievement, but she suddenly realised that she didn't care.

The whole project had started as a way to get the children involved in something that would take them out of themselves; something that would keep their minds and hands too busy to let them continue with their sniping at each other and everyone around them.

She'd been so delighted when Ross had taken a hand in the project that it had spurred her to keep up the momentum, but she'd never thought that he'd take her suggestion about the floor and put it into effect quite so quickly.

She whirled back to face him and her pulse stumbled when she found him looking at her rather than the results of his labours.

'Have…have you any idea what colour the wood will end up?' she asked, glancing away at the floor when she couldn't meet the intensity of his gaze any longer.

'Probably like this.' He squatted down, the fabric of his jeans faithfully outlining the taut muscles of his hips and thighs as he licked his finger and touched the smooth pale wood. She dragged her eyes away from his body to see that the moisture darkened the timber several shades to a deep golden honey.

'Oh! That's just how I imagined it!' Callie exclaimed with delight. 'And when we've got the tree up in that corner beside the window and the settee and chairs grouped around it's going to look so cosy.'

'A Christmas tree,' Ross groaned. 'That's all Fliss and Mark could talk about at breakfast this morning. They were determined we were going out to buy it as soon as they came out of school this afternoon.'

'Do you want me to explain that the needles will all drop off if you buy it too soon?'

'Perhaps with both of us saying it they might believe us,' he said darkly. He glanced down at himself and pulled a face. 'It's going to take more than a quick rinse under the tap to get me fit for duty,' he said with a scowl. 'I look as if I need going over with a yard broom before I can get in the bath.'

'You'd probably do better with the shower—much easier for getting the muck out of your hair apart from the fact it's closer.'

'You're right. I'd probably drop half of it all the way up the stairs, as if there wasn't enough dust flying around. You'd never think I did it with the door shut.'

Callie hesitated a second before she offered her services. 'I could get you some clean clothes...to save you going upstairs.'

His wicked dimple appeared briefly and she tensed

as she waited for him to make a teasing comment but all he did was explain what he wanted her to get and where to find it.

Her cheeks felt warmer than usual as she hurried away from him up the stairs.

It wasn't that she hadn't been in his room before—she'd helped him to get everything unpacked and organised in there just days ago and this morning she'd even woken up in there.

The difference this time was that she was going to have to open his drawers and wardrobe and take his underwear and shirt out and carry them to him, and for some crazy reason that seemed just as intimate.

The woman who collected the children from school was late delivering them home that afternoon so Ross had already left for work. Before Callie could find out the reason for the delay, Fliss burst into tears.

'I haven't got a costume!' she sobbed. 'Oh, Callie, I won't be able to be an angel if I haven't got a costume.'

Callie wrapped her arms round the miserable child and looked over her head to Andy for an explanation.

'It's the school play tonight,' he said glumly. 'We told Uncle Ross when we were living at his flat but he must've forgotten.'

'Are you in the play too?' That might explain his long face, too, although at his age he probably felt crying was beneath him.

'I'm not in the Junior plays any more,' he said, affronted. 'But Uncle Ross said we were going to give some buns or mince pies or something for the refreshments afterwards, and I was supposed to be taking them.'

'And when does the play start?' Her mind was whirling with everything she would have to do if the evening wasn't going to be a total disaster. There was no way she could call Ross home to deal with the problem; he had a job to do and was counting on her to cope.

For some strange reason that thought stiffened her resolve. This would be some sort of final exam which would let her know once and for all if she was doing the right thing by trying to adopt Zoe.

'Seven o'clock,' he said, with a hopeless shrug.

'Right, then, we'd better get moving,' she said briskly. 'There's a lot to do and you're all going to have to help if we're going to be ready in time.'

'But what can we do? You can't buy angel costumes in a shop,' Fliss sobbed.

'No, but with a sewing machine you can *make* one,' Callie pointed out. 'Andy, will you go to the little cupboard in the corner of my room and get out two of Zoe's white sheets and get two white pillowcases from the airing cupboard? Mark, you need to find the box with the Christmas decorations. Fliss, you need to blow your nose, wipe your face and come into the kitchen to make some buns.'

After a startled second of surprise they scattered like chickens released from a coop.

Callie took a deep breath and crossed her fingers, first that she had the ingredients she'd need and, second, that Ross would approve of what she was attempting.

'What are we making?' demanded Fliss, her face far more cheerful in spite of the tear-stains.

'We're going to call them chocolate angels,' Callie

announced as she assembled the ingredients for the quickest sponge mixture of her life.

Ten minutes later the trays of buns were in the oven with the timer set and she was ready to deal with the other half of the problem.

'Did you boys find everything?' she asked as she reached the doorway to her room and surveyed the chaos. The room had only looked tidy for a couple of days before the furniture from the sitting room had been stacked in here so that Ross could re-finish the floor.

'Yes, and I found your sewing machine, too,' announced Andy, with a hint of his uncle's smugness in his smile. 'Where do you want to put it?'

'Good thinking, Andy. The kitchen table, please.' It was probably the only flat surface suitable at the moment. 'Mark, can I borrow one of your crayons?'

The youngster looked up from the game he was having untangling the garlands of tinsel. 'Why?'

'So I can draw round Fliss to turn her into an angel.'

'Can I watch?'

Knowing the garment would probably only be worn once, Callie wasn't too worried about perfection—it was a good job because there wasn't time to do more than cut out a shift shape from the baby's sheets and attach long pointed sleeves cut out of the pillowcases.

'Now for the tinsel—' Callie began just as the timer went off.

'Mind the oven door. It's hot,' she warned as the children crowded round. They stood back a step and she bent to remove a tray of perfectly risen chocolate buns.

By half-past six the tinsel had been attached to the neck and hem of the costume and outlined the slightly medieval wide sleeves. The tops of the buns had been sliced off, divided into two 'wings' and reattached with butter icing made by Andy.

Mark had been detailed the job of sieving icing sugar 'snow' over them and then, after the sticky residue had been wiped from his face and hands, it was time to go.

By the end of the performance Zoe was decidedly cranky, even though Callie had taken the precaution of bringing a bottle with her.

Still, in spite of the fact that her arms felt as if they were falling off from holding the baby for the last two hours, Callie felt as if the evening had been a triumph.

Fliss had shone in her role as the Angel Gabriel and Andy and Mark had been the proud bearers of the most popular items on the refreshment table. It was just such a shame that Ross had missed it all.

The children were so excited by the successful outcome that by the time she got them home they were still almost bouncing off the walls. She had a feeling that it was going to take a lot more than five minutes to calm them down enough to go to sleep, but the calcium in a mug of hot chocolate would help. And in the meantime there was Zoe to sort out.

A ring at the front door was the last thing she wanted when she'd just told the three of them to go upstairs to brush their teeth and get into their pyjamas.

'Can I help you?' she asked over the wailing of the baby in her arms.

The young man on her doorstep looked utterly

shocked for a moment, as if he'd seen a ghost, but then he gathered himself.

'You must be Callie,' he said, and she saw a deep sadness in his eyes. 'I'm Jason.'

Callie blinked. He'd said it as if she should know the name but she was pretty certain she'd never met him before.

'Jason who?' It was difficult to concentrate with Zoe's voice growing louder and louder and the sound of shrieks and running feet upstairs.

'I—I used to live here…with Steph. I'm…I *was* her boyfriend.'

'Zoe's father,' Callie whispered in horror as she suddenly realised what he was trying to tell her.

'I got a letter from a solicitor when I got home from work this evening and I've been trying to ring you ever since.' The words came out so fast it was obvious that he'd been rehearsing them, then he paused and drew a steadying breath. 'Can I come in? I think we need to talk.'

Callie wanted nothing more than to slam the door in his face and run to the furthest corner of the house and hide. This was the man who could take Zoe away from her and, in spite of the fact that she was shouting at the top of her lungs, Callie loved her with all her heart.

'He has rights,' she heard Ross saying inside her head, and she forced herself to open the door wider and invite him in.

'I've only just got back from the children's Christmas play so things are a bit chaotic.' That was an understatement if the noise going on upstairs was any indication.

She had no idea where to take him. The kitchen

seemed a little informal for such an important conversation but there was no furniture in the sitting
room.

'Oh!' Jason stood in the sitting-room doorway,
having automatically turned that way, and gazed in
amazement at the changes she and Ross had brought
about in the last few days. 'This looks fantastic,' he
said. 'I'd never have believed it.'

In spite of her apprehension, Callie was pleased
that he liked what they'd done.

'The children helped to strip the rest of the paper
off, Ross and I did the painting and he hired a sander
to do the floor. It wasn't very expensive, just time-
consuming.'

'Well, it looks great. You're obviously the right
people to have the house.'

Silently she led him towards the kitchen, the movement quieting Zoe's complaints for a moment.

'I had to do some baking and haven't had time to
do the washing-up yet,' she apologised, suddenly
realising when she opened the fridge door for Zoe's
bottle that there was still a fine film of powdered
sugar over everything after Mark's enthusiastic sieving session.

'Look, I realise that I've come at a bad time but I
wanted to tell you… Look, I'm sorry about what happened to Steph but I didn't know… I *honestly* didn't
know what was happening.'

His halting words were very convincing but was it
just another practised speech?

'How could you not know?' she challenged hotly.
'Steph told me you'd had an argument and she told
me that when she told you about the baby you left
her. She tried to contact you again when Zoe was

born but you weren't even interested enough to reply.'

The expression that crossed his face was one of pure misery. 'That's probably what she believed happened,' he agreed. 'We had an argument because I accepted promotion to a job that meant I was going to have to do a lot of travelling—I'm a troubleshooter for a computer company with connections in Britain, Eire, Holland and the USA.'

He seemed far too young for that sort of position but so many of those sorts of jobs were being done by young people these days.

'My mother is very keen for me to do well and when Steph tried to contact me she put her off. The same thing happened when she wrote, but I didn't find out about that until I confronted her this evening. She admitted she destroyed Steph's letter because she thought it would hold me back. She and Dad married young and life was always a struggle. She was determined I wasn't going to make their mistakes if she could help it.'

Callie could see how the whole tragic thing had happened, with Steph caught up in it like a victim in a whirlwind. If her own background had been a little more stable perhaps she could have weathered the storm, but it hadn't worked out that way and Steph was gone.

'What about Zoe?' Callie asked fearfully. It couldn't be clearer that Jason had loved Steph. Would he want to fight for Zoe so he could hold onto that last connection with her?

'I don't know what to do,' he said earnestly. 'She's my daughter but until today I didn't even know she existed. I wouldn't know where to start if I were to try to bring her up, but to give her away...'

There was a sudden crash above their heads and, after a brief ominous silence, a wail of pain.

Callie only hesitated for a second before she leapt to her feet and deposited Zoe in the startled man's arms.

'Here. Look after Zoe. I've got to see what's happened.'

Her heart was in her mouth all the way up the stairs as she imagined one disaster after another, all of them involving broken furniture or copious quantities of blood.

It was almost an anticlimax to find the children huddled in a group on the floor beside Andy's bed.

'All right, then, what happened?' she demanded as she tried to catch her breath. 'What were you doing? It sounded as if something got broken.'

'Something did,' Andy admitted in a shaky voice, his face totally white. 'Me.'

Callie drew in a shocked breath, suddenly realising that he was cradling his arm gingerly against his chest.

'We were bouncing on the bed,' Fliss added in a frightened whisper. 'Andy said he could do a somersault but he fell off and his arm bent round the corner.'

Mark hadn't said a word, big tears rolling silently down his cheeks.

For a moment Callie completely forgot that she was a qualified doctor specialising in paediatric medicine and her reaction was pure emotion. All she wanted to do was pick the frightened youngster up and cuddle him; promise that the pain would go away. Then training stepped in and she began to issue instructions.

'Fliss and Mark, go and sit on the edge of the bed for a minute while I have a look at Andy.'

'You won't touch it, will you?' Andy begged. 'I know it's broken—I heard it snap.'

'I need to make certain where the break is and what sort it is so I know how to prevent you doing any further damage,' Callie explained calmly. She was glad that at least he'd got as far as taking his shirt off so his wiry little arms were easy to inspect.

Silently she catalogued the fact that at least one of the two bones in his forearm was badly broken, the ends clearly visible under skin rapidly darkening into a bruise. He was going to need to be taken to the hospital, but how was she going to do that with the other three to take care of, too?

'You can lean back against the bed if you want to, Andy. I'm just going to get something to make a sling so your arm doesn't get jogged. Fliss and Mark,' she added sternly, 'I want the two of you to go very quietly into your rooms and get your pyjamas on, then come back and sit on the bed. Do *not* run and do *not* jog Andy.'

'Yes, Callie,' Fliss whispered, stricken. 'We're very sorry.'

'Callie, is Andy going to die?' Mark said, his little face nearly as white as his brother's.

'No, Mark,' she said, and scooped him up off the bed for a swift comforting squeeze. 'Andy's not going to die, but he's going to be very uncomfortable while his bone mends.'

Callie's half-formed plan was complete by the time she reached the kitchen.

'Jason, I need your help,' she announced as she walked in. She didn't know whether to be pleased or frightened that he seemed to have quickly got the knack of cradling Zoe in the crook of his arm while he held the bottle for her.

'What happened? What can I do?' he offered quickly, and she could see in his calm acceptance that he was far more mature than his appearance suggested. He would probably have been the perfect partner for Steph once they'd ironed out their teething troubles...

'Andy fell of the bed and he's broken his arm. I need to take him to the hospital but I can't take the other three with me. Will you stay here with them until I can get back?'

He was silent for a moment, clearly startled by her request.

'But you don't know me!' he exclaimed. 'How do you know you can trust me?'

Callie grinned and pointed at Zoe, rapidly falling asleep in his arms. 'I'd say that was a fairly good reference,' she said as she rummaged in the first-aid box and drew out the wrapped package that contained a calico sling. 'The other two probably won't want to go to bed until they know how Andy is, but if you can put up with the world's largest video collection of Disney cartoons they'll probably fall asleep before long.'

'I'm game,' he agreed. 'There are several of those I haven't seen yet. Where's the television?'

Callie beckoned him to follow her as she led the way, pointing out the television and video machine in the jumble of her bedroom and grabbing Zoe's bassinet to take it upstairs where it would be quieter.

While she gently immobilised Andy's arm and helped him to his feet she introduced Jason as a friend of the family.

Fliss and Mark begged to come to the hospital but when Jason intervened with a question about Disney videos Mark was side-tracked long enough for Callie to persuade Fliss that her little brother needed her to look after him.

'We'll be back as soon as we can,' Callie promised as she led a very wobbly Andy out to the car, his dressing gown wrapped carefully over his shivering body.

She had driven almost halfway to the hospital before she allowed herself to think about what she was going to say to Ross. Would he blame her for not keeping a proper eye on the children? She'd certainly been distracted by Jason's arrival and at a time when the three of them had still been flying high after a gala evening.

If only she'd insisted on settling them down before she'd spoken to him, it wouldn't have happened. But she'd been so desperate to know whether he was going to take Zoe away from her that it had superseded everything else.

She almost dreaded facing Ross, but there was no option. He was the paediatrician on duty this evening and if she'd judged the situation right Andy was probably going to need an anaesthetic while the broken bone was realigned—if he didn't need anything more drastic doing.

'Will Uncle Ross be there?' Andy asked, his voice sounding very young and unsure in the half-light of the car. 'Will he be very cross with me…? Only he's told me off for jumping on the bed…lots of times.'

'I don't think you'll be doing it again in a hurry,' Callie pointed out wryly. 'And I think he'll be more worried about sorting your arm out than anything else.'

'What happened?' Ross demanded as he came hurrying into the room with his white coat flapping.

Callie had been left in the cubicle to keep Andy company but she found herself wondering if she was really there to hide behind Andy.

'I'm sorry, Uncle Ross. I was bouncing on the bed and I fell off when I tried to do a somersault.'

'Hmm,' Ross said with his lips tightly pursed. 'Is this where I say I told you so?'

'I never fell off before,' Andy pointed out. 'The new beds are much more bouncy than your old one.'

'So it's all *my* fault for buying bouncy beds, is it?' he challenged as he stepped back from making his examination. 'I think, when this is mended, we're going to have to do something about getting you some lessons on a real trampoline.'

'What happens now?' Andy asked, much of his apprehension gone in the presence of his uncle.

'Now you have some X-rays taken and we decide how to get your arm straight again so it can mend properly.'

It didn't take long for plates to be taken and developed and Callie joined Ross in front of the view box.

'He's going to have to go up to Theatre with this,' Ross murmured out of Andy's hearing. 'The orthopod *might* be able to align it with a cast but I've a feeling he's going to say it needs plating to keep it in position.'

'How long before we know?'

'I asked the radiographer to let him know as soon as the plates were ready to view, so hopefully he's on his way now.'

Callie was amused to see that the strong resemblance between the orthopaedic consultant and Father Christmas was growing more pronounced by the day. Apparently it had become a hospital ritual several years ago that he started growing his neatly trimmed silvery beard during the run-up to the special day so that he could don the familiar red costume with a really authentic touch.

Even Andy, a confirmed Santa sceptic at eleven, stared up at the man in amazement as he conferred with Ross.

'If you give them a buzz to tell them I'm on my way up, I'll go and get ready,' he said genially, then directed a kindly smile at Andy. 'See you in a few minutes, young man. Got to get you sorted out so you can enjoy Christmas.' He threw a quick wink at Callie and bustled out of the cubicle.

'Uncle Ross,' he hissed, wide-eyed. 'Did you see? He looked just like—'

'Shh!' Callie warned. 'We know. But nobody talks about it just in case he *is*.'

Ross stayed talking to Callie and Andy until the porters came to take him up in the lift to Theatre.

'I'd better get back to the others,' Callie said, knowing Ross would want to accompany Andy until he went under the anaesthetic.

'Where are they? Did you persuade one of the

nurses to keep an eye on them or are they causing havoc in the waiting room?'

'They're at home,' Callie began.

'What?' Ross queried sharply. 'You left Fliss looking after Mark and Zoe?'

'Of course not. She's far too young. Jason's looking after them while they watch Disney videos.'

'Jason? Who on earth's Jason?' he demanded, but the porters weren't going to wait for her reply and Andy was holding tightly onto his other hand.

The last sight she had of Ross was the furious glare he was directing at her as the lift doors closed.

CHAPTER NINE

THE children were fast asleep by the time Callie returned, one leaning trustingly on either side of Jason on her bed.

She didn't know him well enough to be able to read his expression but, having dumped him at the deep end, she'd expected him to want to leave as soon as possible. Instead, he insisted on helping her to carry them up to their beds.

Fliss had woken up just enough to ask how Andy was but Callie doubted that she'd stayed awake long enough to listen to the answer.

'Any problem with Zoe?' she asked quietly as they went back down the stairs. She'd tiptoed to her bassinet to check up on her but she was still fast asleep.

She paused at the bottom of the stairs, not quite certain what the protocol might be for this sort of situation.

'Zoe was no problem at all. She's a beautiful baby.' He added quietly, 'Look, I know it's late and you've had a stressful evening but we didn't get a chance to finish talking.'

For a moment Callie didn't answer, still hearing him saying that Zoe was a beautiful baby.

'Can I offer you a cup of coffee?' she said, with a conscious straightening of her shoulders. Putting it off wasn't going to change anything he wanted to say so she might just as well get it over with.

She busied herself with the mechanics of getting

two cups of instant coffee, taking advantage of the moments while she waited for the kettle to boil to begin wiping down the work surfaces and stack the sink with dirty utensils.

'If you want to start washing that lot I'm quite happy to wipe,' Jason offered, and startled her again.

'No, I'd probably break something or cut myself because I wasn't concentrating,' she said wryly. 'All I can think about is whether you're going to take Zoe away from me.'

The silence probably didn't last for more than a second or two but by the time Jason spoke Callie's fingers were knotted tightly together and she was almost ready to scream.

'I'm not going to go for custody,' he said quietly, and she watched him staring down into the dark, steaming brew for a long time before he looked up to meet her worried gaze.

'You don't sound very certain,' she said, afraid to hope for too much.

'If Steph were still alive it would be a different matter,' he admitted sadly. 'If I'd known that while I was feeling terribly important flying from one side of the world to the other she was carrying our baby...and believing that I didn't want either of them...'

He stopped and shook his head and Callie knew that he was close to tears.

'Anyway, I know I couldn't manage to look after her properly on my own. She's a beautiful baby and she's healthy and happy and I think she's in the right place.'

'Oh, God, thank you,' Callie breathed, and swallowed the lump in her throat as she tried to fight down the tears of relief welling in her eyes. 'I promise I'll look after her as if she were my own.'

'Will you tell her about Steph? Please? I wouldn't want her forgotten, because she was a lovely person and I...I loved her...very much,' he finished in a whisper.

'Jason, if you think it would help...you could always drop by to see how she's doing. Or I could send you photos?'

He was silent, obviously thinking about her offer.

'Can I let you know? Perhaps after all the legal stuff is finished.' He gave a wry laugh. 'The worst part about all this is the fact that my mother has recently begun hinting that it's about time I started thinking about finding myself a suitable wife so that she can keep up with all her friends who are starting to become grandmothers. Now I've got to go home and tell her that she's missed her chance and she's got no one to blame but herself.'

'Oh, Jason,' she murmured sadly. 'Taking your pain out on your mother won't bring Steph back, and if she's your only relative...'

He pulled a face but eventually he nodded. 'I suppose you're right. We can choose our friends but we're stuck with our relatives, good, bad or indifferent.'

'And how would you class me?' she teased gently. 'Half of Zoe's genetic inheritance comes from my side so in a way *our* genes are linked through her.'

'Hey, that's right.' There was still a shadow in his eyes but there was less bitterness in his smile. 'Perhaps, when you've adopted her, I could call you my sister-in-law?'

Suddenly Callie found herself fighting a yawn but it was Jason who caught sight of the time.

'I've kept you talking for hours and I bet you've got to get up in the morning and see to the children.' He carried his mug over to the sink. 'Are you sure you don't want a hand with this lot?'

'If you're that keen to offer, I might be forced to adopt you, too!' she teased. 'I've decided I'm going to leave it for Ross to do in the morning. It was his fault that I had to do all that baking at such short notice, so that can be his payment.'

Jason paused by the front door, his hand resting on the latch.

'Thanks for being so...' He shrugged. 'I was really screwed up about the whole thing when I came here but sitting with those kids while they fell asleep...it put a whole different perspective on everything. Then talking to you...'

'Well, if it's time for tell-the-truth, I nearly slammed the door in your face when I realised who you were. I was terrified you were going to take her away from me there and then. I know I've only had her for a short time but she's already a big part of my life.'

Zoe woke just as Callie was getting ready for bed but she was quickly satisfied with a dry nappy and a bottle. Within a short time they were both tucked under their covers and ready for sleep.

Callie drew in a deep breath and blew it out slowly, conscious that for the first time in weeks the big black cloud that had been hovering over her head had lifted.

Wait till I tell Ross, she thought happily as she began to drift off. Wait till I tell him that Jason is going to let me adopt Zoe. She's really going to be my little girl...

She could feel the smile creeping over her face as she imagined his pleasure. He'd been so adamant that Zoe's father had the right to know about his daughter so that he could make his choice and, much against her will, Callie had been forced to agree.

Now everything was going to be done legally and if Ross was half as delighted as she was...

She imagined herself giving him the good news; imagined the smile on his face and the way he'd wrap her in his arms and swing her round before he kissed her and...

'Callie...? Callie!'

The voice was accompanied by tapping on the door and she frowned and tried to bury her head under the pillow to get away from it.

'Come on, Callie, you're going to be late. Didn't you hear your alarm?'

Alarm?

Her eyes flew open when she realised she couldn't remember setting it. Now that Zoe wasn't waking her so early she needed the reminder to get her up. On checking, she *hadn't* set the alarm, and Zoe was sleeping peacefully.

'Oh, no!' she exclaimed, and flung the covers off. 'I'm supposed to be out of the house in fifteen minutes.'

'If you *will* stay up till all hours,' he said, the disapproval in his voice travelling very clearly through her door.

That reminded her of who she'd been talking to and a smile replaced her frown. With good news like that to pass on, nothing could get her down. Not even a grumpy Ross.

She must have broken several world speed records for showering and dressing and it was only when she was hurrying towards the kitchen to beg a cup of that delicious coffee Ross always brewed in the morning that she remembered about poor Andy.

'What did the orthopod have to do to Andy in the end?' she asked as she dumped her bag and keys on the table and reached for a mug.

Ross remained tight-lipped for a moment before he answered, almost as if he was considering whether to tell her.

'He decided to plate it in the end because he couldn't get good enough alignment any other way,' he said gruffly. 'Andy was already out of Recovery and settled on the ward by the time I came home.'

'Oh, good. I'm glad. He was so brave when I was immobilising it and bringing him in.' She was eyeing the loaf of bread and wondering whether she had time to make a piece of toast.

'He told me you had a visitor last night while the three of them were getting themselves ready for bed,' he said, and the words were almost an accusation. 'How long did you leave them unsupervised? How long was your visitor down here keeping your mind off them so they could get up to mischief?'

Callie gasped at the implied charge.

'They were only up there alone for about five minutes while I got Zoe's bottle.'

'And before that? They should have been in bed much earlier than that. What on earth were you thinking of? Is this the way you're intending bringing your sister's baby up—routine goes to pot as soon as you have a male visitor?'

Callie clenched her teeth as she fought to control her anger then gave in and slammed her coffee mug down so hard that the contents slopped over the top and onto the work surface.

'I do *not* deserve that and you have no right to say it,' she said tightly as she grabbed her keys and her bag. 'I'll be taking Zoe into work with me today to make sure I can keep an eye on her.'

'Callie…!' he called, but she ignored him to hurry into her room and snatch up handfuls of clothing and stuff it into Zoe's bag.

'I'm sorry I'm going to disturb you, sweetheart,' she told her sleeping charge as she piled everything into the bassinet around the baby's feet and grabbed the handles. 'I'll make sure they feed you as soon as you get to the crèche.'

She shouldered her way out of her room fully expecting to find Ross waiting to harangue her again.

'Callie?' called a little voice at the top of the stairs, and she looked up to see Fliss. 'I forgot to say thank you last night so I'm saying it now. Thank you for making me an angel.'

'You're welcome, Fliss. You were a beautiful angel.'

'Are you going to see Andy today?'

'Yes, sweetheart. Do you want me to give him a message?'

'Just tell him I love him and to come home soon.'

'I will, Fliss. Now you go and get yourself dressed or you'll be late for school.'

She had a feeling that Ross had been listening to her conversation with Fliss but there wasn't time to challenge him about it. If she wasn't careful, she was going to be late again.

Andy had been put in the bed furthest from the door and was looking a bit sorry for himself when Callie caught sight of him.

'Hey! How are you feeling?' She perched herself on the edge of the bed, glad of the chance to sit down for a minute. She seemed to have been running non-stop ever since she arrived at the hospital.

'It aches,' he said glumly, and lapsed into silence.

'Do you need some more pain relief?' she offered when he lay so still and quiet, and felt the frown pleating her forehead when he only shook his head without bothering to speak.

It wasn't unusual for her young charges to feel miserable after an operation but, having got to know him a little over the last few days, she still had a feeling that this was something more than that.

'If you need me for anything, all you've got to do is ask one of the nurses and they'll get me,' she said softly. 'Fliss asked me to tell you that she loves you and she wants you to hurry home.'

She waited a moment but he didn't respond so she slid off the edge of the bed.

'I'll see you later, then,' she said, and began to walk away.

She was almost out of earshot when she heard him draw in a ragged breath. Knowing he'd wanted her to go, she had to content herself with glancing back at him over her shoulder. As she'd expected, she saw the faint silvery track of the first tear as it ran down the side of his face and fell onto the pillow.

'Oh, Andy,' she breathed, her heart aching for him

in his silent misery. She would love to help him but she was beginning to think he would never let her get close enough.

She kept an eye on him at intervals throughout her shift, hoping to see him perk up a little after his tears, but he just seemed to be getting more and more withdrawn.

Ross arrived soon after lunch to spend some time with him and Callie hoped that this would provide the boost that Andy needed.

She could see that Ross was speaking to his nephew and from the expression on his face she could tell that he was doing his best to cheer him up but it wasn't working.

Almost without her permission her feet took her over towards them.

To even the most disinterested observer it was obvious that Andy was showing all the signs that he was going to grow up to be almost a clone of his uncle, and not just in appearance.

The entire family had become very important in her life since she'd met them such a short time ago and she would do anything to help these two resolve whatever problem was keeping them apart.

'I can remember when your father broke his arm,' Ross was saying as she drew nearer. 'He only had to have a cast on so you'll be able to boast louder than he can.'

He was met by stubborn silence.

'Did he ever tell you the story of the time he fell off the top bunk when we went to stay on a farmhouse for a holiday one year?' Ross began again. Callie could tell from the slight desperation in his tone that he'd realised that things were far from right but he wasn't going to give up trying.

'When he comes back from his trip you'll have to ask him about it,' he continued. 'And if he tries to tell you that it was my fault—'

'He won't be able to tell me because he's dead,' Andy shouted suddenly, taking everyone by surprise so that there was a lull in the usual noise in the room. 'They're both dead but you won't tell me. You keep pretending and pretending but I know it... I know they're dead.'

'Andy, no.' Without realising that she'd moved Callie found herself cradling Andy's sobbing shoulders with one arm and reaching for the curtain with the other to give him some semblance of privacy. 'It's not true, Andy,' she said, hoping in her heart of hearts that she was telling him the truth.

'What on earth makes you think they're dead?' Ross demanded in a shocked voice as his eyes met Callie's above his nephew's head. She shook her head, indicating that she'd neither told him nor heard anything from him about his parents' disappearance.

'I *know* it,' he said fiercely as tears streamed down his pale cheeks, 'otherwise they'd be here. Mummy always said she'd be there to look after us, especially if we were hurt, and she's not here so I know she's dead. Either that or she doesn't love me anymore.'

'Oh, Andy, that's not true. You know your mum and dad went right to the other side of the world—I showed you where it was in that big atlas and we worked out how many hours it took to travel there.'

'But she was supposed to be back before the Christmas play to see Fliss be an angel and make the buns, and she wasn't there. You forgot all about it and Callie had to make the angel dress...'

Everything was becoming more and more muddled as he simply gave up and wept.

Ross looked haunted as he realised for the first time that in trying to protect his nephew he might actually have been putting greater strain on him.

Callie gently relinquished her place so that it was Ross who held the sobbing child against his chest and stroked a comforting hand up and down his back.

'You'll have to tell him,' Callie mouthed when Ross looked up at her.

He shook his head with a look of desperate indecision.

'Yes,' she said, holding his gaze resolutely. 'He needs to know. It's eating him alive.'

Ross stared angrily at her for several long seconds before he closed his eyes and nodded.

'How did he take it?' she demanded, beckoning Ross into the gaudily over-decorated little interview room as he made his way out of the ward and headed for the main door of the department.

She'd been lying in wait for a chance to speak to him, needing to know how Andy felt about the news of his parents' abduction.

Ross rubbed both hands over his face then dropped them down to hang limply at his sides with a sigh.

'I'll never understand kids as long as I live!' he exclaimed, with a disbelieving shake of his head. 'He actually seemed *glad* that Tim and Megan had been taken hostage. He couldn't ask questions fast enough and even when I didn't have the answers it didn't seem to worry him. Doesn't he realise that until they're actually back here he *still* might never see them again? Anything could go wrong.'

'And they could get hit by a taxi on the way to the hospital to visit him, or mugged, or any one of a thousand different things. In his mind, the reason they aren't here for him when he's hurt *isn't* because they don't love him any more and it *isn't* because they're dead. That's all that really matters to him at the moment. The rest is too much like the storyline in one of his cartoons for it to be a real threat.'

'I knew he wasn't happy but I kept hoping it was minor things like being cramped up in my flat. I should have listened when you told me to come clean with him.'

'He's a bright lad. You were never going to be able to keep it from him for ever and you don't want to break his trust in you, especially if the worst happens and you need to rely on it later.'

'He must be the only bright one in the Kendrick family, then, because the only thing I'd win a medal for in the last twenty-four hours is leaping to conclusions.'

He met her eyes and she could see that he was far from happy. 'I made a complete ass of myself this morning, throwing accusations around like that,' he said quietly. 'It was indefensible and I've got no excuse…except I was so jealous that I could hardly see straight.'

The last words were added on in a low, slightly husky voice and for a moment Callie wasn't certain that she'd heard right.

'Jealous?' she repeated. 'Of what?'

'Of Jason and the thought that you might have spent the night with him,' he said hoarsely, then looked round quickly as though afraid someone in the department might have overheard him.

'God, I can't believe I'm having this conversation,' he muttered, dragging his fingers through his hair as he turned to stare blindly out of the tinsel-framed window at the uninspiring winter landscape. 'I can't afford to start a relationship, not while I've got three children depending on me for emotional support.'

'Neither of us wants to start a relationship,' she agreed quietly, her heart feeling very heavy when she heard the confirmation of her fears and had to agree with it. 'We've both got too much on our plates at the moment without that sort of distraction.'

Suddenly, he whirled to face her, his eyes almost blazing sparks at her as he grasped her shoulders in his hands and gave her a frustrated shake. 'But it doesn't seem to matter *what* we want or don't want—it's happening anyway…' And he brought his lips to hers as if he could no longer resist.

The loud click of the safety latch on the nearby door had sounded like a rifle shot and startled the two of them apart.

'I…I must go,' Callie stammered as she took another step away from him, her mouth still heated from its connection with his and her body missing the powerful strength of his wrapped around her.

'Dr Bell?' Naomi Henzie's voice accompanied a polite tap on the half-open door.

'Yes?' Callie wrapped her professionalism around her and went out to speak to the nurse even though she would far rather have stepped into his arms again. She'd never realised that she could feel so…so *connected* with another human being.

'Is everything all right?' Naomi murmured softly on their way back into the ward. 'I'm not asking for details, but, well, half the ward heard Andy shouting and the other half heard enough to speculate.'

'I think he'll be all right now,' Callie replied, amazed how quickly she'd forgotten Andy's problem once Ross had touched her.

'I'm not so certain about the young man I've just put into the bed next to him,' Naomi said. 'He only went home yesterday and he's back again today. Last time it was a bicycle accident, this time he says he slipped on the stairs at school and hit his head.'

Callie didn't need to hear the scepticism in the older woman's voice. They both obviously thought there was something nasty going on here and didn't like any of the possibilities.

Her visit to his bedside only confirmed her suspicions.

'What do you want?' he demanded belligerently.

His attitude certainly hadn't improved since she'd seen him last, nor had the bruising around his neck. In fact, it seemed even more livid and widespread, with what looked very much like fingerprints.

'Just checking on you to make sure you haven't got concussion,' Callie said calmly as she produced a penlight from the depths of her bulging pocket and shone it in each eye in turn.

Up close, she was even more certain that the bruising she could see had a human origin. All she didn't know was whether the perpetrator was adult or child.

Either way, she was duty-bound to note her findings and would make certain that the nursing staff on the ward kept their eyes and ears open for clues. It wasn't completely unknown for an abusing parent to use the cover of a hospital visit to deliver threats to their victim.

She was just about to go off duty, her thoughts already flying ahead to the fact that Ross would be waiting for her at home, when she paid a final visit to Andy.

'Feeling a bit easier?' she asked, carefully wording her question as innocuously as possible.

'It still aches, but Uncle Ross said I should be able to go home tomorrow because I've got my own doctor to look after me.'

'Round-the-clock service,' Callie agreed, with a smile. She was pleased to see him looking so much brighter but noticed that he was casting wary glances in the direction of the young lad in the next bed. 'Anything I can do for you before I go?'

He paused and she wondered what new worry was putting a frown on his face when he surreptitiously beckoned her to come closer.

Callie sat down on the edge of the bed and leant forward.

'He had some visitors,' Andy whispered nervously, glancing quickly towards the next bed. 'Bigger boys. They were being mean to him, and one of them called him a…a weedy stepbrother and they poked his bruises and laughed when it hurt him. They said if he told what they'd done they'd kill him.'

'Well done, Andy,' Callie praised quietly, giving his good hand a squeeze. 'We knew someone had hurt him but we had no idea who. Now we'll be able to stop them.'

'Is being a stepbrother bad?' he asked, clearly confused. 'Is it like a wicked stepmother in story books?'

'No.' Callie chuckled. 'All it means is that some-one who already has a child marries someone who isn't the father of that child.'

'Like you?' he persisted. 'You've already got Zoe and if you got married...'

Callie's heart gave a silly skip when she suddenly had a vision of marrying Ross but she ruthlessly squashed it down.

'Then Zoe would be that person's stepdaughter,' she finished for him.

She waited in case he had any other questions but he retreated into silence again, his expression rather glum.

Oh, Andy, she thought as she collected Zoe from the crèche and set off home. Your life would be so much easier if you weren't quite so bright. I've got an awful feeling that you've just found something else to worry about.

Then she was drawing into the driveway and the only thought in her head was that she was going to see Ross.

With memories of their interrupted kiss clear in her head her hand was shaking as she tried to fit her key in the lock.

'Oh, Callie, thank God you're home!' Ross ex-claimed as he met her in the hallway. Her heart leapt into a flat-out gallop when she got a good look at his face.

'Ross, what's happened?' She put Zoe's bassinet down and shed her armful of bags. 'What on earth's the matter? You look dreadful.'

'I had a phone call not ten minutes ago. They think the hostages have been killed.'

'No!' Callie could see the agony in his eyes now.

'Oh, Ross, I'm so sorry.' She wrapped her arms around him, needing to offer comfort even though it couldn't possibly change anything.

Every muscle in his body was rigid with tension as she held him tightly, trying to soothe him the same way she did Zoe by stroking his back.

'What am I going to do now?' he demanded wearily as he finally unbent enough to rest his head against hers. 'I took your advice and explained everything to Andy and he made me promise faithfully that I wouldn't hide anything from him. How can I possibly break the news that his parents are dead?'

CHAPTER TEN

SOMETIMES, Callie didn't know if she could cope with any more tension.

Outwardly, their lives seemed to be running smoothly, with the division of labour at work and home dovetailing neatly between the two of them. Sharing the load had certainly been a good decision as far as that was concerned.

It was the emotional side of things that seethed and boiled beneath the surface.

The attraction between Ross and herself was as strong as ever and she'd finally begun to believe that they really stood a chance of finding something good and lasting.

Unfortunately, ever since Andy had returned from hospital he seemed more determined than ever to keep the two of them apart.

He was perfectly pleasant and helpful all the time he was with Callie, even rescuing the dreaded spider she'd found in the bath. But once Ross came home it was a different matter as Andy tried to monopolise his uncle's time and attention whenever he tried to speak to Callie.

Ross tended to let Andy get away with his ploy but Callie knew that was largely out of guilt. She knew he was feeling uncomfortable about keeping things from Andy after making his promise of honesty, but Callie had pointed out that there was absolutely no proof yet that Tim and Megan were dead.

She knew he'd been grateful that she'd found a temporary way around his conscience and he'd compromised by telling Andy that the authorities had temporarily lost contact with his parents, probably because their captors had moved them to a new location.

Callie was never quite certain whether Andy believed it and tried to make allowances for his moods, putting them down to insecurity, but it all added to the levels of stress.

She shook her head when she remembered the day Ross had suggested making a family outing out of choosing the Christmas tree. In the end, Andy's antipathy towards her inclusion had been so obvious that Callie had made an excuse to stay at home. She would have loved to have spent the time with them—it would have been the first time she'd done such a thing with a real family—but she hadn't wanted to spoil the trip for the rest of them.

Decorating the enormous thing had been a similar disaster, with Andy insisting that everything had to be done the way *they* always did it, and Ross making a special trip to his brother's house to bring their decorations over.

Fliss and Mark were a delight, throwing themselves into everything wholeheartedly, whether it was decorating the house for Christmas or helping to cook some of the festive goodies Callie was trying to stockpile ready for the holidays.

'I made a special wish,' Mark confided after they'd ceremoniously stirred the Christmas pudding. 'I wished that my mummy and daddy could be home for Christmas.'

Callie's heart nearly broke at the thought that his

parents might never have the chance to share Christmas with him again.

She had almost no private time alone with Ross any more, not now that the children had broken up from school, so the right time had never happened for her to find out how deep his feelings were for her.

She already knew that she was deeply in love with him and, given the chance, would willingly marry him and help him to bring up their shared brood.

She sent up a heartfelt prayer that she would never be called on to do it; that Tim and Megan would be returned to their children with their present peril fading to no more than a bad dream.

In the meantime, the last batch of patients were going home after their various stays in hospital. One was a profoundly deaf child who'd been in for the positioning of a cochlear implant that would be switched on after everything had healed. If all had gone well, her belated Christmas present would be the first time she actually heard her parents talking to her.

There had been two patients in for tests on their hearts, the tiny sensors fed right up into the heart itself through an incision in the big blood vessel in their groin. At the end of their session in Theatre, one had been given the all-clear but the other would have to return in the New Year for corrective surgery.

There weren't many patients left in the ward as all who were fit enough had been allowed home for the celebrations, but one who was going to have to stay in was Andy's erstwhile neighbour, Jack.

Callie remembered the way the poor lad had looked when he'd arrived for the third time, this time with his leg attached to a series of weights and pulleys as part of the treatment for a badly broken femur.

At least there had been a witness to his step-brother's brutality on this occasion, the elderly lady phoning for the police and giving an amazingly detailed description of his assailant that didn't give the culprit a chance to wriggle out of the charges.

With the knowledge that something was finally going to be done about the bullying, Jack had undergone a complete change of personality, reverting to the bright, outgoing character he'd probably been before his life had gone sour.

He'd sent a couple of messages home to Andy via Ross and Callie, comparing notes on computer games they'd played, and Ross had suggested that they could all call in to the ward on Christmas Day to wish him a happy Christmas.

Now it was Christmas Eve and the children had finally gone to sleep.

Callie had found some large bright red climbing socks in the bottom of a drawer, courtesy of Ross and a former holiday walking in the Peak District, and had found a way to anchor them at intervals along the mantelpiece with a child's name on each of them.

She knew from things Fliss and Mark had said that this was not a usual Kendrick custom but she'd noticed that Andy hadn't objected to the prospect of more toys.

It had been difficult finding time to do any shopping for presents without children in tow, but she'd managed to find something special for each of them and to get it wrapped and hidden away without anyone being any the wiser.

The one thing she had promised, as her present to herself, was that she was going to sit up and wait for Ross to arrive back at the end of his shift. Unless there was an emergency admission there was every chance that the two of them would finally get the chance to spend a couple of hours together before the children woke up and the festivities began.

Callie shivered with a mixture of excitement and apprehension as she put her prettiest nightie ready on the end of her bed and gathered up her wash kit for a long, pampering bath.

She knew now beyond a doubt that Ross was the only man for her—the man she'd been waiting for all her life without ever realising it.

Tonight, if all went to plan, she would have the chance to talk to him, to tell him how she felt, to share her hopes for the future and maybe even a few moments of stolen pleasure.

It was nerve-racking waiting for him to arrive and she'd changed her mind several times by the time she finally carried Zoe's bassinet upstairs and settled herself into his big bed.

It felt like very brazen behaviour to invite herself like this, totally unlike the time she'd fallen asleep here accidentally, but the thought of the two of them cramped together into her much smaller bed wasn't nearly as enticing. She hardly wanted her memories of her first night with Ross to be punctuated with one of them falling out of bed. It would be hard to explain the circumstances to Andy if they were supporting matching casts.

As the bed warmed up she began to relax and her eyelids grew heavy as she breathed in the familiar scents of the shampoo and soap Ross used.

They almost seemed to be wrapping around her senses, as warm and comforting as a pair of strong arms cradling her while she slept...

*   *   *

'Good morning, Callie,' rumbled a deep voice under her ear. 'I *do* hope you're my Christmas present.'

Callie stretched and found herself rubbing up against a very large, very warm, very naked, very aroused man.

'Ross,' she breathed as her eyelids flew up and she found herself looking straight into a pair of smiling blue-grey eyes. 'When did you arrive home?'

'Hours ago,' he murmured, with a glimpse of that wicked dimple to tantalise her. 'Do I deserve a reward for being a good boy? I didn't open my present until the morning.'

Callie chuckled. They'd had to resort to just such bribery to stop Mark poking and prodding at the presents under the tree.

'Oh, Ross, I'm sorry. I didn't mean to fall asleep. I was going to wait up for you so we could spend a little time together without the children.'

'Great minds think alike,' he teased. 'When I arrived home the first place I went was into your room. I can't tell you how pleased I was to find you up here instead.'

'Why didn't you wake me?' she groaned, and turned to face him. 'The children are bound to wake up soon and I don't really want them to walk in on us like this.'

'That's one reason why I didn't wake you,' he said as he traced one finger around the edge of her face then outlined her lips. 'If I had, I wouldn't have been able to resist making love to you, and once I start a couple of hours isn't going to be nearly long enough.'

Something deep inside Callie began to unfurl and blossom. The emotion in his voice was matched by the heat in his eyes and both were in danger of setting her on fire. After twenty-eight years of wondering what all the fuss was about she was beginning to think she might just not survive the conflagration, but, oh, what bliss finding out...

'Callie, I've got so much to tell you but... Forget the rest; the most important thing is I love you and I want you to marry me.'

'Oh, Ross.' He'd quite taken her breath away but it was what she'd been longing to hear. 'You must know that I love you too. Of course I'll marry you.'

'I hoped you'd say that,' he said, with a mischievous glint in his eye. 'It was sheer hell watching you sleep and holding you while you wriggled all over my exhausted body so I had to do something to occupy my time.'

He pulled the quilt aside just far enough to reach for her left hand, tugging it out from the warmth to hold it up between them.

'I couldn't wait to see what it would look like,' he whispered as he showed her the delicate diamond ring already in place on her third finger.

'Oh, Ross, it's so beautiful...' she gasped, and threw her arms around him to press a fervent kiss to his willing mouth.

The trouble was, a single kiss was never going to be enough.

Within seconds his hands were stroking and roaming up and down her back and then up under the hem of the pretty nightdress that he'd never had the chance to appreciate.

She knew exactly when he discovered that she'd deliberately neglected to put on any underwear, and a slim ray of sanity pierced her heated preoccupation.

'If you start anything we don't have time to finish,

I'll kill you,' she muttered fiercely as she twisted to
try to pull his hands away from their exploration.

'Keep wriggling up against me like that and I'll let
you kill me…very slowly,' he chuckled, then gave a
heartfelt groan when he heard an excited squeal from
further along the corridor as Mark found the little parcel she'd left on the end of his bed.

'Action stations,' he said wryly as he rolled away
from her with gratifying reluctance. 'I didn't have
time to tell you the rest of my news, but there'll be
plenty of time for that. It'll keep a bit longer. First,
I've got to get out of here before I end up having to
give an impromptu ''birds-and-bees'' talk before
breakfast.'

Callie waited till he'd left the room before she
spread her hand out and gloated at the ring glinting
at her in spite of the muted winter light in the room.

Ross was right when he said that they still had a
lot to talk about, but this was definitely starting out
to be the best day of her life.

They had a wonderful breakfast all together at the
kitchen table and then Callie insisted that the washing-up was done and the turkey put in the oven to
cook before they all went through to the sitting room
to open the presents under the tree.

'Clever idea, giving them some little things in the
Christmas stockings,' Ross murmured as he grabbed
her hand and pulled her down to sit close beside him.
'It meant they were more amenable to the idea of
waiting till after breakfast for the main event.'

'That's the good thing about combining different
family traditions—you can get the best of both
worlds,' Callie pointed out. 'I've only ever spent

Christmas in a hospital if I've been on duty. This will be the first year I've gone in as a visitor to the children's ward.'

Andy had decided he wanted to take a present to Jack to cheer him up and Ross had promised he would make sure that Father Christmas knew all about it when they got to the hospital.

Now it was time for some serious demolition and there were three children just waiting to begin on the small mountain of presents waiting under the tree.

By the time they'd finished there was a bag full of shredded wrapping paper and three children pink-cheeked with delight.

'Andy, I think there's one last present on the tree,' Ross directed, to Callie's surprise. 'Could you get it, please?'

There was a definite air of excitement humming through the man. She could feel it very clearly through the arm he'd wrapped around her shoulder as Andy read her name on a thick envelope and brought it over to her.

'I contacted my friend yesterday and he told me he'd sent you something in the post,' Ross began by way of explanation as she slid a nail under the edge of the flap and pulled it open. 'I told him his letter hadn't arrived—it's probably caught up in the Christmas post somewhere—so he sent a photocopy across to the hospital so you could have it today.'

Intrigued, Callie pulled a sheaf of papers out and read the top one.

'It's the adoption papers!' she squealed, and twisted in her seat to throw her arms round his neck. 'Oh, Ross, thank you! The day just keeps getting better and better!'

'What adoption papers?' Andy demanded suspiciously. 'Who's getting adopted?'

'Zoe is,' Callie said, with a happy laugh. 'These are the papers that say I can go to court and they will make her really mine for ever and ever.'

'But she's already yours,' Fliss said, her expression totally confused.

'Not yet,' Ross explained carefully. 'Zoe's mother was Callie's sister, Stephanie.'

'You've got a sister? Where is she?' Now Fliss was intrigued, but it was Andy who seemed most startled by recent events.

'She...she died just after Zoe was born, and now I want to make sure that no one can ever take her baby away from me.'

'Do you love Zoe?' Andy challenged.

'Yes.' Callie smiled as she glanced across at the bassinet Ross had carried in so that Zoe was part of the events even though she was too young to appreciate them.

'Even though she's not yours?' he persisted urgently. 'Even though you'll only be her stepmother?'

Suddenly Callie understood just what had been going on in his mind—the torments that had forced him to be so obnoxious the last few weeks.

He must have convinced himself that, if his parents didn't return, the only way he could be certain that Ross would always love him and want him was if he stayed a bachelor. If Ross were to marry anyone, he would end up a stepson, just like poor Jack.

'Yes, Andy, I love Zoe even though she wasn't mine to start with. And if I decided to adopt any more children in the future, or had any of my own, it would be because I loved them, too.'

She paused for a moment, trying to think of a way

to convince him, and realised that the only way was to tell him a little about her own childhood.

'Andy, Steph and I lost our own mother and father when we were quite small and we never found any-body who wanted to adopt us because we refused to be split up. But we did have one foster mother who told us that the more people you love, the more your love grows. It isn't something like a cake that you have to keep cutting into smaller and smaller pieces to share it out.'

'Do you love us?' demanded Mark.

He'd been sitting quietly surrounded by a sea of books and toys as his eyes went from one to the other. He might not have understood everything they'd said but he'd managed to cut right to the heart of the matter with one question.

'Yes, Mark, I love all of you.'

'Even Uncle Ross?'

'Especially Uncle Ross,' said Uncle Ross firmly as he captured her left hand and brought it up so that her ring caught the light. 'Because I love her too and I've asked her if she'll marry me. Then we can all be part of the same big family.'

There was uproar for a moment as everyone spoke at once but it was one plaintive voice that got through.

'Callie? Can I be bridesmaid? Please?' begged Fliss, and Ross laughed, the happy sound filling the room.

'We're not late, are we?' demanded Andy over the sound of Christmas music as they hurried through the main entrance towards the lifts.

They had to share the space with several other vis-itors carrying brightly wrapped parcels but everyone was in a good mood and squashed in quite happily.

'No, we're not too late. There'll be plenty of time to get to the ward before he comes.'

Fliss and Mark were almost dancing with excitement and Andy was having to fight hard to maintain his 'older brother' control.

Before they entered the ward Ross relieved Andy of the present he'd brought for Jack and promised with a conspiratorial wink to make certain that it reached the Right Person in time.

Callie led the way with Zoe in her arms and took the other three round the room to introduce them to the unfortunate few who'd had to stay in hospital for the holidays.

Everybody had visitors and there was plenty of teasing and talk that everyone could join in.

Andy had made a beeline for Jack's bed and was obviously finding it very hard not to spoil the surprise while he inspected the presents Jack's mother had brought in.

There was a sudden commotion at the door and all eyes turned to see a jolly-looking man with a full silvery beard and a familiar red suit.

'It *is* him!' Andy exclaimed in a piercing whisper to Jack, his eyes almost standing out on stalks as he recognised the face of the man who'd operated on him.

Callie had to bite her lip to control her grin but she'd never believed a bit of fantasy did children any harm—especially on a day like this.

Father Christmas was just making his farewells before leaving the ward when Ross appeared in the doorway.

There was a moment of quiet conversation between the two of them and then he began speaking again.

'I believe there are three children here called Andy,

Fliss and Mark,' Father Christmas announced impor-
tantly.

A squeal from Mark drew his eyes to the far end
of the room and he beckoned them over.

'I've just been told that a very special present has
arrived especially for the three of you. It's a late delivery, I'm afraid, but I hope you won't mind.'

He turned towards the door and Ross pushed it
wide to reveal the man and woman standing just outside the opening.

'Mummy! Daddy!'

Poor Father Christmas had to move out of the way
quickly or he would have been flattened as three children rushed towards their parents.

The red-suited figure gave the room a large wink
and a very quiet 'Ho! Ho! Ho!' before he slipped
quickly out of the door.

Ross let it swing closed, hiding the tearful reunion
from the enthralled ward, and met Callie and Zoe in
the middle of the room.

'When did they get back? How long have you
known?' she demanded, fighting to contain emotional
tears.

She tried to fish for a hankie one-handed and Ross
scooped Zoe out of her hands with practised ease.

'A group of them escaped from their captors just
before the rescue team got there—that was when we
got the message that they were presumed dead. Tim
did his boy scout bit and led them to safety but the
first I knew was when they arrived at the hospital last
night.'

'They arrived here? Last night?' Callie didn't know
whether to hug him or kill him for keeping it to himself.

'The authorities insisted they had to have a medical

check-up before they could go home, and Tim countered by insisting it was done here so he could find out how the children were. I was going to tell you when everyone woke up this morning, but then I found you in my bed and I got a little…side-tracked.'

When he tightened his arm around her shoulders and gazed down at her Callie could tell that he was in danger of getting side-tracked again.

They definitely needed to get out of here. There were entirely too many pairs of eyes watching them.

'Do you think they've finished hugging each other out there? Only there's a large Christmas dinner that needs some attention before we can all sit down and play happy families.'

'I certainly haven't finished hugging *you*,' Ross grumbled. 'But I suppose I'm going to have to wait until we've got a bit of privacy.'

'Give her a kiss, Doc,' called one of the parents.

'It's your perfect chance—you're standing right under the mistletoe,' another pointed out.

Ross glanced up at the greenery above his head and grinned, flashing that wicked dimple and making her knees grow weak.

'What a good idea,' he said aloud, to a chorus of hoots and chuckles as he bent his head towards her. 'I've been wanting to do this ever since I first met her.'

Just before his lips touched hers he whispered for her alone, 'And I'll be wanting to do it for the rest of our lives. I love you, Callie.'

'I love you too, Ross,' she whispered, and gave herself up to the soaring pleasure.

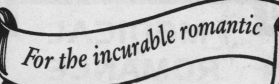
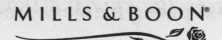

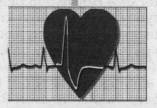

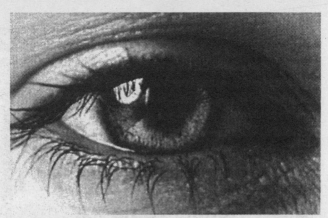

SWEET REVENGE
NORA ROBERTS

Adrianne led a remarkable double life. Daughter of a Hollywood beauty and an Arab playboy, the paparazzi knew her as a frivolous socialite darting from exclusive party to glittering charity ball. But no one knew her as The Shadow, a jewel thief with a secret ambition to carry out the ultimate robbery—a plan to even the score.

The Shadow was intent on justice.

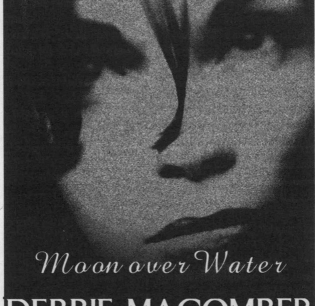

MILLS & BOON®

Makes any time special

Enjoy a romantic novel from
Mills & Boon®

Presents...™   *Enchanted*™   TEMPTATION.

Historical Romance™   ⎮ **MEDICAL ROMANCE**™